# UNKNOWN

### NEW YORK TIMES BESTSELLING AUTHOR
## WENDY HIGGINS

# DEDICATION

**To Brooke Leicht,
Friend extraordinaire**

# PART ONE

# BEFORE

# PROLOGUE

"IT'S NEARLY TIME, BAHNTAN." Bahntan. Keeper of the people. He was the first male leader of his kind, raised for one single, monumental purpose. And the time to fulfill that purpose was upon them.

The Bahntan lifted his heavy chin from where he stared out of the window into Nevada's night sky; his every thought a betrayal of his life's work. On the outside he appeared handsome and capable in a crisp Italian suit, but on the inside he had never felt more broken, his thoughts scattered.

"You have reservations," his female comrade remarked. The Bahntan focused on the stars and imagined what lie beyond them, too far for his eye to see—places humans had never been—places he could scarcely imagine himself.

"We knew it would be difficult for you," his comrade continued. "Being forced to live as one of them. But we are beyond the point of turning back, Bahntan." The woman put a hand on his shoulder. "You have been chosen. Do not doubt one hundred years of careful planning. You are honored."

*I am cursed.* The Bahntan turned, not daring to voice the

thought. His comrade had lived in hiding all her life, surrounded only by other Bahnturian people in one of many subculture camps hidden on every continent on the earth. This woman was well-trained, well-manicured, to speak any language and fit in to nearly any culture, but she did not have the firsthand knowledge that he had.

He met his comrade's eye and gave a stiff nod. "Of course."

"Earth, its people, *need* our cleansing. They beg for it in their despair; the soil and sky cry out for it. And yet they are not willing to do what is necessary."

The Bahntan closed his eyes. "But five and a half billion people . . ." Then he clenched his teeth and shoved his hands in his pockets, turning away again.

"It is the only way." The woman of Bael took his shoulder and forced him to turn again. This woman, who should have been leader, planted her hands on the Bahntan's shoulders. "In every nation they are poisoned. They abuse their own bodies, their own lands. Their minds are rotted by evils of murder and hatred and all manner of perversion."

"Not all," he whispered in response.

The woman gave him a firm shake. "Too many."

Never had he questioned his people and their ways. He knew the earth wept, and drastic changes were the only way to set things right, but five and a half billion souls were a great many to carry on his shoulders.

"Bahntan, do not doubt," she said gently. "Those who perish will be at peace. And those who live will be thankful and embrace their new life."

"As slaves?" The Bahntan gave a dry laugh. "I fear they will not bow to us as easily as you assume."

"History says otherwise. They will succumb. They will adapt. Slavery of some sort has been in these lands since the dawn of time. It is the nature of the masses to be led by those stronger than them. And humans are no strangers to genocide. In the end, our ways will be good for them. There will finally be equality for all. No petty reasons for war. No differences to overcome. They will come to see that—if not in this generation, then the next. And our people will finally be free. Don't you see? The cost is great, but the cause is greater."

The Bahntan swallowed down every argument on his tongue. This was the only way. He had to believe the end justified the means, otherwise what was to come might destroy him. Humanity had its good and bad attributes, its weaknesses and strengths. When he concentrated on the bad, on those weaknesses, he knew this was the only way for his people to have a chance. He couldn't allow himself to fear what was right.

"Please," the Bahntan said. "Ignore my reservations. I am ready."

The woman smiled and rubbed his shoulder. "There now. You make us proud."

# ONE

VEN IN RETROSPECT, IT'S difficult to pinpoint exactly where we went wrong. After the bombings, things were . . . confusing. Chaotic. I'm not sure if it was hope or desperation or simply naiveté that caused us, the United States, to sit back and watch as an eraser was taken to our Constitution. Perhaps it was fear. Whatever the reason, we handed over our freedoms, allowed everything to be stripped away for the sake of supposed safety, even when it felt wrong. Because we didn't know who we were fighting. We only knew who we were protecting.

Us Tates and the Fites. Rylen Fite. Oh God . . . *Ry.*

I feel like I need to talk about him before I can explain the dismal state of our world. Because for me, he's the core strand around which everything else in my life is woven. He's more than just my older brother's best friend. He's more than our neighbor on the potato farm with a screwed up family. He's an integral part of me . . . and I'd die if he ever knew I said that.

Without electronics or electricity, I find myself reminiscing a lot. If I let myself get lost in those safer, sweeter memories, the horrors of the present momentarily dissipate, and I've come to crave that. So when I close my eyes and try to sleep, I think about the day we moved to Lincoln County, Nevada. The day I met Ry.

I was six. He was nine. Dad got stationed just outside of Vegas as an Army recruiter, but he wanted me and Tater to grow up in a small town. Hence Lincoln. Home to Coyote Springs Golf Course, spectacular mountain ranges, green valleys, brown deserts, cattle ranches, wild horses, and UFO folklore. It was the middle of nowhere, but still a lot prettier than Ft. Bragg, North Carolina where we'd been stationed last.

The younger me stared out from the porch of our new one-story rancher at the acres of potato fields with a run-down house in the distance, flanked by a series of sheds, a chicken coop, and a leaning barn. Beyond those eyesores were the mountains, glorious, rocky, and snow-capped.

Dad put his hands on mine and Tater's shoulders and said, "I want you kids to stay off that property. From what I hear, it's owned by a family called the Fites, and they've got a lot of problems."

"What kind of problems?" Tater asked, nosey, know-it-all nine-year old that he was.

"Problems with the law." Dad's face was stern, but Mom walked up, looking softer, pitying, as she stared out at the property.

"They've had a lot of tragedy," she explained.

Tater looked to her with wide eyes. "You met them?"

"No, *Jacobcito.*" *Little Jacob.* "Small town." Mom ruffled his brown curls. "People love to talk. A lot."

They left to unpack and we raced to the tire swing. Tater beat me, as usual, and we were fighting over it when we saw a boy watching from between a couple orange trees at the edge of our property. His hair was so blond. Overgrown like a yellow helmet. His jeans were an inch too short and his T-shirt a size too big. A hound dog puppy with oversized ears sniffed the tree and hiked a leg on it. Tater let go of the swing like he was going to go talk to him.

"Daddy said to stay away!" I hissed.

"He said for us not to go *there*," Tater corrected. The thing about Tater was that he would talk to anyone. He didn't have a sense of 'stranger danger' like I had. So he walked right over to the boy and I followed, wary.

I expected to see meanness in his eyes after what Dad told us. But as we got closer, the boy stayed real still, watching us, just as wary. A weird sense of calm overcame me when he looked at me with thoughtfulness, all serious, like he was taking me in. The puppy came running over, tripping over its ears and paws. I bent down to pet him, but he slobbered a lot. We'd never had a dog. Mom was allergic.

"Hey, I'm Tater."

"Your name's Tater?" The boy's voice was soft. No judgment.

"Well, no. Our last name's Tate, and everyone calls me Tater."

"His real name is Jacob Lee Junior," I chimed in, wanting the boy to look at me again. And he did. And I felt that weird calm again, this time laced with an even weirder tingle of gladness.

"Are you guys Mexican?" the boy asked.

Tater pursed his lips. "You got a problem with Mexicans?"

"No," he said easily.

Tater deflated a little. "Oh. Well, we're half-Mexican. Our

dad's white."

"He thinks maybe he has some Native American in him 'cause he gets real tanned in the sun, and he has brown eyes and hair—" The boy nodded, but my stupid brother cut me off.

"What's *your* name?"

"I'm Rylen. I live over there." He pointed to the old house on the potato farm where we weren't allowed to go. "This is Roscoe." He nodded down to the pup, who ran after a lizard that darted around the tree trunk.

"How old are you?" Tater asked him.

"Nine and three quarters."

"Shoot, I'm nine and a half."

They compared birthdays. Rylen was two months older.

"Well, I'm six and a quarter," I said.

Tater nudged me. "Nuh-uh, you just turned six like two weeks ago. You don't even know what a quarter means."

I shoved him and he laughed. I hated when he tried to humiliate me in front of other kids. I waited for Rylen to laugh like most boys did when Tater teased me, but he just gave a little smile. His teeth were really white against his dirty skin, and his eyes were a dark bluish gray.

"What's your name?" he asked me. I felt pride when he acknowledged me like an equal or something.

"Amber Maria Tate."

"That's pretty."

I stared, and Tater eyed him. The boy's cheeks turned a little pink and he looked down, scuffing his toe in the grass. No boy had ever given me a compliment.

From then on I'd do just about anything for his attention.

"Hey man, wanna swing?" Tater asked. Rylen nodded, and the three of us ran for the hanging tire. The smell of cigarette smoke clung to Rylen's clothes. Tater tried to elbow me out of the way, but Ry spoke up.

"Let's let her go first since she's little."

I frowned at the 'little' part because it felt like a jab, but he was serious. Again. Tater looked baffled, but said, "Okay. Yeah." And together they swung me super high; I clung to the rubber tire, screaming, filled with joy, while Roscoe ran around us in a circle, barking his head off and tripping over his ears.

That night I told mom all about Rylen while she was tucking me in. "He's the nicest boy I ever met. I don't want him to have to stay away."

"Ah, pequeña princesa." My mom was the daughter of migrant workers in southern California. Dad met her when she was working at a taco truck outside of his base, and he was starving after PT. He swears he knew he would marry her when she laughed at him as his mouth was on fire from squirting on too much green hot sauce. "I'm glad he's nice. He can come here any time, but the grown-ups at his house . . . that's who we want you to stay away from."

I remembered what she'd said earlier. "What bad things happened to them?"

Mom sighed. "Rylen had a little brother and a little sister last year." She paused, and my stomach filled with dread. "They're both in heaven now."

My heart started beating super hard. "Why?"

"They were in a car accident. The boy was a baby and the girl was six, like you. Their aunt was driving, and she didn't make them put on their seatbelts." Mom kissed my head.

I'd never heard anything more terrible. I thought about Rylen, and how nice he'd been to me, and how he didn't have his little brother and sister to play with anymore, and I imagined losing Tater. He was annoying, but I did love him. And if a little boy and girl died, that meant I could die too. The exhaustion of the move and the sadness pummeled me, making me shake.

"Why do bad things have to happen? It's not fair."

Mom lifted me and held me close. "I don't know, baby. Life is filled with good and bad. We have to appreciate the good while we have it. Some people, like little Rylen, have learned that the hard way." She'd stroked my wavy hair, murmuring gentle things until I fell asleep.

Growing up in the shadow of two older boys was a challenge, but I was up for it. I wanted to do everything the boys did: skateboarding, rock climbing, rope swinging into the lake, fishing, digging trenches, shooting the bb gun, playing Army. Tater always tried to make me be the nurse, but I wanted to be a soldier too, with a Nerf gun of my own.

"Just let her," Rylen would say in that steady voice of his. And Tater would roll his eyes and grumble, *"Fine."*

As I got older, I agreed to play a medic soldier because I kind of liked bandaging and fixing. Blood didn't gross me out. When me or one of the boys would get hurt, I would watch every step of how Mom cleaned it up and sealed it. She'd be grimacing the whole time, looking pale at the gorier cuts as I openly stared with fascination.

"You'd make a good doctor or nurse someday," Mom said when I was eight, and those words stuck.

Rylen came to our house almost every day. Roscoe would follow him over, and then Ry would pat his rump and say, "Go on home, boy."

He'd sometimes spend whole weekends with us and even weeknights. I learned about his family by eavesdropping on grown-ups.

A lot of people lived in the Fite house, most unemployed

with addictions. Aunts, uncles, cousins, his parents, and his grandfather. His dad and grandfather worked the land. They hired immigrants to help during harvest. I mostly over-heard my mom talking quietly on the phone with Abuela in California, giving her updates on us. Three of Rylen's cousins had been taken away by social services from his aunt. The dad was out of the picture, but a boyfriend lived with them. His aunt and her boyfriend would get jobs as gas station atten-dants, then find ways to get fired to collect unemployment.

". . . can't believe Len Fite lets those leaches live in his house," I heard Dad saying to Mom.

"They're his family," she responded with a sigh.

"They're trash."

"Sh, baby, don't let the kids hear you say that." *Too late.*

"I've got no tolerance for people without work ethic. They're lucky Rylen hasn't been taken away yet." Cold fear sliced through me. Could Rylen be taken away?

"I wish we could keep him here."

Dad mumbled his agreement. He always sounded so an-gry when he talked about the Fites, and Mom just sounded sad.

"His father and grandfather are the only ones who have their acts together, but even Lenard's a loose cannon. That man's got a temper, and when he drinks, he drinks hard. I know he's done jail time."

Mom stayed quiet. I'd seen Len Fite from afar, and also the couple of times he'd shown up at our house to get Ry when he needed him to work. Len was a huge man with a scruffy long beard and he never smiled. His arms were cov-ered in faded tattoos. He smelled like dirt and chickens and sweat. He had that same seriousness of Rylen, but where Ry was gentle, his dad felt dangerous. But Rylen's devotion was obvious in the way he looked at him.

His mom never came over to get him. I only saw her when we were out. She'd be coming out of the liquor store while we were coming out of the little studio room Mom rented to give dance lessons. Mom would say hello and Mayella would halfheartedly wave her cigarette at us.

"Self-medicating," Mom told Abuela on the phone, always in Spanish. "The woman needs help, but she won't talk to me or anyone else. There's no getting through."

It was always a relief to have Ry with us. Just like the day we met, I'd still do anything to impress him. Including trying hot peppers and hot sauces that Tater wouldn't dare put in his mouth. I put my tongue to a ghost pepper on a dare until my nose and eyes ran. And then I hurled a pepper at Tater when he said I looked gross. Rylen followed suit, trying the peppers too, but he had to spit and chug a glass of milk. Honestly, I think he only tried it to make me feel better. And seeing him with runny eyes and a red nose did help.

"You're kinda like a hot pepper, too, you know that?" Rylen told me after I jumped on Tater's back to try and force a pepper to his lips. "Feisty all the time." He took to calling me Pepper after that. I pretended like it was no big deal, but to be given a nickname, something special that was just between us, was the best thing in the world.

Rylen never missed a Sunday supper with us. I began to think it was less about the supper and more about what happened after we ate. The dancing.

Mom was a dance instructor. Salsa and Tango were her specialties, but she could do just about any ballroom style. On Sundays she would turn on her favorite Mexican band CD and her hips would move like *POW, POW*. Daddy would grab a beer and sit back in the recliner, watching Mom with a grin. Rylen would sit in the corner of the couch, eyes soaking us in with that small smile of amusement. Me and Tater had the moves like Mom. Tater was especially funny because he really got into it. When his hips started to swivel fast, Daddy would shout, "Go, Pit Bull!"

The three of us danced until we were sweating and out of breath. Mom took turns leading us, spinning us, sashaying us hip-to-hip. Sometimes she would implore Daddy to get up and join, but he'd laugh and say, "You know I'm just a gringo, baby." Rylen would let her pull him to his feet, but he'd just stand there, red-faced, while we danced around him.

I still dreamed about those nights, longing for that easy laughter and togetherness. But those days were long gone.

# TWO

HEN TATER HAD OTHER friends over, I was never allowed in his room. But Rylen didn't care if I snuck in while they were playing video games. He'd even give me his turn with the controller which really pissed off Tater.

"You afraid a little girl's gonna beat your score?" Rylen asked him. This made Tater battle harder.

"I'm not little!" I insisted. Ry tickled under my arm as I worked the controller, until I wiggled and said, "Leave me alone, you're messing me up!" I tried to kick him, but he grabbed my foot and tickled my arch, making me fall back on the bed screaming.

"I won!" Tater yelled, throwing his arms up. "Take that, pipsqueak!"

I glared at Rylen, but he just grinned in return. I could never stay mad at him. Especially because, as strong as he seemed, I knew he was hurting on the inside. He stayed overnight often, and I always slept lightly those nights, listening. Tater's squeaky bedroom door would wake me, and I'd come out to find Rylen sitting in the living room by himself, reading one of his incredibly boring looking books on the mechanics of airplanes. I sat next to him and eyed the detailed images and complex words.

"How can you read that?" I asked.

He shrugged. "What's wrong with airplanes?"

"Nothing, but that looks confusing."

"It's aerodynamics. It's awesome."

I giggled at how excited he sounded, and his cheeks turned pink.

He let me curl up next to him on the couch. When I was half asleep, I felt him start wiggling, rubbing his back against the couch.

"What's wrong?" I asked.

"Gottta itch right in the middle where I can't reach."

I pulled him forward and scratched with my short nails. Rylen went to mush under my hands, moaning. I laughed at him.

"Are you gonna kick your leg like a dog?" I asked, scratching harder.

He started kicking his leg until we both had the giggles.

I still have a picture on my bedroom corkboard that Mom took when she found me and Rylen asleep on the couch the next morning, snuggled under a throw blanket together. We looked like babies. And it's funny because I never liked being touched when I was trying to sleep. Only with Ry was it okay.

I was eleven the first and only time I saw Rylen cry. I'd seen Tater cry hundreds of times, but this was nothing like that. When Ry got hurt and scraped up, he'd grit his teeth and his face would scrunch up tight. He'd breathe real deep while he clutched his injury, and it would pass without a tear. Then he'd shake it off. But this . . . this was different. I came running out of my bedroom at the sound of the screen door slamming, Mom's hurried murmuring, Ry's deep sniffling.

Tater ran out with me, just as Mom and Dad were sitting Rylen in a chair. We stopped short. Tater's face when he saw his friend crying was as horrified as I felt. They were fourteen now. Even Tater hardly cried anymore. Outside, Roscoe let out a long howl from our front steps.

"It's okay, son," Dad said. He squatted in front of Rylen with a hand on his knee. "You're safe. Tell us what happened."

Mom handed Ry a tissue, and he wiped his nose. His hand was shaking. *I* was shaking. And then Ry took a deep breath and his tears went away. He turned into his serious self. Only his red eyes remained as proof of his breakdown.

"My dad was gone the past two days, working out a market delivery. My mom . . ." Rylen's eyes met Dad's for a second and then dropped. "She let one of the worker men in the house . . . he was in their room, and my dad got back early."

I tried to imagine Mom letting some man in their bedroom while Daddy was away, but it was an impossible thought. It would never happen.

"Did they get into a fight?" Mom asked.

Rylen nodded. His face was grim. My stomach began to tighten. I didn't need to know all the details to know this was not good. And then we heard the sirens from afar. Our heads snapped up to the windows.

"I called the police and then ran here. I think . . . I think Daddy might have killed him."

*Oh my God.*

"Stay here. Lock the door behind me." Dad ran from the house with Mom hollering for him to be careful. She locked the door behind him and turned to us with a face so readable, so grave. It was clear Rylen's life had just taken a turn for the worse. Mom came and sat by his side, pulling his head down to her shoulder so she could hold him. He gladly let her, but he didn't cry anymore. Tater and I stood there, stupidly in shock, at a loss.

That was a long night. The man survived the assault, but just barely. Len Fite was arrested. And while the police were there, they found that Rylen's uncles and one of his aunt's boyfriends had set up a meth lab in their largest shed, so they were both arrested too. Triple whammy.

When Dad got home, he said, "I've told Mayella we'll be keeping Rylen here with us for now. She agreed it was best. She'll even grant us legal custody if it'll keep him out of foster care." We all looked at Rylen, who nodded solemnly at Dad.

"Thanks, Mr. Tate." Ry's eyes were such a deep blue after having cried. He kept his hair, still so blond, cropped in a buzz cut. Unlike when he was a kid, his jeans fit him well now in the length, if not a little loose in his waist, but his T-shirts were still too big for his thin frame. Rylen looked so vulnerable in that moment. I sat next to him and wove my fingers through his. He let me, holding tight, giving me a grateful look.

And that's how Rylen came to live with us when he was fourteen.

That was a crazy year. Mom gave Rylen the guest room. But two months later our grandma Tate passed away in Virginia, so Grandpa Tate came to live with us. Tater's twin bed went away, and he got a bunkbed instead—one of those kinds with a full bed on the bottom—so Ry moved into his room.

Grandpa was a quiet, proud man, who needed more privacy than our guest room allowed, so he turned the attic storage room over the garage into his own personal space. It was a good thing, too, because three months after that Papá Antonio had a heart attack in California, and Abuela ended up coming to live with us too.

That year the house seemed smaller with so many people, but also comfier. Safer. We did a lot of fishing with Grandpa Tate. We'd drive out to Nesbitt or Frenchy Lake, or one of the springs. And then Abuela would make her fish stew or Aroz con Pollo—rice with chicken. In between all of these events, Rylen would disappear home. None of us knew what he did there. Perhaps checked on his mom, the house, the land, who knows? But he always came back in time for a shower, his homework, and bed. Or to watch us dance.

I turned twelve. The boys turned fifteen. Seventh grade, AKA Hell, started for me, and tenth grade started for them. I made my first ever best friend, Remy Haines. She'd been homeschooled through sixth grade, but her mom's real estate career was taking off, so she needed to work full time. Remy and her dad started butting heads right around that time. Remy said it was because she had boobs now, and her dad, a Baptist pastor, couldn't handle her growing up.

Truth was, Remy was boy crazy. And she had fully developed long before the rest of us girls, earning lots of attention, so I could see how it was hard on both her and her father. Funny thing about Remy was that she was a complete dichotomy: super smart with more compassion than anyone I knew, but her two weaknesses, boys and alcohol, were always at odds with the rest of her 'good girl' personality.

Remy ended up spending a lot of time at our house. She and Tater clashed like crazy. When Remy said, "Good lort, your brother is annoying," I knew we'd be best friends forever.

Rylen and Tater became somewhat of football stars. Sophomores on the Varsity team. They seemed to sprout up overnight and I suddenly found myself looking way up at them, a fact Tater loved to rub in as he leaned an elbow on my head like an arm rest. But I was now in the perfect position to punch him right in the gut, something that always gave Rylen and Remy good chuckles.

Rylen became more obsessed with airplanes than ever. He announced at dinner one night that he wanted to be an Air Force pilot, so Dad signed him up for CAP: Civil Air Patrol.

"You'll meet two hours a week and one Saturday a month," Dad told him. "You'll get to fly in their planes and help the Air Force with recovery of parts and eventually compete for scholarships to get a pilot license."

Rylen's face looked like a golden egg had just split open and revealed a world of possibilities to him. I loved my dad for putting that look on Ry's face. Remy was at our house that day. I caught her staring at me as I stared at Rylen, and I quickly focused on my plate. Later she cornered me and asked, "You like him, don't you?"

"What?" My heart felt like it was in a bouncy-house. "He's my friend."

She eyed me, then gave her all-knowing Remy smile. "Mm-hm."

I'd never really thought of my feelings like that until Remy brought it up. After I realized she was right, I couldn't ignore it anymore. Suddenly, everything changed.

# THREE

MONTHS LATER, ON A fall day when the leaves were changing on the valley trees, Mom, Abuela, and Tater were sitting on the couch looking sullen when I came in from the school bus.

"What is it?" I tossed my bookbag to the wall.

"Rylen's grandfather died today."

My heart sank. "Is Ry okay?"

"He's with his mom," Mom said. "But I'm worried. That whole family has been relying on Mr. Fite to support them while Len's in prison. He's the only one who worked the farm. He hired the help and made the sales. When I went over there today, Mayella was crying to Ry about how they'd lose the land. . ."

Her jaw clenched, and she shook her head. I had a bad, bad feeling about where this was going.

"Can't she hire someone?" Tater asked.

"With what money?" Mom retorted. "Mr. Tate was only able to pay his help once his crops were sold. She doesn't know the business side of things, and she's not in her right mind to do it anyway."

"I no like that woman," Abuela said in her clipped accent.

My insides knotted. "Rylen's going to try and do the crops himself, isn't he?" I asked.

Tater snorted. "He can't. He's got school and football and CAP." The room quieted. The *tick tock* of the minute hand on our clock echoed until Tater's eyes got big. "He can't, right Mom?"

"I won't let him quit school," Mom said quietly. "But I can't stop him from quitting sports or CAP."

Tater stood up, his face reddening. "She can't do that to him!"

"It's his choice," Mom said.

"Yeah, but she's manipulating him! She doesn't even care about him! The only time she ever calls is when she needs him to come do something for her."

Mom's eyes began to water. "I know, Jacobcito. But I can't stop him."

We all knew Rylen. His loyalty and need to protect what was his was unparalleled. It didn't matter if 'what was his' deserved him or not. He was honor bound to those he cared about.

"This is bullshit!" Tater stormed to his room and slammed the door, shaking the house. Mom shut her eyes and a fat tear rolled out from each side. She wiped them away. My own throat constricted.

"Sí, es caca de la vaca," Abuela said. I nearly choked on a cough and Mom stared at Abuela before looking at me, caught between mirth and sadness.

"I make fried plantain," Abuela said, standing. "For Rylen. When he come back."

Somehow, I didn't think Ry's favorite food was going to fix this.

Ry didn't do football that fall or baseball in the spring. He cut his school load down to the bare minimum core classes and signed up for work study to get out early. Eventually, CAP had to be let go too. Rylen went from being a happy athlete with good grades to being stressed and barely scraping by with Ds. Each day he would come over at 5:30 on the dot for dinner, scarf it down to rush home, and be back at 8:30 when it got too dark to work. He took over paying his family's bills, communicating with produce buyers and workmen. It was like watching a grown man caught in a teen's lanky body. It seemed that overnight his voice abruptly lowered into somewhat of a rumble, like his dad's. Hearing him talk on the phone with them, spouting off numbers and being a hardass negotiator, blew my mind.

Tater stayed quiet, watching with ire in his eyes as his best friend came and went, conducting business, Roscoe dutifully on his heel. Mom bought a dog bed for our covered porch. Tater stopped asking Ry to hang out, or if he was coming to watch the games. The answer was always the same. They didn't joke around or laugh anymore. The tension was awful, and even Remy stopped trying to goad Tater into arguments when she visited.

The boys turned sixteen that spring, and Rylen started missing dinners. We'd wait until six and then put his plate in the fridge and reluctantly eat without him. I hated those nights. Nobody talked. It was like we'd lost him, or like he'd lost an irreplaceable part of his youth.

One of those warm evenings after dinner, I slid my feet into a pair of flip-flops and told everyone, "I'll be back. Just taking a walk."

The sun had dipped behind the mountains, turning the sky into a peach. I knew where my feet would take me, and I didn't bother to stop them. All these years and I'd never gone on Fite property. At first it had been out of fear, and then out of respect for Rylen's privacy. But lately I'd been missing him too much. I needed to see him and know he was okay. A perfectly straight row of sprouting potato vines led the way. How many of them had been planted by Rylen's own strong hands?

As I got closer to the house, I heard the clucking chatter of chickens, and saw lots of hens and one rooster, all free roaming, pecking at the dirt. Details of the house's dilapidation became apparent now; paint flecking off, missing siding and roof tiles, drooping drain pipes, tilted half-porch with rotted stairs. Stone slabs had been stacked to use as steps instead. Three old cars sat to the side with long weeds growing up around them. Further down was farm equipment in front of the barn. I felt nervous, like a trespasser. Roscoe came out from between two of the cars and gave a deep howl, making me jump. Then his tail wagged and he trotted over, ears swinging. He'd gone gray in the muzzle. I patted his head, and he rubbed his giant face against me, sliming my upper thigh and the top of my shorts.

I laughed, and a clank came from near the barn. A familiar figure pushed out from under the tractor, causing my belly to swoop.

"Roscoe, no." Rylen's deep voice made me shake. He stood up and cocked his head at me from afar, taking off his work gloves and tossing them next to the tire. "Amber?" The muscles in his arms flexed. Ry was nearly as tall as his dad now.

"Ye—" It came out squeaky, so I cleared my throat. "Yeah. Hey."

He walked over, and it felt like I was seeing him for the first time, this new, grown-up version of Rylen Fite. He seemed so much . . . bigger, standing in front of me, appearing worried, smelling of motor oil and dirt with a hint of his familiar soap.

"What are you doing here?" He glanced toward his house and all around, shifting his feet as if embarrassed. "Everything okay?"

"Yeah. Yes. I was just checking on you. You missed dinner." Again.

Why did I feel so nervous and stupid? Rylen's eyes slid down to my chest in the tank top. His gaze became like my personal sun, heating me. He blinked and jerked his head toward the fields. I crossed my arms. I was still getting used to the whole boobs and bra thing. Certain bras lifted them up and made them look bigger. Lots of boys stared at school, which always made me uncomfortable, but to have Rylen look made me feel scorched in a satisfying way.

"I had to drive my mom to the store," he said quietly.

"You . . . drove her?" I was so confused. "Is she not able to drive anymore?"

"She tried to, but ran into the mailbox."

Oh. She'd been too drunk. I kicked a rock, still keeping my arms crossed. "But you don't have your license yet."

"You gonna tell on me, Pepper?" His mouth lifted in a small grin, and I couldn't help but smile a little in return.

"Just be careful, 'kay? I don't want you getting in trouble."

"It's all good. I'm signed up for driving school this summer, so I'll have my permit and license soon."

"Don't get too big for your britches," I teased.

"No need to worry about that. A hick always knows his place."

I frowned at his self-deprecation. "You're not a hick."

"Sure I am. It's all right, though. Someday I'll get the hell out of this town."

He gave me an easy grin and reached around to pull my ponytail. I slapped at his hand and tried to smile back, but all I could think about was Rylen leaving town someday, and how much I hated that idea.

"So." He gave my arm a slow-motion punch. "You're finishing middle-school, huh? You'll be at the high school with us next year."

My shoulders rose and fell in a 'no-big-deal' shrug, though I was beyond excited. "You gonna let me ride to school with you guys or make me take the bus?"

"Me and you get the back seat. Tater can be our chauffeur."

I laughed, imagining what Tater would have to say about that. Though Tater had different girlfriends every week, so he probably wouldn't be alone in front. I imagined being in the back seat with Rylen, and I had to tighten my arms over my chest.

"Sun's gone down," Rylen said. "You cold?"

Nevada was funny like that. Hot as heck when the sun was out, then suddenly cold when it went down.

"Nah, I'm—"

"C'mere." Rylen reached out and wrapped his arms around me, pulling me to his chest, resting his chin on my head as he ran his hands up and down my upper arms to warm me. Through his shirt I could smell his soap stronger now. The same smell that always wafted from the bathroom after he showered. I freaking loved that smell. Not to sound creepy, but I sometimes used his gel-soap too, just to smell him throughout the day.

The way Rylen held me, turning his face to put his cheek against my forehead now, made me feel like this was about more than just keeping me warm. Like he'd needed a loving touch. How long had it been since I'd hugged him? Since *anyone* hugged him? I slowly released my arms and let them slide around to his back. I tried to keep a little space between us, but Rylen pulled me to him and my boobs pressed against his chest. I held my breath at first, afraid I might hyperventilate at the sensation. I let my fingers splay out against his back, and then I scratched the spot right in the middle.

He gave a groan and kicked a leg, making me laugh.

"Ew!" came a kid's voice from the doorway. "Are y'all gonna do it?"

Rylen broke away so fast I stumbled back a step. A round boy stood behind the screen door. Heat burst into my cheeks as I registered what the boy had said. I'd heard in school that Rylen's aunt got her three kids back. This must be the fifth grader, Marcus.

"Don't be disrespectful, Marc. This is my friend Amber."

"Aaaamberrrr," Marcus said, making kissing sounds and grotesquely circling his tongue.

A younger boy and a toddler girl pushed beside Marcus, staring out from the behind the screen. Man . . . they looked like they really needed baths. It hurt my heart.

Rylen made a move forward, like he wanted to teach his cousin a lesson, but I grabbed his arm. A man in a ratty T-shirt with long hair came to the door and pushed his way through the kids. He shuffled out and past us, ignoring us, boots kicking up dirt, and went to the side of the house. Then proceeded to stop and pee on the wall. Rylen turned away and closed his eyes, his jaw locking. The tiny girl came out in her bare feet, dirty nightgown dragging the ground. She came straight to Rylen, and he picked her up. She laid her head on his shoulder and stared at me through stringy locks of blond hair.

"Macy, this is Amber," Rylen said. Macy stared at me silently. "How 'bout I give you a bath tonight, Mace." Still, she said nothing. Just clung to Ry and watched me carefully.

In that moment I had a flash of the future, of Rylen as a man holding our child in his arms. A flush of surprise and embarrassment ran through me. Were these the kind of thoughts other thirteen-year-old girls had when they looked at boys? Is this what Mom meant when she told me hormones would make me feel strange and confused sometimes?

"Who's out there?" came a woman's scratchy voice from inside.

Rylen locked his jaw and set down Macy. "Go on in. I'll be there soon."

"You should go," Rylen whispered to me, but it was too late. His mom swung the screen door wide and let it clatter shut behind her. She sauntered down the cinder block steps with a red plastic cup in her hand, eyeing me. Mayella was curvy and probably killer-gorgeous in her prime. She swished bleached hair from her eyes and looked me up and down.

"Well, look at you. You're growin' up real nice, aren't you Autumn?"

"Amber," Rylen corrected.

"Hi, ma'am," I said quietly.

"Don't *ma'am* me. I ain't that old." She watched me over the rim of the cup as she drank.

*Sir* and *Ma'am* had nothing to do with age in our household. Military personnel and their families were just sort of conditioned to call everyone that.

She looked at Rylen. "You be careful, boy. Remember what I told you. Girls who think they're better than you . . . they'll eat you up and spit you out. You might be a catch right now . . ." She raised her cup and it sloshed. "Mr. Good-Looking Star Quarterback. But that ain't gonna last."

Rylen's face tightened. "Yeah, Mama. Got it. And I'm not the quarter back no more." He turned his head to look at me with blank eyes and said again, "You should go. I'll be over once I get Macy to sleep."

A huge, ratty knot formed in my stomach. I wanted to drag him away with me, but instead I nodded and gave his mom a nod good-bye too. Then I turned and jogged back into the potato field, all the way home to our manicured lawn, which looked and smelled more pristine than ever. Everything was wrong. I sat on the porch steps—the perfectly shaped and painted wood steps that I suddenly felt guilty to have. Mom peeked out the door at me.

"Why are you sitting out here in the dark? Are you okay?"

"I'm fine."

I wrapped my arms around myself, jumbled up inside. Behind me, I barely registered Mom tossing out my jacket and me sliding my arms in. An hour and a half passed before I saw Rylen's shadowy figure trudging through the field toward me. When he got closer, he stopped and surveyed me a few seconds, then came and joined me, sitting by my side in silence.

"I don't think I'm better than you," I finally whispered. "I would never think that."

He pulled his earlobe, a nervous gesture. "She wasn't talking about you."

She clearly had been. Hadn't she? If not me, then what other girls was she talking about? Rylen didn't have a girl-friend. Never had, that I knew of. There were always girls flanking him. Maybe she was talking about all girls, in general. I wanted to tell him she was wrong, but I didn't want to make him more uncomfortable.

"Who was that man?" I asked.

"Don't know. There's always men in and out of the house." He turned his head away and I couldn't see his expression. Rylen always seemed strong, but he had to be hurting inside. I slid my hand into the crook of his arm and leaned against him.

A *whoosh* began in the distance, getting louder. Rylen looked up into the starlit sky. My grip on his arm tightened as a fighter jet zoomed over head, shaking the ground beneath us. Two more followed, filling my ears with their blasts of sound. Fighter jets flying low over our county was a normal occurrence, living so close to Nellis Air Force Base.

Rylen stared wistfully upward until it was silent again. He pulled his arm closer to his body, thereby pulling me closer too, and put his hand on top of mine. Together, we stayed like that a long time until Mom told us to come inside for bed.

# FOUR

**T**ATER WAS BROODING AT dinner. Again. He kept shooting glares across the table at Rylen, who was surely aware, but chose to ignore him and take a third helping of tamales.

"Dude, the team needs you," Tater said. "You took a whole year off already."

"Jacob." Dad leveled him with a hard look. "That's enough."

Abuela unwrapped another tamale and put it on Tater's plate, covering it in her rich, dark mole sauce, then patted his hand. He sighed down at it.

Rylen said quietly, "I'm sorry."

Those two words seemed to blanket the dining room in thick sadness, because he truly did sound sorry. Regretful. Stuck.

"You don't need to be sorry," Mom told Rylen. "And just a heads up . . . we've got a surprise for you tonight."

"What is it?" Tater asked with his mouth full.

"You'll see." She smiled and took a bite. We ate in silence, but a bit of the tension had seeped away and been replaced by curious excitement.

The silence was broken by three hard knocks on the door. We stared around at one another as Dad got up and opened it, and two sets of feet walked back in. A blast of air slid into my lungs. Lenard Fite filled the entrance, as large and beard-ed as ever. Rylen leapt from his chair and sprinted through the space. The two of them collided in a hard hug, burying their faces in each other's necks, clinging with tight fists. Moisture crept into my eyes. I looked at Mom's beaming face and realized this was the surprise.

"Are you out? For good?" Rylen asked.

"I'm out, son. And I ain't going back."

When Rylen and his father became aware of all of us watching, they broke away, looking down, bashful. We all stood to welcome Len back. He nodded, appearing uncom-fortable with all the kindness. Then he addressed Rylen.

"Your mama and her sister don't live at the house no more. It's just you and me."

Rylen squinted with worry. "Where's Mom gonna live?"

"Movin' in with her sister's boyfriend, I guess. Not my concern." Rylen opened his mouth, but his father took him by the shoulder. "You can still see her—I'm not gonna stop you, but she ain't coming to my house no more. I know you been taking care of her and the house and the land, but that's over now. You understand me?" Rylen stood very still while his dad spoke. "I'm proud o' you, son, and you can still help out, but you're gonna be a grown man soon enough. Right now you need to be a kid while you still can. And I need to be a man who gets to see his son play ball."

The timing could not have been more perfect. Tater sniffed and lowered his head to wipe his nose. When he raised his head again I saw he was trying hard not to cry. I wanted to hug him and punch him at the same time.

Lenard looked between Mom and Dad. "Thank you for all you done. I'll work to pay you back—"

"No," Dad said. "That's not necessary."

"It's been our pleasure." Mom sniffled, sounding just like Tater. "He's a good boy. We love him." Rylen's cheeks flushed pink.

Grandpa Tate stepped forward and introduced himself. Grandpa was shorter and leaner than Mr. Fite, but formidable enough in his personality that they might just get along well.

Abuela stepped up, tiny, but fearless. "You eat tamale?"

Lenard looked toward the dining room. "Uh, it smells mighty good, but I better not—"

"Okay." She took him by the wrist as if he weren't twice her size. "You eat."

I covered my mouth, trying not to laugh as Lenard let himself be led. Rylen saw me and grinned. He looked so strong in that moment, so alive. Tater jumped high onto Rylen's back and got him in a headlock. They tumbled to the ground, wrestling loudly.

"Boys," called Mom. "Get in here and finish your food."

They stood, shoving and smiling. And just like that, the strain between them vanished in that miraculous way of boy friendships. For the first time in a long time, I felt like everything was going to be okay.

~

I will never forget freshman year. I will never forget the deep, aching, longing—the *need* which could not be satisfied by anything less than his attention. I crushed so hard on Rylen Fite it wasn't healthy. He made my heart and stomach and head dance and expand and twist. I'd become a straight-up mess for him, and only Remy knew. And Mom . . . but only because she was so observant. And Abuela, because those two had no secrets.

Sometimes I tried to pass Rylen in the hallway at school without saying anything, mostly because the senior guys and girls he and Tater hung out with were so intimidating. But he wasn't having any of that. Ry would snatch me by the waist and spin me into his arms in a bear hug, lifting me off my feet and saying, "What, you can't say hello?"

Sometimes Tater would chime in, tickling my waist with his crab-claw hands. He'd reach out for Remy, too, only to reel back at the viper gaze she reserved for him.

"Damn, why you always so salty?" he asked. She walked away with an eye roll and swish of her hips, and I punched Tater for staring at her butt.

I turned a corner where Remy awaited me, hip propped against the lockers with a grin, and I leaned my head back against the cool metal, feeling sensitive everywhere his hands had touched.

"You've got it bad, Amb."

"Nope."

"Like, *bad* bad. You should tell him—"

"No." I spun to get in her face and show every ounce of horror that her words dredged up inside me. "I swear if you ever say a word, I'll never speak to you again."

Remy merely smiled at my psychotic threats. "What are you so afraid of? You're gorgeous and he obviously cares about you." She didn't understand. She was never afraid when it came to boys. They made her nervous and excited, but when Remy set her goals on a guy there was no doubt she could have him. I'd never had that kind of confidence when it came to Rylen, and I doubted I ever would.

I was instantly popular by no means of my own. Every

freshman girl wanted to be at my side when Rylen Fite and Jacob "Tater" Tate took notice of me and lavished me with silly attention, but Remy was my only trusted friend. We went together to all the games and traveled to districts and regionals, then onto state semi-finals where they narrowly lost. Colleges were in full recruit mode.

As acceptance letters and scholarship offers began to roll in for the boys that fall and winter, a sickening sense of finality and urgency began to fill me. They would be graduating soon. Leaving home. Which school would they choose? How far away would they go? How often would I get to see Rylen? Forget about Tater; I was sure however much I saw him would be plenty. But Ry . . . the thought of him living a life outside of here, outside of *me* . . . I had to make him realize before he left just how perfect we could be. What girl knew him better than me? None. And I wanted to keep it that way.

If only I knew how.

Tater and Rylen decided to attend the University of Nevada where they would play Wolf Pack football and do ROTC. Reno was nearly six hours away. *Six hours.* My heart ached just thinking about it. Tater wanted to join the Army as an officer, just as Rylen wanted to join the Air Force, despite Tater's mocking about how wimpy the AF was.

"You'll be on a stationary bike for boot camp while I'm working my ass off . . ." Blah, blah, military competitiveness, blah.

"I just wanna fly, man," Rylen said. "And I'll still be able to kick your ass."

As always, the taunting led to a wrestling match wherever they happened to be.

Spring came, and baseball season was in full swing. Rylen acted a little weird around me sometimes. Nevada's dry heat required lots of shorts and tank-tops in my wardrobe, but it seemed the more skin I showed the less he'd look at me. And all the while, boys my age circled like annoying gnats. I didn't get it. When he came to our house, I had to throw on a hoodie just so he'd acknowledge me. Remy didn't believe me until she came home with me after school one day and watched carefully, seeing it with her own eyes.

"That is weird," she whispered to me in my bedroom. "He's not normal."

Maybe that's why I liked him. "Maybe he's just respectful," I whispered back.

"I don't even know how to advise you, Amb. I give up. May the force of weirdness be with you." She gave me the Star Trek "V" with her fingers.

"Wrong fandom."

"Whatev."

# FIVE

FRIDAY, MAY SIXTEENTH, WOULD forever stand out in my mind for not just one, but for two horrible reasons. It started with Rylen ringing my cell phone after school, sounding kind of nervous.

"Hey, Pepper, you busy?"

I could have been busy with the most important task of my life and my answer still would have been, "No, what's up?"

"Wanna come to the mall with me? I need your help with something."

"Sure!" I cursed myself for sounding so excited.

He hesitated and mumbled, "You heard on the announcements today, right? About me and Tater being nominated for Prom King?"

"Yeah," I said. My tummy started wobbling at the mention of prom. "That's awesome."

He groaned. "Not really. I hate that kind of stuff. But I feel like I have to go."

"Okay . . ." Major tummy wobbling, like the kid on that

old movie The Goonies doing the truffle-shuffle.

"Can you help me pick out a tux and stuff?"

"Of course!" Agh, again with the over-excitement. I took a deep breath. "Yeah." No biggie.

"Okay, cool. Thanks. I'll be over in fifteen minutes."

We hung up and I ran for my room in a sprint. Mom followed me in, her arms crossed.

"What's going on?"

I grabbed my makeup bag. "Rylen's taking me to the mall so I can help him pick a tuxedo for prom." I smashed the blush brush into the dark pink powder and crushed it against my cheekbone.

"Whoa, whoa." Mom came forward and wiped my cheek with the back of her fingers in an upward stroke. She took the bag. "Let me." In a flash she'd dabbed everything on. Just enough.

"Does he have a date?" she asked as she ran a hand through my hair. She tried to make it sound like an offhand question, but I could feel the heaviness of expectancy in her voice.

"I don't think so." It came out as a husky whisper.

Mom looked at me now. I could see excitement in her eyes, which fueled my own eagerness tenfold. I let out a little squeal.

"Don't jump to conclusions, princesa."

"I'm not." I totally was.

She hugged me and sent me off to brush my teeth. Then reapply my lipstick.

Ry picked me up in the old Chevy truck he'd spent the last year fixing himself. It still needed a paint job, but it purred nicely.

He opened the door for me and I climbed in. Our eyes met as he closed it, and he seemed sheepish. Nervous. Holy truffle-shuffle.

Rylen looked completely out of his element standing in the small tuxedo shop in his dusty boots, beat-up jeans, and T-shirt. His T-shirts fit perfectly these days, by the way.

A sharp-dressed woman came up and smiled. "Can I help you?"

"Uh, yeah. Yes, ma'am. My prom's in a couple weeks."

She took down all of his information and measured him. I stood watching, trying not to smile as he lifted his arms, giving me a grin. Then it was time to choose a style.

"Just . . . pick something," he told me. "Whatever you want."

Whatever *I* wanted. I bit my lip as I walked the rows. Rylen wasn't flashy. No shiny cuffs or tails. He needed something classic, black and white. His gratefulness as I chose was so cute. He nodded, looking happy about my selection.

As he went to the counter, a guy behind us said, "Yo, Fite!" Rylen turned and the two of them grasped palms, then bumped knuckles. I recognized him as a football player.

"What's up, Smitty?" Rylen said.

"Not much, man. Listen to this—I came two days ago to get my tux, right? Then Lanna sent me a picture of her dress and told me I had to come back to get a bowtie and cummerbund to match. Can you believe that shit?" Both of them laughed. "Is Becca making you match with her?"

A wave of dizziness crashed over me and I reached for the counter to steady myself.

Rylen shook his head. "Nah, man. I'll make sure the corsage matches, though. She's wearing blue."

"What kind of blue?" Smitty asked. "Sky blue? Royal blue? Navy blue?"

Rylen turned ashen. "I don't know."

"You're fucked if you mess it up, dude."

Rylen and Smitty continued to talk and laugh, but their words were like storm clouds in my ears.

Becca. Becca Rinefeld. I imagined the tall, dark-haired senior from the dance team on Rylen's arm. Jealousy made my stomach spasm, hot and nauseating. I stood there in absolute silence while Rylen finished up his transaction and said good-bye to Smitty. He politely held out an arm for me to go ahead of him. I walked robotically. We were silent all the way to the truck—him seeming comfortable, me more uncomfortable than I'd ever been.

As he put the truck in gear and headed out of the parking lot he said, "Thanks for your help."

"Why didn't you ask Becca to help you?" It came out venomous. I stared straight forward, but in my peripheral I saw Rylen's head snap to me.

"She's working. Are you okay?"

Oh, God. I was going to cry. I swallowed hard and willed the moisture to back off.

"What's wrong?" He sounded so worried. So freaking clueless.

"When you asked me to come today, I thought . . . I didn't know you had a date."

Oh, God. Oh, God, oh, God. I said it. It was out there. The words hung between us like a fat blob of awkward. And as much as I wanted to take them back, I was glad he would know now. My secret was out. The ball was in his court.

"Aw, Amber. It's just a stupid dance. It's nothing special. Everyone makes prom seem like such a big deal, but it's not. People dress up and dance and get stupid."

"I don't care about the *prom*," I said. My hands were shaking. I clenched them shut.

"What then?" Absolute confusion in his voice. He still didn't get it.

"I care about *you*! You're leaving in a couple months, and, and . . ." Freaking tears, go away!

He looked aghast. Rylen whipped the truck into a side road so quickly I had to grab the Oh Shit handle. He put it in park and faced me.

"Pepper, come on, I'm not going to forget about you when I go away to college. I could never. You and me, we're gonna write each other every week, right? Tater and I will come home to visit whenever we can. And we'll hang out before I leave. I'll take you to the movies. We haven't done that in a long time."

He was trying to appease me, like I was a little kid having a tantrum, not a fourteen-year-old girl who had basically just declared her feelings. He searched my face. My tears dried up as sheer disappointment and mortification settled in. I looked straight forward again.

I felt him staring at me, like he was trying to figure me out. Then he shook his head, at a loss. "Shit, I'm sorry." The confusion in his voice was still there, my secret still intact as if I hadn't just laid it all out there for him.

"Just take me home," I whispered.

He put the truck in first gear and did just that. I jumped out of the truck before he could put it in park, and ran inside. I blew past Mom, who frowned. Then I slammed my bedroom door and fell face down on my bed in a full dramatic meltdown.

Moments later I felt the bed sink and Mom's hand brushing over my back. "Three years seems like a big difference when you're young," she murmured. "But before you know it, you'll be a grown woman, and the age thing won't matter. Don't rush it, princesa. You know Rylen loves you. But you're like a sister to him right now."

"Mom, *please*." Not helping. I pushed my face further into

my pillow, until she sighed and left me.

Hours later she tapped on my door. "Dinner's ready."

"I'm not hungry." I knew I was being a baby, but I couldn't face anyone. I felt like such a fool. After a minute her feet pattered away, followed by sounds of all the family gathering around the dinner table, voices lowered as if they were afraid to bother me. Afraid of my hormonal female teenage wrath. I didn't hear Rylen, so if he was there, he wasn't talking.

I texted Remy, who was furious that I hadn't texted her right away, but I told her it all happened so fast. She wanted to call me, but I couldn't talk. My emotions were still too raw. We texted for over an hour, releasing all our frustration, disbelief, and pure confusion about Rylen Fite.

By the time I heard dishes clanking in the sink, my stomach was grumbling. Prideful embarrassment was the only thing keeping me in my room. I would wait until everyone dispersed before I'd sneak into the kitchen to grab something.

The television in the family room came on. Dad and Grandpa watched the news every night after dinner. A low rumble of rock music came from Tater's room. I waited half an hour more before cracking open my door and slipping out. In the kitchen, I grabbed a mozzarella stick from the fridge and a bag of chips. I was filling a cup with water when I heard all of the adults in the family room, their voices terse. Something was majorly wrong.

"Jesus . . ."

"No . . ."

"Dios mío!"

I dropped my stuff on the table and ran into the family room. Mom, Dad, Abuela, and Grandpa Tate were all standing, staring in horror at the television.

The screen showed an aerial view of some massive, smoking ruins. The bottom of the screen read, *Bombings at Three*

*Major Hollywood Film Studios.* The reporter was saying, "We're not sure yet if this is an act of terrorism . . ."

"Bullshit," Dad murmured, looking fierce. "Simultaneous bombings is terrorism." Mom shook her head, eyes watering.

"One moment . . ." The reporter stopped, reading something that was handed to him. For a moment his face went slack, and then he regained composure. "It looks as if there's also been a bombing at Disneyland . . . and Universal Studios Orlando." A harsh line creased the reporter's forehead.

"No!" I yelled. There had to be thousands of children at those places! Mom came to me and we grasped hands, staring at the TV. I felt like I couldn't breathe.

"What kind of monsters would blow up Disney?" Grandpa asked.

Tater and Rylen came running in from his bedroom. "What's going on?" Tater asked.

"Bombings at studios and theme parks," Dad said.

"*What?!*" Tater's face went red with anger. Rylen met my eyes in a crestfallen moment of guilt. I looked away. We had bigger problems.

The boys fell in to our semi-circle around the television. The news only got worse. By the end of the hour, it was reported that six theme parks across the U.S. and five film studios had been hit. Besides Disneyland in California and Universal Studios in Florida, there'd been bombings at Sea World in Orlando, Six Flags over Dallas, Six Flags in New Jersey, and Kings Dominion in Virginia. The two other film studios were in New York City. The bombings were major. Huge.

This was the largest simultaneous attack to ever hit the U.S. The number of casualties were rising at an alarming rate. The pictures . . . oh, good Lord, the pictures. Mom, Abuela, and I ended up on the couch clutching hands, our faces tear-streaked. To see all those families, spring-breakers. People running, screaming, with limp babies in their arms. It was impossible not to imagine that being us on one of our family vacations.

Whoever had done this, they'd blatantly hit the heart of our country, our soft spots, our hallowed family grounds. Our entertainment industry—the very symbols of our freedoms and joy. I couldn't fathom a world where masterminds set out to hurt children.

Dad paced the room spouting, "Fucking cowards!" over and over. Mom never bothered to tell him to stop cussing like she normally did. He'd called a fellow soldier to make sure nothing had happened in Vegas, but all was clear there. Rylen and Tater stood with their arms crossed, like angry statues facing the television. Grandpa sat on the edge of his rocker, staring helplessly.

I felt so powerless. I wanted to help those people. I wanted to do something. I wanted to stop all of the evil. And yet, what could I do? We sat there all night, unable to tear ourselves away from the news.

"*No organizations have come forward to claim responsibility . . .*"

"*Death toll rises to over ten thousand . . .*"

"*Military and police on the highest alert . . .*

"*Theme parks nationwide being evacuated and shut down to be scoured for danger . . .*"

And finally, the President, with bags under his eyes.

"We do not yet know the perpetrators of these unforgiveable crimes, but I can assure you our country's highest personnel are seeking answers as I speak. We will find who's behind this." He jabbed his finger down on the podium and enunciated each phrase with anger. "We will have justice. This was an act of war, and we will act accordingly." I was glad to see the fire in his eyes. I wanted vengeance, and I wanted it swiftly.

At three in the morning I was curled in the corner of the couch, trying my best to keep my eyes open, when I heard Rylen say something to Dad.

"I want to talk to you about joining the Air Force this summer."

I stayed curled up real still, but my eyes blasted open, fully awake. Rylen and Tater were sitting on the ground with their arms across their knees. Dad was in the recliner now, Grandpa Tate having retired to bed at one along with Mom and Abuela.

"Me too," Tater said. "Army."

"Now, just hold on a minute boys. I know you're both fired up, and I understand, but you have a plan already in motion. A good plan."

"With all due respect, Mr. Tate. I want to change my plan."

I sat up now. Rylen's serious eyes flicked to me, then back to Dad.

"Take it from me as someone who went straight into the military from high school," Dad said. "It will be worth it for you both to go to college and join as officers. The pay is better, the opportunities—"

"I don't care about any of that," Rylen said. He sounded more passionate than I'd ever heard him. "I don't really care about college either. I just wanted to play football a little longer, but that doesn't matter now. I don't want to wait."

"You won't be a pilot if you're not an officer," Dad told him.

At this, Rylen's jaw rocked, contemplating. "I know. But I applied for the CAP scholarship to get my pilot license. If I get it, I'll have my license before I graduate. That will be enough for now."

"It's enough for you to just have a civilian pilot license?" Dad challenged. "Because having a license doesn't mean you get to fly Air Force jets, son. Isn't that your dream?"

Ry's jaw locked for a handful of tense seconds before he said, "Dreams can change, sir. I'm ready."

A tremble began at my core and spread outward until my hands shook. Rylen was not impulsive. He was thoughtful and decisive. If he joined the Air Force now they would own him and move him anywhere they wanted. He wouldn't be in Reno for the next four years with the freedom to visit every summer and holidays.

"I'm ready now too," Tater said. "I don't care about being an officer. I've watched you my whole life. There's nothing wrong with being infantry. Soldiers are badass. The Airborne—"

"Jacob, I've shown you what I wanted you to see." Dad's voice with Tater was much sterner. "From the outside it looks like fun and games. Jumping out of airplanes, working your ass off at P.T., Drill Sergeants screaming in your face." *That* sounded like fun and games? "But it's hard damn work with a lot of unnecessary drudgery."

"I don't care, Dad!" Tater jumped to his feet and pointed at the television. "They need us. You saw that. I don't want to wait!"

Dad's body was tense as he rubbed his face in his hands. Dad had badly injured his knee in a jump as an Airborne Infantryman years ago, forcing him to become a recruiter. I know he'd seen a lot during his stints overseas, but he never spoke of it. Not once. From the tension rolling off him, I'm pretty sure those scenarios were running through his head right now . . . only with Tater's face instead of his own.

He lifted his head, eyes rimmed in red. "I want you both

to give it one week. One week from today, if you still feel this passionately about joining, then we can talk. But there is no shame in getting your education and waiting it out. The country will still need you three or four years from now. Maybe even more so. And as officers you'll have more power to help. Just . . . think about it. Okay?"

Both boys nodded their heads. Dad stood and came over to me, leaning down to kiss my head. He crouched and met my eyes. His were dark and round.

"I love you."

I immediately choked up. He hadn't been as affectionate with me lately since I began 'blossoming'. I didn't realize how much I'd missed it. "I love you too, Daddy." He stood and left us.

Watching Tater and Rylen sitting there, staring off into space, it was hard to see them as anything more than just *boys*. I tried to imagine them in boot camp in three months. Then heading out into danger. I wanted to beg them to go to college, but my opinion wouldn't matter. I could only hope they'd change their minds in a week's time.

Tater eventually stood and trudged to his room. After a minute of awkward silence, Rylen got up and came over, sitting close. He watched his hands as he rubbed them slowly together.

"You still mad at me?" he asked.

"I'm not mad," I whispered. I was never mad, exactly, more like hurt. Disappointed. Humiliated. Broken-hearted. "I'm just gonna miss you."

"I'll miss you too, Pep. More than you know."

He didn't mean it in the way I meant it. I knew that, but I took his words and held them close anyhow. Rylen leaned across me and grabbed the remote. He switched it to a light-hearted movie and pressed play.

"Lay down," he said gently. He scooted down so I could lie, and he pulled my feet into his lap, then tossed the throw blanket over me. His hands rested on my ankles. Now and then he'd absently touch my feet, kneading the pads of my toes in his tough fingers. I wondered if he used to do that with his tiny cousin, Macy. I wondered if he ever saw her anymore.

My vision blurred as I relaxed into Rylen's touch.

I woke early to the sound of a *click*. My groggy eyes cracked open enough to see Mom, camera in hand. She gave a small smile before walking away. Rylen had fallen to the side, onto me, and was sound asleep. His head was on my hip, his arm slung down the length of my back, his other hand splayed against my stomach as if holding me like a pillow. My feet were still across his thighs. I was covered in Rylen.

It was seven in the morning, and I really needed to pee, but I didn't want to move. Warm breath bathed my hip from Ry's lips through my pajama shorts. His arm on my back moved a little, fingers nuzzling the back of my neck. I wanted to run my hand over his short strands of light hair. I wanted to stay like this forever. But Tater came into the room, giving an obnoxious groaning stretch and yawn. He began to scratch his crotch until he caught my look of revulsion. My brother's brown hair was a big curly mess.

Rylen lifted his head, revealing creases on his cheek from my shorts. He looked at me, bleary-eyed, no embarrassment or shame as he mumbled, "Mornin'." We'd woken up like this together so many times that it was nothing to him. He had no clue how much it meant to me.

"Morning," I whispered. Rylen planted a hand on my hip and the other on the side of my thigh to push himself up lightly, his arms flexing. The heat of his hands sent a strange quiver in my most sensitive areas. I pulled my knees up and yanked the blanket over my legs. Tater gave me a funny look.

"What?" I snapped.

"Nothing, freak." He ruffled his hair and walked out. Rylen looked down at me quizzically and I stood up, brushing past him to my room where I could brush my hair and get dressed away from inquiring eyes.

Abuela made egg and chorizo breakfast burritos, but as we watched the morning's aftermath news, none of us had much of an appetite. It felt wrong to be doing something as normal as eating breakfast when there were so many people traumatized in the country. All of last night's emotions came rushing back. A sense of mournfulness filled our home. And as I watched Tater and Rylen staring at the screen with fervent expressions and crossed arms, I knew with sinking certainty that they would not be changing their minds.

# SIX

N THAT HOT JULY day after we took them to the recruiting office to be picked up by the Army and Air Force buses, we came home to find Roscoe sitting on our porch. My parents silently passed him, but I sat and let him move next to me. He watched me imploringly through his droopy eyes.

"He's not here, boy," I whispered, scratching behind his ear. "He's gone."

Roscoe let out a huffing breath and lay at my side, pressing close despite the heat. Together, we stared out at the Fite land until the darkening sky matched how I felt inside.

I thought about the month before, when the boys graduated and Rylen got his pilot license. We'd all gone to the airfield to watch him take his first official flight as a pilot. One of the instructors had taken a liking to him and allowed him to borrow his plane. My heart had soared with him, even from the ground, as I'd stared up at the sunny sky, blocking the glare with my hand. Rylen was going places. Without me.

I patted his hound on the rump and said, "Go on home,

boy." I never saw Roscoe again.

Though Rylen wasn't in college, he stayed true to his word about writing me. We wrote a lot. At first it was emails, and more recently he told me he had to go offline, and to expect snail mail. I regretted that we only got to see him briefly, once a year, but each letter felt like a gift, like they were lit with Rylen's warm sunshine.

The summer before my senior year was the first time we saw both Tater and Rylen together in two years. Neither could seem to get leave at the same time. They'd spent their first year in the military doing training for their specific jobs. Tater wanted to go Airborne, of course, and he ended up being stationed at Ft. Benning, Georgia. Rylen's off-the-charts math scores, CAP experience, and high school ROTC time allowed him to climb ranks quicker than usual, and to gain top-secret clearance. He'd done jobs like Combat Control Team and Pararescue, and learned how to work on jets. More recently he wasn't able to tell us as much about his job specifics, which meant he was involved in dangerous situations, securing drop zones in war areas. But of course he would be. I was kind of glad not to know all of the specifics. My own imagination was bad enough.

Years had passed and no organization had taken responsibility for what was now being called Fatal Friday, a day America and the entertainment industry would forever mourn. In the past, someone always claimed blame for attacks, quickly and boastfully. A mysterious attacker, after all these years, was simply terrifying. And the fact that they hadn't attacked since then kept everyone on edge. Every continent had faced similar simultaneous attacks since Fatal Friday, all by an unknown enemy who killed by the thousands and never attacked the same place twice.

I always hoped for even the vaguest of news or insight from Ry's letters, but though he filled the space with heart-felt words, he never told anything we couldn't find out from world news. He never gave details of what he'd seen or been through.

Rylen's station changed a lot. Andrew's Air Force Base, then some undisclosed location in the Middle East for a whole year. Six months in Korea. Now he was back in the U.S., but he couldn't tell us where exactly he was stationed.

Rylen didn't have any social media pages, but Tater did. Six months ago, when Tater and Rylen crossed paths in the Middle East, my brother posted a picture of the two of them in full BDU gear, Battle Dress Uniform: camo in desert shades from top to bottom, belts filled with ammo, black boots laced up their calves. Tater had a wicked looking gun propped up on his shoulder with a cigarette dangling from his lips, eyes slightly squinting against the smoke. Rylen's arms were crossed and his face wore a hardcore expression. They both looked huge, like they'd been working out nonstop, and their faces were lean, all sharp angles. They were men now.

I refuse to admit the total amount of time I spent staring at that picture. Or how I'd cover Tater and just examine every speck of Rylen's body. His stance. His badass expression. Looking at him, wondering how cut he was under those BDUs, turned me on more than anything I'd ever experienced. He's what I thought about when I explored myself in the dark of night. His deep voice murmuring that I was beautiful and all he wanted was me.

Imagine how hard I blushed when Ry walked in with Tater that summer day when I was seventeen and he was twenty. He looked at me from the doorway, a half-grin on his face, and then his gaze seemed to unwillingly dive down

my body and swoop back up. For the first time ever, I truly felt shy with him, like maybe he was a different person,
like he could see into my mind and know all the thoughts I'd
had about him. Tater hugged me tight, tossing me side-to-
side like a ragdoll, even though I was a solid 5′5 and muscular
from school athletics.

"Looking good, Pep," Rylen said from behind him, reaching out to yank a lock of my hair while I was being held by
Tater. I wiggled away and smacked his arm. He laughed and
pulled me close, holding me tightly. Oh, holy crap . . . that
familiar scent of him. The feel of him, all hard muscles in
his back, his flat, hard stomach pressed against mine, strong,
heavy arms draped over my shoulders. My hips instinctively
wanted to mesh upward against his. I abruptly pulled away,
afraid I might rub against him like a cat in front of my family.

Mom bumped me out of the way to hug him next. As the
living room filled with family, all smiling and talking anima-
tedly, I just watched Rylen. I wanted to soak in every detail,
not knowing when I'd see him again. His hair was shorn close
to his scalp, with the front part slightly longer than how Dad
kept his. He wore a T-shirt that fit his arms and chest so spec-
tacularly, it looked like it was tailored for him. Cargo shorts
hung from his hips to his knees, showing off his sculpted
calves. And then he was wearing ugly slip-on Adidas sandals,
which almost made me laugh. His feet were long, always had
been, but for some reason even his long feet made me feel hot
right now. I blinked and looked away. Having dirty thoughts
while surrounded by your chattering family was just wrong.

Mom and Abuela went to the kitchen to start cooking—
we'd feast tonight on carne asada and then play cards and
dance for hours—and Grandpa Tate and Dad took Tater out
back to show them Grandpa's new rifle. Rylen hung back,
making me immediately nervous and excited by the way he

sized me up. I crossed my arms over my tank top, just as I had when I was fourteen. Stupid Nevada heat.

"Thanks for writing me," he said softly. "Means a lot."

"Yeah . . . you too." My heart swelled thinking of all the letters I'd received from him, his messy scrawl laced with loneliness, always asking me to please write back and tell him every mundane detail of my life. Which I always did.

I eyed the bottom of his T-shirt sleeve. I thought I'd seen something when he lifted his arm.

"Did you get a tattoo?" I asked.

"Oh, yeah." He started to pull up his sleeve, but it was too tight, so to my absolute wonder he pulled his shirt lazily over his head and turned to the side. A shiver of pure arousal went through me at the sexy sight of his glorious skin and the markings he'd chosen—from the rounded tops of his shoulders, down the backs of his arms to his elbows were black, tribal designs swirling thickly and ending in intricate spikes. They were the sexiest things I'd ever seen.

"Ry . . . those are amazing."

"Thanks," he said softly. He started to put his shirt back on, but hesitated, his back still to me. "And I got one more . . . but it wasn't as thought out. Don't be mad."

Okay, now he was making me nervous.

He slowly turned and I saw a two-inch red chili pepper on his left pectoral, above his heart. I rocked back on my heels.

OH. MY. GOD.

He quickly tugged his shirt back down and gave an embarrassed chuckle. "I drank a little too much sake in Japan. That was my first tat."

OH. MY. GOD.

All I could do was stare stupidly as he peered at me, waiting.

"What made you get that?" I whispered.

His head drooped like he was embarrassed, and I hurried to say, "I mean, it's totally cute—"

Now he threw his head back and laughed. "Yeah, cute. That's what the guys say too." He shook his head. "I guess I just needed a reminder of home."

My blood was buzzing. My nickname had been needled into Rylen's chest. Over his heart. Forever. *I* was his reminder of home.

OH. MY. GOD.

"You got any?" he asked.

"Huh?" I forced myself to focus. "Oh, tattoos? No."

He nodded his chin down to my shoulder. "What's that?"

"What?"

He reached out and touched the bottom of my neck. The warm graze of his finger over my skin made me shiver. I brought my hand up to cover the spot, suddenly remembering. Heat flooded upward into my face. Oh, shit. Four days ago the boy I was seeing gave me a hickey. I'd been so mad. But now it was barely visible, just a yellowish spot. Why did Rylen have to be so observant?

"Nothing," I said with a shrug, but I kept my hand over it.

"You lettin' some boy mark you?" His voice was half-joking, underscored by half-deadly.

Burning face. Truffle-shuffle. I peered up into his eyes. Those serious cloudy-day eyes. Then I let my hand drop, feeling challenged and needing him to know I wasn't the young girl he'd left behind almost three years ago.

"I'm old enough."

He didn't react. Didn't blink. Just held me in his stare.

"Don't give any part of yourself to some boy who doesn't deserve you. The right man'll be worth waiting for."

My heart accelerated so quickly I could hardly breathe. Was Rylen giving me big-brotherly advice, or was he telling me to wait for him? He had no idea how long I'd wait—how long I'd already waited, and how much longer I'd hold out if I knew he wanted me.

"We're not serious," I said lamely. I didn't want him to think I was in love or something.

He studied me, then gave that half-grin again. "All right. Have your fun. But be careful. Let me and Tater know if anyone bothers you."

*Have your fun.* Was Rylen out having his fun with women all over the world? Those lucky bitches. My stomach turned over, pushing up sour bile.

He gave me a nod and went to go join the guys, when I practically shouted at his back.

"I'm very patient, Ry." He turned his head, giving me a funny look until I elaborated. "When it comes to waiting."

My heart. Once again I was handing it to him, praying he would see my offering for what it was, to see in my eyes that it was *him* I waited for.

"Good." His voice was a low rumble through the room. "Hope he can handle you, Pepper."

"I'm sure he can."

Rylen grinned and shook his head before slipping through the back sliding door. Once again, I'm pretty sure he was clueless, and I was a fool. I gathered my composure before I went outside to join them. I wanted to text Remy, but she was at youth camp for her church. She'd want a complete detailed rundown of every moment of our encounter when she returned. And she was going to die when she heard about the tattoo. Just thinking about Rylen marking his skin with a symbol of me made me feel strung tight, hot all over. Perhaps a bit of target shooting was just what I needed.

Not gonna lie; when Tater and Rylen went out to a party that night and didn't invite me, I moped around the house all night. Were they hanging out with people they'd graduated with? Would Becca what's-her-name be there? I mean, what the heck? I was seventeen now. I went to parties all the time. Why did they still act like I was a kid?

I sat outside on the old tire swing, lost in thought until late in the night, determined to see them come home. At nearly two my eyes were drooping from boredom. I was just about to go inside when I saw headlights crest over the hill at the top of our street. My stomach wobbled and I held the tire tighter. I'd probably be covered in dirt and black marks, but I didn't care.

I didn't recognize the sporty coup that pulled up or the girl in the driver's seat. I stayed very still until I realized it was Tater in the front with her, and Rylen in the back. Rylen got out and Tater proceeded to swallow the girl's face. Actually, I couldn't really tell, but that's what it looked like from far away. Rylen came straight toward me.

"Saw you when we pulled up," he said, leaning against the tree. I could smell beer and cigarettes on him. "What are you doing out here in the dark all by yourself?"

"Waiting for you," I said. The words sent a tremor of nerves through me like roller skates on rough pavement.

A sly grin pulled the side of his mouth upward and he shoved his hands in his pockets. "We're big boys. You don't need to wait up for us."

"Maybe I just wanted to see you again."

He cocked his head at me, as if trying to study my face in the dark.

The door of the car closed and tires crunched in the drive-way as the girl reversed. Tater strutted over with a cigarette in his fingers, and I gritted my teeth in irritation.

"What are you still doing up?" he slurred. "Dontchu got school?"

"It's summer, duh," I said. "And you're trashed. You should go drink some water and go to bed." I smacked the burning nub right out of his hand and he smirked as it went sailing into the dirt.

"Imma eat everything in the fridge first." Tater patted both of my cheeks and squeezed them in his fingers, pinching me. I could smell liquor on his breath mixed with tobacco. "Aw, my wittle sissy."

"Stop it." I pulled back, laughing at his stupidness. He grabbed the tire and gave me a hard swing, making me squeal as I flew high. And to my joy he walked toward the house, and Rylen stayed.

When I started to slow, Rylen pushed off from the tree and his hot hands touched my back, gently pushing me. I swung like that for five minutes in the silence of night, looking forward to each downward swoop when his hands would touch me to push me upward again. Then he grasped the tire with a jolt to stop it, and spun it so that I was facing him. He stood close. His eyes glistened in the moonlight, slightly unfocused. I wondered how much he'd had to drink.

"It's weird to see you all grown up," he said in a deep rumble.

My stomach did that truffle-shuffle thing as my brain searched for a response.

"You know," he said, "when you were little I used to pretend you were Krystal." Oh, my God . . . his little sister who he lost. I held my breath as he looked away, still talking. "I used to get mad at my mom for making me take Krystal everywhere I went, like I was her constant babysitter or something. I'd get mad at my mom and take it out on Krystal. I was mean as shit to her."

"Rylen . . ." He'd definitely had a lot to drink. He never let himself talk about his past or his feelings. "You were just a boy."

He shook his head. "Doesn't matter. And no matter how mean I was, she still stuck to me like a loyal little puppy."

I swallowed hard. "I'm sure she knew you loved her."

He didn't say anything for a minute, just stared off toward his darkened house. "I just always wanted to do right by you."

"You have," I whispered. *But I'm not your sister*, I wanted to say.

He stepped even closer, enough for us to really see each other's eyes in the starlight. "There's so much shit out there in the world. So much fucking evil. There's times where I'm so submersed in it I start to wonder what the fuck the point of life is. And then I get a letter from you, and it's like this little light is shining from across the world. Like a piece of gold, making me remember the good that's out there. The things that are worth fighting for."

What do I even say to that? I was like gold to him? *Swallow. Breathe. Do not cry.*

"If I'm gold, Ry, you're like . . . *titanium*. Stronger than you know."

My words made him rock back slightly on his heels and he grasped the tire to steady himself, reminding me he was buzzed. When I kept my gaze locked on his, letting him know I was completely serious, he shook his head in wonder and let out a huff of disbelief. He absently rubbed his earlobe.

I reached out and touched his chest with my fingertips, gently at first, and then fisting his shirt in my palm, urging him toward me. He stumbled slightly and stared into my eyes as I pulled him closer. He began to breathe harder. Our foreheads touched. Then our noses. My body felt light enough to flutter right out of that tire if I let go of him. Rylen wet his lips and my heart pounded a steady rhythm, chanting *finally, finally, finally.*

With a *bang,* the screen door slammed and Tater tromped out with his hands full. "I found the mother lode!" he called with a mouthful. "Dad's stash of Oreos!"

*Damn it, Tater, no!* My hand released the fabric of Rylen's shirt. He let go of the tire and stepped away, shoving his hands in his pockets and clearing his throat. *I want that moment back!* Tears of frustration threatened as my heart stampeded inside my ribs. I could feel the angry scowl on my face when I turned back to Rylen. He flinched, perhaps from my grimace, so I schooled my face into something calmer.

"C'mon, man!" Tater yelled.

"You okay?" I asked Rylen.

"Yeah." He cleared his throat. "I'm sorry about that."

"About what?" Why was he acting weird, like he'd done something wrong?

He let out an embarrassed sound and shook his head. "Will you still write me?"

"Of course." *Always.* Rylen looked at me for a long moment before listing to the side and righting himself.

"Good." He ran a finger down his ear and pulled on his lobe. "Maybe we should...go in?"

My heart sank. "Okay."

He held the swing while I climbed out of it. I'd never wanted to punch my brother's smiling, oblivious face more than I did as I passed him that night. Instead, I snatched the half-eaten sleeve of Oreos from his nearest hand and gave him a death ray glare when he reached for them. He pulled his hand back.

"Damn, you're like a viper."

Rylen chuckled at the exchange. When I stared at him, he

hushed and gave me a quizzical stare back, cocking his head. I had almost kissed him. Would he remember? It would have changed everything, for better or worse. I don't know where the bravery of the moment had come from, maybe the fact that I knew he wasn't sober, but it was gone now.

"Enjoy your cookies." Tater's way of saying *get lost*.

"I will," I snarled.

I went to bed that night with a belly full of too much sugar, and a mind full of precious metals, wondering what might have happened if Tater hadn't interfered. And then I gave my mind permission to imagine the possible scenarios. I fell asleep still cursing my brother's name.

# SEVEN

**A**T EIGHTEEN, AFTER I graduated, I attended nursing school to get my Associate RN degree. I stayed busy with an overly-full class load, hanging with Remy when I could make trips out to the University of Nevada in Vegas, or whenever she visited home.

Mom and Dad didn't care that I still lived at home; in fact, I don't think they were ready to be empty-nesters. They gave me space and I took care of my own laundry. I offered to try and make dinners, but Mom and Abuela wouldn't hear of it. They were total control freaks in the kitchen. Abuela cleaned up all around me while I did something as simple as making a sandwich, wiping crumbs before I was even finished.

Nursing school was awesome. It was freeing to be in classes about things I wanted to know, rather than boring stuff I was forced to learn. Give me arteries, clots, and bone structure any day over Shakespeare and geometry.

At twenty, I graduated nursing school but jobs were scarce. Our small county clinic wasn't hiring. I went down to Clark County and the hospital H.R. rep told me their nursing staff was pretty full too, but they needed EMTs and I could be put on the nursing waiting list. So, I took EMT training to become a paramedic.

I felt a driving need to stay busy and useful, and to push myself to the limits, much to my mother's chagrin. But my trainers commended me for being able to think and react quickly in dire situations, and to still manage a kind, compassionate bedside manner for the injured and their panicking family members. I'd finally found my calling.

It was only a matter of time before work calls began to break my heart. I couldn't tell anyone the things I'd seen. I'd once tried to tell Mom why I'd come home with bloodshot eyes, trembling, but partway through my story she covered her face and shook her head, begging me to stop. Yeah, I saw some awful stuff.

I was crying in my car after a shift one night when a fire fighter who'd been at the scene knocked on my window. Ken—I think it was short for something Japanese. My stomach gave a small swoop. Ken had been trying to get me to go out with him since we met. Remy thought I was crazy—she'd taken one look at his face at a party two weeks ago and declared I needed to date him, stat. I wiped the tears from my face, but it was no use. He leaned down, resting his forearms on the ledge. I looked up into his beautifully slanted brown eyes, at the black hair long enough to tuck behind his ears.

"It won't always be this hard," he promised. "Hang in there." I'd heard it from Julian, too, about how I had to build scar tissue around my heart, otherwise I'd imagine every patient as someone I love. "Look, I know this sounds fucked up, but you can't think past the scene in front of you—you can't think of their lives. You have to look at each call matter-of-fact, mind over matter."

I nodded, but stared at the steering wheel.

"You wanna . . ." He cleared his throat. "Go get a coffee or something?"

"Ken." I made myself face him. Remy was right—he was incredibly good looking, but I couldn't help but hold back. I felt bad every time I rejected him, but my heart was on the other side of the world. "I think I should probably go home. But thank you."

He patted the car door and gave me an understanding smile. "All right then. Get home safe, Tate."

I tried to avoid Ken after that, but it was hard when we kept ending up at the same scenes together. Each time, he looked at me with hope in his eyes. Hope that I continued to smash. He was right about what he'd said about the job, though. Eventually the shock lost its power, and I was able to partially numb myself. But only partially.

In late winter, I got a letter from Rylen with a question thrown seemingly innocently into the mix—something he'd never asked me before—*Any man lucky enough to steal your heart these days?*

The way my heart danced, I could have run a hundred sprints around the house. I worked up every ounce of nerve and wrote back: *By now you must know you're the only man who can have my heart, Rylen Fite.*

I nearly chased down the mailman the next day to get the letter back from him. I called Remy and could hear her jumping up and down on her springy bed as she laughed maniacally and cheered.

"Finally! It's about dang time, Amber! I'm so freaking proud of you!"

But I didn't share her excitement. I was in full panic mode. I had ruined everything. Rylen was going to tell me he didn't think of me like *that*, and then everything would be strange between us. He'd probably stop writing me. When I shared these fears, I could sense Remy's eyes rolling back in her head through the phone line.

"Way to ruin my euphoria," she said. "I refuse to listen to any more of your negativity. You will lift your chin and speak to me only of rainbows and true love's kiss until Prince of the Potato Fields responds. Mm-kay?"

I snorted, still shaking on the inside. "Yeah, Fairy Queen. Mm-kay."

"Many thanks, Unicorn Princess."

Five weeks passed. It always took a long time to receive a response, but this time seemed especially long. I felt like my stomach was plummeting down over a hill every time I thought about it. Of course, my paranoid mind began to wonder if he was avoiding responding. Was he trying to find a kind way to let me down? The only time I wasn't overthinking was when I was at work. And that day, in particular, was crazy.

We got a call to a house in the middle of nowhere. Rural land. Hundreds of acres of crops: alfalfa, barley, corn, and oats. As we raced up the gravel road, kicking up a cloud of dust, my redheaded partner, Julian, pointed out at the field. About a quarter of a mile away there seemed to be a huge area smoking.

"Fire?" I asked.

He shrugged, staring. "Could be a controlled burn, but it's in the middle of the field." Thankfully the fire department would be coming soon too. We peered out, trying to see what could be causing the faint circle of smoke, but it was hard to see anything through the tall corn stalks.

"That is weird as hell," Julian said. I agreed. The call came from an older man, who said his wife had come in the house barely breathing, white as a ghost, and unable to talk. He thought she was having a heart attack.

We skidded to a stop in front of an old two-story, white farmhouse. I jumped from the back of the ambulance with my pack and sprinted to the front door. It was hot—the sun seemed to sizzle on my skin. An older man answered, a worried look on his face. He pointed to the couch, where a gray-haired woman sat. Her face was nearly as gray as her hair, but at least she was upright. Make that tilting. I ran in and knelt beside her, reaching for her wrist. She was cold and clammy, her pulse weak but fast.

"Ma'am, can you tell me your name?" I asked. Sweat dotted her brow and lip.

"She hasn't spoken since she came in," the man told us.

Julian shone a quick light in her eyes, which were unfocused. "Dilated," he said. Her chest rose and fell irregularly with shaking breaths.

"She's in shock," I said. "Ma'am, we're going to check you for injuries. I'm Amber, and this is Julian. We're going to take care of you." I lifted a bottle of water to her lips and she drank a sip, still with a vacant stare, dribbling slightly. Julian grabbed a throw blanket from the back of the couch and wrapped it around her.

Her husband stood close, watching.

"Sir, did you see anything happen?" Julian asked him.

"No. She just came stumbling in like that."

"How about out in your field?" I asked. "What happened out there?"

His face scrunched. "My field?" He walked to the window and pulled the flowered curtain aside while I got the woman to take another sip. The man gasped raggedly.

"What in the Sam hell . . . ?"

Sirens from afar and tires on gravel told me fire and rescue were arriving.

The woman's chest lifted with a sudden intake of air and she said in a scratchy voice, "The aliens."

My heart gave a hard pound of surprise. Julian and I looked at each other.

"Come again, ma'am?" Julian said.

Her husband rushed over and fell to his knees in front of her. "What is it, Gracie? What did you see out there?"

"His face . . . was handsome . . . but his arms." Her eyes grew unfocused again and she began to shiver violently.

"What about his arms?" her husband asked.

The woman met him eye-to-eye and her gaze seemed to clear. "He had four."

What the *what*?

The screen door burst open and four men rushed in. Two in firemen uniforms and two in suits. FBI or a state investigative unit? Why were they here for a routine call? They surveyed the room and then nodded at Julian and I.

"She's in shock," I told them.

One of the men stepped forward, nodding. "Thank you both. We'll take it from here."

Julian and I shared another glance. We weren't usually dismissed so quickly.

"She needs fluids and warmth, possibly oxygen—"

The man shut Julian up with a hard pat to his shoulder. "We know how to handle shock, son."

*Alrighty, then.* The four men converged on the couple in the small space, so Julian and I headed out. One fire truck and two unmarked cars stood outside. Men were walking through the field. A strange sense of trepidation chilled me. I was glad to climb into the ambulance and leave.

We were quiet for a long time until I said, "Okay, was that weird as shit or is it just me?" Julian had been an EMT for a couple years longer than me.

He shrugged and chuckled. "I've seen weirder. People do fucked up things, or see fucked up things, and then their brain deals with it in fucked up ways."

I let out a deep breath and tried to relax. I pulled out my work laptop and began to type up the incident report. I included every detail, including what the woman had claimed. I usually didn't check back on reports after I filed them, too worried that what I'd find out would be bad news, but I'd definitely be looking into this one tomorrow.

My phone dinged with a text and I looked down to see a message from Ken. It had been nearly a month since he'd contacted me.

**Not to be a stalker, but I saw ur schedule and ur off Sat. Dinner? U have to eat, Tate. May as well eat with me.**

Julian asked, "Who's that? Your friend Remy? Let me know next time you and her go out. I might just happen to show up."

He winked at me from the driver's seat and I shook my head, smiling. Last time we'd gone out had been at a fire fighter's house party. No cop friends were there, so everyone turned a blind eye to Remy's underage drinking—and in all fairness, she looked at least twenty-one. Remy met Julian shot-for-shot. She nearly drank him under the table, but I had to carry her out and babysit her all night. I didn't care for a rematch. I shoved my phone back into my pocket without responding. I'd let him think the text was from Remy. Julian didn't know about Ken's persevering attempts for a date, and I wanted to keep it that way.

I was still weirded out when I got home that evening. Until I saw the letter waiting for me on the table with Rylen's messy script. My heart leapt, then sank, then leapt again as I opened it with shaking fingers.

His letter began: *Dear Pepper, Haha, very funny. You'd better be setting your sights higher than that . . .*

And he proceeded to talk about the massive tropical birds he'd seen, one of which sat on his shoulder at an outdoor bar and didn't want to leave him. There wasn't another single mention of my bold admission. He'd written it off as a joke.

"What's wrong, Amber?" Mom asked. She was looking at the letter, which I'd crumbled in my sweating fist.

"Nothing." I forced a smile and went to take a long shower. Unfortunately, there wasn't enough water or soap in the world to wash away the strangeness and disappointment of the day. I texted Remy right away and spent the next hour scrolling through her tirade of male-bashing texts as they came in. Hearing her call Rylen a bone-headed, cave-dwelling, award-winning-idiot-of-the-century didn't make me feel any better. Because deep in my heart I knew I would never have the nerve to tell him again. Because maybe he wasn't dismissing it as a joke. Maybe he was gently telling me he wasn't interested in me like that. The spark of hope I'd been holding onto for so long had dimmed.

I was tired of feeling this way. Tired of the roller coaster of hoping and then having those hopes crushed. I couldn't keep living like this.

As I sat on my bed, filled with a sense of loss, I pulled out my phone and read Ken's text several times through.

**Okay**, I texted back, **let's have dinner.**

The next morning when I arrived at the hospital, the first thing I did was to open my laptop and search for Grace Fondent's file to see if any information had been added. Nothing came up. I double checked the spelling of her name. I typed in Gracie instead. Still nothing. Baffled, I went to my supervisor's office.

She held up a finger as she finished her phone conversation, then hung up and smiled at me. "What can I do for you, Amber?" Her phone rang again, but she ignored it.

"I can't find one of the files from our run yesterday. Grace Fondent?"

"Ah," she said. "The FBI are taking over that case, so we passed the file along to them."

The FBI? Why? Utterly bizarre.

"I thought we kept files of all our stops, even when they get passed to an agency?"

"Sweetie, when the FBI asks you to delete a file, you do it without question. It's best if you put it out of your mind. Understand? Criminal activity is touchy business. Don't speak of it to anyone again. Even me."

Criminal activity? Did they think Grace Fondent started that fire in her field? Even if she had, why would it be FBI business? Insurance stuff, maybe? The phone rang again, but this time she answered it, giving me a final smile before turning her attention away. I backed out of the room, unsatisfied and even more confused than yesterday.

# EIGHT

STOPPED FOR FUEL on the way home and went inside the gas station for a bottle of water. As I stood in line I grinned at the local papers on display and the magazines with pictures of green alien heads and fuzzy pictures of round UFOs. My eyes landed on one article title in particular: HANDSOME ALIENS WITH FOUR ARMS!

The back of my neck prickled sharply. I stepped out of line and picked it up off the rack, ignoring the scoff from the man behind me. I flipped through until I came to the article. A New Mexico woman, age 59, was quoted: "I was out for a walk 'cause I couldn't sleep, and I saw a big group of people sort of wandering near our property line. I stood real quiet behind a tree, 'cause I'd never seen so many people out our way before. There were hundreds of them, all moving the same direction. Nobody made any noise. But one of them, he looked my direction. Even in the dark I could see he had a face like an angel, with a full head of dark hair . . . but his body . . . that's when I got scared. He had four arms. I looked around 'cause I thought I was going crazy, but it was the same for the others. Some of them had four arms, some three. Only a couple had two. I ran straight home and called the police!"

The magazine slipped from my hand with a clatter against the floor. My heart was pounding. The gum-chomping cashier and the man checking out stared at me. I bent down and grabbed it, trying three times before I got it back into the slot on the rack. I don't even remember paying for my drink or driving home. Next thing I knew I was sitting at the dinner table with everyone chatting around me.

"Bad day at work, hun?" Dad asked carefully.

I blinked. "Have you noticed all the alien stuff in the tabloids lately?" I asked.

Dad chuckled and Mom gave me a funny look.

"There's always alien stuff," Dad said. "We're a stone's throw from Area 51."

Not really, it was a couple hour drive, but I knew what he meant.

"It just seems like more than usual lately."

They got quiet, exchanging worried glances, as if I might finally be cracking under the pressure of my job.

"Sorry," I said. "Yeah, bad day at work."

This seemed to appease them; my bad days being something they were accustomed to. Abuela put a giant scoop of yellow rice with diced veggies on my plate. I picked at my food as I thought about Grace Fondent and the woman from the article. There had to be a logical explanation for why they'd both seen multiple-arm beings. My mind turned and turned until it hit me. Grace Fondent must have done or seen something awful, just like Julian said. But she also must have read that stupid tabloid this week, and for whatever reason her mind replayed it and made it her reality.

Relief trickled through me, clear and sweet. I nearly

laughed at myself for getting so freaked out. I put a helping of black beans on my rice and relaxed.

Remy was more excited about my date with Ken than I was. I swore to her I'd call her the minute I left him. My stomach was a bundle of nerves when I showed up at the Japanese steakhouse, but his bright smile put me at ease right away. *Time to relax. Enjoy his company.*

"Want a drink?" he asked, nodding to the cocktail list.

"I'm only twenty," I whispered.

He winked. "The owner is my uncle. And the bartender is my cousin." I looked around.

"I don't want to get anyone in trouble."

"Don't worry about it. They've been serving me since I was sixteen."

My eyes went wide and he laughed. I agreed on a fruity rum concoction in the belly of a porcelain Buddha glass. And after dinner, he got me to try a shot of sake with him at the bar. I tried, and failed, not to think about how Ry had been drunk on sake when he got his pepper tattoo.

*You'll always be like a sister to him. Move on.*

The shots were gross, but they warmed me up inside and I found myself smiling. A lot. I switched to beer, and we sat there talking for two hours. Mostly work stuff, which was kind of nice to be able to blow off steam and tell the stories that other people in my life could not handle hearing. He stopped drinking and bought me another.

By ten, I was pretty buzzed and feeling so relaxed I'd actually been staring at his mouth as he talked. I think I wanted to kiss him. The thought was so shocking, so welcome, that it made me giddy.

This was what I needed. I started to touch him as we

talked—a hand to his wrist, my knee bumping his thigh—small touches, but they didn't go unnoticed by him. When I finished my beer he cleared his throat and ran a nervous hand through his strands of black silk.

"You wanna maybe come over to my place and watch a movie or something?"

"Sure," I said without hesitation. His eyes popped wide with surprise, and I giggled, which made him laugh too.

"All right. We can leave your car here," he said. "I'll bring you back when the movie's over if you're okay to drive."

"Okay." I let him take me by the hand and lead me to his car. The feel of my hand in his larger one was nice. We drove with the windows half-down while he blasted EDM. I felt alive and young in that moment. This was what I should be doing. Going out, having fun. Living my life. Giving nice guys a chance.

We got to his apartment and he put on a new Greek war drama. But by the time the title was across the screen, he'd sat next to me, looked at me, and then we were kissing. I think I surprised him when I leaned back and pulled him down on top of me, because he let out a moan and then chuckled at himself. My head was buzzing and my skin welcomed his touch. It had been a long time since I kissed anyone, and Ken knew what he was doing.

Things progressed quickly. I'd dated guys during college, and done some stuff, but I'd never had sex. The full desire had never been there. But tonight I felt something inside of me pushing. Something seeking. Something begging me to fill that longtime void inside of me. And Ken was more than willing.

His shirt came off, and his smooth brown skin hovered over mine. He pushed up my shirt and gently shoved a hand under my bra to cup me in his palm. I felt strangely . . . disembodied, like I didn't want to think about it. I just wanted to keep going, as quickly as possible, before I could talk myself out of it. I squirmed underneath him until I'd pulled my shirt and bra off. He moaned again and took each of my breasts in his warm mouth, one by one, until my back was arching for more.

"Amber . . ." he murmured.

I reached between us and stroked the outside of his jeans, eliciting a guttural cry from his throat. Then I unbuttoned his pants and he sat up. His eyes stayed on me, hungrily eating me up as he dropped his jeans and stepped out of them. His eyes roamed down to my hands where I was unbuttoning my shorts. That's when the first small bout of nervousness hit me.

*Keep going,* I told myself. *It's okay.*

I lifted my hips and he tugged down my shorts before climbing on top of me. Now there were only boxers and panties between us. I felt an underlying panic, like if I didn't hurry up and do this I would lose my nerve and never move forward in life. As he kissed me, I reached down again. He lifted his hips and let me pull down the elastic of his boxers and take him in my hand. His eyes squeezed shut for a moment as he composed himself, and then he reached for his wallet inside his jeans on the floor. Within moments he had a condom in his hand and was ripping it open with his teeth.

*Oh, my God . . . this is happening.*

I pushed down my fear. He rolled the condom on and looked me in the eyes again. This was my chance to stop him. But I didn't. Reckless rebellion against years of nothingness urged me to push my underwear down. Ken touched me and said my name again with such adoration. He licked his fingers and touched me again. Then I felt him, right there. I held my breath as another shock of nervousness ratcheted through me.

Ken thrust his hips and I cried out at the stinging pinch of discomfort. He must have taken my gasp as a sound of pleasure because he thrust hard again and I yelled, pressing my forehead into his chest and gripping his sides as hard as I could. My entire body went rigid. What was I doing? What was I trying to prove?

*The right man's worth waiting for . . .*

"Ken," I said breathlessly. "Wait. Stop."

His hips immediately stilled and he wrenched his head back to look at me. In a panic, I pushed him so I could sit up. He pulled out of me, making us both hiss. Then he looked down at the condom, which made me do the same. There was brownish-red on it. His head swung up to me, his eyes wild.

"Tate? Please tell me this wasn't your first time."

I opened my mouth to lie, to tell him I was on my period or something, but I hesitated too long.

"Fuck," he whispered. He hung his head, pressing his face into his hands.

"I'm sorry," I whispered. My head suddenly cleared as all traces of lust faded. I spotted my underwear on the floor and snatched them up, shoving my legs into them. I was trembling all over as I tried to find the correct holes for my arms and head in my shirt.

"I didn't even think . . ." Ken stuttered. "I wouldn't have been so . . ."

"It's okay," I said. But it wasn't. I shouldn't have let it go so far. "It's my fault. I should have told you."

"Amber . . ."

Once my legs were in my shorts again, I headed for his bathroom and closed myself in. I splashed cold water on my face, breathing hard, refusing to look at myself in the mirror.

How could I go out there and face him again? I was humiliated, and I hated that he obviously felt guilty for being rough
with a virgin.

Oh, my God . . . I wasn't a virgin anymore. Did it matter?
Kind of. I'd just always thought it would be different. I'd only
ever imagined being with Rylen . . . I shook my head at that
lost dream, and felt a moment of irrational anger toward Ry,
as if he were to blame for my actions. I stood upright and
shook my arms out, releasing a deep breath.

Unless I planned to live in his bathroom, I had to get back
out there. Ken stood in his living room, completely dressed.
His eyes were full of remorse, which made me look away.
The room spun a little from the buzz that clung to me.

"I think I should go home," I said.

"Tate." He came forward and took my hands. "I'm sorry. I
don't even . . . I didn't expect this to happen."

"I know," I said. I'd taken us both by surprise. "I didn't
either."

"Are you mad at me?"

I looked into his eyes and said strongly, "No. I'm not mad,
Ken. I swear."

"But you think it was a mistake." I watched him swallow
hard. I knew he wanted me to say no, that it wasn't a mistake.
That I liked him and wanted to be with him, but I couldn't
give him false hope. I, for one, knew how much false hope
really hurt someone.

"I thought I was ready, but I was wrong. That's on me,
not you. It's not because of anything you did. You're . . . awesome. I'm a mess." I tried to smile, but he looked like I'd
kicked him in the balls. I'd totally left him hanging. I let out a
trembling sigh. "Can you take me to my car?"

He was silent a second, and I prayed he wouldn't make
things any worse by begging me to stay or something.

Thankfully, he asked, "Will you be okay to drive?"

"Yeah," I answered quietly.

I felt near tears the entire drive back to the lot with my car. Then there was the awkward moment when we arrived, where I didn't know if I should hug him good-bye. I ended up clutching my purse in both hands and blurting, "Good night, Ken. Thanks for dinner." *So lame.*

He let out a huff of air and a disbelieving chuckle. "Yeah. No problem." I couldn't tell if he was mad or sad or what, but I didn't take time to find out. I got out and shut the door. Ken waited until I was in my car with the engine on before he drove away.

Guilt consumed me whole at that moment, like a giant, slimy mouth. I sat there disgusted with myself on so many levels. I'd tried to appease my aching heart by pulling the wool over its eyes, but my heart knew what it wanted and would accept no substitutes. I wanted to bitch-slap my stupid heart.

I knew Remy was waiting for a call, but I didn't think I could stomach it. In fact, I was mortified at the thought of telling her. If anyone could understand and love me without judgment, it was Remy, and while she was an open book about her own escapades, I'd always been more hesitant and private. And right now I couldn't think about what had happened, much less talk about it. Besides, Remy would sense my guilt and probably try to take partial responsibility for pressuring me to go out with Ken.

I pulled out my phone and texted: **On my way home. So tired. Nice guy, nice dinner, but I'm not feeling a 2ⁿᵈ date. Sorry. Luv u.**

She texted back right away: **Aw, boo. :( Luv u 2.**

And that was that.

I turned twenty-one at the beginning of that summer. I didn't take the day off or tell anyone it was my birthday. But Remy knew, and she asked to take me out after work. Funny thing is, Remy ended up being the drunk one while I was the DD. I'd been drunk plenty of times, especially in high school, but for the past year I'd had no desire. It was like I'd seen too much. Drunk driving, alcohol poisoning, bar fights . . . hooking up with dudes you had to see *way* too often at work. Yeah, no thanks.

"I can't believe you didn't bother to bring a change of clothes," Remy complained.

I glanced down at my navy work pants and my under T-shirt, then at Remy's cute skirt and beaded top. I looked around at the other girls with their hair flowing and shiny. Mine was up in a ponytail. Suddenly I felt incredibly frumpy and old. Remy sipped her pink drink with her glossy lips, and I suffered a pang of jealousy.

An older guy in a flannel shirt came over, puffing out his chest. "Can I buy y'all—"

"No thanks," I said. Remy's eyes bulged. I guess she wanted that free drink.

The man looked back and forth between us and muttered, "Lezzies."

Remy gasped and I shot him the bird as he walked away. Then she glared at me.

"Sorry," I said. "I'll buy you a drink myself, but men like that will act like you owe them something if you accept a drink from them."

Remy studied me. "I feel like your job is sucking the life out of you. When's the last time you hooked up with someone?"

My face heated as I thought back to Ken's apartment.

"Maybe it's not your job. Maybe it's Rylen," Remy said.

His name was like a punch to the chest. Remy finished her drink and pushed it away. I nodded at the bartender to bring her another. "You know I've shipped Ryber for a long time, but—"

"I thought we were Amlen?"

She shook her head. "The point is, his half of the ship refuses to sail, and it's screwing up your life."

"It's not because of him." Big, fat lie.

"I'm not trying to be mean . . ." Oh, she was totally about to be mean. "But don't you think if Rylen thought of you like that, he would have made a move by now? You've been legal for three years."

I grit my teeth to avoid telling her to shut up, and when her drink came I almost snatched it up and sucked it down myself. Instead, I sat quietly and watched her sip.

"All I'm saying is that you either need to flat-out tell him how you feel, no small hints that can be taken as jokes, or drop the fantasizing and move on. You're freaking gorgeous. You're going to regret wasting your youth."

Geez. I turned to face the bar and scowled at the rows of bottles. Remy slid her arm around mine and put her chin on my shoulder, gazing up at me with a pouty face.

"I'm sorry," she said. "I shouldn't have said all of that. It's the vodka talking."

"No, you're right." I rested my cheek on the top of her head.

Behind me I heard a man cough loudly, and imbedded in the cough was something that sounded a lot like *Lezzies*. I saw flannel pass us.

Remy started to turn, saying, "That's it," but I grabbed her arm.

"Just ignore him. I promise to let him bleed to death if I get called to the scene of his accident. He's bound to get stabbed by someone someday."

She giggled. As the night went on, I got to hear all the dirty details of Remy's sorority life at UNLV and their brother fraternity with its myriad of hot, future businessmen. She was in her last year and would have her biology degree soon. Remy's future sounded glamorous, and as much as I wouldn't trade my job for anything in the world, I began to wonder if I wasn't cheating myself out of something. But then, as I stood in the tight bathroom stall of the bar two hours later, holding Remy's hair back, I realized we all had our place in life. I'd rather be the helper than the puker. Perhaps that made me boring, but I was happy. Ish. Happy-ish.

# PART TWO

# AFTER

# NINE

HEN IT RAINS, IT pours. And floods. And washes away adolescent dreams.

That Thanksgiving, for the first time since the bombings on Fatal Friday, a true sense of dread had settled over the U.S. There'd been so much hearsay of imminent danger over the years. So much talk of threats and possible enemies, but it seemed like hot air because nothing ever happened. Today felt different. Every news station was abuzz. I sat with my family after our Mexican-American feast, watching the coverage. My phone sat on my lap, ringer on high in case I got called in to work.

"Tomorrow is being hailed a monumental day in U.S. and world history," the anchor said. "Every U.S. Senator and House Representative, along with our President and Vice President are headed to Washington DC to meet with leaders from allied countries. Never before will so many leaders be together outside of a decreed summit of the United Nations: Britain, France, Spain, Turkey, Belgium, and Canada to name a few. Those who cannot join will be present via satellite. The security level of the nation's capital is on the highest alert it's ever been.

"For those of you just joining us, U.S. intelligence gained undisputed evidence that three undisclosed nations have nuclear weapons that are not sanctioned by the U.N., and are refusing to disable or allow the U.N. to further research. Our sources suspect the countries are Russia, North Korea, and one of the Middle East Emissaries, but representatives will neither confirm nor deny those rumors. They have, however, confirmed that our country is under a dire threat. The House speaker was quoted this Monday saying *'Time is of the essence. We are overriding the U.N. and taking matters into our own hands.'*"

At this, my father shook his head from the recliner. "About time." Grandpa Tate murmured his agreement. Mom, Abuela, and I continued watching in silence.

"Once the international panel has met this evening, the U.S. representatives will immediately vote on whether or not the U.S. should declare war. The meeting is expected to last through this evening, possibly into morning hours."

There had always been known threats—countries and groups that were hostile to western culture, but it sounded like the current perpetrators were taunting us, with bombs pointed and fingers on the triggers. The news switched from the anchor to demonstrators on The Mall lawn in D.C. Some cried out for peaceful negotiations, while others hollered for the swift justice of war. And though it was all a bit unsettling, I felt a grateful sense of distance from the danger. I was glad to live in the middle of nowhere.

I stood, ready to hit the sack early, but a special alert flashed across the screen.

"Senator Bradford Navis of Nevada is being flown from proceedings in the nation's capital back to his home state.

We've received word that his wife has been in a car accident and is in critical condition."

What? I pressed a hand to my heart as Mom and Abuela gasped.

"Not the senator," Mom said.

My heart ached. Bradford Navis was young and vibrant. He took office at thirty, his gorgeous wife at his side. The two of them were clearly in love, the way they always smiled at one another, caught on camera. They couldn't have children and it was common knowledge that they were in adoption proceedings.

"That is a damn shame," Grandpa said softly.

"I light candle." Abuela stood and disappeared to her guest room to pray.

I sat next to Mom, feeling too heavy to get up and go to bed now. I saw tragedy all the time, but it was always hardest with young couples and families. So full of life and energy. To see someone's candle snubbed so soon, so suddenly, it filled me with an aching hole full of questions.

My phone buzzed with a text message, filling me with disappointment at the thought of getting called in. But when I looked, my heart rose into my throat. It was Rylen.

**Happy Thanksgiving.**

I grinned like crazy. He rarely texted me unless he was somewhere in the U.S., off duty. I texted Happy Thanksgiving back to him. Where was he?

Then he said: **U home? I'm coming by. Got a surprise.**

I bolted to my feet. "Oh my gosh! Rylen's coming over!"

Mom jumped up too, clasping her hands and beaming at me, then she ran off to straighten up the kitchen. She knocked on Abuela's room on the way, telling her in Spanish that Rylen was on his way. Dad grinned and kicked the footrest down on his recliner.

I typed back with a shaking hand: **Yes. See u soon!**

Rylen! I dashed into the bathroom, feeling giddy as I brushed my teeth, then into my room to change into something cuter and brush my hair. I was swiping on lip gloss when I heard the door open and happy voices ringing out. I ran down the hall and into the family room, stopping in my tracks at the sight of not one, but two people.

Rylen . . . damn . . . he looked so amazingly good, dressed in his BDUs. But at his side was a girl. A cute, petite, shy-seeming, Hispanic girl. Rylen gave me a half-smile from across the room. He seemed almost nervous, the way his eyes darted around to each of our faces, stopping on mine for an extra long moment before focusing on Mom. Then he put his arm around the girl's shoulder and said, "Tate family. I'd like you to meet Livia . . . my wife."

Dizziness overcame me. The room was silent as a beat of shock settled over us. Mom shot a worried glance at me, but at the sight of my stony face quickly looked away and recovered with a beaming smile. And then my parents converged on them, making happy sounds, giving hugs, asking questions that I couldn't hear through the storm in my ears. My entire Thanksgiving meal threatened to make an ugly reappearance. I vaguely felt Mom's hand on my shoulder, pulling me forward, casting another anxious look at my face before she plastered on that smile again.

I went forward numbly and gave Rylen a quick, weak hug around his waist. I tried to pull away, but he held me.

"Wow," I said quietly to his chest. "I . . . congrats."

I couldn't look at him. I felt like I had no control over my body. I knew I should be smiling. Hugging with gusto. Showing excitement for them. But my body and heart fought against those basic rules of propriety. The girl was so close, right there beside us like an unwanted elephant in the room.

"Hola," I heard the girl say in a small voice. Rylen released me and I gave the girl a robotic hug, kissing both her cheeks. I managed to whisper in return, "Hi."

"You Amber?" she asked.

I pulled back and nodded. My eyes were burning. I wanted to run from her sweet face. She gazed at me with nervousness.

"Ry-*len* tell me . . . of you." She seemed to struggle for the words in English. And the way she said his name, putting the emphasis on the second syllable of his name, making it sound like something different, something uniquely hers . . .

"Yeah?" I said. I had no idea how I was still standing there. Especially when Rylen put his arm around her again and pulled her closer in an awkward side embrace, as if trying to make her more comfortable. This girl seemed nice, however I felt a vileness toward her that made me ashamed.

"Yeah," Rylen said to me. "Liv's gonna be staying at my dad's until I can get us housing at my permanent duty station." His eyes raked me, searching me. He sounded uncertain, which I knew was because he couldn't read me, but he kept going. "I was hoping you might be able to help her out when I have to go away. She's twenty, so you two are close in age."

No, this wasn't happening. It couldn't be. He wanted us to be besties.

His eyes bore into my unfocused ones as if he were pleading with me. Or apologizing. I couldn't read him either. I nodded without words, and Mom was suddenly at my side, speaking for me.

"Of course, Ry!" She smiled and acknowledged Livia, speaking to her in Spanish. "You are welcome here any time. No need for an invitation. We'll give you our phone numbers—"

"Already done," Rylen said. Though he never spoke in Spanish, he always seemed to understand the gist of what we said. "I got her a phone with everyone's numbers programmed."

"Perfect! Now, tell us where you two met."

The girl looked up at Rylen.

"Guatemala," he said. "She's from a really small town near where we were doing drills."

The girl smiled, that nervous air never leaving her. "I know . . . little English, pero I learn."

"My mother is originally from Mexico, and she's still learning English," Mom said with a laugh. She motioned to Abuela, who had come into the room at some point and stood with her hands twined in front of her. Abuela came forward and kissed both of Livia's cheeks, then moved away, watching the girl carefully. Then Abuela looked at me. I tried to smile, to reassure her, but my half-hearted attempt only made her eyes droop further.

"So," Dad said. "Where is your new duty station?"

"Nellis," Rylen answered.

God, that was so close. For a second I felt joy—I'd dreamed of him being stationed near us for so long, but now—oh, God, now . . . I didn't know if I could handle it. How could he be married?

Dad laughed. "You gonna be checking out all the aliens over at Nellis?"

Rylen laughed too. "I sure as hell hope not."

"You hungry?" Dad asked. "We've got plenty of Thanksgiving leftovers."

"No, Mr. Tate, but thanks. We ate."

A lull of silence passed. I felt Rylen's eyes on me, but I couldn't look straight at him. The room seemed to spin like a funhouse maze. Or a nightmare. Or a torture room. The ache inside of me—the attack on my emotional state—felt like it would glitch my entire nervous system.

"So," Grandpa said. "How'd you meet?"

"My unit had some business in Guatemala." Rylen paused and glanced down at Livia. She gave him a soft smile and then dropped her eyes. "We met outside of the market in town."

That was it? Typical Rylen and his typical private nature and lack of details. Not that I really wanted details.

"The ceremony in Guatemala was quick, just enough for the government to allow her to leave, but we still have to get a U.S. marriage license and make it official here."

"Ah, a wedding!" Mom clasped her hands.

"Nothing big," Rylen said, shifting his stance.

So, they weren't technically married. Well, in his eyes I'm sure they were, but not *legally*. Ugh, my stomach was a wreck.

"Have you told Tater?" Mom asked.

"Yep. Gave him a call as soon as I got stateside. But I asked him not to tell."

I let myself look up again. At him. At her. This was real. This was happening. This wasn't something small. She wasn't some random girlfriend. She was his *wife*, and Rylen was loyal to a fault. It's what I loved about him. And this girl, Livia, was from a culture where women weren't likely to seek divorce the moment things got hard. She was probably in this for the long haul. This was permanent.

I had waited for Rylen, but he had not waited for me.

He had not loved me like I loved him.

He never was, and never would be, mine.

My eyes burned as tears filled and spilled over. "Pepper?" Rylen sounded horrified. Livia regarded me with sadness before turning her eyes back down to her feet.

"I'm sorry." I snuffled and wiped my eyes, forcing a smile and a psychotic-sounding laugh. "I'm just . . . wow, what a surprise."

From the couch my phone let out a blazing ring. It was my work tone. I turned and snatched it up. "I have to go."

"Called in on Thanksgiving," I heard Grandpa mutter to the group. "They work that girl to the bone."

The tears that had snuck up were rising, filling my eyes and making my chest ache with unleashed, powerful emotion. I knew it was rude of me to leave without a good-bye, but I grabbed my jacket and ran past all of them, not meeting their eyes, and not looking back. It's the first and only time I'd ever been glad to be called in.

# TEN

**M**OM WAS WAITING FOR me on the couch when I came home close to one in the morning. She stared blearily at the television, but her eyes cleared when she focused on me. She opened her arms wide and I went straight into them. We cried together, me a bit louder than her.

"I always thought he would marry you," Mom said, which made me cry even harder. "It's okay to be sad." She ran a hand down my hair. "But eventually we have to move on and be happy for him. We have to support them."

"I know," I said, though it pained me to admit it.

"They need us," she said. I nodded and pulled away enough to wipe my swollen eyes. I was still in shock, an aching chasm dented into my chest. I had no idea how long I'd feel this way, but I prayed it wouldn't last forever. Right now I just wanted to go to bed and sleep for days.

The television broadcaster's somber voice shook me from my own pitiful thoughts.

"We regret to inform you that at 12:35 this morning,

Ashlyn Navis, wife of Senator Bradford Navis, passed away from injuries sustained in an automobile accident earlier this evening . . ."

"Oh, no," Mom murmured.

For the millionth time that day, my heart constricted painfully in my chest. The poor senator. I felt a weird sort of kinship with the man. He'd lost the woman he loves on the same day I lost the dream of the man I loved. But at least Rylen was still alive.

I gently extracted myself from Mom's embrace and wiped my eyes, taking a deep breath. Senator Navis's unfortunate situation somehow helped to put my mind into perspective. Rylen was alive. I loved him. I would always love him, and I wanted him to be happy. I wanted him to be a part of my life forever. I just had to let go of the romantic feelings I'd harbored for so long, and start to see him the way he'd apparently always seen me.

As a sibling.

The thought made my stomach roll, but I swallowed the feeling down and took a deep breath. Sadness and exhaustion weighed heavily across my back, like physical things threatening to bend and crush me.

"Get some rest," Mom whispered. Without a word, I nodded and pushed to my feet, thankful beyond measure to have the rest of the day off.

I wish I could say I rested, but my body never relaxed enough for full sleep to come. A tension headache had begun in the back of my neck during the night and eventually spread upward into a promising migraine. It hurt too much to even get up and take pain meds. I was beyond grateful when Mom stuck her head in that morning to check on me.

She pressed a hand to my forehead.

"Migraine," I whispered. Thirty seconds later she was

there with a glass of water and pills. I took them gratefully, wincing against the throb of pain.

Mom set the glass down on my bedside table and grasped my upper arms in her strong hands.

"Close your eyes," she whispered. "Now relax your lower back. Let it go completely limp. Let yourself feel heavy." I knew what she was doing. It was a simple exercise in relaxation, one body part at a time, that she often did with her dancers. "Now relax up your spine, all the way up to your shoulders." I listened and followed her quiet directions, until the tension in my muscles shed, and I immediately fell asleep.

❧

I woke hours later with Mom sitting on the edge of my bed again, touching my face.

"Princesa, I want to let you sleep, but the news is on. They're about to tell us the results of the discussion and have their vote. I knew you'd want to know, but I can record it—"

"I'll get up," I whispered. The throb was back as I sat up, my face scrunching. I reached for the glass of water from earlier that morning and downed the rest of it. I glanced at the clock. It was nearly noon.

Mom went back into the living room and I trudged behind her. Abuela was there on the couch. She glanced at me with concern and patted the spot next to her. I went to her side, and she took my hand, rasping her wrinkled fingers over my knuckles. Grandpa Tate gave me a nod and I tried to smile.

"Mornin'," Dad said.

"Mornin'," I said back in a scratchy voice.

"You hungry?" Abuela asked. It sounded like *hoongr-r-ry* with the rolled r's.

"A little, but mostly I need coffee."

She tried to stand, but I held her hand tightly and said, "I'll get it in a minute."

The news was showing a grand room filled with officials from the U.S. and worldwide allies. I felt a flitter of nervousness in my gut, wondering what the outcome would be today. For so long the U.S. had been fighting small sects and groups, but it hadn't been since WWII that congress declared outright war against another country, let alone three countries at once. A war of that scale would most definitely affect our family. Rylen, Tater, even Dad would be up to his ears with work. It was a frightening possibility. But even more frightening was allowing those other countries to be reckless with nuclear weapons and threaten us in a power play.

The congressional and worldwide leaders on the television took their seats and settled down. As the camera panned around the room, it was clear that the officials were weary. They'd been at their discussions since the day before. In the next moment, the president's face filled the screen, bags under his eyes. He opened his mouth, and then . . . nothing. The screen went black. Our family stared a moment before Dad let out a grunt and stood.

I looked up at the ceiling fan, which still whirred around and around, so the electricity was working. And the television icon was now bouncing around the screen, so the TV was clearly working too.

"Station go out?" Grandpa Tate asked, sitting forward.

Dad switched channels with the remote. Every news station was out. He got to a cartoon station, which still played. But then it suddenly cut off too.

"What the hell?" Dad whispered. "Of all the damn timing. I wanted to hear that."

"Try the radio," Grandpa Tate told him.

I jumped up while Dad was messing with the television and turned on the stereo. Latino music blared from the station we listened to while we danced. I pressed the buttons to get to the local Vegas news. The station was static. My eyebrows came together, and the headache I'd had earlier started creeping around from my neck to my temples and behind my eyes.

"The Vegas station is out," I told Dad. He stepped over and switched it to AM. I never really listened to any national news on the radio, but he did.

"This one's out too," he muttered. "I think it's New York based." He continued to scan until he came to a man talking.

"—stations out across the United States with no response—"

And then something altogether bizarre happened. I started to shake. I couldn't understand it. I looked to Mom, who leapt to her feet, panic on her face. I realized then that it wasn't me shaking. The entire room was shaking. Abuela cried out and Grandpa Tate gripped his chair handles with white knuckles. A family picture fell from the wall with a *crash* of broken wood and shattering glass. The ground beneath me shifted so violently I fell to my knees.

"Earthquake!" Dad yelled. "Out of the house!"

Mom and I grasped Abuela by her upper arms while Dad helped Grandpa. We rushed from the house with the *thuds* and shattering of falling things ringing out behind us. Abuela sat in the yard, grasping her chest. I fell to her side and put my arm around her. Pieces of siding fell from our house and a metal gutter screamed as it drooped. From afar I heard a strange *woosh* and ear-splitting crashing that seemed to go on forever. I looked out to see one of the dilapidated old barns on the edge of Fite property falling.

Rylen! Were they okay in that old house? I jumped to my feet just as the trembling waned and stopped. A still hush passed over the land, followed by sounds of more things falling and settling. From the neighborhood behind our house that lined our property, I could hear people screaming behind the dividing wall. We were all breathing loudly. We'd never had a quake out here before. I didn't even know there were fault lines.

And then my mind went into work mode. Surely there were accidents and injuries. I kissed Abuela's head and jumped to my feet, running past Mom and into the house. Inside was a mess, but the walls, floors, and ceilings were intact. I dove for my phone on my bed and cursed when I saw no bars. No reception. When I ran back into the living room, Dad was there fiddling with the radio.

"Power's out," he said. His face was fierce as he yanked the cord from the wall and upended the small stereo, opening the battery compartment. "Four D batteries." He ran to the kitchen.

Voices sounded from outside and I went to the door to see Rylen running into our yard, eyes quickly scanning Mom, Abuela, and Grandpa until they landed on me and halted. His tight shoulders loosened and he let out a breath before springing up the steps and throwing his arms around me. He squeezed me to him. In that moment, after experiencing such fear, I melted into his embrace and held him too.

"You okay?" His chest heaved from the run over.

I nodded, my heart a hammer. Rylen suddenly tensed and his arms disappeared. I looked up and followed his gaze to the doorway where Livia stood, also out of breath, watching us.

"Uh, everyone here is okay," Rylen told her. He tugged at his earlobe.

Livia stared hard at me and said softly, "Es bueno."

Dad rushed back into the room and put the batteries in, then clicked the compartment shut. I moved closer to him, away from Rylen, feeling guilty and peeved. Immediately we could hear the newsman again, and my feelings shed away as I listened.

"—here in Cincinnati, but news is starting to trickle in from other networks. I'm not sure how much of this is speculation or fact, but there is word of an attack on Washington D.C., New York City, Los Angeles, and Las Vegas so far—"

"Shit!" Dad cursed.

Vegas. Remy was in Vegas! I allowed my entire body a moment of reactionary pain and nausea, and then I pulled myself together.

"My phone's not working," I said. "I need to get to the hospital."

Dad checked his phone too, and shook his head. "I should go see if the blast was anywhere near my office."

"Mind if I go with you?" Rylen asked him.

"Not at all, son."

Another tremor shook us, but it only lasted a few seconds. A splitting crack wrenched through the air outside, and I held my breath as Mom and Abuela screamed. *Whoosh-crash.* Crunching metal and broken glass. We ran for the door, and spilled onto the porch to take in the sight. One of the old, taller pine trees next to our house had fallen right into our driveway, and right onto—

"My car!" I shrieked. It wasn't a nice car by any means, but that thing was my lifeline, and the front end was completely crushed.

"I'll run you by the hospital," Dad said. "Come on." He gave Rylen a wave toward his car.

Livia took Rylen's hand. "You leave?" She glanced over at me. I turned away and walked to Dad.

"Mrs. Tate," Rylen said. "Do you mind if Livia stays here with you while I'm gone? She might be more comfortable here than with my dad."

"Not at all," Mom said. Rylen kissed Livia on her forehead at her hairline and jogged over to Dad and I at the garage door.

Mom came over and gave Dad a kiss good-bye.

"You should be able to go back in the house now," Dad told her. "But listen. You might want to run to the store before things get too crazy. See if you can buy some bottled water and non-perishables. Who knows how long it'll be before the power comes back on."

Mom nodded and reached for me. I hugged her tight, then looked over at my smooshed car under the giant tree. It didn't leave a ton of room for them to get their cars out of the garage. Dad and Rylen pulled the garage door open by hand.

"Think he can make it out?" I asked Mom.

Mom nodded gravely. "He'll just have to drive through the yard." The thought saddened me since my parents worked hard to keep the yard looking nice, a constant battle with water restrictions in the area.

I kissed Abuela and Grandpa.

A few minutes later, Dad pulled his oversized utility vehicle out of the garage, narrowly missing the tree, and making tire tracks in the lawn. Rylen jumped in the back and I took the front. Dad peeled off down the road. We were silent, but their faces were as tense as I felt. Dad flipped to the AM station.

More bombings were announced. So many cities. I covered my mouth in horror as the announcer rattled them off: "Dallas, Seattle, San Francisco, St. Louis . . ." He went on and on. "But the blast in Washington D.C. is feared to be worse than the others. Specialists are testing the area for nuclear activity. At this time, I can neither confirm nor deny that there are no survivors from the Global Summit that took place . . ."

"They're all dead," Dad murmured. "Every last one of our leaders."

Dear God . . . we were a nation without a leader. Except—

"Senator Navis!" I said. "He wasn't there!"

Dad's face lit up. "That's right. All be damned, our own senator."

"If he wasn't near Vegas," Rylen said from the back seat. I peered over my shoulder to see him lounged, arms crossed, legs splayed, no seatbelt.

"Buckle up, Ry," I told him.

His eyebrows came together like he hadn't heard me right—like I was crazy for worrying about his safety inside the car with everything going on in the world.

"Please," I said none-too-gently.

Rylen must have seen something in my eyes, the knowledge I held from things I could never unsee with my job, because he nodded and grabbed the seatbelt, clicking it securely and giving me a softer look. So handsome. I swallowed hard and turned to face forward, pressing my head back hard against the headrest. I could not think things like that anymore. I had to stop.

When we got close to the hospital, I motioned for Dad to go around back where the ambulances loaded. My partner, Julian, saw us pulling up and jogged over to my window, leaning in. He gave Dad a nod then looked at me.

"Glad you're here, Tate. Since most phone lines are down, we can't really make calls. A lot of minor injuries are coming in from the quake, but they've got a ton of hands on deck here. They're looking for medics to head out, closer to Vegas to help with the relief there. Wanna come?"

"Yeah, absolutely."

He nodded and grinned, but put up a hand when I started

to get out. "Do you have your car? The ambulances are pretty full."

"We can take her," Dad said. "We're headed that way."

Julian gave us a thumbs-up and patted my window before jogging away. We followed the procession of three ambulances, listening to the radio as we drove. The problem with the news was that so much was hearsay—reporters were getting their news from other stations and passing it along. They'd even had to correct themselves about cities they said were bombed that actually weren't.

Dad yelled and slammed the breaks, swerving. "Damn lunatics." He glared over his shoulder at the car that was headed down the center of the road, zooming in and out around other vehicles. I cringed, watching until it was out of sight.

"Some people are always ready to take advantage of bad circumstances," Dad muttered. "No concern for others, just because they can."

I stayed quiet as he grumbled. I really hoped he'd taken his blood pressure meds that morning.

As we got closer to Vegas, the traffic became congested until we came to a stop. Some cars did three-point turns and went back the other way. The ambulances in front of us kicked on their flashing lights and sirens and took to the shoulder with Dad hot on their tail. We got to the outskirts of Vegas, and as the ambulances came to a stop, Dad pulled around the side of one, and I gasped at the sight before us.

Parts of the Vegas skyline that weren't hindered by mountains were filled with black, billowing clouds of smoke.

"Holy . . ." Rylen leaned forward and breathed out.

I ripped off my seatbelt and jumped from the car, racing to the ambulance in front of us.

"Why are we stopping?" I asked Julian. "We have to get down there!"

Julian shook his head. "They're worried it was nuclear. We can't get any closer. They're putting up barriers. If people can make their way up here to us, we can treat them." I looked at the roadblock. A semi-circle of cop cars and ambulances stood facing the destroyed city. I covered my mouth with a shaking hand. An unmarked white van was opened, and four people in safety suits stood pouring over their electronics. I assumed they were searching for nuclear particles. I couldn't stop shaking as I looked out at the city again. Had the university been hit? Was Remy okay?

I reached for my cell phone in my back pocket, wanting to check the news, and then cursed under my breath at the lack of signal. It was beyond bizarre to be cut off. A rumbling came from behind me, and I turned to see a convoy of military vehicles kicking up clouds of dust. They stretched out across the desert landscape, barreling over brush, not bothering to use the road.

"Air Force from Nellis," Rylen shouted over the noise. I raised an arm to block my face from a dirt cloud as the vehicles came skidding to stops.

Rylen jogged over to the driver of the nearest Humvee, a young man in light green Army fatigues.

"Tech Sergeant Fite," Rylen said, introducing himself. "On leave this week, but soon-to-be stationed at Nellis. What can I do?"

The other man shook Rylen's hand and said, "Not really sure what the hell's going on, to be honest." The man took off his camo hat and ran a hand over his short hair before putting it back on. "A lot of our comm is out. We're here to secure the area. You're welcome to fall in."

Rylen nodded and the guy jogged off. He and I both turned to see American Red Cross vans and more military vehicles arriving. I felt sick to my stomach with helplessness. As

Rylen ran off to talk to more people, I paced the invisible line we weren't supposed to cross. I stared out, down the road to the city, for what felt like forever. A frenzy of activity to the side caught my attention as a dark sedan pulled up, flanked by police vehicles.

Shock pummeled me as Senator Bradford Navis jumped out and was quickly surrounded by body guards. A wave of whispers rushed through the personnel on scene. The senator walked forward until the CDC people made him stop. He stared out at the destruction with a tight, pained look on his face that matched how I felt inside. He wore khaki pants and a cream button-down shirt with the sleeves rolled up to his elbows. His dark hair still managed to look good in its disheveled state, but there were dark crescents under his eyes.

Behind him, a news crew leapt from a white van and pounced, filming every detail of the senator's reaction to the devastation. I watched in fascination as he spoke to the CDC official, then Army and Air Force officers. The media was pushed back for those moments, but allowed to move closer again once they finished discussing. I wished I could hear what they were saying. When he turned to address the cameras, I weaved my way through the crowd to get close enough to hear.

"Like all of you, I'm . . . in shock. Heart-broken." His voice cracked and he paused, looking down to compose himself before lifting his face to the camera again. "I am working as closely as I can with remaining government officials, though our means of communication are sparse. It's imperative that we reestablish new leadership, raising up those who are next-in-command until we can have official elections. I will do my best to oversee the process personally, but I ask for your patience and cooperation during this process.

"I do not want to cause widespread panic, but I need

everyone to be cautiously aware . . ." He paused and his face grew so serious that a chill ratcheted up my spine. "Threat to remaining survivors is imminent. Whoever is responsible for these attacks is still out there, and is likely not finished. We have reports of possible water contamination throughout the country, food contamination, biological warfare. Please listen to your local news station, and if your town is at risk, follow the guidelines that will be outlined for you.

"We are forming a nationwide organization called the Disaster Relief Initiative, the DRI, from local government officials. These persons will have the authority of police to arrest and obtain suspicious and uncooperative persons of interest. Their first job is to take a census of all towns in order to determine our remaining population and our greatest needs. If your town is under any biological threats, you will be notified and given instructions within the next week during the census taking."

I watched, rapt. Just seeing him there, confident and composed, gave me such hope.

"Please, I cannot stress this enough . . . in order to weed out those who are responsible, we must require complete compliance from citizens. No looting. Anyone found taking advantage of our country's predicament in a negative way will answer to the law. We are under high alert and there will be zero tolerance as we move forward.

"I understand most of the country is without cellular and internet service, unable to contact loved ones. This issue is being worked on around-the-clock as top priority. It's pivotal that we cling to our loved ones in this trying time." His jaw set, and I knew he was thinking about the wife he'd just lost. I covered my mouth, overcome, and watched as he swallowed hard. "We must remain positive. We must cling to hope and goodness. I urge you to stay strong as we fight this unknown enemy. Let us show them that this great country will rise from the ashes, and rebuild even stronger. In every tragedy there are unsung heroes. I urge you all to be those heroes."

He turned to face Las Vegas again. The media was given a few more seconds to tape him from behind, and then they were ushered away.

"Damn," Rylen whispered from behind me. His words brushed the side of my face, and I jumped at his nearness, at the heat he garnered in me so easily. "You okay?"

I nodded. "I'm just . . ." I nodded toward the senator.

"I don't envy him right now," Ry muttered. "He's the only elected leader left, so it all falls on him, you know?"

"Yeah," I agreed. "We're lucky to have him."

Around us, the crowd surged toward the senator, but his guards ushered him quickly into the sedan and they sped away. I turned toward the city with growing dread.

"They need us," I said.

"We can't take the chance of going in there and getting radiation poisoning." Rylen's voice was filled with warning, as if he knew my thoughts to ignore all warning and just go.

"Remy's in there," I whispered.

He put a hand on my shoulder and squeezed. "I know."

In that moment, a speck of dark moved in the distance and I stiffened. It was a car . . . no, a big SUV, and it was speeding toward us. I pointed and shouted, "Look!" Others began to murmur until our entire mammoth group stood watching, waiting. As the vehicle got closer, it became apparent it had a flat tire and was listing to the side, bumping and swerving. My heart lurched as sparks flew from the hubcap and the vehicle went off the road, hitting a rock and spinning to a stop about a hundred yards away.

"Wait for them to come to us!" one of the CDC yelled. "That's in the danger zone." I held my breath to see if anyone would get out, but none of the doors opened. My anxiousness reached a peak and I took off at a sprint.

"Amber, no!" Rylen shouted. When I didn't stop, I heard him mutter, "*Shit*," and then his footfalls were right behind me. We reached the SUV together and I pulled three times before I was able to wrench the front door open. A man caked in bloodied dirt with a bobbling head stared at me blearily.

"Sir, can you walk?" I asked. "We have to get you to the ambulances up there." I pointed, but his eyes didn't move. I lifted his arm, pushed my shoulder under his pit, and shoved my arm around his waist, then I heaved him toward me. He nearly fell on me, but managed to stay standing. "That's it," I said. "Let's go." But he was so heavy.

"Here." Rylen came up on his other side and took him, then inclined his head at the SUV. Get one of the others."

I helped a woman out of the back and looked at the other four people in the car, all adults in torn business attire. "If you can walk, I need you to get out and follow me. Now." I hated to be stern with them, but they were clearly all in shock. "Come on. Up! Let's go!"

We all made it up the road, dragging, slowly, but the moment we passed the safe line the medics converged, taking over in an orderly, efficient fashion that calmed me.

The CDC took Rylen and I to one of their vans and waved wands over us, asking a myriad of questions.

"Do you feel nauseated? Headache?" No, no.

"They're clear," one of them said.

"So, was it definitely a nuclear bomb?" I asked them.

"That is classified, ma'am," the man said in an all-important voice that made me want to roll my eyes. What the hell was the point of classifying that? Mass panic was already a given.

Rylen pulled something out of his back pocket and flashed

it at the woman next to him. She raised her eyes at the man by me. "TS clearance, Air Force." Of course Ry would have Top Secret clearance.

The man nodded stiffly. "All right. No. No radioactivity that we've been able to detect."

My eyes bulged as I jumped to my feet in a fury. "Then why aren't we down there?"

"We still have two final tests we're waiting on."

I gritted my teeth and stormed away to check on the five people who'd made it to us. And to my relief, a stream of cars began to steadily make their way up the dusty highway from the city to us. The military directed them where to park and helped people to the medic stations that were erected with cots. We worked fast. Most of the injuries were topical. I realized those with the most damage were probably not able to make it to cars and were stuck down there with no help. Some of the survivors were in shocked silence, but others were eager to talk as we worked, to tell us what they'd seen and experienced—hotels leveled, buildings falling, people trapped, jumping over dead bodies as they ran. Most were traumatized, frantic about family and friends they couldn't find as they fled.

I had no words to comfort them, so I began telling people about Senator Navis and what he'd said. His words seemed to clear people's eyes. To focus them. Each and every person clung to those words, like a beacon of light, our solitary hope.

With each person I helped, I gently asked, "Do you know anything about the university?" They each shook their heads, having been in different parts of the city. Until the last woman nodded.

"I work in the financial aid department. The school is mostly okay. A lot of injured are being brought to the campus for treatment since the hospital was damaged during the earthquake. I was out to lunch at the outskirts of the city when the bombs hit."

Bombs? Plural? "There was more than one?"

She nodded, her eyes fluttering closed for a second. "There were two. Planes flew over. They hit one end of the strip, then the other." Planes had dropped bombs?

"Ma'am." The loud voice from behind me made me spin in surprise. A man in a suit with sunglasses reached out a hand to the woman I was tending.

"Come with me," he said.

"I'm not quite finished bandaging her arm," I said.

"We'll take care of it," he said. The woman took his hand and he helped her to her feet.

"I'm sorry, but who are you?" I asked, standing to face him.

"Your local DRI." He quickly turned and walked away with the woman, leaving my head spinning. What the hell was DRI? I wracked my brain and then felt relieved. Oh . . . the Disaster Relief Initiative. Damn, they worked fast! The senator must have literally formed that organization overnight and had his people working double time to get them up and running.

So many people were coming and going. The woman's words blew away from my mind like dust in the hustle and bustle around me.

Tents were set up in the nearby field of dirt where people could rest, and then be shuttled to a high school that was being turned into a makeshift temporary hotel for survivors. The line of people coming for treatment seemed never ending. Now and then I'd catch glimpses of Rylen checking on me, and then he'd disappear again.

The other medics and I worked without stopping until the

stars were bright in the sky above us. It was the longest day of my life. When I finally stood, I stumbled into the side of the ambulance in a wave of dizziness.

"Whoa, Tate," Julian said. I shook my head and blinked.

"I'm all right." But I was suddenly so hungry and thirsty I worried I might vomit. Like a magician, Rylen was there by my side, looking me over.

"I'm fine," I said, but my voice sounded tired.

"You haven't eaten a thing."

I vaguely remembered him trying to hand me a sandwich earlier, urging me to stop for a minute, but I'd refused it and called over the next limping person.

"Tate, let him take you home," Julian said. "We've got plenty of medics here now, and you can come back after you rest a little." He rubbed his face. "I'm heading out too."

It's true that another round of medics from nearby hospitals had showed, and for all I knew I might be needed back at our own hospital. But I'd be no help to anyone if I passed out. So I nodded and let Rylen lead me through the many vehicles until we came to Dad's SUV in the last row. I wondered how long he'd been waiting there for us.

Dad looked me over as I climbed in and gave me a nod of respect. Rylen handed me a bag of chips and bottle of apple juice, and I downed them in a minute flat. Then I leaned my head against the window and passed out.

# ELEVEN

I WOKE CRADLED TO a warm, hard chest, feeling the movement of feet beneath me. It was dark, so dark. No artificial light anywhere. My senses were filled with his smell. His body against mine. My eyes blearily opened and I lifted my chin. Rylen's cheek was beside my lips. His strong arms were beneath my back and under my knees. He was *carrying* me.

All at once I remembered he was now married, and my entire body stiffened. I kicked my legs. Rylen stopped and leaned down so I could leap from his arms. I spun to face him, feeling irrationally angry. My whole body shook and in the moonlight I saw his eyes widen.

He held his palms up. "It's just me, Pepper."

"You didn't have to . . . hold me," I said.

His face flashed through a series of surprise and agitation before he shook his head and said, "Well, I'm sorry, but I couldn't wake you and I didn't want to leave you in the truck all night. I won't touch you again if it bothers you so much." He put his hands up, pursing his lips.

"Fine," I said.

"Fine," he huffed back.

I looked around at my dark yard, breathing hard, feeling a pang of upset at the blurry sight of the tree still laying across my car. Wrong, so wrong. Everything was wrong. I grabbed my head, which was about to split open.

"Amber," Rylen said in a ghost of a whisper. "You've been through a lot today."

I opened my eyes and looked into his solemn eyes. A painful crack split my heart. Why did I have to love him so much? Would it always hurt like this?

"Let's get you inside." He reached for my arm and I shifted, turning and jogging toward the house.

"Pepper, what the hell?" His voice trailed off behind me. I didn't stop.

Inside, I found Livia standing by the window with her arms crossed. She studied me as I passed her, heading straight for the hall. I wondered if she'd been watching from the window. Probably. I didn't wait around to witness Rylen greeting her. I knew I was being a bitch, but I couldn't seem to stop. I didn't want to acknowledge any of it.

Despite my complete exhaustion, I slept restlessly with thoughts of Rylen and work. It was weird not to have a working cell phone—not to know if there were local dire emergencies where I was needed. I felt guilty trying to rest. All night I kept glancing toward my alarm clock to check the time, only to be greeted by darkness and the reminder that we had no electricity. It was eerily quiet without the white noise of my fan. When I heard the quiet opening and closing of my parents' bedroom door at dawn, I got up and joined them in the kitchen.

Abuela was already up too, sitting at the table in her night-gown and quilted robe. She took my face in her hands and kissed the top of my cheek as I sat next to her. Mom and Dad were looking out the front windows of the house.

"His truck is back," Dad murmured.

"Whose?" I called.

"Grandpa Tate's," Mom said. "He told us he was going to get something from the storage room he rents, but he was gone all afternoon. Must have gotten back after dark." Grandpa was funny like that. Very private.

They came and sat across from us at the table. I noticed a stack in the corner of family photos in frames that had bro-ken or lost their glass during the earthquake. It made me sad to see our history piled there like that. I remembered what some of the people had been saying yesterday.

"They think the earthquake here was caused by the bomb in Vegas. Like they shifted the earth's plates or something."

"Unbelievable," Dad said. "To think a single bomb could do that."

"It might have been more than one bomb," I told him. "Some lady said she saw to planes drop separate bombs."

"What?" Mom's eyes bulged, and Dad's narrowed.

He shook his head. "There's no way. No way these were from bombers. The Air Force is right there in Nellis—they would have stopped any foreign aircraft."

I shrugged. Maybe she'd seen wrong. I had no idea.

"Did Rylen and . . . his wife stay here last night?" The words felt like grit in my throat.

"No, honey," Mom said quietly. "They went to his house. Why don't you tell us what happened when you three left here."

I told them about Vegas and how the people had to make it up to us for treatment, though by the end of the day they were ruling out nuclear radiation. I told them about how we'd seen the senator, too.

"I heard that speech on the radio!" Mom said. "He's just what this country needs right now."

Dad pinched the skin between his eyes.

"What's wrong?" I asked him.

"I hate this feeling of sitting around, being disconnected. Our main comm systems are down at work, but we blew the dust off an old telegraph machine yesterday and I was able to get through to Tater's squadron leader. He hasn't seen him. They're all out helping with local relief in the Atlanta area."

"Was Atlanta bombed too?" My heart thudded as Dad and Mom both nodded. I hoped Tater was okay.

"Is there any major city that wasn't hit?" I asked, appalled.

Dad sighed. "We really don't know." He glanced longingly toward our coffee pot, and my gaze followed. Everything in our house was electric, including the stove. This sucked hard. My eyes felt weighed down by rocks.

"We shouldn't use the tap water," I said. "Senator Navis mentioned possible bio warfare. Do we have bottled water?"

"Some, but I need to try the bank and the store again today," Mom said. "It was packed yesterday with a line out the door." Dad shook his head.

"I don't want you going out there again, baby. The Harrises down the street said when they went to the store yesterday afternoon there were fights, and cops out there pepper spraying people and hauling them off. It's gonna be the same today. And even if the bank is on a generator, everyone's going to be trying to cash out their assets, and banks aren't equipped for that. They'll run out of cash and shut their doors."

A feeling of horror ran through me, matching the look on Mom's face.

"We won't be able to access our money?" I asked.

Dad shook his head. "Nope. And chemical warfare or not, we won't be able to access our plumbing water without electricity. The Fites might be able to; I think they're one of the rare old houses on well water still."

"How will we get food and stuff?"

Mom and Dad shared a glance. Abuela brought a hand up to her cheek, murmuring, "God help us," in Spanish.

Just then the front door opened, and my heart gave a bang, expecting to see Ry. But it was Grandpa, holding something bulky and metal . . . a camping stove?

Dad jumped up and went to take it from his arms. A French press coffee maker was on top of the two-burner gas stove. My mouth watered. Dad asked, "Where you been, Pop? You disappeared on us yesterday." He set the things on the table and faced Grandpa.

"Just picking up a few things we might need. You all might want to follow me."

We looked around at each other with interest before standing. I gave Abuela my arm and we followed Grandpa Tate out of the house into the dawning morning that felt cool on my bare arms. The sight of my smashed car made me grimace. We went to the side of the house and took the outdoor stairs up to the loft above the garage. Grandpa's loft had been off limits since he moved in. He locked the door every time he went in or out. He'd even added a padlock to the outside.

Abuela and I were last to make it in. Dad was standing there with a surprised, goofy kind of grin, his hand on his head as he stared around. Abuela smacked a hand to her chest.

Whoa.

"Shut the door," Grandpa commanded. I quickly did, then

turned to survey the dim room. Against one wall was a twin-sized bed, neatly made, a dresser, and a tall, wide bookcase. The rest of the room was packed full. Piles of canned food went nearly from floor to ceiling in the corners. Cases of bottled water and giant jugs, bags of rice, propane tanks, sleeping bags, boxes of matches . . . it was like a camping supply store. Or a zombie apocalypse safehouse. All that was missing were guns.

Mom picked up a can of green beans and looked at the label.

"They're all within date," Grandpa said. "I keep them in order of date and chuck 'em when they get bad."

"Pop?" Dad said, still with that quirky smile on his face. "How long have you been doing this?"

"You never can be too careful," Grandpa said in a gruff tone, as if he didn't want to answer any questions or hear any teasing. "I knew after Fatal Friday it was only a matter of time."

This was extreme. Part of me felt like Grandpa was batshit crazy, but was he?

"This was very . . . smart of you," Mom said, seeming to choose her words carefully. "This is exactly what we'll need to get us through until things are back to normal. Thank you, Papá Tate."

He grunted. "Things ain't getting back to normal anytime soon, sweetheart. Bet on it."

Mom frowned and I swallowed hard.

"And don't go telling anyone about this," Grandpa continued, pointing at his piles of goods. "Otherwise they'll all be over here trying to take our rations. I know how you ladies have soft hearts, but this is for *our* family. Do you all understand that? The Fites are the only ones we share with, and that's because I know damn well they'll share their fresh crops with us too."

An awkward lull passed in which he stared around at all of us until we nodded our understanding.

"One more thing," Grandpa said. He limped his way over to the tall bookcase and proceeded to grab it on both sides and pull. To my shock, it moved forward as if on wheels, and he pulled it to the side, opening it like a hidden door to reveal a wooden panel in the back and within the wall behind it. The doors had two padlocks. He must have constructed this entire convoluted thing himself. We all gawked as he unlocked it and swung both doors wide.

*Holy freaking zombie apocalypse.* There were the guns.

Dad whistled low and stepped forward. Mom gave Abuela and I a frightened glance. She'd never been comfortable with guns. Some of these were straight out of Rambo. There were handguns, rifles, and shotguns—manual, semi, and automatic. A variety of at least twenty-five. Along with axes and boxes of ammo lined along the bottom.

"You don't whisper a word about these," Grandpa said in a low tone. He shook a finger. Abuela's eyebrows were practically grazing the ceiling. "The government will try to take 'em."

Oh, Grandpa. He'd lost his mind. But once again, when he nailed us all with that dire look, we nodded our promise not to tell. He closed the doors and clicked the padlocks shut. I almost burst out laughing at the look on Dad's face, as if caught between amusement, worry, and absolute admiration.

"Now." Grandpa clasped his hands. "Let's go make some coffee."

Amen.

French press joe with a scoop of sugar was rich, dark, smooth, and every other wonderful adjective that might describe perfect coffee. I was sipping with my eyes closed, letting it sooth my soul when Dad said, "I always thought Tater would be the first to run off and elope."

My coffee became bitter and turned my stomach.

Mom and Abuela both glanced at me. Dad took another big drink, oblivious. I looked at my cup, swirling the dredges.

"That's a soldier for you," Grandpa said. "Most are married before they even turn nineteen."

"Jacob no marry," Abuela said, pronouncing his name like *Jyae-cobe.* "No yet. He like mas chicas too much." Her *much* sounded like *mush.*

I snorted. Gross. Mom rolled her eyes, and Dad and Grandpa both chuckled.

"He's better off," Dad said. "Too many of these young guys end up cheating, or being cheated on while they're away, then getting divorced." We all got quiet. Dad's first wife cheated in their first year of marriage when he was gone for eight months. They didn't have any kids together, thank goodness. He'd drilled it into mine and Tater's heads not to be quick to marry, as it was his most regrettable, rash decision in life.

"What am I gonna do about a car?" I asked, wanting to change the subject.

"You can take mine," Mom said. "I think I'll stay here with Abuela. I'm sure there's nothing left at the store now anyway. And we seem to have enough." She smiled at Grandpa.

I really wanted to shower, but I knew there was limited water available to houses during outages, and I was afraid of contamination. I really hoped the town would be able to get us up and running again soon.

I brushed my hair and put on work clothes. When I came out, Rylen was standing there talking to Dad in camo cargo pants with his boots planted a foot apart and his arms crossed over his fitted white T-shirt. That same irrational anger from last night rose inside me at his effortless hotness. Now that he was married, he should have the decency to grow a beer gut or something.

I jolted at the feel of someone's eyes on me, and found Livia sitting at the table, watching me watch her husband. She looked so small sitting there in a worn gray dress and black leggings, her tiny frame sitting up straight in the chair. I wanted to just ignore her—pretend she didn't exist—but ugh. I walked over and pushed my hair behind my ears.

"Would you like coffee?" I asked, nodding toward the French press that still had a little left.

"No, no," she said, shaking a hand.

"She likes tea," Rylen said from behind us. Dad kept on talking, and I realized Ry had probably been on his way in to help Livia when he got stopped by Dad's motormouth.

"Rylen, no," Livia said. Again with the Ry-LEN. I wondered if they'd had sex last night.

Oh, God.

"I can make it," I told her, bustling over to the pot with the boiled water. It had cooled, so I lit the burner again. Propane fumes stung my nose. My stomach was a knot, coffee halfway back up my esophagus. A wave of dizziness hit me as I turned toward the cabinet and reached up for a mug and the box of teas. I closed my eyes and leaned against the counter.

"Please." Her voice was close. Livia had moved to me and taken the mug and box. I gave her a single nod and bit my lip as she turned away to make her own tea. My eyes burned. Two seconds later Rylen was at my side, scrutinizing me with those gray eyes.

"You okay?" I knew he was talking about last night, too, not just my current state.

"I'm fine. Just over-tired," I assured him. Then I walked in an arc past him, careful not to touch him. Dad reached out and put an arm around me, pulling me in for a hug. I was so tense.

"I have to get to the hospital," I said.

He kissed my head. "Don't burn yourself out, Amber. If you need to take a day off, do it. You're no help to anyone if you're falling down."

"Okay," I said to appease him.

I finished getting ready and grabbed Mom's keys from the hook when a knock sounded on the door. I followed Dad, who called through without opening it, "Who's there?"

"Nevada State DRI," came a man's voice. "Here for the mandatory census."

"The Disaster Relief Initiative," I whispered.

Dad raised his eyebrows. "That was fast."

He slid the deadbolt and opened the door. A gorgeous woman with flowing brown hair and new highlights stood there with an equally handsome man, both with glowing ol-ive skin, both in suits. They looked like flight attendants. Did the senator hire DRI people from the Vegas modeling agen-cies or something? Geez.

"Please, come in," Dad told them. I moved aside and they walked in, smiling at the room. Dad called for Mom. Grandpa slid in the door behind them, staring at their backs with dis-trust. I really hoped he didn't embarrass us by spouting any conspiracy theory nonsense to them.

Rylen and Livia walked in from the kitchen, her blowing steam off her cup of tea. The room was full and I focused on the two government workers.

"Can you please tell us how many people reside here?" the woman asked.

We went through the entire family, genders, ages,

races—they were very particular, needing to know precise percentages for each race—a precise census. We had to explain that Rylen and Livia were our neighbors, newlyweds. They became especially interested to learn that Rylen was Air Force based there in Nevada.

"When was the last time you were at Nellis?" the woman asked.

"Actually, never, ma'am. I'm supposed to report in five days, but I think I'll go today to see if—"

"You can wait," the woman said. Rylen appeared taken aback, so she smiled with assurance. "The base is in chaos. I suggest taking your remaining days and allowing them to reestablish communications before you bother reporting."

"Oh," he said, his brow still furrowed.

The woman forged ahead with their questions. My head spun until it sounded like they were finally wrapping up.

"Your water here is still testing fine, but I would boil before consuming for now," said the man. "They're working rapidly on vaccines to some of the strands, and antitoxins, so if your area is affected, DRI personnel will be set up to take care of the community."

"Wait," I said, running my hands over my arms. "Would it be safe to shower in?"

The man shook his head. "We recommend bathing in boiled water, as well. But as I'm sure you know, there is only a limited amount of water available because the pumps are run by electricity, so once it runs out, there is no more."

"I'm sure electricity will be back on before that's an issue though, right?" Dad asked.

The woman gave him a pleasant smile. "Let's all hope. We're doing our best." The woman casually added in a chipper voice, "And do you have any weapons on the premises?"

They couldn't see Grandpa's saucer-sized eyes, but I

could, and I had to look away from him for fear of bursting into laughter.

"You're cataloging weapons?" Dad asked. His face appeared casual, but I could tell from the stance he took and the way he crossed his arms that he didn't approve.

The woman looked to the man, who gave a tight grin. "As you know, sir, these are trying times. The enemy could be anywhere. To be completely transparent, we need to know who's able to defend themselves, if necessary, who's willing and able to help, and who's not."

Mom cocked her head. "So you *want* people to be armed?"

"The right people, yes," he said.

Dad nodded imperceptibly, and eventually uncrossed his arms and shoved his hands in his pockets. "I have a conceal and carry permit. I've got a Glock and a hunting rifle. Also a bb gun, if that counts."

"Of course it counts." The woman was so serious. I couldn't help myself.

"Yeah, Dad, you can shoot your eye out."

Rylen gave a cough-snort and wiped his nose. Nobody else in the room laughed.

The man stared at Dad. "And where do you keep your guns, sir?"

"In my home," Dad said. The smartass.

"Are they secured?"

"Of course."

"And do you bring your Glock with you when you leave the house?"

"I do." Dad's face had gotten tighter and tighter with the questioning. Grandpa looked like a frozen statue of terror, and Mom and Abuela had also become awkwardly stiff.

"Any other firearms besides the three you listed?" the man asked.

I had to hand it to our family. We played that moment very cool and respected Grandpa's demand to keep his secret. We all shook our heads casually, though my family's minds were probably just as full of Grandpa's insane gun collection as mine. And it was bizarre, because Dad was the most honest, upstanding citizen I'd ever known. He'd once brought me back into a store to pay for a fifty-cent piece of candy he didn't realize I'd taken until we were in the car. And then he'd counseled me about right and wrong the entire ride home. If anyone followed the laws, it was Dad.

So why didn't he, or any of us, tell about the other guns? Was it because Grandpa would most definitely lose his shit and be carted away? Or because we were embarrassed about the extremist supplies on our property? Or maybe because all of my family felt the same amount of strange discomfort around these DRI people and just wanted them to leave? I knew they were only doing their job, but some of it felt invasive. Whatever the reason, we didn't tell. And they finally left.

Grandpa collapsed into a chair, gripping the arms and breathing hard. "It's happening."

"Nothing is happening, Pop," Dad said, giving his shoulder a pat and squeeze. But even Dad's eyes looked troubled.

I looked at Rylen, who also appeared uneasy as he looked back at me.

"I'm sure it's fine," Mom said. "Government stuff is always tedious and detailed."

I let out a breath. I wanted to get away from Rylen's warm eyes, and go where I felt needed. "I'm going to the hospital, but they'll probably send me out on runs. If you need me, tell someone at the hospital and they'll get a message to me."

I gave Mom a hug and she told me to be careful, then I was off.

# TWELVE

I LISTENED TO THE AM radio news on the way to work. The United States was in ruins. Los Angeles had, in fact, been leveled by a nuke, which caused high-magnitude earthquakes to snake violently up the California coast. I couldn't wrap my mind around the kind of devastation they described. Whole cities flattened. Tsunami-type waves and flooding. Bridges, roads, airports, all in rubble.

In the northern states there weren't many bombings, but the biological warfare wreaked evil havoc. States like the Dakotas were facing a toxin in the water that was causing boils on people's skin, and in their mouths, throats, and stomachs. New Englanders seemed to be facing some sort of medieval bubonic plague. In southern states, like Louisiana and Alabama, the crops and livestock were dying from a mysterious virus, cutting off the local food supply to all those people. I was trembling by the time I got to work and terrified to turn on a faucet.

Our small hospital looked like a warzone, and we were in nowhere near as bad of a predicament as the other cities I'd been hearing about.

Medics from the closer cities surrounding Vegas took over the efforts there while smaller towns like ours sent a handful of helpers and used the rest of our personnel to try and pick up the messy pieces. Panic does crazy things to people. Overdosing, alcohol poisoning, attempted suicide, fighting . . . the hospital was packed. There weren't enough rooms. EMT staff were going down the line of people on the sidewalk outside. Tents with cots were going up in the parking lot. Generators were being used for the most dire emergencies, but we were asked to save electricity because the generators weren't meant for prolonged use.

I was a stickler for sterilization, so these were not optimal working conditions, but it's crazy how quickly you adjust when you have to. I kept a box of sterile, antibacterial wipes by my side, and of course changed gloves between each person. If the glove supply ran out, I was screwed.

It was late in the day when the first fever/rash combo came in. A fever and rash was not uncommon, of course, but this rash wasn't like anything I'd ever seen. The woman's arms were spotted with dark red, raised welts that seemed to cover her whole body. It looked like Rocky Mountain Spotted Fever, a tick-borne bacterial infection I'd only seen in textbooks.

"When did this rash begin, ma'am?" I asked.

Her voice was raspy. "The fever started last night, and the rash this morning. I put some cortisone cream on it and took a nap. When I woke it was worse, and it itches." She let out a moan. "I'm sore all over."

Julian, who was working on the man ahead of me, looked over at her. We met eyes, and I could see he was as nervous as me about what this could be.

"We're going to run some bloodwork," I told the woman.

"Sit tight."

I ran to get a blood tech. When I came back I saw another woman down the line with the same rash on her arms. She had a toddler boy with her. Fear clawed at my belly.

"There's another one," I whispered to Julian.

"Get Boss Lady," he said.

While the technician was taking blood, I wove in and out of the people and into the building to find my supervisor. It was stifling inside the ER. I found her at the desk, looking frazzled as she spoke to another nurse.

"I'm afraid we've got bio warfare victims coming in," I told her. She didn't ask any questions, just followed me quickly to the line outside on the sidewalk. The moment she saw the women's faces and arms she muttered, "Shit. We can run the bacterial tests here, but I'll have to send off to check for viruses or toxins, and that could take days."

"Maybe the DRI could get the tests done sooner?" I asked.

She nodded. "I'll ask. In the meantime, I want everyone with these symptoms put in a separate tent."

Julian stepped up, having finished with his patient. "I'm on it."

Our boss took off to find one of the DRI who'd been nosing around the hospital all day, and Julian and I went to clear out a tent so we could bring the women in. The nurses and doctor working in there were not happy about having to move, but when I mentioned biological warfare, they packed up real quick.

We brought in the women, and my heart sank when a teen boy with the same spots came in, too. This was not good. Boss Lady rushed in with a suit-wearing DRI woman, and they began questioning the patients, all of whom had drank unfiltered, unboiled tap water in the past twenty-four hours.

Julian and I stood to the side, watching. I glanced at him and found his normally freckled skin to be a grayish palor, his cheeks sunken. I wondered if that's how I looked too.

"Have you eaten anything today?" I asked. I hadn't, and now that I stopped working for a second I noticed the dizziness in my head and gnawing in my gut.

"I tried to eat a protein bar," he said. "But it tasted like Ebola."

I looked at his unsmiling face and was horrified when something cracked inside me and I let out an uncontrollable burst of laughter. Julian pressed his lips together. I covered my mouth as the mirth continued to bubble out of me at its own accord. Everyone in the tent turned to glare at my insensitive outburst. I couldn't hold it back—I was about to blow like a kid with the giggles in church. I rushed out of the tent with Julian on my heels, heading toward the parking lot, and collapsed between two cars where my inappropriate laughter could be hidden from the world. Julian fell to his knees next to me, and we laughed so hard we couldn't breathe.

*It tasted like Ebola . . .* "You asshole," I sputtered, whacking his arm.

He pulled a bent chocolate-peanut butter bar from his pocket. "Want one?"

No, I really didn't after that disgusting comment, but my body needed it. I took it and opened the wrapper, forcing a tentative bite. He waggled his eyebrows as I chewed. It was too creamy.

"It's like pustules," I said, and we fell over laughing again. Eventually we relaxed, and he took out his last protein bar, eating it in two giant bites. He was thoughtful as he chewed, as if contemplating what it tasted like.

"Don't say it," I warned. "Whatever you're thinking, just don't."

He grinned and got to his feet, helping me up. "If there's really something in the water here, we're in for hell, Tate." All traces of humor were gone now.

I brushed off my bottom and sighed. We needed to get back to work, but I was so tired. A few rows over, the DRI woman was walking quickly with a DRI man to a white van. They were as golden and good-looking as the ones who'd come to our house. I don't know why that was so weird to me. She carried a small kit, probably with the blood samples. Again, that nervous feeling thickened like mud inside of me.

I inclined my head toward them and Julian looked. "Ever notice how the DRI peeps are all so—"

*BOOM.*

I had no idea what had happened, but I'd been blown sideways onto the pavement. Julian's warm body was braced over top of mine, my arm burning where I'd hit the ground and skidded several feet. An ear-splitting *fizzle* filled the air and then the loudest, longest crashing sound I'd ever heard.

"Go, go!" Julian yelled. We both jumped up and sprinted, partially squatting, deeper into the parking lot, as a giant cloud of dust rolled over top of us. I balled up behind a van, and Julian hunkered next to me.

A series of *bangs* sounded from the direction of the hospital, like rocks falling, and a sprinkling clatter of rubble hitting the ground and cars. I pulled up my legs and grasped them, hiding my face against the cloud of dust. It felt like forever before it quieted and warm air ceased rushing from under the cars.

"Oh, God." I was afraid to look behind us. My arm stung and throbbed. "Julian . . ."

Julian didn't move. He was panting beside me, then gave a giant cough. His body shuddered as he stood and slowly turned to look toward the hospital. "Holy shit, Tate."

It had been awhile since the scene of an accident made me ill, but when I finally stood and peered through the dust and smoke to see the twisted, smoking remains of the hospital and flattened, scorched tents, I bent over and retched up that entire protein bar.

# THIRTEEN

LL THOSE PEOPLE—THERE couldn't possibly be survivors. Even those outside would have been sent flying from the power of the blast. Down the road the white van with DRI sped away. I hoped they were getting help.

Julian and I took off at a sprint through the cars, many of which had been slammed together and dented from debris. One was on its side. We were so lucky we weren't crushed. We made it to the outskirts of the blast and searched for bodies. Where the sidewalk used to be was now covered in rubble.

Julian ran with me to the edge of the scorched tent, and together we lifted the tarp, grunting as we yanked the stakes from the dirt. We got it high enough to see five bodies in a pile that had been thrown to the back of the tent in the blast, bloodied but whole.

"Check them!" Julian said, holding up the flap.

I bent and pushed my way under. The first body was the teen boy with the rash. I felt guilty for hesitating to touch him, but I didn't have my gloves on. He didn't appear to be breathing. I lay my head on his covered chest and listened. No heartbeat. No breathing. I crawled to the next. Both women were dead. And then I sucked in a breath. Underneath the second woman was her toddler, also dead. His face looked sweet and tender, like he was sleeping. My eyes burned as I moved to the last body . . . Boss Lady.

No . . . I pressed my fingers to her neck. No pulse. "Please," I whispered.

"Any survivors?" Julian called. His voice was strained from the effort of holding up the heavy material.

I couldn't answer. A giant lump had lodged in my throat. I crawled back to him and shook my head. He dropped the flap and put his hands on his knees, breathing hard.

I stood up and looked around. An eerie silence fell, and then the remains of the hospital seemed to become a live thing, hissing breaths of smoke, shifting, creaking. Julian grabbed my arm.

"We need to move."

We backed away.

"Let's see if any of the ambulances made it," I said. Together we jogged a circle around the building until we came to the back. The five ambulances were all either crushed or overturned. A sense of despair bloomed around my heart and clutched it, threatening to squeeze the life from me. We walked as close as we could safely get to the building, listening for voices, though I had no idea how we'd get any trapped people out of there.

"Who would do this?" I whispered. I just couldn't fathom the madness behind this. "What if they're still here? Watching us?" Julian and I both swung our heads around. I was half-expecting to see evil eyes staring out at us from behind vehicles, but not a soul was in sight. Just a hospital filled with lifeless bodies, and manicured trees, now mangled and bent.

Inside that building had been nurses and doctors—my friends and coworkers—and innocent people, all with families at home, expecting them to return. What if Julian and I hadn't had our stupid bout of laughter? We would have been killed in that tent. I should be dead! My parents, Tater, Rylen . . . how would they have felt to hear that news? My eyes burned, and I wiped them with the back of my shaking hand.

Sirens sounded from up the road. Police cars and firetrucks, followed by the black government sedans the DRI were now driving. Julian and I ran back around the building to head them off as they arrived.

We answered their questions as best as we could, and we told them that DRI had taken samples of possible biological warfare victims. At that point, I noticed a stream of new cars trickling their way down the roads and into the parking lot. When spots began to fill, they parked on the medians and in the grassy areas.

Julian muttered a curse as people began ambling toward us, covered in whelps, staring at the dead hospital in confusion and panic.

"They're infected," I told the nearest cop. The DRI man beside us heard me and ran to his car, popping the trunk.

"We've got to steer them in a unified direction." He pulled out a white cardboard sign with stakes in the bottom, like election signs, which he wrote instructions on. Then he pointed to the elementary school next door. "Send all possible infected persons to the elementary school for treatment. I'll notify the DRI that more hands are needed here since the hospital staff . . ." he gazed in the direction of the hospital, but didn't finish. My gut clenched.

As he jogged off to put up the signs, I stared. "He had

signs ready?"

The cop shrugged. "I guess they were anticipating the worst."

The sun was setting. A pink hue hovered over the mountainous landscape, the beauty clashing with the ugliness of our circumstances. People were crying in the parking lot, upset by the sight of the hospital ruins, not knowing what to do. I felt like I should somehow let my family know I was okay, but I didn't have the time to make the forty minute ride home and then back. I would be so tired. And I was one of the only medics on hand. Julian had already made himself useful, guiding people to the school.

I took a deep breath of smoky air and joined him.

It was almost midnight before I made my way to Mom's car to drive home. I knew better than to drive when my eyes were heavy slits that I couldn't keep open. So I lay back the seat, just for a quick nap, and then I'd go home.

Seconds later, I was hard asleep with visions of rashes dancing in my head. And across my skin.

Loud, rapid rapping made me scream at the top of my lungs, echoing in the small space. I sat up in a panic, confused as hell about where I was in the pitch dark. When I saw the crazed face in the window, I screamed again, then covered my mouth as Dad's features became clear. I yanked open my door and tumbled out into his arms.

"Jesus Christ almighty, Amber!" He squeezed me tightly, and I felt his chest heaving. "I thought you were dead!" Dad let out a sob that broke me. The wails that rose from deep in my soul were unlike any sound I'd ever made. It was like the laughter earlier that day—I couldn't control it. I cried in my father's arms as he kissed my head over and over, murmuring,

"It's okay, baby girl. I've got you."

It wasn't until I finally pulled myself together and pulled away that I saw Rylen beside us, leaning against the car, watching me with this look of combined relief and heartbreak. My heart galloped. I quickly wiped my face.

"Rylen's gonna drive you home," Dad said.

"I can drive—" I began.

"Ry will drive." Dad turned toward his vehicle as if to say *end of discussion*.

Rylen walked me around to the passenger side and opened the door. I slid inside and he closed the door. When he got behind the wheel, he didn't start the car right away. He stared over his shoulder at the hospital. Even in the dark, I could make out the moisture in his eyes.

"When we saw it, Pepper . . ."

The sharp bloom around my heart squeezed, pricking me with thorns. They'd really thought I was dead.

"I'm so sorry," I whispered.

He grabbed my hand and held tight, his eyes fierce on mine. "I've never been so happy as when I saw you laying in here." He let out a dry laugh and his chin quivered. So help me, if Rylen cried I would break all over again. But he swallowed and cleared his throat, sniffing once and taking his hand from mine to face the steering wheel again. We were quiet a long time.

"Oh . . ." He leaned to the side and pulled something silver and crinkly from his back pocket. "Sorry, it's probably broken."

A PopTart. I tore it open like an animal and moaned at the smell of cinnamon and brown sugar. I nearly choked on the dry-ass pastry as I shoved it in my mouth. Rylen gave the road a small smile as he drove us away, leaving the wreckage and sickness far behind.

For now.

We were halfway home, both lost in thought, before he finally spoke again.

"I know you've been upset with me," he said. My body tightened at the onslaught of grief and guilt. I stared down at the crumpled wrapper in my hand as he continued. "I'm sorry I didn't tell you about Livia right away. I know you don't take surprises well. I should have called or something." He ran a hand over his head and let out a long breath. "It . . . I don't know, I think I was still in shock myself. It happened sort of fast."

My gut twisted hard. I had to force myself to say something. "She seems . . . really nice."

"She is," he said, grasping my words eagerly. "She's a good girl, Pepper."

I nodded.

"She's been through a lot."

*Just like you*, I thought. I wondered what she'd been through, but he said nothing more. Part of me wanted to know everything, but that broken part of me still wanted no part of it.

"I'm sorry," I whispered. "For how I've been."

He shot me a small smile, as if to say *no worries*. And I vowed not to let my feelings make me act rude to him or Livia anymore. I had to get over this. I loved him too much to treat him badly, and if he loved Livia . . . well then, I needed to treat her well too.

"It's funny," he said quietly. "When you're overseas, in warzones, after a while the people you love start to feel like fairy tales or something intangible. So far away they're not real. You start to look for any small human interaction that makes you feel something." He grasped his earlobe. "Sorry, I'm not making sense."

"No," I said. "You are." I'd been watching him, hanging on every word.

He watched the road for another minute, staring at the beams of headlights.

"I guess the point of all that was to say that when I saw Livia . . . I felt something."

I watched the side of his face as he stared ahead. He'd felt something. Something big? Or just . . . something good? I didn't know. All that mattered was that I'd been far away—a distant memory—and he'd felt something in that moment with her right in front of him, something special enough to hold on to. And now he would stand by that choice.

"Okay," I whispered. I faced forward and didn't look at him again.

# FOURTEEN

I SLEPT UNTIL NINE thirty the next morning. That was long for me, but I still awoke groggy with my head pounding. In the bathroom, I stared down at the water in the toilet. The plumbing was working for now, but that water . . . it seemed so innocent, so normal, but I'd spent the last part of the day yesterday seeing how organisms in that water were killing people. Being terrified to use the bathroom was a whole new level of strange.

I went to the backyard and peed against the wall. I couldn't believe it had come to this. An antibacterial shower would be amazing right about now.

I joined my family in the kitchen and saw my mom lifting a bottle of water to her lips. I cried out and raised a hand. She jumped and said, "What?!"

My heart was pounding erratically.

"It's bottled water," Dad said soothingly. "It's not from the tap, Amber." He, Mom, Abuela, and Grandpa were all staring at me.

I collapsed into a chair, holding my aching head, my heart

slowing. I was sure Dad had told Mom everything last night because I vaguely recalled her sitting next to me on the bed and petting my hair.

"Don't even wash your hands in it," I said.

"We haven't let any tap water touch us since the DRI gave us the warning," Mom assured me. In truth, my headache was probably due to dehydration. I'd been too terrified to drink any water yesterday as the infected patients streamed in.

"We boil the hell out of the water before we use it," Grandpa said. I nodded and eyed the coffee. I knew the germs had to be dead, but I still could not stomach the idea of drinking anything that had come from those faucets.

Abuela got up and went to the camping stove, filling a bowl with scrambled eggs, black beans, and rice. She put it in front of me and sat beside me, rubbing my back.

"That's the last of the eggs," Mom said to Dad. They shared a look. They'd been keeping the eggs and dairy stuff on ice in a cooler, but the ice was now melted.

"It's been days," he said. "They should be getting the power up and running now. This is getting ridiculous. I asked the grocery store manager when their next shipment would be in and he said he had no idea, and that their generator was about done."

Grandpa shook his head and gave a gruff grunt. "Don't tell anyone about our goods. They'll be over here trying to get their hands on it."

Nobody said anything to that. Times weren't desperate enough to ravish neighbors' homes. But if the power remained out, and stores weren't replenished, and people couldn't access their money to be able to buy or trade . . . what was going to happen? Especially with the water being infected. Water was a necessity, and bottled water sources in local stores were already gone.

I shivered, and Abuela rubbed my back again.

I ate all of my breakfast and then made my way to the pantry where I picked up a bottle of water. I wasn't prone to anxiety, but I felt panic symptoms as I unscrewed the cap and tilted the bottle up to my mouth. What if these water bottling companies had been infected as well? People could live without food for a while, but not without water. My body needed the liquid so badly that I chugged the entire thing, despite my terror. By the end there were tears in the corners of my eyes. *Please don't let me get sick.* I stood inside the pantry, breathing hard, trying to hide my near-anxiety attack from my family.

My arms prickled, as if the burn of whelps were rising on my skin. I rubbed my hands up and down my arms. I couldn't see anything. But I was so hot I broke out in a sweat. Was it a fever? I could feel hives rising.

The pantry door suddenly swung open and Mom's eyes widened when she saw me hunched over on myself, sweating.

"Dios! Baby, what's wrong?" She pulled me out and the others rushed over. The kitchen was so much cooler than the pantry. Mom ran a hand over my forehead, smoothing back my hair, the worry apparent on her face. Dad looked me over.

"Are you feeling okay?" he asked.

"Is she sick?" Grandpa yelled too loudly.

I looked at my arms again, then down at my legs. Normal. I felt my cheeks. Cool. Oh, my God . . . it had all been in my imagination. And now I was shaking all over.

"I just . . ." I stammered. "I'm okay."

Mom wrapped an arm around me and led me into the living room, down onto the couch. "Listen to me, Amber." She took my chin and forced my eyes to meet hers. "You need to take this day off."

I shook my head. There was no way.

"You listen," she said again. "Take the morning off. You are going to make yourself sick."

I closed my eyes and leaned my head back, slumping. I really could not imagine getting in the car and driving to that elementary school right now.

"Okay," I said. "I'm going to take some ibuprofen and rest until after lunch. And then I really have to go." I looked at her again. "They need me. So many people are sick from the water—"

"I know." She squeezed my forearm and got up to get me another bottle of water and some meds for my headache. She watched me as I looked hesitantly at the water, even sniffing it, before I finally drank. "Just promise me, Amber . . . if you see any suspicious people walking around . . . any suspicious packages or boxes or bags, you run. Don't worry about anyone else. You can't save everyone. *You run.*" The adamancy in her voice made me nod.

My stomach was too full. I lay my head back again, hoping I would not puke up all of the water I'd forced down. I took even breaths, trying to relax. When I felt better, I went into the bathroom and scrubbed myself down from head to toe with antibacterial wipes, then pulled my hair back into a slick, high bun. Mom tried to talk me into going back to my room, but I wanted to be with them. So she had me curl up in the corner of the couch with a pillow and blanket.

Dad turned on the radio and we all sat together, listening. The news was dire, even more so today.

"*The Eiffel Tower has fallen,*" the newscaster announced. Holy shit. "*I repeat, the Eiffel Tower. . .*"

"God damn it." Dad grasped his head in his hands and leaned his elbows on his knees.

Things were not getting better. They were worsening.

Hearing the details spout from the radio, I felt like I might sink under the despair. It was as if whoever was responsible wanted to wipe out all of the world's history—every symbol of culture and pride. They wanted to leave us with nothing, and it felt like they were against everyone on earth. Anyone who thought the attacks were from the Middle East was flabbergasted when oil refineries were blown sky high. The ruler of North Korea and half his army? Gone. That shady Russian leader? Adios. This was like a serial killer of epic proportions, leaving lands in anarchy.

Looking around at my family, it made me miss Tater and Rylen so much. Even though Rylen was only a potato field away, he seemed so much farther than that. And Tater . . . I wondered how he was. I hoped he was keeping safe, and not drinking the water.

I nearly jumped out of my skin when the front door flew open. Ry's key was in his hand, and his face swiveled over our family members until his eyes locked on me.

His face was ghostly white. "Pepper . . ."

"What's wrong?" I sat up, flinging off the blanket.

"My dad."

# FIFTEEN

GRABBED MY MEDIC kit from Mom's car and sprinted behind Rylen through his potato field. We rushed up
the steps, through the creaky screen door that slammed
behind us. Inside smelled musty, like old furniture and old
scents of grease that had yellowed the walls and ceilings. The
throw rugs were threadbare and faded. The place was clut-
tered, with junk piled up in corners, but otherwise clean.

I followed Rylen into a family room area with a television on a card table and a velvet picture of dogs playing pok-
er above a worn out couch. Livia was sitting on the floor by
Len Fite's head, dabbing a damp cloth to his face. He took
up every inch of the couch. My breathing quickened when I
saw his arms and those telltale splotches. His long, gray hair
was wet with sweat. I dropped to my knees next to Livia,
and she scooted out of my way as I put gloves on. We still
weren't sure if this thing was contagious, so I wasn't taking
any chances.

He didn't move or react as I took his vital signs. I sat
back on my haunches. Rylen stood with his arms crossed,

watching us, chewing his thumb nail. Livia perched on the end of a rocking chair.

"He has it," I whispered. "We still don't know what it is or if it can be cured. I'm hoping someone from the DRI will have more information today from the samples they took."

"Is he gonna . . ." Rylen began, then stopped. "I mean, were people yesterday . . ."

"Nobody died yesterday, but some became nonresponsive by the end of the day, like this." I was frightened to return today and see how the victims were faring. But an urgency rose in me to do just that. "I need to go in."

"Can I take you?" Rylen asked. We both looked at Livia. "Do you mind staying with him while we try to find out what to expect?"

Her eyes darted, and I didn't think she fully understood, so I translated into Spanish for her. The look of complete gratefulness she gave me at the sound of her native language broke my heart. She nodded and looked up at Ry.

"Sí. Yes. I stay."

"Thank you." Rylen leaned down and kissed her forehead before darting out of the room to grab his keys.

In Spanish, I told Livia, "Go to my house if you need anything at all. And here." I handed her a pair of gloves. "Don't touch any of these open sores with your bare hands. See if you can get him to drink any broth or tea made from boiled water. We have some at our house."

She nodded again.

We set off for Clark County, and it was weird to see so few cars on the streets. No cops either, so Rylen went twenty over the speed limit.

"I guess everyone's conserving their gas," I said.

He sighed as he looked out over the ghostly town. Even the fields seemed abandoned and sad. Rylen had a crease in the middle of his forehead that made me reach out and touch his forearm. He tensed so I let go. I wanted to tell him everything would be okay with his dad, but that could be a lie. So instead, I gave him the only promise I could.

"If there's a vaccine, I'll bring it to him."

Rylen swallowed hard, his Adam's apple bobbing down and back up. We drove in silence a bit longer.

"Have you seen your mom since you've been back?" I asked.

"Yeah." It came out as a grunt. "I checked on her last night before I went to see your folks. While everyone else was at the grocery store, she was raiding the liquor store, so she's all set."

I clamped my teeth together at the pain in his words.

"I told her I'm married, but I haven't taken Liv to meet her. She wasn't exactly happy about having a *foreigner* in the family."

Ouch.

"How about your cousins?" I asked.

"Haven't seen them. My aunt took them and moved to Reno two years ago."

I didn't ask any more questions after that. Since we were speeding, we made it to the elementary school in record time. It was still a shock to turn onto the street and see a giant hill of demolished cinder blocks and twisted metal where the hospital used to be.

Hundreds of people milled around the full parking lot. A line snaked out of the building, just as it had at the hospital yesterday. Two policemen with a K-9 roamed the area, hopefully sniffing for bombs or any other possible threats.

I wove my way through the crowd at the entrance and looked around for Julian, but didn't see him. I spotted a DRI woman with a clipboard in the office area giving a nurse directions.

"Hi," I said. "I'm one of the medics, Amber Tate—"

"Yes, I remember seeing you yesterday. Thank you for coming back in. We'll need you in room 205 today treating wound victims."

"Yes, ma'am," I said. "Thank you. But can you tell me first if there's any news about the water illnesses?"

Her face tightened, as if she were annoyed. "It's viral. Non-airborne. Can only be spread by ingesting or sharing bodily fluids. Kills within two to four days." Rylen hissed a breath in, but she thoughtlessly kept rattling off facts. "Eighty-eight percent kill rate from what we've gathered from the towns hit before us, all in the Midwest. Affects humans and animals, though other species simply become lethargic and then die, no rash. We're calling it the Red Virus. No cure, but they've created a preventative vaccine in record time. The first batch should be here by tonight or tomorrow."

She turned away from us to direct a man in scrubs pushing a gurney with a body covered by a sheet. Dear God above. My insides shivered. Len was going to die within days.

I was shaking as I faced Rylen. He stared at the gurney being wheeled away down the hall. Another gurney with a covered body came after it. The wrecked look on Rylen's face made me grab his hand and pull him. I rushed us out of the dank, smelly school with its suffocatingly tight halls, out into the warm autumn sunshine. He let me pull him to the side of the building where I went up on my toes and circled my arms around his neck, pulling him close. He buried his face in my neck, wrapping his arms around my waist and holding me tight.

Why? Why were these things happening? What was the point of it all?

"I'm so sorry," I whispered. He said nothing, and didn't cry, just held me like I was a lifeline he was afraid to let go of. Like his world might crumble if he didn't have me. I know, I was being ridiculous—it could have been one of my parents or Tater, or his wife here to hold him and he'd probably be clinging just as hard. But I was glad it was me.

When I became overly aware of his hot breath on my shoulder and his taut body against mine, I gently released his neck and he let me go. His eyes were red, but not wet.

"Go home to him," I whispered. "I'm going to work." His eyes blurred for a second, lost in thought. He still stood close, our bodies brushing.

"What time should I get you?" His voice was hoarse.

"I don't know," I admitted. What time was it? Eleven in the morning, maybe? "You don't have to come, Ry. One of my parents can get me."

"What time, Pepper?" he asked again with patience.

"Maybe midnight?"

His eyes narrowed. "That's over twelve hours."

"Hospital staff work twelve-hour shifts all the time."

He put his hands on his hips and let out a long breath. "One of us will be here at eleven." Without giving me a chance to argue or say good-bye, he walked away from me. I watched his long strides, his lean waist and strong hips, and I felt a swelling buzz deep at my core—a feeling I had no business having anymore. I imagined Livia's face and it was like stepping into an ice water bath. Now it was my turn to let out a long breath.

He was hers. She would be there for him today, at his side, helping to nurse his father in his final moments. Helping to comfort Rylen as he watched the man he loved most in this world face a downhill battle. As that familiar bout of jealousy began to claw its way up through the sludge of despair and grief, I turned and speed-walked to the entrance. Nothing like death, blood, and disease to take my mind off Rylen.

# SIXTEEN

**T**HERE WAS NOTHING TO do for Red Virus victims except try to keep them comfortable. Our stock of injectable pain killers and I.V. fluids were long gone, with a promise from DRI on premises that more was coming. All we had left were pills, and many of the sick could not get them down. Half of the classrooms had been converted to 'dying rooms,' crammed with cots and wailing family members. Many of the rooms had battery-operated CD players, which we used to play soothing music for those who were sitting there all day and night, holding loved one's hands who'd fallen into fevered sleeps that they might never wake from.

I cleaned and bandaged many injuries that came in throughout the day, people still streaming up from Vegas. At some point I looked over and saw Julian working at my side. I don't know when he arrived; we were both so busy. Around three o'clock he handed me one of those sawdust Ebola bars. I gave him a rueful grin before I forced it down with a bottle of water. My stomach churned like it had that morning, as if water were the enemy. I noticed Julian grimace as he drank his too.

He cracked his neck and made a free shot at the waste basket.

"Score," said a familiar, sweet voice behind me.

My head swung fast enough to give me whiplash and I leaped to my feet.

"Remy!" I had one second to notice how rough she looked before I flew into her arms. We rocked back and forth, both laughing with exhilaration.

"I was hoping I'd find you here." She sounded exhausted. "I had a breakdown when I saw the hospital, until I caught sight of all the people over here."

I pulled back and looked her over. She'd definitely been crying. "Are you okay? Any injuries?" Other than the greasy ponytail and bags under her mascara-less eyes, she looked whole.

"Just tired."

"Please . . ." My heart banged hard. "Please tell me you haven't been drinking any tap water."

"No, I haven't. I promise. I had an entire new case of water in my dorm room and that was the first thing I threw in my car when I was able to get the hell out of there."

Julian sidled up next to me. Remy ran a hand over her ponytail and gave him the once-over.

"Julian, right? I outdrank you at that party."

"Ha, yeah, you wish. I remember your ridiculous fake ID."

She made duck lips. "I remember you threatened to turn me in."

He laughed. "I thought you were gonna cry. I didn't think you'd believe me!"

I nearly rolled my eyes at his dimple-cheeked grin and their flirty manner. Not the time or place. But then again, it was kind of nice to see something happy amidst the shit storm.

"So much has happened," I said. "Have you talked to your parents yet?"

"No, I was stopping at the hospital to see you since it was on my way home. I'm going there next."

As much as I selfishly wanted to keep her there with me, I knew I needed to urge her to go home, to put her parents' minds at ease and tell them about the Red Virus.

"All right, I'll go now," she said once she'd seen a gurney go by with a red-whelped arm dangling down from beneath the sheet. "But just in case I don't see you for a while. Tell me real quick, is your family okay?"

"Yes. They're all okay. My dad got through to Tater's command a couple days ago and he's okay too."

"Tell her about Rylen," Julian said.

I flashed him a deadly look as my stomach swooped. I didn't want to talk about Ry. "That's a story for another time."

"No way," she said. "Tell me. He's not . . . dead, is he?" Her face paled.

"No!" My stomach soured. "I'll come by your house in the morning."

"Don't you dare make me wait. I have to go. Tell me!"

"He married some Guatemalan chick," Julian blurted.

"Julian!" I rounded on him and punched his arm.

"What?!" Remy shouted. "He's *married*?"

A woman with a tear-streaked face jumped and glared at us as she passed. I grabbed Remy's arm and pulled her further into the room.

"Yes," I said, trying to keep my voice flat and face emotionless. "It's . . . whatever. He eloped."

Remy stared at me, mouth gaping, searching my face,

before her eyes drooped. "I'm so sorry, Amb."

"It's really nothing in comparison with all of this." I waved an arm, thought it still didn't feel like nothing.

"I know, but still. I'm sorry." She hugged me, and I hugged her back.

"I really will try to visit in the morning, okay?" I said. "We'll talk more then."

"Okay." Her voice sounded sad, like she'd been the one to lose the man of her dreams. I guess that's how friendship was. You couldn't help but hurt for each other.

I felt slightly lighter after she left, just knowing she was okay and out of Vegas. Hunger hit me, so I went to the vending machine, which someone had busted open, and got the last bag of chips. I felt like crap, physically. My body craved fruits and vegetables, things I'd taken for granted before.

Just as I finished my unhealthy snack, a freaking bus full of old people from Vegas came stumbling in, looking like they'd climbed through rubble to get here. Julian and I raced over to help them in.

The day went by in a blur, just as the day before had. I lost track of time until it was pitch dark out and the wave of injured people waned. Julian left and I sat against the wall in our main room, staring at the felt wall calendar with apples on the pocket of each day. It had been a first grade room. The tiny desks were now shoved into a corner, piled high. I closed my eyes.

"Hey, Pepper."

My heavy eyes peeled open. Rylen was crouched a couple feet from me.

I sat up. "How is your dad?"

"Actually, he took a little bit of a turn this afternoon. Opened his eyes, said a few words, drank some tea and broth. He's a strong bastard."

"That's awesome!" A tiny bloom of hope sprang to life. Would Len be one of the twelve percent who could pull through this?

I stood up, wanting to get home.

As we passed the office, three DRI personnel were rushing in with boxes. The woman who'd given us the insensitive breakdown of Red Virus earlier looked at me.

"We have vaccinations. Get yours before you leave, please."

I shared a bright look with Rylen and we followed them in. This was good.

We went into what was once the nurse's office, and I was directed to sit on the hospital bed, while Rylen took a chair that looked way too small for him.

"Just a few questions first," said the woman. "Amber Tate, correct?"

"Yes." She took my address, social security number, and some other basic medical information.

"Is this your husband?" she asked.

My face flushed with heat. "Uh, no. He's a friend."

She looked at him. "I'm sorry, sir, but I'm going to have to ask you to wait outside —"

"It's okay," I said. "I don't have any secrets from him. He's like family." Ry crossed his arms and relaxed back into his chair, giving me a tired grin.

"Have it your way." She peered down at her clipboard. "Now, what is the breakdown of your race?"

I told her and she scribbled something and cocked her head, smiling. "I'm curious, Amber. Being of mixed-race, do you find yourself mostly attracted to Hispanic men, white men, or men of a different race?"

"Um." I almost laughed. She said it like it was friendly conversation, but it felt so . . . stiff and clinical. What a weirdly inappropriate question to ask. "I don't know." My gaze darted to Rylen, who was staring at the blank wall in front of him, but by the quirk of his lips he was definitely listening. I should have let him be kicked out of the room. "Why do you need to know that?"

She saw me looking at him and turned to peer at him a moment too. He nodded politely at her, but seemed to stiffen under her gaze. She turned back to me.

"Answer the question, please."

I squirmed. "Is this an official question that I have to answer to get a vaccine? Because, not to be rude, but it's really none of anyone's business who I'm attracted to."

The woman's face tensed with seeming anger.

"It is the government's business."

I felt my anger rising up against hers. "No, actually, it's not."

She stared hard, and this time when she spoke, her voice took on a lyrically sharp quality that made my tension turn to mush.

*"Answer the question."*

She held my eyes and a fuzzy feeling overcame me, making me forget why I'd been upset as all of my tension shed away. I had no idea why the question had bothered me. It was no big deal. This lady was super friendly, just making casual conversation.

"I've been attracted to Hispanic, African-American, and Asian-American boys in the past, but it's mostly a Caucasian boy—*man*—who I've liked the longest."

At her tight smile, my ease morphed back into unease. I felt weird, dizzy for a second, but it passed. And then my words came crashing down on me. What the hell? I could not believe I'd just said that in front of Rylen! A wave of heat slammed me, the flame of embarrassment. Because seriously, *why* had I told her that? My eyes flicked to him again, and though he still stared at the wall ahead of him, I could definitely read the amused disbelief in the set of his eyes and lips.

The woman jotted more notes and then opened a sterilized needle package. She chose a tiny vile and tipped it up, sucking the vaccine into the syringe. Still shaken and confused, I pulled the sleeve of my shirt up to reveal my upper arm and shoulder.

"Side effects are nausea and cramping." She injected the vaccine, and I pressed my lips together at the sting. My arm heated. I lay a hand over the spot as the woman threw out the needle.

"You're all finished," she said to me, then looked at Ry. "Ready?"

"Wait," I said. "Can I get a few of these to take to my family?"

"No, these have to be administered by DRI. All local clinics will have vaccines by tomorrow."

"His father is infected," I said. "I don't think he can make it to the clinic. I could administer it—"

"If he is infected, the vaccine will do no good." She looked at Rylen again, and I took that as my cue to wait outside of the door. I slid down and stepped out, but left the door open.

I listened as she asked him all of the usual medical questions. Then she got to, "Are you married or single?"

"Uh . . . engaged, technically."

*Engaged.* Wow, that sounded so much better than married. I frowned at my thoughts.

"Congratulations," the woman said flatly. "And what is your fiancé's ethnicity?"

What the actual hell. Why did she keep asking race questions?

"Yeah, see, I agree with Amber on this," Rylen said. "I

don't see what it has to do with getting a vaccine." His voice was hard. Again, the woman used a casual, lyrical tone that seemed to calm my heart.

"*Answer the question, sir.*"

He paused for a long time. I waited, expecting him to tell her off where I had failed, but instead he said, "She's Guatemalan."

My eyes flew wide.

"Ah, how nice." I heard her unwrapping a needle and the tinkling of her grabbing a vial. "And do the two of you plan to have children together?"

If possible, my eyes widened even further. And then it was as if a bomb dropped directly on top of my head . . .

"She's pregnant now." He said it quietly, and I knew it wasn't meant for my ears.

I leaned heavily against the wall, my knees becoming almost too weak to hold me. A prickle shot up my body, from my heels up to the top of my head. I had to close my eyes.

"Lovely," murmured the woman. "Be sure she tells the Disaster Relief Initiative administrator when she goes to get her vaccine."

Pregnant. Livia was going to have a baby. Rylen's baby. Ry was going to be a dad. I felt like my body was breaking down into a pile of dried particles on the floor.

Half a minute later, he was walking out, that deep crease between his eyes again. We walked to his truck in silence. I was in a daze.

"I don't like her," he said.

"Me either." I wanted to ask him why he'd given in, but I felt so ashamed and weirded out about what I'd blurted that I didn't want to bring it up. We climbed in.

"Hungry?" Rylen started the truck and held out an apple.

I took it. He watched as I managed a small bite. The burst

of fresh fruit on my tongue cleared my mind. It was so perfect that I took another bite, much bigger this time.

"So . . . who's this white guy?"

I sucked apple juice down into my lungs when I gasped, and then bent over to cough like I was dying. Rylen patted my back hard, chuckling.

"I'm just messing with you," he said. "That was weird as hell. I thought you were going to kick her ass."

I finally stopped coughing, but my face was still hot.

"I should've," I admitted. "I think I was too tired to fight it or something. I don't know."

"Yeah," he said.

I took another bite. I usually couldn't eat when I was upset, but my body overrode its usual starvation-sadness protocol. Once I polished off the entire thing, only leaving a thin strip of core, I said, "Thank you for coming to get me."

"No problem," said the soon-to-be-father. I wondered when he planned to tell us. This news felt so much bigger than him getting married. I hated myself for not being able to be happy for him. He deserved my support, and I wanted to give it, but damn it. It hurt so bad.

I rolled down the window and chucked the core as hard as I could into the dirt field. I left the window down and stared up at the bright stars as the air whipped my hair and the loud *woosh* drowned out all thoughts.

# SEVENTEEN

'M NOT SURE WHAT time it was when the cramps began, but my room was still pitch-black. It was like the worst period cramps I'd ever experienced. I curled into a ball until the pain was unbearable, and then I grabbed my wastebasket, spitting up acidic apple before collapsing onto my bedroom floor.

So heavy. My face pressed into the carpet, body convulsing, arms wrapped around my middle. Curled up in a ball was the only position I could handle. At some point Mom and Dad were there, hovering over me, asking questions. I think I saw Abuela's silhouette in my doorway. I wanted to ease their minds, but the pain . . . the pain was everything.

Oh, God, did I have the Red Virus? None of the victims I'd seen had reacted like this. Then I remembered the vaccine, and how she said I could have some cramping. If that's what this was, she had vastly minimalized that side effect.

"Cramps," I managed to whimper before I vomited again, this time only dry heaving.

I lay on the ground, curled up and moaning for hours.

They put a hot compress to my belly, gave me ibuprofen, but none of it helped. I wondered if this was what labor felt like. Stabbing, twisting, sweating, stomach muscles shaking from the exertion of contracting. I felt like I'd run a marathon with a knife in my gut.

When the rising sun cast a hazy hue over my room, the pain finally began to ebb. Spent, I passed out in Mom's lap. I felt her shift out from under me, putting a pillow under my head and covering me with my blanket. Voices murmured out in the hall, and my door opened. A heavy, large hand cupped my face, sliding my hair back.

"She's not feverish, at least," Rylen said softly.

"Yes, I took her temperature every twenty minutes," Mom said. "It never got above ninety-nine, but she was in such pain."

I forced my eyes to open and focus on their faces leaning over me.

"The shot," I whispered.

Rylen slowly shook his head. "That could be it, but I haven't had any of these side effects. I was gonna take Liv to get it this morning, but not if this might happen."

"Let's wait and see," Mom said. She placed a hand on my hip. "You're taking the day off, princesa. Like it or not."

They left me, and my eyes drifted closed again.

When I woke the room was bright. A lingering thrum of discomfort resided in my lower abdomen and I was still nauseous, but I forced myself to stand. I clutched my stomach, slightly hunching, as I went out into the living room. Abuela held open her arms at the end of the couch and I went to her side, letting her hold me. The radio voice murmured on low as Grandpa looked me over from his recliner. Mom set a bowl of canned raviolis in my lap.

"Can you stomach these?"

"Sure," I said. I took a tentative bite and ate slowly. I hadn't had canned pasta since I was a kid. They tasted much better to the younger me, but I wasn't about to be picky. I slowed when my stomach cramped, stopping to give it time to pass, then continued and finished the bowl.

Dad came in the front door, shaking his head.

"What happened?" Mom asked.

He sat heavily in the recliner. "Well, I stopped by the power company to try and get an update. You'll never believe what I found."

"What?" Mom asked.

"Nothing. Nobody. There wasn't a single employee."

My forehead tightened. "That makes no sense. Maybe they're all out working on the power lines or something."

He shook his head. "No idea. You'd think if they were working to get power up and running for the town there'd be someone there."

"What about Tater?" Mom asked. "Were you able to contact his base?"

Dad's forehead scrunched. "Nobody is answering the telegraphs or the Morse code we sent through the lines. I tried contacts at several bases and got nothing. It could be that they're all away from the base, working in nearby cities, but it's unlikely they'd leave the comm lines unmanned. I'll try again tomorrow."

We all sat back, silent. I hoped everything was okay.

"How you feeling?" Dad asked me.

"Better." I didn't want to worry them about the residual pain. "I don't know if it was some random bug or the shot they gave me, but it's wearing off. I still think you guys should all get the vaccine. The Red Virus is . . ." I thought about all the bodies piled up behind the school by last night. "It's worth a few hours of cramping."

"Okay," Mom said after a moment of hesitation. "We'll go today." She looked worried, probably anticipating an afternoon of pain.

"I'll take care of you," I promised. Mom came over and kissed the top of my head.

"I'm glad you're feeling better. You scared us."

I pushed to my feet and went to go rinse my bowl out. The sink had been filled with boiled water. Still, I put on a pair of kitchen gloves that went up to my elbows and used a huge squirt of antibacterial dish soap. A bowl had never been so clean.

And speaking of clean, I really needed to bathe, but that wasn't going to happen, vaccine or not. A pot of boiled water had been placed in the bathroom for washing up. I dunked a wash cloth and cleaned my body and face, rinsing the cloth by dipping a cup into the pot and pouring it over top of the cloth in the sink. What a huge pain this was. I couldn't wait to get things back to normal. But when would that be? Especially considering nobody was at the electric offices? It made no sense.

Thankfully my hair didn't get greasy like Remy's. I could let it go without a washing for a few days before it started to look dank. I pulled it up into a messy bun and went out to join my family. The tightness in my abdomen was still there, making me unable to stand straight.

Mom and Abuela both had their purses on. Dad and Grandpa Tate were at the door.

"You guys going to get the vaccines?" I asked.

"Yes," Mom said. "I would offer for you to come, but I think you should stay here and rest, just in case you've got a bug."

"Okay." I collapsed on the couch, kicking up my feet. My stomach spasmed and I rolled to my side, curling in.

Rylen and Livia were at the door when they opened it. I gave them a wave and forced a smile.

Ry came over and crouched next to me.

"Is she getting the shot?" I whispered to him.

"I don't know. I told her what happened to you, but she says she wants to."

That was scary. If it hurt her nearly as much as it hurt me, she could surely miscarry. But if she got the virus, she could die. That would be a hard choice. I didn't envy them.

When he started to stand, I grabbed his arm.

"Make sure you tell them," I whispered. "Before they give her the shot."

Rylen squinted at me. "Tell them what?"

I raised my brows as if to say, *You know what*. His face went slack when he realized I knew—that I'd heard. I felt bad admitting to eavesdropping, but this was serious.

He looked away and gave his earlobe a tug. "I will."

I kept hold of his arm. "They'll let you know if it's a risk. And then you need to let Livia decide what she feels like she should do."

Though he looked torn, he nodded. I let go of his arm, but he lingered in front of me with an expression I couldn't quite decipher. He looked like young Rylen making adult phone calls while his father was in prison . . . like he wasn't quite ready for the responsibility, but he would fake it like a champ. He was the picture of determined strength with hints of vulnerability and fear around the edges. But he never ran away.

I caught a glance over his shoulder of Livia sending us furtive looks as Mom talked to her.

"Go on," I whispered. They were all waiting. He gave me a meaningful nod before standing. I watched them leave and then got up to turn off the radio. I could only take so much doom each day. I forced down a bottle of water and more pain meds before crashing on the couch again.

Unfortunately, I was wide awake now. With nothing to do. No internet to browse, no television shows to watch, no phone line to call Remy. It'd been forever since I made time to read. I wondered if the library or bookstore was staying open these days. And was I really willing to waste gas to seek entertainment?

Footsteps shuffled up our front steps followed by a knock. I went to the door and opened it a crack, thinking someone in my family forgot something. But it was an unfamiliar man who stood there, unshaved and thin. He gave me a smile when he saw my face through the inch of open door.

"Hi there, Miss," he said in a dry voice. "I got some kids at home with no food. I was wondering if you had anything you could spare."

"Oh," I said, feeling a rush of guilt about just how much we had to spare. "Sure, hold on just a second."

It was probably rude of me, but I'd seen way too much not to be cautious. I totally closed the door on him and locked it. In the kitchen, I took two cans of soup, two bottles of water, and a sleeve of crackers. I put them all in a grocery bag. If I took more Grandpa Tate would notice and have my head. He probably would have told the guy we had nothing.

I went back to the front door and gave him the bag.

"Thanks, sweetheart," he said. His eyes raked me, and he looked past my shoulder as if checking out the inside of the house, then back to my face. "You got a real nice smile."

"Thanks," I said, getting squigged out now. "Have a good day, sir."

He shoved a boot into the doorway when I tried to close it. "Now, hold on just a second, pretty thing."

Panic, along with a hell of a lot of training, set in. I

wrenched open the door enough to slam my bare heel into the spot just above his kneecap. When he pulled back his leg with a shout, I slammed the door shut and spun the deadlock into place with a shaking hand.

"Stupid, fucking bitch!" I heard him shout.

I ran to the back sliding glass door in the dining room to make sure it was locked, then the garage door. If he tried to break in, I'd go straight for Dad's hunting rifle. But when I peeked through the window, he was hobbling away, stopping every few steps to lean down and grab his knee with one hand while holding the bag in the other. He probably didn't have any kids to feed. I wanted to snatch that soup back from him, the bastard. I watched until he was out of sight. I wished I could call the cops. What if he tried to get into someone else's house? I had no idea what his intentions were—to steal or rape—but neither of those were on my to-do list.

I covered my mouth against another bout of nausea. It was one thing to hear stories about people taking advantage of the current situation, and another horrible thing to see it firsthand. I didn't want to lose faith in humanity, but damn. People made it hard.

# EIGHTEEN

I WATCHED MY FAMILY closely when they returned home.

"Did you all get the shot?" I asked.

Mom nodded. "It took forever. They're understaffed."

"Are they?" That surprised me. I'd tried to get a job there after my schooling, but smaller clinics in small towns rarely had turnover.

"What about Livia?" I asked. "Did she get it?"

"Of course," Mom said. Then I remembered she didn't know Livia was pregnant, otherwise she and Abuela would be making a huge fuss over her. The fact that she'd gotten the shot made me nervous. As jealous and hurt as I was, whether I had a right to be or not, I didn't want anything bad to happen to her.

My family appeared normal as the day went on. My own stomach still held a deep, aching cramp, and my head throbbed, but I was able to get around. It wasn't until hours had passed and my family still seemed fine that I began to relax.

"I'm going to check on Livia and Len," I told them. It would be good to stretch my legs.

"You bring food." Abuela bustled into the kitchen and I realized it was nearing dinnertime. She handed me a covered Pyrex dish with a layer of rice, canned tomatoes, and canned chicken. It didn't sound appetizing, but she probably worked some magic with spices. I kissed her cheek and headed out with my medical bag slung over my shoulder.

I was careful to look all around me for that creepy man, as if he might be lurking behind our front bushes or the citrus trees that lined the road. I'd never had reason to be nervous or scared in our small town, especially on our own property. Once I was in the potato field, certain I wasn't being followed, I thought about Len. This was right around the time when Red Virus victims took turns for the worse. My heart was a heavy, burdensome rock in my chest when I thought about Rylen losing his father.

I noticed the absence of chickens when I got up to their house, but I could hear them clucking in their closed pen. I climbed the cinderblock steps and opened the creaky screen door, then knocked.

Rylen pulled the cloth curtain aside and unlocked the door.

"Hey, Pepper." He stood aside and let me step in before taking the dish.

"From Abuela," I explained.

"Give her my thanks." His face was serious, as always, but not grim.

"How's Livia? And your dad?"

"Fine, actually. Come on in and see for yourself."

Relief. My heart lightened as I followed him into the living room, stopping so he could set down the dish on the way.

I couldn't believe my eyes. Len was sitting up on the

couch. He looked half-dead and sweaty, but he was *sitting up*. His forearms and face were still splotchy with spots, but as I got closer I could see they looked darker, like they were drying. None of the other patients I'd seen had recovered.

"Hi, Mr. Fite," I said. "Mind if I check you over real quick?"

"Nope," he rasped.

I put on my gloves and took his temperature. It was down to one hundred. All of his vitals were slightly elevated, but nothing alarming.

"Wow," I said, giving him a smile. "I think you're one of the twelve percent."

"I ain't ready to die," he said. "Gotta find out who stole my chickens first."

"Someone stole your chickens?"

"Yeah," Rylen said. "When we got back today I noticed our main hen and the rooster were gone. We've got the rest locked up in the pen now."

My lips pursed in anger. I hadn't planned to tell anyone about the man at our house, but I found myself blurting out the story now, wondering if the thief had been the same guy.

I watched Rylen's hands form fists when I got to the part about him sticking his foot in the door, and though he nodded appreciatively when I told him I'd kicked the guy's knee in, Ry's fists never relaxed. He bounced them on his thighs, in thought, when I finished.

"Don't open the door like that anymore," he said.

I rolled my eyes. "I know, I know. I've learned my lesson."

He turned to Livia and said, "Please, do not unlock the door for anyone you don't know."

She watched his face as if concentrating on each word really hard, and she nodded. I looked her over.

"Are you feeling well after the vaccination?" I asked her in Spanish.

Again she nodded. I gave her a small smile and she returned it.

"Bien." I stood to go.

"Take some eggs with you," Rylen said, standing as well.

"Do you have enough?" I asked. "'Cause you know the Tates will never turn down eggs."

He laughed. "We've got over two dozen just from the past two days. I'll give you a dozen to take."

"Awesome." Eggs!

In the kitchen he handed me a full carton. He leaned against the old counter and crossed his arms. "I need to report to base tomorrow."

"I thought you still had a couple days."

"I do, technically, but . . ." He shook his head.

"Yeah, I know. I get it." He felt like he needed to be doing something.

"I should wait," he said regretfully. "Until my dad's stronger. I'm worried if things keep up like they are someone'll try and break into our barn for the spare gasoline and he won't be able to stop them."

It sucked that we had to worry about things like that.

"Will you keep an eye on my dad and Liv when I go? Just check on them now and then?"

"Sure, of course."

"She likes you, you know." I swallowed hard and looked down at the eggs as he kept going. "She doesn't say much, but I know she's grateful to have you and your family."

"Good," I whispered.

He walked me to the door and held open the screen. Once I was out, he stepped out on the top block and crossed his arms, eyes scanning the field and our property beyond. His arms bulged when he stood like that, and his hips jutted out. I cleared my throat and yanked my eyes away.

"I'll watch till you get in your house."

I didn't bother telling him he didn't have to do that, because I knew he would anyway, and I also appreciated the comfort of knowing I was safe. So, I walked home with Rylen's eyes on my back, wondering why I'd been the only person to react to the vaccine as I had. Or maybe I had some twenty-four hour bug? That was more likely, considering all the germs I'd encountered in the not-so-sterile school the past two days. Whatever it was, I was glad it was just about gone because I couldn't stand to sit around at home another day. I needed to stay busy.

I looked up, startled, when I heard running footsteps on the pavement up ahead and panting breaths. I stared, in shock, at the sight of Remy's father, Mr. Haines, running down my road. As a Baptist preacher, I'd only ever seen him well put-together, pressed pants and collared shirts. Right now half of his shirt was untucked and sweat marks colored his armpits and chest.

A burn of panic sizzled up my spine. I nearly dropped the eggs. Something was wrong. Oh, my God, *Remy*.

I set the eggs on our lawn and ran to him. In my peripheral I could see Rylen running toward us too.

Mr. Haines nearly collapsed, bending over and grabbing above his knees to catch his breath. He lived in the housing development down the road, but it would have taken him twenty minutes to get here by foot.

"What's wrong?" I asked.

"*Remy . . .*"

No!

"Is it . . ." I needed to find out if she had the virus, but I faltered when my body convulsed in a tremor of fear. Rylen caught up, staring at Mr. Haines.

"It's okay," I told him, but my voice shook. "This is

Remy's dad." I looked at the man again and took a huge breath. "Does she . . . have spots?"

He stood up so he could look at me, still breathing hard. "No. She's on the bathroom floor, throwing up, in so much pain. We don't know what to do."

My eyes went wide. "Did she get the vaccine?"

He looked surprised. "Yes. We went this morning."

I closed my eyes and exhaled sharply, the fear draining palpably from my chest. "I think she's going to be okay. The same thing happened to me last night. But I want to check on her just in case. Did you run all the way here?"

"My car ran out of gas at the exit to our neighborhood."

"I'll drive," I told him. I looked up into Rylen's worried eyes. "It's okay. You can go back home. Thank you."

He nodded and took a few steps back, watching me another moment before turning to go home.

I rushed into the house and gave my mom the eggs, quickly explaining what was going on before I ran back out, keys in hand. When we got to the top of the road and turned the corner, I gasped at the sight of the gas station. The glass door was broken and people were pushing in and out with things in their hands.

"Oh, my gosh!" I pointed.

"Keep going," Mr. Haines warned. "It's happening all over town. People are dangerous when they're desperate." His voice was forlorn, and I felt heavy with grief for our town.

We got to Remy's parents' house in record time. The number of cars abandoned on the side of the road, out of gas, was disheartening.

Remy's house was gorgeous. Her mom, the leading real estate agent for the town, was the breadmaker for their family. I ran in and took the white-carpeted stairs two at a time up to their hall bathroom outside Remy's bedroom. She was curled up in a tight ball, shivering on the floor just as I had been. Her mom was at her side, face red from crying. I crouched over Remy and brushed the sweaty hair back from her face. Her mom stood and I heard her ask what had taken so long, followed by Mr. Haines telling her that his car had run out of gas. I took all of Remy's vitals. Low grade fever. Definitely no spots.

"You're going to be okay, Rem," I murmured. "I spent last night with this, too. I think it's from the vaccine, or maybe just a stomach bug, but if it's what I had, you'll feel better soon, okay?"

She gave me a weak, "Okay," and reached her shaking hand for mine, pulling it to her chest with surprising strength.

"Thank the Lord," her mother said. Her dad closed his eyes, his shoulders drooping.

Remy held my arm like a doll. I stretched out next to her on the cool, pristine tiles and kept stroking her long, blonde waves back from her face. She moaned and curled tighter as a wave of pain contracted her abdomen. I stayed with Remy several hours until her stomach was relaxed enough to take some pain medication, and we got her into bed.

Her parents both hugged me, their eyes red.

"Thank you for coming to get me," I told Mr. Haines. "How are you guys doing on food and water?"

"Actually," he said, "we're just about out of food, but we've been using the pool water and boiling it."

My eyebrows went up. I hadn't thought about the pool.

"We'd been putting off converting it to salt water, and now I see it was a blessing in disguise," he told me. "Tastes a little like chlorine, but it's better than nothing."

"I'm so glad," I said.

I left with the promise that I'd be back to check on Remy in the morning on my way to work.

In the car I listened to the news and remembered it was December. This was when Christmas songs usually started on the radio, but there was none of that this year. I doubted there would be any tree stands or festively lit houses either, unless by some miracle we got electricity back.

". . . one step closer to rooting out the enemy," Senator Navis was saying. "We have obtained breakthrough intelligence, information about cells of the unknown organization in certain towns across the United States. We are calling these culprits *Outliers*. Your local Disaster Relief Initiative representatives will be in touch in all areas that are in danger. I urge each of you to comply with their instructions. I repeat, it is *essential* that each and every citizen do their part by following instructions and remaining calm. I know you want the perpetrators of these heinous crimes caught just as badly as I do. And I promise you, they will be. We will root out the evils of this society and rebuild. We will be an even stronger nation."

I turned the car off in the driveway. His words reverberated through me. Each time I listened to him I felt that lively spark of hope, but there was always a feeling of doom, as well. As if we had a whole hell of a lot of bad to overcome before we would reach the good.

# NINETEEN

**T**O BE HONEST, I didn't feel like going to work the next morning. It was strange not having a set schedule, or a check-in clock. I didn't know if I'd be paid for any of this work now that the hospital was demolished. Would I contact the state with my hours? It was kind of a ridiculous worry since I wouldn't be able to access my auto-deposit funds anyhow. Money didn't seem to be of value anymore.

I knew I would keep working, paid or not, because the guilt would eat me alive if I didn't. Even yesterday had felt wrong staying home all day. But I felt better today, so I dragged my butt out of bed and ate my egg and salsa breakfast burrito. Then I savored the French press coffee with sugar. The only thing that could have made the morning better was a hot shower. I had to settle for leaning over the sink and letting Mom pour a cup at a time of cool water over my hair as I washed with a tiny amount of shampoo. I didn't want to make too much foam to have to rinse out. It did the trick, and I felt clean.

I returned the favor and helped her wash her hair in the sink, too. When we finished, I found Rylen and Livia sitting on the couch talking to Dad. The couple sat close, holding hands. When Rylen saw me standing there with a towel on my head, he gave a smile and let go of Livia's hand, rubbing his palms down his thighs. She gave him a quizzical look and glanced at me. I walked to my bedroom to brush my hair, experiencing that weird residual sadness and awkwardness.

When I came back out, Dad asked in a stern voice, "What's this about some guy trying to get in the house yesterday, Amber?"

My head flew to Rylen, but his face remained unfazed under my glare.

The traitor. Although, I guess my family should be on the lookout. I sighed and told them the story.

"You didn't think this was important for us to know?" Dad asked.

I looked down at the rug. "I'm sorry. I should've told you, but I didn't want everyone worrying."

Grandpa Tate stopped rocking. "You shoulda kicked him square in the family jewels, Amby."

Oh, my gosh. Rylen half grinned and Mom covered her mouth.

"What is this family jewels?" Abuela asked. She was wiping her hands on a rag.

"It's a man's . . ." I motioned to my crotch.

She nodded emphatically. "Ah, yes. This is good to . . ." She struggled to find the word "kick," and instead lifted her flexed foot in the air.

Now everyone laughed. Abuela continued to look serious. She was accustomed to us laughing at her expense now and then. Amidst it all, I could feel Livia watching me, and I avoided eye contact. I didn't want to examine whatever weirdness was between us.

"How's your dad this morning?" I asked Rylen.

"Still worn out, but better. Even got up to relieve himself outside. Too stubborn to die." I heard pride in his voice and I smiled.

"That's wonderful," Mom said. She looked over at me. "Rylen brought some gasoline to refill my car so you can get to work."

"Thank you," I told him. I definitely didn't want to end up walking down the highway. "I guess I'd better get going." I went to my room to finish getting ready. I pulled my hair up in a high ponytail and dug through my clothes. My primary work clothes and scrubs were all dirty, so I put on some comfortable jeans and a long-sleeved T-shirt. It wasn't exactly cold, but I was a wimpy desert girl who liked her sunshine. Sixty-five degrees was chilly to me. I dug my medic pin out of my jewelry box and put it on.

Unfamiliar feminine laughter greeted me as I left my room, and I noticed Livia and Abuela working in the kitchen together, both smiling and chatting in Spanish. Livia was really pretty when she was happy. I watched them working together for a moment, boiling water and organizing pots on the counter. They made a good team. I couldn't bring myself to be jealous of their seeming closeness, because it was nice to see Liv and Ry not clinging to one another. Was Livia close to her own grandmother? Was she missing her? If I weren't so consumed by bitchiness, those would be the kinds of questions I'd ask. A heavy sigh heaved from my chest.

Time to get to work.

In the living room, I kissed my parents good-bye and gave Rylen a wave. He examined me, as if wondering why I hadn't come over to hug him, but it felt wrong with the way Livia kept studying me like she knew my thoughts. I quickly

looked away. Grandpa must have gone up to his room because his rocker was empty. When I got outside to the car, he
was coming down his stairs, using caution with each step. He
had something under his arm.

"One sec, Amby."

Grandpa walked toward me and I noticed the handle of
a gun. He motioned for me to get in the car. I slid in and he
crouched in the open doorway, knees cracking. Grandpa set
the small handgun on my lap. It was a 380 pistol that I'd never seen before. I would have remembered that deep cherry
panel on the handle. It was pretty. His eyes darted up to the
house before he spoke.

"This was your grandmother's. I want you to have it."

"Really?" I ran a finger over the slick handle.

"I wanted to give it to you when you first started your job,
but when I asked permission, your mother said no. I understand her feelings, but I'm overriding her now. You need to be
protected out there. Let's just . . . keep this between us."

Grandpa was afraid of Mom's wrath, and I couldn't blame
him. She had never been comfortable with the fact that Dad
took me and the boys to shoot. I'd handled many guns, and
while I wasn't afraid like Mom was, I had never felt the need
to own one. Now, though, I felt very grateful for his offering.

"Thank you, Grandpa." I kissed his sun-spotted forehead.
"It'll be our secret."

"Good. This'll help me sleep at night when you're gone."

He took it from the case and showed me how to eject the
magazine and turn the safety off, and rack the slide. When
he was secure that I understood the workings of it, he patted
my hand and stood. He dug a box of bullets from his pocket,
and I put everything in my purse. Grandpa watched me pull
away and drive down the street. When I got to the end of
the drive, I remembered what Mom had said about the local

clinic being understaffed yesterday. I was used to driving almost forty-five minutes into the next county to work. But that was taking a lot of gas. On a whim, I turned the opposite direction and headed to our local clinic. I wanted to check on their staffing, just in case.

And it's a good thing I did. There was a line out the door, and I was horrified to see most of them had Red Virus. Apparently, sixty percent of their nursing staff had stopped coming to work after the earthquake, because they had children and no childcare with the schools being out. At the front desk was a DRI woman who looked like she belonged on one of those super-rich-housewives shows. She let me in after asking who I was and if I'd been vaccinated.

I found Dr. Persus, our ancient family physician, in his stagnant exam room finishing up with a patient. The fevered woman was led out by her non-spotted husband. Dr. Persus gave me a heavy, burdened look when they were gone.

"Can I help you here?" I asked.

"I don't know how I'll pay you, Amber." The man had given me all of my shots growing up. He'd been old then. I was willing to bet he was regretting not retiring years ago when he probably should have.

"Don't worry about that," I told him.

He patted my shoulder, a soft touch. "I wish I could have hired you last year when you came to me."

"It's okay," I said. I thought about the two ambulances on the side of the clinic. "Are your EMTs here?"

"No . . ." His eyes fell. "They were in Clark County at that hospital that was bombed."

My insides twisted. "I'm sorry. I was there too, and I'm lucky to have survived. Look, I can do anything you need, okay?"

He leaned against the bed. "I don't know what to do. I just

keep sending them home. Telling them to rest, but we both know what will happen. At this point I just want people to die somewhere other than here."

I knew he said it out of weariness, not meanness, but ouch.

"I know of one survivor. Lenard Fite. He had it and now he's healing."

The doctor chuckled. "Why does that not surprise me?"

I grinned. Yeah. "Have you had anyone show up with severe abdominal pains? Vomiting?"

"Yes. Low fever. Seems to go away after a few hours?"

"Yes! Both my best friend and I experienced that after getting the vaccine."

He nodded. "Could be a side effect for some. Strange, though. Let me know if you feel anything else unusual."

"I will. Put me to work, doc. I'll do anything."

"Anything?"

I should have thought twice about that offer.

Even with bio boots strapped over my sneakers, heavy duty gloves, and a medical mask, I was not comfortable moving dead bodies, even when they were in body bags. At least I couldn't see their faces. I was sure to know some of them. I would check out Dr. Persus's list of deceased later, but for now I was glad not to see. A male nurse and I worked together to haul the bodies into the back of an open ambulance. Thankfully, he was young and strong. He looked like a giant redneck in blue scrubs, all scruffy. We had twenty-three bodies and could only fit ten at a time. We were to take them to the county morgue and retrieve more body bags from them.

The male nurse was quiet, but worked hard. He looked about the same age as me, but he must have gone to our rival high school because I didn't recognize him.

"What's your name?" I asked when we shut the doors and

pulled down our masks.

"David Wyatt." He held out a beefy hand and I shook it.

"Amber Tate. You wanna drive this over or stay here?"

"I'll take it," he told me. I saw him off and then went back to the clinic. I left my boots and gloves outside. I instinctively started walking toward a sink to wash up, then remembered I couldn't. In the medical profession it's drilled into you head to wash your hands frequently. Now the best we could do was use a squirt of antibacterial gel between patients, which wasn't quite as effective. I felt germy all the time.

It was a long day, and even more depressing than working in Clark County, if possible. I knew most of these people, or I knew their kids or grandkids. Hearing all of the stories happening right here in my hometown, and how many had died or been arrested, hit me hard.

When I drove home that night, the number of abandoned cars on the side of the road in the dark was alarming. Even more alarming were random people trying to hitch rides, or just standing outside of their houses, looking around like they needed something.

Food and water, to begin with. How much longer could the town live this way?

It was ten at night when I walked into the house, and I was surprised to find my entire family awake in the living room, candles lit on various surfaces. Their faces were pinched with worry.

"What's going on?" I locked the door behind me and set my stuff down.

Mom held up a paper. "There's a town meeting tomorrow at the high school. Every person is required to go, by law."

"Okay," I said. That wasn't such a bad thing, was it? Maybe we'd finally find out when electricity would be back on. "So, what's the problem?"

Dad let out an unamused huff of laughter as Grandpa shook his head, arms tightly crossed. "They've discovered an infiltrator cell in our county."

A drip of melting ice slid down my spine. "What?"

"Yep." Dad's face was deadly. "Right here in Lincoln. I'm going to see about joining the local force tomorrow to help sniff them out since my office is shut down for now. I'm tired of sitting around."

I moved across the room and slid into the spot next to Mom. Were some of the people responsible for all the bombings and biological warfare really hiding in our county? We did have some mountains and miles of abandoned fields. It was possible. But this was a family-oriented place, and I couldn't come to terms with that kind of hatred being so close to home.

"What time is the meeting?" I asked.

"Six o'clock at night." Mom took my hand and rubbed my arm. "They're asking everyone who has spare nonperishable items to bring them for the food bank."

Grandpa grunted. "In times like this it should be to-each-his-own."

"To be fair," Mom said, "if it weren't for you, we'd be one of those families needing the food bank. We can afford to share a little."

Grandpa grunted again. "Just don't let 'em know what we've got. They'll be over here trying to take it all. If they were smart they'd set up some sort of trading market."

"Don't worry, Pop," my father said. "Nobody's saying anything. And we'll get some answers tomorrow about when they're gonna get this town up and running again."

"That's right," Mom murmured. She kissed the side of my head. "Try to get some rest, princesa."

I tried. I really did. God knows I was exhausted, but my subconscious was an evil villain. I woke, heart-pounding, over and over, as ceilings caved in on me, babies covered in spots were tossed into my arms, and friendly-seeming neighbors morphed into throat-tearing monsters. I must have had three anxiety attacks during the night. The signs of PTSD were clear after nearly dying in the hospital bombings and seeing so much death. Half of America probably suffered from PTSD now.

I lay back in the dark and closed my eyes, concentrating on my breathing. A vision wiggled its way into my mind like a serpent—Rylen moving on top of Livia—making me flop over onto my stomach and press my face into the pillow. None of those horrible dreams had brought tears to my eyes, but that vision had done it, the way he'd been staring down into her eyes, all passion and intensity. I cried as quietly as I could, heaving deep breaths, until sleep finally took me.

# TWENTY

**M**ORE RED VIRUS VICTIMS. More death. More bodies.

I couldn't believe the number of people in Lincoln County who contracted the virus. Even with all the vaccines being given daily. There were also an alarming number of young women who had the same side effects I did. It hurt just to watch them writhing in pain. I was glad when five thirty rolled around and the clinic shut down so everyone could attend the town meeting.

I met my family and the three Fites in the parking lot. After my inappropriate visions last night, I avoided eye contact with Rylen and Livia. But, as always, I felt his presence like a heated lamp pointed right at me. We waited in a long line to get in as Disaster Relief Initiative personnel checked people off a list. A tense, expectant atmosphere blanketed the line of people. Our family was uncharacteristically quiet. Mom held two cans of tuna, which made me realize how hungry I was.

I felt knuckles bump my arm and I looked over at Rylen

holding a fruit and nut bar out to me. "Hungry?"

Beside him, Livia stared straight ahead at the line.

"Thank you." I took it and immediately tore it open.

Abuela handed me a to-go cup. "Juice," she said. "I squeeze."

My mouth watered. "Orange juice?"

Mom smiled. "We had some ripen on our tree. We wanted you to have the first cup."

Geez, that made me emotional. "I feel bad. Can we share it?"

"Well, we already took sips," Mom said with a wink. "To make sure it was okay."

I laughed and took a drink—it started tart but then got sweet. I downed it all and ate the bar. And though it did the trick, I couldn't help but wish I'd had a giant burger with fries.

Len began coughing. He'd stood a ways away from all of us, and I'd forgotten he was there. He did not look well enough to be standing like this, and his breaths were wheezy. He wore long sleeves, but there were dried, dark scabs on his hands, neck, and face from the spots. I wanted to tell him to wait in the car and we'd get him when it was time, but I knew his pride wouldn't allow it.

At the entrance there was a sign that read: No Red Virus Infected Persons Permitted. I wondered if they'd give Len a hard time, but they didn't. He was too much on the mend. We answered a million questions. Other families with children were having their kids ushered off to a nursery and kidzone. The meeting was for anyone over twelve. We filed into the gymnasium, which was already packed. Every seat in the bleachers was filled, and the floor was lined with rows of chairs in every available space. Since we were in the back of the line, we made sure Len, Grandpa, and Abuela had seats, and the rest of us stood along the back wall. A small platform had been erected at the other end under the school's giant mascot mural. I peered around until I spotted Remy and her parents in the stands. She looked well, if not bored. She found me too, and we both waved.

The room was hot and stuffy with all the people and no air circulation. It felt like forever before three DRI personnel came onto the stage. When the room quieted, I could make out the hum of generators that kept the emergency lights burning. A giant screen was pulled down on the wall behind them. I guess they were going to show a video?

Beside me I felt Rylen's elbow, and I followed his gaze toward the doors of the gymnasium where six police officers stood with gigantic guns. On his other side, Livia noticed them too and moved closer to him, as if afraid. He immediately took her hand.

"Since when do our cops carry assault rifles?" he muttered from the corner of his mouth. I shook my head. I guess since enemy cells were supposedly found in our midst. I elbowed Dad for him to see. He narrowed his eyes and looked around at all of the exits, each flanked with heavily-armed officers.

"I don't recognize any of them," he said quietly. I didn't either. And they weren't any kind of police uniform I'd ever seen. They looked like some sort of fancy flame-retardant material. Where was our hometown force?

I suddenly felt a little claustrophobic. I lifted my ponytail to fan the back of my neck with my hand. Mom and lots of other ladies were waving paper in front of their faces.

Finally, one of the DRI reps took the podium. She tapped the microphone and it gave a high-pitched screech that made everyone flinch.

"Citizens of Lincoln County, I thank you for coming out tonight. I will try to keep this brief so you can travel home before it's too dark." Gee, that was kind of her since tons of people had to walk now that they were out of gas. I don't know why I felt irrationally angry toward her all of a sudden, but I did. Maybe it was because as I looked around at all of the hungry, dirty, tired faces, she had the nerve to stand up there with a non-wrinkled blazer, pencil skirt, and flawless hair and makeup. For once I'd like to see a DRI in unclean jeans with their hair messy like the rest of us.

"I'm sure you all have many inquiries and concerns. I will get straight to the point, and hopefully your questions will be answered along the way." She lifted her chin, speaking from memory with no notes. "A threat was made to the local power companies. They received message that if they attempted to restore power, they would be bombed. The bombing of our power companies would set the city back, and we do not want that. So, we've taken the precaution to stop power restorations until those who threaten them are found and captured."

A loud murmur of voices raised in the room. She spoke over the din of unrest.

"We have little information about the perpetrators, but I will tell you what we know." She paused until there was complete quiet again. "Government intel has found that the enemy is neither a particular race nor religion. There is no particular label we can apply to them. They could be your neighbor. Your coworker. Your family member." She stopped and peered around. The room was silent with shock.

"And this is why our predicament is more difficult than any we've faced before. There is something that bonds these people. They are a union of sorts. It seems they want to break down our society, and many of the larger societies of the world, for purposes unstated. It is clear that their goal is to force change. Perhaps they wish to stop Global warming or radically reduce the population. Or bring western civilizations back to their roots of a simpler time. Whatever their purpose, they know no bounds. Their ways are extreme, and their organization seems to have unlimited funds."

My stomach was tied up in an intricate series of knots as she continued.

"It is due to this vagueness that we must be more vigilant than ever. As you read in your flyers, our intelligence has traced persons of interest here to Lincoln County."

She looked out gravely over our townspeople as another murmur rose.

"We do not wish to cause alarm, only caution. Meetings such as this one are taking place all across the United States in towns where the enemy are believed to be in hiding. Senator Bradford Navis has sent a message to you, and all of these towns."

She stepped aside and the room seemed to hold its breath as a film reel flickered to life across the wide screen. Moments later the senator's handsome, albeit weary, face appeared. His white dress shirt collar was unbuttoned. His brown waves looked pushed back, as if a nervous hand had run through them over and over. I felt for him.

He sat at a desk with a window behind him, but only blue sky showed. I wondered where he was.

"Good evening. As I'm sure you've been told, we're making great strides toward rooting out our adversaries, but we are to the point where your help and your compliance is essential." He inhaled and rubbed a hand over his mouth, circling his chin before exhaling. "If you have followed my career at all, you know I am a proponent of Constitutional rights. I have fought to uphold them at every turn. I have been an advocate of equal rights for all, and the pursuit of justice and happiness. That will never change. Please know that my heart is in the same place it always has been, but we are facing a situation unlike any in history. These are extremely desperate times, and they are going to require us to make some temporary changes."

His face took on a fierceness as the camera panned in that made my breath catch. His voice was utterly passionate, his tone beseeching. His tanned hands made fists so tightly that his knuckles whitened.

"Work with me to find these infiltrators. Work with your local law enforcement and the DRI to help them distinguish between who is causing this terror and destruction, and who is innocent. Because right now, as much as it pains me to say it . . . both look the same. At this point, it is our actions, and *only* our actions, that will make it clear what side we are on. We stand together on unprecedented ground. Let us work together to swiftly overtake those who would destroy our way of life." He brought one of his fists down on the desk and the entire room erupted in a cheer that surprised me.

My family stayed silent. Dad's face was tight. Rylen kept his hand linked to Livia's and thrust his other hand into the pocket of his jeans. I wondered if they felt like I did. The senator's speech was no doubt genuine, but it sounded an awful lot like constitutional rights and laws were about to be overturned, and even if it was only temporary, it kind of freaked me out.

"I thank you in advance for your cooperation. The sooner we work together to find our foe, the sooner we can resume our regular lives." His voice cut through the chatter and the room quieted again. "Please listen as your local representatives discuss the details of your town's fight. Please remember . . . we are at war. *You* are at war. Your own town is the unfortunate battlefield. By now we've all lost loved ones or know personally someone who has. If we work together and follow this simple plan, we will soon right the wrongs without further unnecessary death, and be able to begin the process of rebuilding. I commend you, sincerely, for your efforts in this. We will fix this. We will get our lives back to normal." His eyes glistened. "I promise you."

The film flicked off, followed by a brief moment of silence, and then once again everyone cheered. Grandpa Tate turned in his seat several rows in front of us, and gave Dad a huge-eyed look. Dad raised a calming hand, as if to tell him to settle down. Grandpa turned back around, his spine straight with alertness.

"I don't like this," Rylen said as the DRI woman took the stage again.

"Me either," Dad whispered. Mom tucked her hand into the crook of his arm and he patted it.

The woman stood at the podium an uncomfortably long time before speaking. The air was thick with expectancy.

"We are calling the enemy . . . Outliers. And as I look around this room, at our list of names of those in attendance, there are many under suspicion of being Outliers or helping Outliers."

My heart began to pound as I looked around, like everyone else, whispering and trying to search out villainous faces. Everyone looked so ordinary. So worn.

"Outliers do not stand out. They work to blend in. That is what has made our search so difficult." She raised her chin in that way that told us she was about to say something big. "It is customary in our system that persons of interest are innocent until proven guilty. That cannot be the case for this war. In order to be absolutely thorough, we must move forward under the assumption that all persons are guilty until proven innocent."

A collective gasp whooshed through the room, and I felt dizzy. I saw Rylen slightly shaking his head in disbelief.

"The first order of our plan is to unarm the Outliers. This will feel unsettling to those who are innocent, and I assure you, this is a temporary measure. All guns, explosives, or weaponry outside of a normal kitchen utensil will be confiscated, labeled with the owner's name, and stored in a nearby facility for safekeeping."

A burst of angry voices cut her off.

"Holy fucking shit," Rylen murmured.

As Grandpa started to turn around again, a sheen of sweat on his forehead, Dad waved his lowered hand at him and whispered, "God damn it, Pop." Grandpa turned back, and I could see him shaking.

"For the next twenty-four hours," the DRI woman shouted. "All Lincoln County residents are ordered to stay in their individual homes. I repeat, for the following twenty-four hours, there is a mandatory county-wide restriction. Do not leave your homes. DRI and police will be coming to each residence to take your weapons into safekeeping. In this way we can be sure the Outliers are unarmed."

The room had not quieted. One man in worn out work pants shouted, "How am I supposed to hunt for my family's food?"

"Each person who turns over a firearm will earn a box of nonperishables from the food bank."

Another uproar. Dad covered his mouth, shaking his head. "This is bullshit."

"I'm not giving up my guns!" another man shouted.

"Well then, sir, you will be put under arrest."

That quieted the room.

"You heard what the senator said," the DRI spokeswoman said. "This is not what any of us want. But it is temporary. I know right now it feels as if your rights are at risk, but I assure you it is temporary, and it is for your own good. Do you want the enemy to be stopped?"

She looked around. "Your water supply is being treated as we speak, and in the near future it will be ready for safe use again. Do you want another virus to kill off your family members?" More silence. "We must stop them, and *this* is how you can help! If you fight against these efforts, we will have no choice but to assume you are an outlier and to take the appropriate measures."

The room was so silent I could hear the generators buzzing again.

This was serious. This . . . was terrifying. On one hand, I understood, but on another hand I felt like we were making ourselves so vulnerable. I thought of handing over my late grandmother's handgun, and I felt a jolt of desolation.

"Trust us," she whispered. "Senator Navis and the DRI have been working tirelessly to find a way to win this war. In the past four days alone we have increased our police ranks tenfold, so as to keep the innocent citizens safe during this time of upheaval. *Trust us.*"

I couldn't believe it had come to this. Somewhere in the crowd a woman began to cry. Some people covered their mouths or shook their heads, or stared off with blank faces as if this new reality were too much to process.

"In a few moments you will be dismissed. For those of you who have not made it to a clinic for the mandatory vaccination, we will have them on hand when we visit your homes. Remember . . . the representatives of the state who will come to you are not your enemies. They are doing their job. I cannot urge you strongly enough—go home, comply with this decree—and we have faith that this will all be over soon. Stay inside your homes or you will be assumed armed and dangerous. Good night."

She was quickly ushered through a set of doors behind

her, which I knew led to the locker rooms and exits in the rear of the school. I expected all hell to break loose in the gymnasium, but as police with their guns filtered in and began motioning people in lines toward the doors, it was eerily quiet, like people were afraid to talk. No one in my family spoke either, but I knew they'd have plenty to say once we got home.

# TWENTY-ONE

"**T**HEY'RE NOT GETTING MY guns," Grandpa said the moment the door to the house was closed behind us. The Fites had gone to their own house, having driven separately, and I wondered what they would decide to do.

Dad sighed and sat heavily, pinching his nose.

"Don't you dare give them over, son," Grandpa said. His jowls were trembling and he pointed a finger down at Dad.

"Pop, they know I have three guns. I told them, remember? What do you want me to do, be arrested?"

"They can arrest me before I'll let them take my guns!"

"Fine!" yelled Dad. "Be arrested! But I've got a wife, daughter, and mother-in-law to look after."

"Okay, let's all calm down," Mom said.

"We have to be able to protect ourselves," Grandpa insisted. "This whole thing . . . it doesn't feel right. That woman is out of her damn mind if she thinks I'm going to trust them!"

Mom wrung her hands together and paced the room. "I agree that we need to turn over our three guns since they know about them. The last thing we need is to be placed on some outlier suspicion list. But as for yours . . ." She looked at Grandpa. "Maybe they won't find them? I mean, they *are* well hidden."

"We'd be taking a big risk," Dad said. "If we're caught lying—"

"You won't be," Grandpa said. "They're my guns. You could say you didn't know."

"We're family," Dad pointed out. "I highly doubt they'll put just one of us on the suspicion list and not all of us."

I'd been standing against the wall, but I felt dizzy and my stomach gave a loud growl, so I went to sit next to Abuela on the couch.

"Tonight," said Dad to Grandpa, "you will sleep in Tater's room and make it seem as if you live here in the main house with us. With any luck, they won't notice the room over the garage. I'll hand over my guns, and we won't say a word about yours."

Dad's foot began to bounce up and down nervously as he stared up at Grandpa, who nodded. Then Dad looked toward Mom and me. "Is that okay with you two?"

Like he said, it was risky—so risky. I didn't want us lumped in with the bad guys just because we wanted to have a way to protect ourselves, or because we had a loco old man in our house who hoarded supplies and weapons, and would rather die a fiery death than give them up. But I had this hollow feeling inside me at the thought of being without protection, a hollow feeling that had nothing to do with hunger.

"Yeah," I whispered.

Mom closed her eyes and whispered, making the sign of a cross. It was something I hadn't seen her do in a while. Then she nodded at Dad. "Okay."

"Good," Grandpa said. "And did you notice how they

made us bring food so they could use it to bribe people? Using people's starvation as a way to get them to hand over their weapons peacefully!" He stuck an angry pointer finger in the air and hissed. "They're manipulating the masses."

"Yeah, they got us there," Dad said wearily. He lay back in the recliner. At that moment I envisioned years of Dad's dealings with Grandpa's rantings etched into the lines on his forehead.

"I'm going to make us all some tea, and then we need to get to bed," Mom said.

"I go to bed now," Abuela told us. I helped her to her feet, although she was nimble as could be on her own. She patted one side of my face and kissed the other cheek before shuffling away.

Dad jumped up to help Mom in the kitchen, leaving me with Grandpa. When my parents were out of earshot, his head swiveled to me.

"Where is it?" he whispered. I knew he was talking about Grandma's gun.

"In the glove compartment of Mom's car," I whispered back. "I was afraid to bring it inside."

He nodded. "I'll put it with all of mine. Tell your parents I went up to get a change of clothes and my other things."

"Okay." I stood and went over, giving him a hug. His arms were still strong. He might have lost a few marbles, but I knew he loved us. I had an awful fear that something would happen tomorrow. "Promise me," I said. "No matter what, that you won't try to fight them when they come. Even if they find your guns."

Grandpa stepped back and left his hands on my shoulders. "Don't you worry about this old man." He walked out the door and all I could think was *that's not a promise.*

By now I should have been accustomed to no sleep, but my body only became angrier with each day of exhaustion. It was like my brain and subconscious were on nonstop and at war with my body's need for sleep. No amount of coffee or ibuprofen could quale the thumping headache that spanned the base of my skull. However, the smell of pancakes definitely perked me enough to make me roll out of bed.

Mom was working over the gas griddle. We had pancake mix, water, and a quarter bottle of syrup. My mouth watered. She handed me a flimsy paper plate and I sat. Then she scooped two peach halves from a can and put them next to my pancakes. Without speaking, I scarfed down the entire plateful in a shamefully small number of bites. Mom laughed.

"Please don't choke. I've made it all these years without having to use the Heimlich on anyone and I'd like to keep it that way."

I grinned and whispered, "Sorry." She narrowed her eyes at me.

"Do you have a headache again?"

I gave a soft nod. It felt like my bobble head would fissure and fall off.

She made a cup of coffee and handed it to me with a bottle of water and two pills. "Drink all of that." She pointed her spatula at the mug and bottle. "And then go lay back down. I'll wake you when they get here."

My stomach turned at the thought of them coming, but I obeyed. To my utter shock, I actually fell back asleep. In fact, I slept so hard that Mom had to shake me.

"They're coming down the road, Amber."

It took a few seconds to realize she was talking about the Disaster Relief people. "What time is it?" I muttered.

"Three."

Three in the afternoon? Holy crap! My head was groggy

as I stood and quickly fixed my hair, nearly toppling over as I rushed to put my legs in my jeans.

I joined my family in the living room. The DRI man and woman came in and declined to sit in the chairs we offered. The rest of us took our usual spots: Dad in the recliner, Grandpa in the rocker, Abuela and Mom sandwiching me in the middle on the couch. I could feel Mom shaking.

Dad stood and pointed to the hunting rifle, handgun, bb gun, and bullets that he'd placed on the table by the door. "There's everything," he told them.

"Ah." The woman gave him a warm smile. "Thank you for your cooperation. We'll just have a quick peek around the rest of the house and inside your vehicles, then we'll be on our way."

She motioned to the man, who motioned outside. Four men in full SWAT-like gear with masks and guns came into the house and passed us. Abuela put a hand to her chest. I wanted to laugh at the ridiculousness of it. Overkill, much? But then I got nervous. I resisted the urge to take Mom's hand or look at Dad and Grandpa, anything that might rouse suspicion that we were hiding something.

I chanted silently in my head, *Please finish, please leave.*

Nearly ten minutes later the men came back in and gave a hand signal to the male DRI. I stood to the side, and the police man standing closest to me, angled himself toward me, shifting close. He lifted his mask enough to give me a leering grin. I sucked in a shocked breath. His face was fuller now, but I immediately recognized the man who'd come to the door asking for food.

He quickly pulled his mask back down and filed in with the other three men. My eyes darted around the room, but the others had all been distracted and hadn't noticed. A disgusted chill slithered through me. How had that sleezeball been hired?

"All clear," the DRI man said with a smile, and the four police guys marched out. "Just one last thing. We'll need to see into the garage and the room above it."

Shit. My attention completely switched from the creepy guy to the situation at hand.

Without hesitation, Dad said, "Of course." He pulled his keys from his pocked with complete poise and handed it to the man. "This is to the storage room upstairs. You'll find that my father has been in crisis-savings-mode for years." He chuckled. The DRI looked toward Grandpa with amusement, but he only glowered from his rocker.

Dad put his hands in his pockets and rocked back on his heels. The male DRI headed outside while the woman stayed with us, her hands clasped in front of her skirt. A pleasant expression remained on her face while sounds of scuffling came from the adjacent wall above the garage. Grandpa stopped rocking.

"I hope everything has gone well today," Dad said.

The woman gave a tight smile. "Things have been . . . expedient."

"That's good," Dad said.

Oh, God. With each passing second I thought I'd be sick. A bump sounded against the wall and we all looked up as if we'd be able to see something. I tried to place where the sound had come from. The bed area? But the hidden gun cabinet was right beside the bed. *Oh, God!*

"I hope you find them all," Dad said. He looked intently at the woman, trying to garner all of her attention. "And if the DRI or government need me, I am happy to help in any way."

"That's right, Top," she said, shocking us all by using his Army nickname. "I take it you haven't been able to work since this all began."

"No," he said, crossing his arms. "And it's driving me crazy."

"I'll bet." Still with that smile. "Thankfully we've had no shortage of volunteers, so you'd do best right here with your family for now."

He looked prepared to argue, but the front door opened and the DRI man came back in. My stomach flipped. The two of them met eyes and he slowly raised his hands, giving her a signal. She nodded tightly then turned to my father.

"We are finished here. Thank you for your cooperation."

I felt Mom's entire body shiver next to mine. I tried to let out my tight breath as quietly as possible.

"One thing," the man said, stepping forward. "That's an awful lot of food you have up there. Did it occur to you to bring more to the donation last night?"

Dad cocked his head innocently. "The paper said for each family to bring two items. We did that."

The man laughed. "Well, yes, but . . ." His smile disappeared. "There are many people in your county who are in far worse need than you. So I'm sure you'll understand if we don't reward your compliance today with a box of reserves."

Dad gave a curt nod. "Of course. I understand."

"Good. Remain indoors until tomorrow morning unless notified otherwise."

They turned and walked out. On a whim, I ran past my gaping parents and called out the DRI woman on the porch. She needed to know.

I whispered to her, watching as the men walked away. "I just think you should know that the last man there," I nodded toward them, "tried to force his way into our house last week."

She looked toward the men and gave a solemn nod. "Mm,

yes. Starvation makes people act in deplorable ways. But I can assure you he passed all of our measures." I opened my mouth to say I didn't think hunger was his only driving force, but she cut me off in a curt voice, saying, "Remain inside until the morning." And she walked away. My hands clenched.

I went back inside and Dad locked the door behind me.

"What was that all about?" he asked.

I weighed whether or not to tell them. The thought of Dad freaking out and causing a scene made me decide to lie. "I was just asking her about the clinic. Making sure I wasn't needed today." Acid churned inside of me. The way the guy had looked at me had been a power play. He'd obviously remembered me, and he hadn't been at all worried about repercussions for his actions. Dad patted my shoulder and gave me a proud smile. I tried to put the man from my mind.

"We did it!" Grandpa whispered. His straight face turned to the hugest crap-eating grin I'd ever seen. He looked like the freaking Joker. I had to slap a hand over my mouth. Mom pressed her lips together and leaned back, bringing her knees to her chest in glee. Dad shook his head, also grinning.

After a minute passed and the DRI were far down the street, Abuela said, "I no like them."

And we all burst into laughter.

# TWENTY-TWO

I WAS STARTING TO get used to the complete darkness at night. It sort of signaled bedtime to everyone, whereas before we would have stayed up past dark to watch television. Now we preferred to save candles and propane and just go to bed. And if it weren't for the battery-operated kitchen clock, none of us would even know we were going to bed so early. My body certainly wasn't complaining about the rest.

I was nearly asleep when I heard a *pop, pop, pop* in the distance. Gunshots? I flung off my blanket and slipped my feet into sandals. Dad and Mom came out into the hall at the same time as me. I recognized their silhouettes in the sliver of moonlight shining through the windows.

Dad whispered, "I think it came from out back, maybe Coyote Springs."

Coyote Springs was the small neighborhood that our property backed up to. It was an older neighborhood. The development was surrounded by a wooden fence, but in the past five years the place seemed to be falling into disrepair. Some of the older residents had sold their homes or passed away, and the market for the older homes was down. Drugs and crime had become a problem.

We looked around for government people before jogging through our acre of low-cut lawn toward the fence, where smoke rose in the distance. Voices yelled from the streets. It was hard to see through the overlapping slats of the fence, so Dad grasped my waist from behind and lifted me up to look. I hoisted myself to the top of the fence until my elbows locked, putting all my weight on my arms while my legs dangled. Dad held my calves. I had a good view of a row of unkempt backyards and backs of small houses.

Flames and smoke rose from the next street over, sending a billowing cloud of gray up into the dark blue sky. "One of the houses is on fire."

Between the houses I could see to the street. Everything was hazy but my eyes adjusted to the small bit of light from stars and the moon. Shadowed figures darted in the street.

"People are running . . ." I whispered down to them. I had to squint to make everything out. Except the fire rising even higher. That was clear.

My eyes widened at the sound of simultaneous stomping feet. Dark-dressed men were running down the street— it took a second to realize they were police—like the creepy man and other ones who'd searched our house earlier. And then a loud voice rang out through the screech of a megaphone.

*"A mandatory curfew is in effect. Return to your homes at once."*

People in the streets were shouting back. It sounded like they were refusing. Rebelling. And then, to my horror, the police opened fire. Screams sliced the air. Bodies fell. People ran. Oh, my God! My arms gave out and I fell back into Dad's embrace.

"What's going on?" came Rylen's voice behind us.

Dad nearly dropped me as he spun, and I got my footing.

"Jesus, Ry," Dad said. "You scared the shit out of me."

"They're killing people!" My voice trembled.

"What?" Mom grabbed my hand.

"We have to get inside!" I kept hold of her hand and pulled her as we ran back to our house. Rylen was just ahead of me and I squinted as I made out something long slung over his shoulder.

"Do you have a *gun?*" I hissed. He didn't answer until we wrenched open the sliding glass door, slipped inside, and locked it behind us. Mom lit a single candle as Dad closed all the shutters.

I gawked at Rylen and his hunting rifle. "You didn't hand it over?"

Rylen gave a shrug. "My dad's been hiding things from the cops for years."

"You can't run around outside with it, Ry!" I whisper-yelled, feeling panicked. "They'll kill you! They're shooting people for being outside during the curfew!" My whole body trembled, and Dad pulled me to him.

"Sh, honey, we're all safe. Rylen won't do anything stupid." I pulled back in time to see Dad sending his *you better not* look to Ry, who gave a nod.

"How'd it go at your house?" Dad asked him.

"We gave over two of our four guns. When I told them I was reporting to base tomorrow, they told me not to bother. That the base was shut down. Can you believe that?"

Dad's face scrunched. "I haven't been able to get ahold of Tater's base in days."

"Yeah, they said the bases are dispersing so that individuals can help their communities locally." Rylen shook his head. "She said only the elite were being used for war efforts. I guess the bombers?"

"That makes no sense," I said. "They should be utilizing the military."

Dad crossed his arms and seemed to be having dark thoughts. Another series of gunshots rang out from a distance and I jumped.

Dad eyed me. "What exactly did you see in Coyote Springs, Amber?"

I circled my arms around my torso. "They're shooting people who are out of their houses."

"Who are?" Mom asked. "The DRI?"

"No. The cops like the ones who checked our house for weapons today."

"Damn," Rylen whispered. "They're calling them the DRP. Disaster Relief Police. Were the people trying to attack them? Did they have guns?"

"No!" I shook as I remembered. "They were unarmed as far as I could see. They were just standing in the road and in their yards, yelling stuff." I wish I could have heard.

Mom looked as horrified as I felt. "What on earth is happening?"

"Well," Dad said gravely. "They made it clear they were assuming everyone to be guilty until proven innocent."

I recalled that comment at the town meeting. But God . . . were they just going to literally kill anyone on the spot, even for protesting or whatever they were doing in Coyote Springs?

Rylen rubbed his hair. "After they told me the base closed, I asked about joining on to the police force to help, but they told me they had enough."

"Same here," Dad said.

I couldn't hold it in any longer. "One of the police guys at our house tonight was the same man who came to our house for food and tried to push his way in."

Their angry faces turned on me. I told them how he'd lifted his mask enough to show me his face and give me a creepy smile. Dad and Rylen both wore deadly expressions like they would strangle him without hesitation if he were in the room right now.

"Why are they hiring men like that," Mom asked, "and turning away men like the two of you?"

None of us had the answer to that, though.

Dad shook his head, exasperated. "None of it makes a damn bit of sense."

I walked to the sliding glass door and pulled the curtain aside enough to peer out. Smoke and flames still rose, but no more gunshots. All was quiet. Rylen sidled up to me and put his cheek close to mine to peer out. His sudden nearness and the scent of him sent a burst of need streaking through me. On instinct, I dropped the curtain and stepped away. His gaze honed in on me, inspecting.

"What is wrong with you, Pepper?" he asked. "Why does it feel like you're mad at me all the time?"

"I'm not *mad*. I'm just . . ." Emotion filled my throat and I had to swallow. I wished I could tell him to keep his distance and not touch me. He was making it so much harder on me, but I couldn't tell him that. How could this man who knew me so well, not know how I felt when it came to him? It pissed me off. And it made me angry with myself that I couldn't get these feelings under control.

Mom, who'd been glancing over from the dining room entrance, came in and sidled up next to me. "I think we're all just a bit overwhelmed."

I felt his eyes on me. "I need to go to bed," I said.

"That's a good idea." Mom patted my lower back.

I brushed past a frowning Rylen, past my dad, down the dark hall and into my pitch-black room.

# TWENTY-THREE

I HAD JUST SETTLED into my bed and cleared my mind of Rylen thoughts when my door shot open. I sat up abruptly as Rylen shut my door hard, and his boots stomped to my bedside. He sat heavily on the edge of the bed and took me by the shoulders, squeezing.

"Why are you mad at me, Pepper? Why?"

"Stop it, Ry." I tried to shrug away. He was too close. "I told you, I'm not—"

"Yes, you *are*." He held me tighter. "You don't think I can tell? Every time I think we're okay, you start acting weird again. I hate it when you're mad at me. I fucking lay awake at night worrying about it."

My breath caught, and my sinuses burned. "It's not anything you need to worry about."

"Just tell me what the fuck I did." He held me tighter.

"Please, Ry," I growled, on the verge of a mental breaking point.

He let go of my shoulders and grasped my face in his hot hands, pulling me closer. "*Tell me.*"

"You shouldn't be in my room like this," I said. "You're married."

He went completely still, as if he'd stopped breathing. He dropped my face.

"We're not allowed to be friends?"

My jaw clenched and released. "If you were my husband, I wouldn't want you in some other girl's room."

"Liv knows we're not like that." His voice was raised, so mine rose to match.

"Liv knows that we're a man and a woman who are very close, and we are not siblings!"

"Is this really about Liv and what she thinks?" he asked. "Or does the fact that I'm married, in general, make you uncomfortable?"

"The fact that you're married, Rylen, makes me *sad*." My stomach dropped.

I thought it would feel good to say it out loud, but all I felt was sick. Those were homewrecker words. I'd had so many years to be truthful with him and I'd not been brave enough. My true anger was at myself. I didn't take the chance when I had it. It was my own fault.

"I'm sorry," I whispered. "I shouldn't have said that. I'm just . . . I'm not good with change. And I'm selfish when it comes to the people I care about."

"I never meant to make you sad." His voice was thick. In my small, stuffy room, his scent overwhelmed me, made me wish for things to be different. I wanted to drink in his emotions. He was right here. I could so easily reach out and put my hands on him.

I needed him gone.

"Everything is fine," I said. "With us. It's fine. I promise. I just need to go to sleep now." I had to make an effort to be nicer to him from now on. Not to flinch away when he got near. To act sisterly. It wasn't fair to punish him because of my broken heart.

Rylen let out a deep sigh. "I've . . . missed you. I mean, Tater, too. Your whole family. But you . . . your letters . . . you don't know how much it meant to me. You're the only person who kept in constant contact with me over the years. I knew wherever I went your letters would find me, and there were times when I felt really lost. But you always found me. And I looked forward to it. I got excited every time I saw your handwriting. God, I know I sound like a pathetic fool, but I read them over and over. I . . ." He stopped and I found I was holding my breath. I couldn't see his face, only shadows, but his words, his breathing, every sound was heightened in my ears. I heard his mouth open, and he wet his lips.

"When I met Livia, she reminded me of you."

I squeezed my eyes shut and hot tears slid down my cheeks. I wrenched my knees up and wrapped my arms around them. The silent tears kept rolling.

"I just, I love you, Pepper. And if it had been you who showed up with a husband . . ." He gave a chuffed laugh. "I would have been sad too. Because I don't know what I'd do without you."

I swallowed hard. Once. Twice. Three times.

He loved me like a sister. And his words were the sweetest things I'd ever heard. His love for me might not be the same as mine, but it was real. We had a bond. It wasn't the relationship I'd wanted, but I was glad to know I'd helped him in some small way. That would have to be enough.

"I love you too, Ry. And your letters were special to me too."

"Please don't cry," he whispered. I'd been so careful not to even sniffle, but he must have heard it in my voice. I quickly wiped my cheeks on my T-shirt sleeve. I took a deep, cleansing breath and felt my tear ducts finally tighten and begin to dry.

Rylen reached out and found my wrist, running his fingers down to my hand, which he opened from its grasp. He enveloped my hand in both of his large, warm ones. Those hands. Those strong palms and able fingers. Oh, God, Rylen's hands felt so good. How many times had I imagined those hands taking my face, those fingers trailing along my skin and cupping me, feeling me everywhere he dared. I prayed for the day when his touch would not elicit those thoughts. When holding my hand wouldn't make me hot all over. I wanted to love him the way he loved me. This was too hard.

Finally he let my hand slide from his palms and he stood.

"Get some sleep, Pepper."

"You too," I whispered.

He left me and I wrapped my arms around my knees again, slightly rocking. Moments later I saw the shadow of Mom looking in my door.

"I'm okay," I whispered.

She closed the door and left me with my jumbled thoughts and the smell of Rylen.

# TWENTY-FOUR

**L**EAVE IT TO HIM to steal another night of sleep from me. Well, to be fair, the whole night wasn't lost, only the first half of it. Then I woke with the sun, and I vowed to have a new outlook.

I went to work with a belly full of oatmeal swirled with strawberry jam and pressed coffee, plus a sponge bath, so my body was mostly happy. My head was still holding a grudge about the half-night of sleep.

As I pulled into the clinic parking lot and rounded the line of tall bushes, everything I'd eaten solidified into a hard lump. There were five Disaster Relief Police standing at the entrance in all black with guns, but no masks this time. I searched their faces, but creepy man was not with them. A civilian man cradling his injured arm was walking away from them. I ran up to him when I saw he was bleeding.

"Sir," I said. "What happened? We need to get you inside the clinic."

The man was probably my dad's age, but really thin and in bad need of a shave. His eyes rounded and darted from me to the DRPs. One of the men stepped forward and said, "Under new law, persons injured by DRP fire cannot be helped."

"What?" I asked. I looked at the man. He shook his head, appearing frightened. I looked at the DRPs. "You shot him?"

"I'm fine," the man insisted in a tremoring voice.

"No, you're not." The towel he held around his bicep was soaked with blood. "I'm a medic, and I'm sworn to help people, no matter what. Let me look."

The DRP who'd spoken before moved closer and said, "He's been told to leave clinic property. He was out of his house during curfew hours and faced punishment. He's not to be treated."

"I'm going." The man shuffled quickly away from me, leaving me there staring at the DRP. He looked like a farmer converted to a police with his tanned skin and shorn hair.

"Are you kidding me right now?" I asked, throwing out my arms. "A law that I can't treat people?"

The man pointed his gun at me and I raised my hands, jumping back and shutting up as fear sliced through me. "Are you questioning the laws of Senator Navis and the DRI?" Was this asshole going to shoot me for speaking? What the hell was going on in this world?

"Whoa, whoa." Another DRP walked up beside him. "I know her. She's good people." I looked at the guy's face and recognized him as a freckled, tall boy who was in the year below me in school, Jeff Adams.

"Good people don't question the law," the other man spat.

Jeff nodded. "I think she was taken by surprise. Sounds like this is the first time she's heard the law. Miss Tate, you should head on in and talk to the doctor. He'll inform you of the new decrees."

I slowly lowered my hands and walked past the men, keeping my eyes on the mouthy one. I wanted to flip him the bird, but he'd scared me too badly. When I got to the doorway, Jeff walked me in and whispered, "Just keep a low profile, okay? Most of these guys aren't from around here, so they don't know us, and they don't care. We have to treat anyone who isn't obedient as an outlier. If they think we're slacking, they let us go like that—" He snapped his fingers. "And there goes our food."

"They pay you in food?" I whispered.

He nodded and glanced back through the doorway. "Be careful."

I gave a curt nod and managed to say, "Thank you."

Inside, I couldn't even relax because the stuffy DRI woman who gave vaccinations was sitting there at the main desk. She smiled big, oblivious that I'd nearly been killed for questioning a horrible new law.

"We've had to turn away many today who were punished," she said. "But word will spread because of this, and people will realize we are very serious and we mean what we say. People will be more cautious."

"Yeah, maybe, but . . ." I scanned her for a weapon before I continued. "It feels wrong to me. I'm trained to heal people, even people at crime scenes who are clearly not innocent."

"I understand." Fake, weird smile. "That was the past. All of our beliefs are being changed and challenged. But it is temporary. In due time all will be right, as it should."

My lips clamped shut. I lowered my head and walked to the doctor's office. He was listening to the radio and his eyes were glazed as he stared at the wall. I closed the door behind me.

"Morning, Dr. Persus."

His eyes flitted to me and cleared before he reached out a hand to silence the radio.

"They're saying most of Africa is wiped out. Did you hear?"

An uncomfortable zing itched its way over my skin. I sank into the chair across from him and whispered, "No. I've been trying not to listen."

"All but South Africa, which has had half of its population spared. The rest of the continent, Amber . . ." His chin trembled. "Have you ever been—no, never mind, you're young. You haven't had chance yet, but I have. I took three trips to different parts of Africa for Doctors Without Borders."

"I'm so sorry. I can't believe this. Were they bombed?"

He shook his head and his voice was strained. "All water sources were contaminated. Every one. Those who survived the illnesses starved."

I closed my eyes, hoping my stomach would settle. I did not want to lose my breakfast. "Dr. Persus. What are the new laws? One of the DRP acted like he was going to shoot me for trying to treat a man who'd been injured by one of them."

The doctor's entire face crumbled and he seemed to become frailer before my very eyes.

"Oh, Amber. I'm so sorry. Those devils. I want the Outliers found, I really do, but this." He shook his head. "This is a sad day. Medical personnel will be killed if we treat anyone who was injured as a form of punishment. They want their suffrage to be a warning to others. I understand their determination—their need for complete cooperation—but I wish there was another way."

"I mean, if obedience is how they'll determine the Outliers, what will stop the Outliers from pretending to be outstanding citizens? They're probably hiding their guns somewhere and doing their evil business during the day, in secret. It's the innocent people who are being treated like Outliers who are getting shafted here!"

The door swung open without a knock and I gasped as I spun to see the pretty, smiling face of the DRI woman.

"I heard a raised voice. Is everything okay?"

"Oh, everything is just fine," Dr. Persus said with his own fake smile. "Amber was worked up when I told her what the Outliers did in Africa."

"Mm." She gave me a sympathetic look. "Well, we'll keep this door open in case you need anything. I'm just a shout away." She pressed the door open, flush against the wall, and gave us a meaningful look.

"Wait." I stood up. This was going too far. "Sometimes the doctor and I need to discuss patient business in private. We *will* need to close the door at some point."

"There's no need for patient privacy in these times. We're all in this together, Miss Tate. Aren't we?"

What. The. Hell. She was giving me that damn perma-smile. I, on the other hand, was not smiling.

Dr. Persus stood and gave a chuckle. "Of course we are. We'll leave it open."

She walked away and I leveled Dr. Persus with a disbelieving look. He held his palms up as if to calm me. He mouthed silently, *choose your battles*. And out loud he said, "We have patients to see. Let's get started."

❦

I was not okay. I had the heebie-jeebies all day. My world had tilted sideways and I couldn't walk straight. Everything was off-kilter.

I came home to the beautiful sight of my parents and grandparents sitting in the living room with Remy. My bag slipped from my fingers as I ran to her.

"Remy!"

She stood and we collided in a hug. Her eyes were red.

"What's wrong?" I asked. I looked around and saw Mom and Abuela's sad faces.

"My dad," Remy said. "He's just being . . . well, you know how he gets about church stuff. Nothing else matters."

Ah. We sat together on the couch. "What's going on?"

"He wants me to be there all the time, helping, trying to give people hope, but it's really hard when I'm not exactly feeling the hope myself, you know?"

"Yeah," I whispered. I hated hearing that, though, about her not having hope.

"It's really awful at the church, Amber. We've nearly drained our pool bringing gallons of water to boil and give away, but people are hungry, and they're begging us for food we don't have." A wave of guilt slammed me. "And they're crying about people they've lost, and they want to know why this is happening to them. And I'm like, I'd really like to know that too. *Why?*"

I pressed my lips together. I'd been hearing similar questions at the clinic, and I saw some horrible cases, but I'd hardened myself to peoples' suffering. Maybe that was wrong of me, but it's how I coped. I murmured kind things to them as I worked, but I kept my heart sealed in a tight chamber.

Remy sniffed. "I told my dad I couldn't do it anymore. I just . . . I had to get away. Can I stay here tonight?"

"Of course," I said.

Abuela pushed to her feet and said, "I make food."

We were all quiet. Dad and Grandpa hadn't said a word. In the kitchen I could hear the *whir* of Abuela opening a can of something and then lighting the gas burner. I almost asked, "Did you hear about Africa?" but that probably wasn't what Remy needed to hear right now.

Remy looked toward the hall to the kitchen. "Is she *cooking?*"

"Yeah," I answered.

Remy stood and I followed her into the kitchen. She

stared at the cans of black beans being poured into a pan, and the second pan which was warming water to make rice.

"Oh, my gosh," Remy whispered. "That looks so good."

I felt the need to explain. I kept my voice low. "Grandpa Tate sort of collected supplies and food . . . just in case anything like this ever happened. We're really lucky."

"That is awesome!" she said. "I ate the last of our fruit snacks yesterday and I've been freaking out a little." She looked at me sheepishly. Remy was hungry. I took her hand and pulled her to the pantry. I lifted her hand and poured some almonds into her palm. Her eyes seriously watered from gratitude, which made another wave of guilt hit me. She threw the handful into her mouth and laughed as she chewed. I would make sure Remy went to bed with a full stomach.

Mom came to the pantry doorway with a medium box. "I don't care what Papá Tate says. I'm going to fill a box and bring it to your church today." Remy threw her hands around Mom's neck and they hugged tightly.

"Thank you," Remy said. "There's so many little kids there. That's the part that I can't take. They're crying and they have no energy. The parents are, like, *desperate*. This will mean so much."

We helped Mom pack the box, and saw her off. I knew she'd let Remy's dad know she was with us, and she was okay.

That night our family and Remy sat around the table eating, trying to make small talk. It was on the tip of my tongue to tell them about what had happened to me this morning with the DRP pointing his gun at me and the DRI making us keep the doors open, but nobody else was talking about unpleasant things so I decided it could wait. We could have one night of no upsetting subjects.

As we were finishing up, a rattle came from the front door,

as if someone were trying the knob. We all stilled. And then came the sound of a key in the lock. Dad's eyes narrowed and he leapt up from his chair with all of us behind him. We got to the living room as the door swung wide and a tall, handsome young man with wavy dark hair stood in the doorway dressed in worn out fatigues.

"Glad to see you haven't changed the locks."

I screamed. "Tater!"

# TWENTY-FIVE

I SPRINTED TO HIS arms and he laughed as I knocked him against the door. He lifted me off my feet and gave me the longest, tightest hug we'd ever shared. Emotions swelled inside of me, tumbling over one another in a rush. I had never been so happy to see anyone. Suddenly my tilted world felt slightly righted.

"My turn!" Mom was clapping and then elbowing me away so she could get to him, squealing. Dad came over too, and the three of them hugged. I watched, feeling such massive joy that my smile was hurting my cheeks.

I looked over at my smiling grandpa, and Abuela who stood with her hands clasped at her chest and tears streaming down her cheeks. Then I looked at Remy, who was staring at Tater as if she'd never seen him before. Her gaze traveled up and down. I knew that look. She met my eyes and her brows bounced.

"Um," I whispered. "You hate him, remember?"

"I hated the *teenage* him," she whispered back.

I rolled my eyes, but still couldn't stop smiling.

Tater and Grandpa hugged, giving each other hard slaps on the back, and then he got to Abuela, who was about half his size. He lifted her up and spun her around as she slapped his arms to put her down. He set her down and she grasped his face, pulling him down so she could kiss both his cheeks.

Tater then turned to Remy. "Damn, Remy."

"Damn yourself, Jacob."

Oh, my damn, they were totally flirting. Gross.

"What are you doing here?" Dad asked.

Tater spun to face him, throwing up his arms. "They closed the base. Sent us all away."

"Fort Benning, too?" Dad's hands flew up, his expression angry.

"I know. Nobody knows what the fuc—oh, sorry Abuela."

"I no care." She waved a hand.

"Nobody knows what's going on. I had to hitchhike the whole way here from Georgia."

"What?" Mom looked horrified.

"I know, right?" Tater was smiling broadly. "People kept running out of gas and shi—stuff. It's the same in all the towns. Businesses closed. Drips got roadblocks so they can check people off."

"Drips?" I asked.

"Yeah, you know, the DRI peeps."

I let out a laugh. "I call the DRPs Derps. Drips and Derps!"

Tater held up a hand and I jumped to slap it, half expecting him to pull it out of my reach at the last second like old times. But he was mature enough to actually allow me to high five him. How far we'd come.

"What's wrong with the DRI and DRP?" Remy asked. "They're good. They're trying to help, right?"

"Well, yeah . . ." I looked around the room. "But they're kind of weird. And really hardcore." I decided to go ahead and tell them about what had happened that morning. I thought Dad was going to blow a gasket about the gun-pointing thing, his face got so red. Mom put a hand on his forearm.

"Amber, you have to be careful!" Remy scolded. "They warned us! And who knows what that guy did to get shot."

I was surprised to hear a viewpoint so different from what my own gut said.

"Well, yes, but . . ." But what? I shook my head. "I don't like it that they're treating everyone like criminals. It just feels wrong."

"It's just temporary," Remy said.

"It's just bullshit is what it is," Tater blurted. "Oh, sorry Abuela."

"I tell you, I no care." She swatted his arm.

"Well, I do care." Mom swatted his other arm.

"Ah, crazy ladies!" Tater scrambled away, stopping right next to Remy. He put an arm around her. I flung it off. Remy gave him a wicked smile.

Stomps came from the front steps and we all turned to see the door fling open. Rylen's eyes scanned the room and widened when they came to Tater. At the same time, both guys dove across the room and fell to the ground, wrestling. They were laughing and shouting inappropriate things like, ". . . *pussy ass mutha* . . ." and Mom was shaking her head, eyes to the ceiling.

Remy elbowed me and nodded to the door. Livia stood there looking unsure.

"Come in," I told her. I went over and closed the door and locked it. Then I gave her a small smile. She stared at the boys, almost worried.

"This is how they greet each other," I told her in Spanish. She gave a stifled laugh.

Finally they got to their feet and finished with a series of punches and head swipes before stopping. Tater's eyes went straight to Livia.

"Is this the Missus?" He headed straight for her and took her hand, speaking to her in Spanish. "You are a beautiful girl. What are you doing with my ugly friend?"

Livia's eyes shot to Rylen over Tater's shoulder.

Rylen told her, "Whatever he says, Liv, ignore it."

I punched Tater's shoulder. "Leave her alone." He smiled at her and let go, turning back to Rylen.

"Was your base closed too, Dude?"

Rylen crossed his arms and nodded. "Benning closed? That's a surprise."

Dad pinched his nose and closed his eyes. "This is insane. Why are bases closing? I need to talk to people, but I'm trying to ration our gas."

"We've been out of gas for days," Remy said. "We've been riding our bikes for miles."

"Here's the thing about gas," Tater said. "Most of the stations have generators, but they closed shop after they sold out of all their food, 'cause they can't take credit and not a lot of people have cash. They're afraid of being held up or killed for gas if they stay open. If you can find a gas station owner and you have something valuable enough to trade them, they might be willing to turn on a pump so you can fill up."

Grandpa stepped forward. "I'm willing to trade goods for gas. Just let me do the talking."

Dad nodded. Grandpa was a hustler. "All right. We'll give it a try tomorrow."

The room was already dimming with the setting sun. Soon we'd have to light the lantern. I had a feeling we'd be up for a while tonight, excited by Tater's presence, and I was right.

We talked for hours, oftentimes shouting over one

another. There was seriousness, and talk of our fears, but there was also laughter. Around eleven, Tater talked Mom into putting one of her salsa CDs into the battery-operated player and moments later we were on our feet. Well, Mom, Tater, and I were on our feet. Then Tater pulled Abuela up and we all laughed and cheered as she moved her little hips in the most adorable way. After that, she was wiped out and went to bed. Grandpa had gone up at ten.

I grabbed Remy by the hands and Tater snagged Livia up by her waist. She let out a squeal and I thought she'd protest, but to all of our shock she smiled bigger than we'd ever seen and she pressed her palms up against Tater's, meeting him move-for-move. Rylen's eyes got big and he laughed, clapping. Mom let out a "Woo!" then grabbed Remy by the hand and spun her. This wasn't Remy's first time dancing at the Tate house.

Dad and Rylen kept their butts in their chairs, Dad with his hands behind his head and Rylen with his arms crossed now, but both of them were grinning. Rylen was watching Tater and Livia as if he was thoroughly entertained, and then his eyes slid to me and his grin softened a touch. I smiled back and spun with dramatic flare, feeling my hair whip out.

"Ow!" Remy shouted. I turned and saw her holding her eye where my hair smacked her.

"Sorry!"

She gave her head a swoop to the side and whacked me with her wall of thick blond waves, stinging my face. We both fell over each other laughing.

Through the blare of music I thought I heard something *boom* outside. Tater stopped and hit the CD player. "Did you hear that? Sounded like gun fire."

Rylen was out of the chair and through the door before anyone else could speak. Tater was right behind him.

We all went for the door but Dad stopped us, whispering, "Turn off the light. Stay quiet. Lock the door."

He left with the guys and we did as he said. When the room was darkened, we ran to the window and the four of us watched through slats as the dark figures of Ry, Tater, and Dad sprinted through the potato field toward the Fite house.

"I didn't hear anything," Remy whispered. "What was it?"

"It sounded like a shot," I whispered back. "Rylen said someone stole two of their chickens a couple days ago. I wonder if someone is there again." My fingers were shaking on the blinds.

"Wait," Remy said. "So, where would the shot come from? What gun do they have?"

"Um." Oh, crap. "I'm sure everything's fine."

On the end, Livia quietly whispered, "Papá Len no give gun."

Oh, dear. I wished she wouldn't have said that.

"He didn't?" Remy asked. "They'll think he's an outlier."

I had no comeback. We watched in silence, but it was too dark out there. And then all of a sudden, it was way, way too bright.

The four of us screamed as the sky lit up from a blast on the Fite property. It was on the side of the house.

"Oh, my God!" I said. "The barn!" All of the gasoline he'd stored in there must have been somehow ignited. The boys!

"Ry-*len*!" Livia cried.

We moved for the door, but Mom sprinted past us and blocked it, her face pale with panic. "We can't go out there!"

"Mom, what if they're hurt?"

"What if there are DRI or robbers?" Mom asked.

I ran back to the window and looked out. I couldn't see anyone, just a massive fire, which I hoped would not spread to their house. God, my stomach was a bundle of nerves.

Were they okay? Having been close to a bomb myself, I knew anyone in the proximity could be hurt, or even killed. I was going to give them one more minute to come back or I would grab my medical kit and run like hell no matter what Mom said. As I watched, with Livia pressed at my side watching too, I saw with horror as the trees between the barn and house began to flame. Every thing was so dry. They went up like flint.

"La casa," Livia whispered.

"Mom, I'm sorry. I have to go."

Mom and Remy both called after me as I ran to my room for my pack. I snatched it up and pushed my feet into my shoes. I made it to the door and Mom was leaning against the wall, covering her mouth with both hands. Livia was quietly crying.

"Please don't go," Remy begged me.

"I'll be careful," I promised.

"Mirame!" Livia said. *Look!*

We rushed to the window and looked out. Our three men were crouching at the edge of the potato field near our property, edging their way back to us. The bundle of sharp nerves in my stomach loosened. As they slunk through the yard and up the stairs, Mom opened the door and closed it once they were all in. The men were breathing hard, covered in dirt from where they'd crawled. None of us could speak. We all looked to Rylen. His brow was so severely drawn it made a V between his eyes. His eyes were rimmed in dark red.

"Did anyone see you?" Dad asked him.

Ry shook his head. "I stayed low till they were gone."

"What happened?" I asked.

"My dad set up tripwires to catch thieves." He sucked in a sharp breath. "Those bastards were showing up in the middle of the night to take our livestock and gasoline. When I got

close enough I heard one of them say something about community goods."

"Who?" I whispered.

"DRPs," Dad said. The new "cops." He looked back at
Rylen for him to continue.

"They had their guns pointed at my dad. He must've giv-
en a warning shot when the wires were tripped, the damn
fool. By the time I got there, he was unlocking the coop for
them and they took all the chickens. Then they followed him
to the barn, but he stopped at the tree and yanked a rope
that was hanging there. He booby-trapped it and the whole
damn thing went up, blew him and the man holding the gun
straight back."

His dad blew up the barn. I held my breath. Remy had
retreated and crumpled onto the couch.

"One of the Derps was busy with the chickens and the
other ran into the house, maybe looking to see if anyone
else was there, or to see what they could take. I ran to Dad
and checked his pulse." His eyes. Oh, my heart, Rylen's eyes
were rimmed in tears. "He made it through that virus, only
to be . . ."

He let his head fall back, closing his eyes.

"He's gone?" Mom croaked.

Rylen lowered his head and when he opened his eyes the
remnant of threatening tears were gone, but his voice was
thick. "Yeah. He's dead. The DRI too."

My chest was so constricted, I could only take shallow
breaths. Len Fite . . . Rylen's dad . . . I couldn't believe it.

I stepped to Rylen's side to comfort him, just as Livia did.
She and I both looked at each other, and I moved back, feeling stupid.

Livia went into his arms and he pulled her close, resting
his cheek on the top of her head.

Now Mom had to sit. Rylen raised his head from Livia's, but kept an arm around her waist. She leaned her cheek against his chest.

"It was definitely DRPs?" I asked. "No DRIs were there?"

"No," Rylen said hoarsely. "And it was definitely Derps, in uniform. They dragged their man's body away and took our rifle."

Dad shook his head "He knew they were going to shoot him one way or the other. That's why he blew up the barn. Didn't want them getting his goods."

"This is such bullshit!" Tater yelled. "Why are the Drips giving these assholes guns and letting them have power over us?"

"How did we get to this place?" Mom quietly cried. "How is it okay for government officials to take people's property and kill people on the spot for any rule broken?"

I felt so ill. I couldn't wrap my mind around the idea of Len Fite being dead. What if Ry had been there? Would they have expected him to sit back and let them take all of their valuables? If he'd been there and tried to refuse them, he could have ended up dead, too. I slunk back and sat beside Remy. We grabbed one another's hand at the same time.

Both of us jumped at the sound of a key in the front door. The men spun to face Grandpa Tate, looking like they were ready to take him down. Grandpa didn't even flinch at the sight of them. He was wearing a light blue pajama set that was too comfortable and cozy for the vicious look on his face. He turned to Rylen, looking up and slapping a hand to his shoulder.

"I watched from my window with my binoculars when I heard the shot. I've been waiting for this day to come. Your father did exactly what I would have done. I'm sorry for your loss, son, but that man needs to be commended." He looked around at the rest of us. "And now, we all need to pack as much as we can and get the hell out of town."

# TWENTY-SIX

"I'M NOT RUNNING," RYLEN said. We all looked at him. His attention was respectfully on Grandpa. "I need to get to the bottom of what's going on here. I need to find out if these were dirty cops or if the Drips are giving them permission to do this."

"Being his son will automatically put you on their suspicion list," Grandpa told him. "He had an illegal gun. Even if the DRPs were dirty cops, the Drips won't overlook the gun possession."

"I'll act like I disagreed with my father, and that I didn't know he'd hidden any guns. Whether they believe me or not is a chance I've got to take."

"Rylen," Mom said. "This is not time to go vigilante. You've got a lot to live for."

They looked at one another and he responded, "I know. But something's not right. Something is going on."

"Yeah," Tater said. "And it's not just one or two corrupt Derps. This is everywhere. And the Drips are weird as hell. Ever notice how they're all *good looking*?"

"Yes!" I pointed at him like he'd read my mind.

His face lit up. "Right? It's so creepy! Not a fat one in the bunch."

We gave each other another high five.

"That doesn't necessarily mean anything," Mom said. "They've got more resources—the longer we go without showers, the nicer they look."

I shook my head. "Seriously, where are these resources? Where are they blow-drying and curling their hair? It kind of pisses me off to know they're using some generator somewhere to primp. What crappy priorities."

Remy lifted her limp ponytail and mumbled, "How exactly does one become a DRI anyway?"

Rylen walked to the window and stared out. Flames from his burning home lit his face with moving light. I wanted so badly to go to him. To hug him. But his wife was close behind him. She placed a small hand on his shoulder blade. I wondered how he could stand there, holding it together so well. I'd be a mess on the floor if I lost one of my parents and my home was in flames. My heart lurched just thinking about it. I knew he had to be dying on the inside. He shoved his hands deep in his jean pockets, locking his elbows. His jaw rocked back and forth as he grinded his teeth.

Oh, yeah. He was feeling every bit of that loss.

"I still say we should leave," Grandpa grumbled.

"Where to?" Tater asked. "It's like this everywhere."

"Somewhere more remote," Grandpa responded. "The mountains."

"Every road between towns has roadblocks. They're taking names to keep track of people."

"What?" I asked. "They weren't doing that when I was going into Clark County for work."

"They just started," Tater said. "When I left Georgia there

were no stops. By the time I got to Nevada there were stops between every major town on every major road."

Grandpa had gone ashen. "They're out of control."

"They're just searching for Outliers, right?" Remy asked.

"That's what they're saying," Tater said. Remy looked confused, so Tater expounded. "The problem is, they're acting like everyone is their enemy."

"But they have to, because anyone could be one." When he lifted an eyebrow at her, she shrugged and peered down at her nails. "I don't know, it made sense when they told us."

Dad sighed and crossed his arms. "We need to come up with an exact exit plan then. First thing in the morning our priority is to fill the tanks with gas and get a few containers for spare. Then we should probably fill the trunks with a portion of our resources, have everything ready just in case we have to up and go. I'll check out some of the back roads and abandoned private lanes that go up into the mountains."

This was so scary. I couldn't even believe we were talking about leaving home.

Rylen cleared his throat. "I'm gonna head to the police station now to let them know what I found when I got home. I think it'll look suspicious if I wait until the morning. When I get back, I'm going to bury him."

"Want me to go with you?" Tater asked.

"No."

"What are you going to tell them?" I asked.

He turned from the window to face us. "I'm gonna bold face lie. Tell them my dad was acting weird." He grabbed the back of his neck and looked down, like the thought of betraying his father's memory hurt. Grandpa grunted and crossed his arms tightly.

"I know it's wrong," Rylen said in a deep voice. "It goes against everything inside me, but I have to find out what's going on, how deep this goes. I need to know if these were three corrupt Derps, or if they were ordered . . ." He shook his head. "I don't know. I don't know how I'll react."

"Rylen," Livia said. Her eyes were slightly bulgy as she reached for his hand.

He took it and looked at her. "Please, don't worry."

Mom stepped forward. "If you're going to do this, you have to do it all the way. Don't let them know you disagree. Don't question them. Find out what you can, and come back to us safely. Promise me."

He grinded his teeth again and nodded, whispering, "I promise."

My stomach twisted itself into the tightest, most sickening knot. I wrapped my arms around my middle, unable to stand straight. Remy was chewing her thumbnail.

"Dude," Tater said. "Just let me come—"

"No," Rylen said again. "I'll come straight back here. I swear."

"Fine," Tater said. "But I need to be doing something. Maybe . . . maybe I can start digging."

Len's death hit me in the chest again. His dead body was over there. It made me ill thinking about it. Rylen gave Tater a grateful nod, and said bye to everyone, getting hugs from each of us. I kept mine brief. He hugged Livia last, holding her longer. He kissed the top of her head and then he was gone.

The room was ghostly quiet for half a minute until a sob issued from Livia and she covered her mouth. Mom put an arm around her, leading her to the couch where they sat. Remy looked at me and I saw the worry in her tight brow.

"I should load the trunks while it's dark," Dad said. Grandpa followed him out, probably to unlock the door to his room, but he didn't come back down. He had to be exhausted. Grandpa liked his sleep more than any of us.

I looked at Tater's worn face. "I'll help you dig." He nodded. Together we went to the garage and got shovels. When we came back out, Mom's face was so worried she looked ten years older.

"Please be careful. Hide if you hear or see anyone coming."

"We will," I promised.

Tater and I trudged through the silent, dark field. Even from afar I could feel the heat of the flames wafting toward us. The fire was like a raging, terrifying beast, reaching for the sky, wanting to obliterate anything that came near it. I could barely make out Len's form on the ground in front of it.

"Let's dig on the side," Tater said. He pointed to their small grove of citrus trees. We made our way over and began digging a Len-sized chasm in the earth until our arms were burning and our backs were sore.

I tried not to worry about Rylen, or to think about a blast powerful enough to kill a large man like Len. Would I ever be brave enough to sacrifice my life to stop an injustice from happening? In that situation, I had no doubt I would have given them the chickens and gasoline and anything else they wanted. Did that make me a coward?

Rylen was no coward. At the moment I kind of wished he was, but what were his other options? Stay at our house? They would find him right away if he were on the suspicion list.

Dad came over forty minutes later when he was done packing the cars and got in on the digging rotation.

"Both our cars are packed," Dad said through panting breaths. "Food, water, flashlights with batteries, cooking equipment, propane, tents, sleeping bags, all of Grandpa's guns. I think we're good."

When we had about five feet in depth, we stopped and made our way silently back home.

Mom was still sitting on the couch, rubbing Livia's back. Remy was sitting against the wall, hugging her knees to her chest. The three of us washed our hands and faces. Then Tater and I sat on the floor with Remy.

Dad took the recliner, and once again we waited. The room was so quiet that the gurgling growl that came from Tater's stomach seemed to echo off the wall. He patted his flat abs.

"There's food in the pantry," Mom said quietly. "Just take it easy."

"I'm the picture of self-control, Ma." Tater stood stiffly, appearing sore. She rolled her eyes, but grinned. I did the same, minus the grin.

Tater strolled back in with two shiny, silver packages of PopTarts. When Mom gave him a glare he said, "It's rude to eat in front of people. I brought this one in case anyone else wanted some." When he opened his and I saw that it was chocolate, Remy and I shot out our hands at the same time. Of course he gave it to her. She ripped it open and handed me one. In the sadness of the past hour, that stupid thing was heavenly. We savored every crumb and then shared a bottle of water.

I looked up and found Livia watching us. "Tater, get one for Livia."

"No, no," she said shyly, but Tater was already on his feet. He brought a package and held it out. She shook her head. "No, I cannot."

"Go on." He gave it a gentle shake. "*Es chocolate*. Rylen would want you to eat."

She hesitantly reached out and opened it. I was relieved

when she began to munch. She was thin to begin with, but lately she was kind of looking gaunt in the face. It couldn't be good for her to eat so little with the baby taking a good portion of her nutrition. When Mom got up to use the restroom, and Remy and Tater were chatting again, I went and sat next to Livia.

"Rylen will be fine," I whispered in Spanish. "He's a quick thinker." She gave a small nod. I glanced at the others, but they weren't paying attention to us, so I went on, keeping my voice low. "If you ever want to visit me at work, if you're ever feeling bad, please come. It's good to have checkups when you're . . ."

Her eyes searched mine with something akin to panic. "¿Ya sabes?" *You know?* Her hand hesitantly roamed to her stomach.

My hands became super interesting to stare at as I whispered in Spanish, "I overheard Rylen when he was getting his vaccine. Nobody else knows."

When I peeked to see if she was upset that I knew, her hands were clasped in her lap and she stared away, expressionless.

I wanted to tell her it was okay, but the sound of a truck's engine hummed outside of our house. We all leapt up and rushed to the window. Rylen climbed out, looking whole and well. His eyes went to the window as he walked up and he nodded.

Dad opened the door and let him in, quickly closing and locking it again.

"Well?" Mom asked.

Rylen rubbed his hands together and we waited, the air between our circle thick with expectancy. "I think they bought it. I didn't see the guys who came to my house. In fact, the two DRI who were there didn't seem to know about the incident, so maybe the other guys hadn't made it back yet, or maybe they really were doing their own thing. They said they'd look into it, but I'm not holding my breath. I didn't tell them about the gun. Just told them I came home to find my dad dead and my barn on fire. They told me to report back in the morning. I asked how I could become a DRP myself, and they said, due to conflicts of interest, DRP are no longer hiring people to work in the towns they're from."

My eyebrows shot up.

"They don't want anyone giving special treatment to people they know," Dad said. He looked at Rylen and cleared his throat. "The uh, the grave is ready."

We all got to our feet. A quiet heaviness loomed over the room. Rylen shifted his stance and looked from the ground around to our faces.

"Do you mind if I do this alone?"

Oh, Ry. It had always been he and his dad against the world.

Dad put a hand on Rylen's shoulder. "Of course not, son. We'll be right here if you need us."

We sat in complete silence when Rylen left. Only a single candle flickered in the room. Tater and I went to wash up and change our clothes. He came out of his room with a too-tight T-shirt, biceps bulging out of the sleeves. His old clothes were too small now.

He let out a dramatic sigh and said, "I'm gonna need some help fighting off all the women who want a piece of this."

Dad snorted and Remy giggled, staring at him until I made a barfing sound.

When Rylen came back, he was covered in dirt, his eyes still red-rimmed, but there were no tear streaks. Tater stood and embraced him. Watching them made the rest of us cry. Even Dad wiped his eyes. I forced myself to remain on the other side of the room as Livia stood and went to Rylen.

When they broke apart, Mom said, "We should get some rest now." She handed Rylen a pack of baby wipes to clean himself.

Tater said, "I figured you'd turn my room into a dance studio."

"Nah, it wasn't big enough." Mom bumped his hip and looked toward Rylen and Livia. Tater picked up on it right away.

"You two take my old room," he said to them. "I got the couch." And before anyone could complain, he dove onto it, grabbing a pillow and manhandling it into a small ball under his head. He closed his eyes and grinned. I grabbed the throw blanket from the back of the couch and dropped it on his face.

"I feel the love," he said from under it.

"Night everyone," I said. I headed to my room before I had to watch Rylen and Livia disappear into a bedroom together. Remy was right behind me. I cracked my window to let in some cool night air. Sounds of crickets drifted in.

Remy and I had shared my bed too many times to count, but it had been awhile. I forgot what a snuggler she was. She had to be touching me at all times, which is exactly how Tater was. Whenever we shared a bed in childhood, I'd wake up with his arms and legs flung over me all night. Right now I was on my back and she was on her side, facing me. She had my arm in a hug, her face pressed against my lower shoulder.

"It's weird to see them together," she whispered. My stomach soured. "I mean, if it's weird for me then I know it has to be super weird for you."

"I'm getting used to it." It was minutely true, but I didn't want to talk about it.

"I'm sad about his dad," she said. "I can't believe he didn't cry."

The shock of it weighed on my chest. I don't think it had sunk in that Len was really gone. It seemed impossible.

"I've only seen him cry once, when he was little. That's just how he is." In some moments he let his emotions show so freely in his expressions and his stance, and in other times he was like a steel vault. But to see his father killed . . . to see him lying there, lifeless. I couldn't imagine the hopeless finality he must have felt.

I hoped Livia was comforting him well. I squeezed my eyes shut, not wanting to think one iota of what that comfort could entail. *Just love him well,* I wished. *Love him for me.*

A humiliating, unexpected sob rose up and I gasped on it, my chest heaving, my eyes burning.

"Amber," Remy whispered, sitting up. And without another word she wrapped her arms around me and I wrapped mine back. She held me while I shuddered, trying to force the emotions back down into their hiding place.

"It's okay," she whispered. "It's okay to be sad."

*No, no, stop,* I wanted to tell her, but I was too busy crying. *Again.* Lord, I was so sick of crying. I pulled away and wiped my eyes.

"I'm all right," I whispered.

"But it's okay if you're not," she reasoned.

"No, Remy, I *need* to be all right. I can't keep feeling like this. Too much is going on. I have to move on. I have to think about the bigger picture and stop feeling sorry for myself."

She was quiet a moment. "You were always so much stronger than me."

"That's not true. We're just strong in different ways."

I lay back down and she slowly relaxed again too.

"I'm glad you're here, Rem."

"Me too. Let's get some sleep."

I rolled over with my back to her. Remy rolled over as well, and squished her butt right up against mine. An unexpected smile pulled at my lips. How many times had I slept butt-to-butt with Remy? So much was changing, but some things were still the same.

# TWENTY-SEVEN

"**L**OOK AT ALL THESE furry creatures," Mom said at the breakfast table the next morning. Grandpa, Dad, Tater, and Rylen were all sporting shaggy short beards of varying color. We'd pulled up folding chairs and squeezed everyone in.

"Es oogly," Abuela said. I snorted my coffee and everyone laughed.

Tater rubbed his face. "Abuela, I look *good*."

"Noo." She shook her head. Remy was dying next to me.

"Aw, come on, Mama," Dad said to her. "We can't waste precious water keeping up our baby faces."

"Es okay," Abuela said. "Use *all* the agua." The laughter continued as Mom passed out paper plates of salt-n-pepper grits with strips of fried Spam.

"You keep feeding us like kings and queens and we'll run out of supplies right fast," Grandpa said.

"We have to eat," Mom told him. "And these are much smaller portions than we'd normally have. So hush." She kissed his head.

He shoved in a bite and said around a full mouth, "Damn, I forgot how much I loved Spam."

Now it was Tater's turn to nearly spit his coffee. Rylen stayed quiet, but kept a small smile on his face. Knowing him, he was hurting terribly, but glad to be surrounded by friends and family, and glad everyone was happy.

When we were finished, Mom looked from me to Remy to Livia and said, "All right girls. Time to wash your hair. I boiled a huge pot of water before breakfast and it's cooling. Tater?"

"Yes, ma'am?"

"Carry that pot into the bathroom for me."

"Hooah." He stood and did what she'd asked, and his tongue stuck out between his teeth as he concentrated on not spilling. Also, his biceps bulged from holding it up. Remy stared at him as he passed.

"Gross." I nudged her.

She hissed in my ear, "When did you brother get so effing hot?"

"Ew!" I hissed back, making her laugh.

Remy, Livia, and I went in the bathroom. Mom came in and shut the door. She had spread out a row of towels on the floor in front of the tub. I took my shirt off so I was in my bra.

"Are we getting nekkid?" Remy asked.

"No, just your shirt," I said, then I knelt in the middle of the tub.

"All three of you," Mom said.

Remy took off her shirt to reveal a gorgeous pink lacy thing that unnecessarily pushed up her perky D-cup. They bounced when she kneeled next to me.

"Show off," I said.

She giggled. "You're not too bad yourself." She poked the side of my black bra. I was more than a full B, but not quite big enough for a C. Mine looked miniature compared to hers.

"Girls," Mom scolded. She looked at Livia, who still stood, appearing frightened. Mom told her in Spanish, "You can leave your shirt on if you prefer. We'll give you a dry one."

She seemed to consider and finally shook her head. Slowly, she raised her shirt over her head and I had to try not to stare. Not at her petite chest or the bones that showed, but at the greenish old bruises along her ribcage and collarbones. They looked like they were from severe injuries sustained a while ago. She squatted at my side and brought a hand up to her chest when she saw me looking. I quickly turned toward the tub.

My God . . . what happened to her?

Livia's chin lowered as if in shame. This time when I turned to her, I met her eyes and gave her a smile. Then I leaned into the tub, pulled out my rubber band, and pushed my hair over my head. The other girls followed suit. Mom poured cups of warm water over our heads and we moaned and laughed as we worked our locks into lathers. We washed our faces too.

"Mrs. Tate, you are my hero," Remy said when we were done and towels were wrapped around our heads. She gave Mom a huge hug. Livia thanked Mom and slipped her shirt back over her damp head before heading out of the bathroom.

"What happened to her?" Remy whispered.

Mom and I both shook our heads and shared a sad look.

"I don't know," she said.

"Me either. It must have happened in Guatemala." I knew there were things Rylen wasn't telling us, and it was none of our business.

We took off the towels and hung them, then brushed our hair.

"What can I do today to help?" Remy asked my mom.

"Well, it's not much fun, but Abuela and I need to get some laundry cleaned. Just the essentials. We have to do them by hand." She raised an eyebrow.

"I'll totally help!" Remy said quickly. "We'll be like pioneer women."

Mom shook her head, clearly amused. "Try to keep that attitude. You'll need it after the first hour."

"Gee, wish I could help," I said. "But I've got to go to work." I winked and Mom shoved me out of the bathroom. Thankfully my shirt was back on because I ran right into Rylen in the hall coming out of Tater's bedroom. I forced myself not to jump away.

"Hey," I said. When he gave me his soft smile, I couldn't help myself. I reached out and hugged him around the waist, enveloping myself in his smell. He fully hugged me back. Standing there in the otherwise empty hall felt strangely private despite a houseful of people. For a few seconds everything else was drowned out, and it was only us. Then I heard Tater's laughter in another room and I slowly pulled away.

"Thank you," he whispered.

"How are you feeling?" I shook my head. "Never mind . . . that's a stupid question."

"No, it's not." He rubbed the blond hair along his jaw. "I'm pissed, to be honest. I've got a lot of questions and I doubt I'll get any answers. But I'll get by. Long as I have you guys."

"You'll always have us." I shuffled my feet. "Well, good luck this morning."

"Thanks." He plucked my nose and we went our separate ways.

*See,* I told myself. *You can do this.* Keep it sisterly. No big deal.

Even though I'd told Livia she should visit the clinic, I was still surprised when I saw her. My face lit up in a true smile and I hugged her gently. We sat down in the small exam room, leaving the door open per the new rule.

"How are you feeling?" I asked her in Spanish. "Any sickness?"

"I feel sick all day, but I never vomit. I feel hungry all day, but when I try to eat it is too difficult. Except the sweet things from your brother . . ."

"The PopTarts?" I asked. "You can have them all! They're yours."

She gave an embarrassed laugh and looked down at her hands in her lap.

"That is normal, what you're feeling. I've heard it can be like that." I took out the blood pressure cuff and got all of her stats. She was doing well. I got a bottle of prenatal vitamins for her. "You have to take these with food or they can hurt your stomach. You can start with just half a pill."

She took it and gave me a grateful smile, then stared down at the bottle. "Ry-*len*, he worries. I want to be healthy for him."

"He's going to be such a good dad." It just sort of slipped out. I stared at the bottle of vitamins too. "I've always thought that about him."

"He loves you."

I looked up at her, shocked. "Yeah. I'm like a sister to him."

She stared at me in a hard calculating way that took me by surprise. "You love him too."

In my nervousness I slipped back into English. "I . . . I mean, yes, I do, but not—"

"Es okay. I know." She responded in English too. She pointed to her eyes. "I can see."

"Livia," I said. My heart felt like it would explode with each pound. I forced myself to concentrate on speaking Spanish again. "It is nothing like that. I swear."

"I believe you. But Rylen was not planning marriage. He saved me, but ruined his own life."

"Wha—" I shook my head. "No. What do you mean, he saved you?"

Her face . . . I watched as her eyes unfocused, as if thinking about the past, and a grimace appeared, making her close her eyes. "My father. He was ashamed of me. He punished me in our market street for everyone to see. I was a helper to our doctor, much like you, and the doctor . . ." She swallowed hard, her eyes glistening. "My father wanted me to marry him. To seduce him so he would marry me."

She sucked in a breath and covered her mouth. Her other trembling hand went to her stomach.

"Oh, my God," I whispered.

"The baby is not Rylen's," she said. "The doctor made me his lover, but he would not marry me. He told my father I was a whore, and my father needed to punish me in public to keep our family name clean."

"Wait." My voice was low and dangerous, filled with anger. "Your *father* gave you those bruises?" I had never been more appalled.

She nodded. Her eyes fluttered open, filled with moisture. "I tried to fight. My cousins held me down. He cracked my bones. I was choking on blood, but Rylen stopped him."

My heart was in my throat, pounding uncontrollably.

"Excuse me," came a sweet voice from the doorway. Mine and Livia's heads spun toward the face of our DRI woman. To my horror, she looked straight at Livia and began speaking in perfect, polished Spanish. "My dear, it is my job to keep records for all of our town. I could not help but to overhear— did you say that the child you carry is not your husband's?"

I was on my feet, feeling like I'd been doused in fire. I opened my mouth and the DRI lady looked straight at me. *"Don't speak,"* she said lyrically. "I am addressing Mrs. Fite."

My mouth hung there, the words dead before they left my throat. I felt all of the anger deflate from my chest, leaving me with a cool numbness.

"This will stay completely private," the woman told Livia. "Just between us. Was the father of Guatemalan heritage, like yourself?"

Livia confirmed this, looking worried.

The DRI woman's voice softened, taking on a gentle tone I wasn't used to hearing from her. "And how do you feel about this pregnancy?"

Oh my freaking . . . hell no . . . why was my mouth not working? This line of questioning was highly unprofessional.

Sweet Livia shrugged, seeming to struggle. The woman stared hard. "It seems you are not happy."

Livia dropped her gaze, and the woman nodded.

"I see. Okay, then. Have you had your vaccination for the Red Virus?"

Liv confirmed. "Sí."

"Good, that's good. Well, I have one more preemptive shot to give pregnant women in these trying times. It is full of vitamins and minerals and will guard you against several flu strands."

I narrowed my eyes, overcome with apprehension, and

my voice finally burst out. "What shot is this?"

"It's new," she said without looking at me. She pulled out a plastic container with a single dose needle inside. My heart began to pound again.

"What's the name of it? I've never heard of it before."

Now she looked at me. She had lost her smile. "Are you an expert on all things, Miss Tate? Are you an obstetrician?"

"Of course not, I just—"

The woman switched to English and said curtly. "Please, let me work. I'm *helping* her."

She smiled pleasantly at Livia, who shot a fearful look in my direction as the woman lifted her sleeve.

"Are there any side effects?" I quickly asked. "She's not feeling well. Will it make her—"

Livia flinched as the woman poked her arm with the needle and squeezed the serum into her muscle.

"There now. Nausea and cramping might follow, but you will be just fine."

She left the room and I had to lean against the table. Livia rubbed her arm.

"It's okay," I whispered. "I'm sure it's okay." I was being paranoid. I needed to calm down because I was pretty sure my actions were freaking her out. Before the DRI woman had come in, there was so much I wanted to ask Livia, but now was not the time. Not that I knew that woman was listening. "How did you get here?" I asked.

"Your papá," she said. I helped her up and walked her outside. Dad was waiting in the car, reading an old Army magazine. I gave Livia a hug and what I hoped was a reassuring smile.

"Thank you for opening up to me today. I promise it will stay between us."

She nodded and walked around to the passenger side.

Dad frowned when he saw our faces. "Everything okay?"

"Keep an eye on her," I said quietly. "And please, make sure she gets a chocolate PopTart."

He chuckled. "Sure thing."

"How'd it go this morning with trying to get gas?"

He grinned. "Turns out it's useful to have Tater around. He and the owner's son played football together. We're all set."

"Nice." I smiled.

"Love ya, Amber."

"Love ya too." I kissed his cheek and went back into the clinic, a place that used to make me feel useful, but now made me feel confined. And disgusted.

I spent the rest of the day teetering between calming myself down over that shot, and feeling gutted about Livia's story. My heart was like this raw thing left jagged by too many emotions. Though it killed me that Rylen was married, I was so thankful he'd stopped Livia's dad from killing her.

As far as the shot went, I had to stop letting my prejudice of the weird DRI people make me act like a psycho. I definitely needed to have more self-control over my reactions too. I finally felt a fraction calmer when it was time to leave work later that night.

I pulled up at our house and Tater flung open the front door. He leaped down the porch steps and sprinted over. The alarmed look on his face made me jump out of the car, going straight into work mode. Alert and ready. Mom was in the doorway waving me in. She appeared panicked too.

"What's going on?"

Tater nearly collided into me. "Livia is sick!"

*Damn it!* My heart sank clear down to my feet and for a second I couldn't move. Tater grabbed my arm and I ran. She was on the lower bunk in Tater's room, crying pitifully, her knees pulled up. Her hair was slicked back with sweat. She let out a scream and her body convulsed. Rylen and I met eyes—his helpless fear gutted me.

Mom had a cold rag in her hand, which I grabbed and ran to her. I practically had to push Ry out of the way to get full access. I sat at her side and wiped her forehead.

"I'm here, Liv." She was in too much pain to do anything but writhe and cry.

"What's happening to her?" Rylen asked.

"How long has she been like this?"

He shook his head and looked at Mom. "Twenty minutes, maybe?"

Livia was wearing dark jeans and her back was to the wall.

"Close the door," I told Mom. It was just her, Rylen, Livia, and me. I scooted back on the bed to get a better look. Her pants looked wet. I gently moved her and I was just as I expected. Blood covered the sheets under her.

"She's having a miscarriage," I whispered.

Mom sucked in a breath. "She's pregnant?"

Rylen's face crumbled. He sat by her side again and used the cloth to wipe her face. "She's been under a lot of stress."

"I don't think this is natural." My mouth was bone dry. "I think this was a forced miscarriage. Ry . . ." He looked at me, his brow tight. "The DRI did this."

I expected him to tell me I was crazy. And for Mom to tell me not to jump to conclusions. But Mom remained quiet and Rylen asked in all seriousness, "She said they gave her a shot today and you weren't happy about it. You think the shot did this?"

"Yeah, I do." The question was, why? *Why* wouldn't they want her to have the baby?

# TWENTY-EIGHT

**T**HAT WAS THE QUESTION of the past couple weeks, wasn't it? Why? Why was the world dying? Why were the Outliers doing this? Why were DRI acting so strangely and enforcing such tyrannical rules? Why were they asking questions about race, and why would they seemingly punish Livia for being impregnated by a man in Guatemala? Was it some morality issue, because she wasn't having her husband's baby? It felt like there was so much they weren't telling us. I could not understand.

The three of us were silent for a long while, thinking, and Livia finally began to hush, too, as if her pain were easing. She whimpered and Rylen quickly took her hand.

"You're okay," he murmured.

Mom placed her hand on Rylen's shoulder. "Let us clean up. We'll call you back in in a few minutes."

He kissed Livia's forehead and left us.

"El bebé?" Livia whispered.

Mom took her hand and whispered back. "Lo siento, preciosa. El bebé se ha ido." *The baby is gone.*

Livia's squeezed her eyes shut and her face crumbled. She threw an arm over her eyes and cried.

"Lo siento," Mom murmured over and over. *I'm sorry.*

"No," she gasped. "No . . . Dios respondió mi oración."

Mom's face turned to me, gaping in surprise.

*God answered my prayer.*

My heart ached for her. I could understand. Not from personal experience, but I could see how she'd feel that way after what she'd been through. I thought of the DRI woman saying, "I'm helping her."

So weird. Like she knew. Or she *assumed* after eavesdropping on our conversation. But that was a dangerous assumption to make on behalf of a pregnant woman. I was still officially pissed, answered prayer or not.

When Livia calmed down, we helped her change into clean clothes, and Mom took hers to be washed, along with the sheets. I brushed her hair and pulled it back. Rylen came in, going immediately to her side. She looked so small and fragile in his muscular arms. I left them alone.

Remy and Tater were side-by-side on the couch, watching me for news.

"She'll be okay," I said.

They both relaxed.

Grandpa let himself in the front door at that moment, locking it behind him. He was carrying a big folded paper.

"What's that?" I asked.

Grandpa gave me a look. "You never seen a map?"

Tater laughed at me and slapped his knee.

"When have you ever used a paper map?" I asked Tater.

"We use 'em all the time in the military." He stuck out his tongue and I did a fake lunge at him, stomping my foot. He flinched and now it was my turn to laugh.

"Girl, don't make me—"

Grandpa interrupted loudly. "I mapped out an escape route."

Escape route. Twenty-four hours ago I would have thought the phrase was unnecessary and even amusing. But after last night, the possible need for an escape route was far too realistic.

We followed him into the dining room where he spread the map on the table. Abuela sat at the end of the table with her hands clasped. Rylen came in to join us.

"How is she?" Mom whispered.

"Resting." The planes of his face seemed sharper than normal. He stared down at the map, his body rigid with tension.

Grandpa stabbed a finger at a mountain range just south-east of our town. "Clover mountains," Grandpa said.

Dad nodded, scratching his chin. "That's all wilderness area. Plenty of trees and valleys for cover."

"A big stream runs through it too," Rylen answered.

"Didn't we camp there once?" I asked.

Dad grinned at Mom and she let out an exasperated breath. "It was my first time seeing a scorpion, okay?"

Now Dad outright chuckled. "It was back when we first moved here. We hadn't even set the tents up yet. We took a short hike, Mom saw a scorpion, and we were back in the car fifteen minutes later."

"You didn't tell me there'd be scorpions there."

"It's the desert!" Dad said. "If we stayed around we would have seen even cooler stuff like snakes and—"

"Ew, no more!" I rubbed my arms and Remy shivered next to me.

"You know I can't handle anything with scales or little whipping tails," Mom said.

Grandpa forged ahead, all business. "I'll take snakes and

scorpions any day over corrupt humans. We can get to this range using all back roads and private, abandoned lanes. In some places we could even cut through on flat dirt expanses, but we have to watch for bigger rocks."

We leaned in and looked at the fingers of ink Grandpa had drawn, all leading to the mountains.

"Looks good, Pop." Dad clapped him on the back. "Thanks for organizing."

Grandpa pulled a perfectly-folded rectangular map from his back pocket and slapped it against Dad's chest. "Made one for you, too."

The sound of tires in our driveway made us all go still. When we heard the opening and closing of doors, Remy and I grabbed hands. Grandpa snatched back Dad's map and shoved them both inside his shirt before falling into the rocking chair.

"Stay here," Dad whispered to us. Mom clutched her chest and ran to Abuela's side. All of the men went to the living room to see who it was. Screw that. I wanted to see too. I creeped out, ignoring Mom's hiss for me to get back there. Remy grabbed the back of my shirt and followed me.

"Fuckin' Drips and Derps," Tater whispered low as he peered through the shades.

Dad cursed a whisper of his own. Rylen's hands curled into fists. Grandpa's chin went up in defiance just as the knock came. Fear jolted through me. My anxiousness was only expounded by seeing the men in my family all stall for half a second, their faces unsure. But when Dad opened the door, his demeanor was poised and friendly.

"First Sergeant Tate?" asked a DRI man I'd never seen before.

"Yes, sir, that's me. How can I help you?"

"The local Disaster Relief Initiative, along with each town

member, is combining our efforts for a Lincoln County food bank." He handed a paper to Dad. "Every household in the county is being ordered to donate all of their nonperishable food items. Each family will be given a voucher good for one trip to the food bank each week. In this way, resources will be shared equally."

Dad's face remained pleasant, but I could see the tightness in his jaw. He held the paper tightly, crumpling the part that was in his hand.

"Sort of like communism?" Grandpa asked.

The DRI shot his eyes to Grandpa. "Sort of like keeping everyone alive."

They were going to take all of our food. My breaths were coming short as the DRP men pushed their way in, heading for the kitchen with boxes. One remained at the DRI's side, his giant gun seeming ten times the normal size. They were maskless. I didn't recognize any of them.

"You don't have to do a thing," the DRI said pleasantly to Dad. "We'll pack everything up for you and be out of your way momentarily."

"What's going on?" I heard Mom say from the kitchen as men tromped in there.

"Just stay where you are," Dad called to her. "Everything is fine."

Remy's hands tightened on my shirt and she moved closer to me. Sounds of cans and boxes being thrown together came from the kitchen.

"I take it you're going to leave us some of our resources?" Dad asked. "We've got quite a crew as you can see."

"Everything goes. Tomorrow at ten AM your town is having a mandatory meeting at the high school. Ration cards for the food pantry will be given at that time. Plan to be there most of the day."

Oh, no. That sounded brutal. Dad rubbed his face. "So, none of us can eat for approximately the next eighteen hours, give or take?"

The DRI faced him, stony. "That is the reality everyone in your town is facing, yes. That is the reality we are trying to combat."

Grandpa was so still in the rocker, his hands so tight on the handles, face so red that I worried he'd blow a gasket at any moment. As long as they didn't go upstairs to Grandpa's room, we'd still be okay.

The men came through the living room, and it took every single ounce of my will-power not to snatch the opened box of chocolate PopTarts from the top when they passed me. God help us, they were even taking our cases of water!

But wait . . . Dad had packed the back of our cars. Would they check there too? Hope and worry stirred in my chest. *It'll be okay, don't panic.* I didn't mind sharing with others, especially with the malnourished people I saw coming into the clinic lately, but I hated the thought of having to rely fully on the DRI.

The Drip remained where he was, like he was waiting for word from the Derps that they were done with their search and siege.

Remy and I walked to the window and watched as they put the boxes in the back of a truck, and then they huddled together as if discussing.

*Leave, please leave,* I silently begged. The men began to look up toward the room over the garage and then down at a clipboard. My hope turned to lead, sinking so quickly I rocked back. One of the men ran up the steps, then back down. *No . . .*

The Derp came back in and said to the DRI, "Says here there are more resources in a storage area above the garage, but it's locked."

The DRI looked to Dad. "We're going to need the key, sir."

Dad looked to Grandpa. "Give him your key, Pop."

Grandpa turned his full, chin-high righteousness on the DRI man, and said, "I worked in this country for sixty years, and I worked hard. I earned every single item in that room, and I specifically got them to care for my family. It's my God-given right to keep—"

"Sir," the DRI cut in. "In these times there is no room to squabble over individual rights. We must care for society as a whole before we can—"

"Don't you interrupt me!" Grandpa shot to his feet.

The DRI's mouth shut tight and the glare he gave Grandpa made me dizzy.

Oh, God. I closed my eyes.

"Pop!" Dad shouted, his eyes beseeching. "Just give him the God damned key."

"This has gone far enough," Grandpa said. I couldn't even believe my ears. Didn't he remember what happened to Len? What I'd told him about those people in Coyote Springs?

"Grandpa, please," I whispered. "It's just food. We'll get more."

His eyes were moist and filled with sorrow when he turned to me. "It's about so much more than food."

"The key." The DRI held out his hand to Grandpa, who did not move. "Are you refusing to cooperate?" At his tone of finality, the Derp pointed his gun. Remy and I both gasped and pushed back against the window. My heart slammed like a basketball in my chest.

Rylen put up his hands and stepped in front of Grandpa, facing the Derp. "Whoa now, take it easy."

"*Move*," the DRI man commanded, his voice making my

insides shake and calm. To my surprise, Rylen slowly moved aside, but Tater stepped right up into the same spot, "He's just a crazy old man. Give us a second, we'll get the key."

Dad lunged forward, grasping Grandpa by the wrist and trying to get his other hand in Grandpa's pocket.

"*Move*," the DRI man commanded Tater. My brother swallowed hard and he moved aside too, like he was being forced by invisible hands, his face scrunched.

Dad and Grandpa struggled.

"Son," Grandpa said thickly. "There comes a time when you got to stand for something."

"This is a time to *shut up*," Dad begged. His voice shook.

"Grandpa, please!" I said again. Tater seemed to break from his trance and moved to help Dad get the key. The DRI raised his hand in some sort of signal. Suddenly pain shot through my ears—a overly loud *bang* and screams—one of which tore from my own throat. I moved forward as Grandpa fell, but Remy caught me by the shoulders and yanked me back, circling her arms around me from behind.

Grandpa's chest was gaping, red, his face a macabre mask of surprise. I crumbled to my knees and Remy came down behind me. My ears rang, thumping, making it impossible to hear. Everything moved in slow motion, blurred. Dad fell over Grandpa's face, holding his cheeks. Mom came running in and fell to her knees beside him. Rylen had Tater in a wrestling move, his arms under Tater's armpits, as if holding him back from going crazy.

Tater's face, the blood splatter on him . . . it matched the utter horror I felt.

The DRI walked over and crouched next to Grandpa's still body. He dug into the trouser pocket and pulled out a set of keys. Then, he stood.

"A mandatory curfew is now in effect. You are not to leave

your home until tomorrow morning when you will report to the high school. Your streets are being watched."

"We have to bury him," Dad croaked.

"Fine. But you are not to leave the vicinity of your own yard, and only on foot, no cars."

He walked out of the house, followed by the Derp who'd shot Grandpa, and our family was alone.

I tore out of Remy's grasp as Rylen released Tater. I shoved everyone out of the way and shouted, "Get his shirt off!"

Dad and Tater ripped from either side. It was a gory mess. I put my hands in, feeling, but his chest was like a soupy bowl of mixed bone, blood, and tissue. I found his heart, but it wasn't whole anymore.

"No." My hands trembled inside of my grandfather's chest. I couldn't save him.

# TWENTY-NINE

E BURIED GRANDPA THAT night under our orange tree, which had been picked clean by the DRI. Remy asked if she could say a blessing over him. It was short, but she knew all the lovely words to say. Words that were a vivid contrast from what we'd witnessed, but inexplicably comforting all the same. When she was done, Abuela crossed herself and dabbed her eyes, pulling her shawl tight over her shoulders.

I don't remember walking back to the house in the dark. Abuela scrubbed the walls first, then the carpet; she wouldn't let anyone help. Tater paced the living room beside her. The rest of us sat, in silence. Livia was on Rylen's lap in grandpa's rocker. Her head was on his shoulder and she still looked tired. All of us had red eyes and puffy cheeks from crying. Dad and Tater had bawled the hardest after we buried him.

"I moved when he told me to," Tater muttered. "I don't even know why. I wasn't scared. I didn't even try to stop, I just . . . moved."

"I did too," Rylen whispered. It *had* been strange. I'd

been relieved when both of them moved, but I'd also been surprised.

"You didn't do anything wrong," Dad said hoarsely. He looked down at Abuela, who was scrubbing fiercely. "Mama, you don't have to do that. We're not staying."

She sat up. "We leave? Now?"

"No. Tomorrow. Right after this damn meeting."

Mom nodded.

"I clean." Abuela put her elbows into it. I picked up the bucket of disgusting water and dumped it out back, then filled it again with boiled water from the pot on top of the camper stove.

"We should all get to bed," Mom said softly. "It's going to be a long day tomorrow."

Nobody moved for another five minutes. I think we were too tightly bonded in our tangled web of emotions. I was afraid to let any of them out of my sight.

"Keep your window closed," Mom called to me. "And locked."

"Okay," I whispered.

"Hey." Tater grabbed my arm and I turned to see his drooping face. He smelled like earth from digging Grandpa's grave. I still had dirt under my nails from helping.

"Oh, Tater." I hugged him for a long time until he let me go. It was late. We were all so exhausted.

Remy and I curled up together in my bed, and for once I didn't mind the snuggling. I didn't want to be alone. We fell asleep hip-to-hip with our arms linked and the sides of our heads tilted together. I woke in the morning alone and chilly. I blinked through the dimness of dawn light and saw a huge mass on Remy's side. At first I thought it was just her balled up in all the covers, but then my eyes popped.

Remy and Tater were sleeping soundly on the other side

of my queen-sized bed, twined together like a Celtic knot, blankets interwoven.

"Um . . ." My voice made them stir. Tater looked down at Remy a moment as if confused, and then gave me a goofy grin. Remy stretched, making her boobs press against him.

"Stop that." I nudged her shoulder.

"Yeah, stop that," Tater said. "I'm not that kind of boy."

His tone wasn't quite as joking as usual—there was still a heaviness about him. Remy sat up and pulled her knees in. Tater lay back with his hands behind his head, staring at the ceiling.

"When did you come in?" I asked.

"Not long after y'all came to bed. You two were asleep fast."

I guess he didn't want to be alone. I grasped a blanket and pulled until I got enough to snuggle down on my side, facing them. "I don't want to go to this thing today. I wish we could leave right now."

"Me too," Tater said.

Remy was quiet a minute. "My parents will be there." She paused. "I guess I should probably stay with them."

I reached out and laced our fingers together. As much as I wanted to beg her to come with, I knew she probably did need to be with her family. Who knew where us Tates and Fites would end up, and there'd be no way to let her parents know.

"That sucks," Tater whispered.

Remy looked down at her toes. "Yeah. I don't want you guys to go. I mean, I understand, but I'm going to miss you."

I held her fingers tighter. The three of us lay there together until the room brightened and we heard others moving about. Obviously there was no breakfast to be had, but the Derps hadn't touched Mom's ceramic storage containers on

the counter, so we were able to have hot tea with sugar before we left. We each packed bookbags with all of the essentials we could manage. For me it was clothes, pads, tampons,
sunscreen, lip gloss, and chapstick. Mom assured me she
packed our bathroom toiletries.

I was really not looking forward to camping in the wild,
but at least we'd hopefully be free from the fears of the DRI.
After last night, I'd never feel safe in this house again. I avoided looking down at the carpet in the living room. Abuela
had done a good job, but you could still tell something dark
had been there. Remembering made me nearly lose my tea.
I closed my eyes and steadied myself on the back of a dining
room chair.

"Now all we need is to be armed," I heard Tater say.

"Your wish is our command," Dad told him.

"Whatchu got, Dad?" Tater asked with excitement.

"Pop's hideaway cabinet was loaded. They're all packed in
the back of the car underneath stuff now. I'll show you everything when we get to the mountains tonight. They took all
our spare gasoline from the garage, but I've got a small one
in the back of each car. Let's head out now. Ry and Liv, you
can ride with us. It's probably best if your truck is left at your
property and not the school." Rylen nodded. We'd agreed to
only take two cars and to leave his truck behind since it was
kind of old and loud. Dad had a newer 4x4 SUV, and Mom
had a quiet sedan.

"Another thing," Dad said. "Act normal today. Don't give
them any reason to suspect that we're upset or preparing to
run." We all nodded.

Tater and Remy rode with me. My heart ached as we left
behind our childhood home. I had so many great memories
there, but the newer memories would forever taint the good
ones. Tater stared over his shoulder.

"Man . . . ten more seconds and we would have had the key. That's all they had to wait."

"It stopped being about the key as soon as Grandpa defied him," I said.

Remy remained quiet.

"A seventy-two year old man," Tater raged. "He wasn't a threat to anyone! Old dudes run their mouths, that's what they do. There was no fucking reason to kill him. I swear to God, if I see that fucker who pulled the trigger—"

"Jacob!" I yelled. "If you see him, you better not say a damn word!" I glared at him hard, but he had that stubborn look of Tate anger on his face. "I'm not kidding. I will personally throat chop you so hard if you so much as side-eye that guy." I was nearly in tears, just thinking about Tater being shot down.

"Please don't do anything," Remy whispered.

"Relax," he said to us.

I gripped the steering wheel hard enough to rip it off. Tater rubbed his tanned palms down his jeans. His dark eyes were bright, but his mouth was tight.

"I'm not gonna do anything," he said. "Seriously, stop popping a blood vessel. I *want* to do something, but I won't. Someday, maybe, but not yet."

I exhaled my frustration and relaxed my hold on the wheel.

We got to the school and there were only about half the cars as there were for the last meeting.

"Where is everyone?" Remy asked.

"Well, let's see," Tater snapped. "Some are dead. Some had to walk 'cause they got no gas." He pointed to a line of bicycles next to the building. "See. But I'd say most are dead."

"Tater *stop*," I begged. He got out and slammed the door. Remy's eyes started watering.

"He's just upset," I told her.

I left my stuff in the car, but made sure to have my ID since they always asked for it. We got in the long line, and I was glad it wasn't hot or cold because it felt like we stood out there forever.

Inside, once the gym filled up, it was only half full, unlike the last meeting when the room was bursting at the seams. I hated the feeling of despair in the air. When I looked around at the sunken faces and crying children, I was glad they'd be getting food vouchers. It wasn't something that my grandfather should have been killed over, but I did see the importance of feeding the masses.

At every entrance and exit, and scattered throughout the room, were armed Disaster Relief Police—Derps. I didn't recognize any of them, nor did I see the one who shot Grandpa. They stared around like they were in a prison camp, and we were going to start revolting or attacking at any moment. I hated how they held their guns, all of them at the ready to shoot. I could not relax.

Many of the people in the gymnasium were friends and acquaintances, local business owners. Remy spotted her parents and I hugged her good-bye. When she started to walk away, Tater grabbed her and hugged her too, whispering, "Sorry I was an ass," before letting her go.

Abuela got a seat. Tater, Rylen, Livia, and I stood against the back wall and watched as Mom said hello to people she knew from her dance studio. Dad stood silently at her side. I wondered if they were telling people what happened. Probably not.

A couple people greeted Tater, welcoming him home, old classmates and parents of classmates who recognized him. They shook Rylen's hand too. But not an ounce of cheer was in anyone's voice. When people asked me how things were going in the medical world, I forced a smile and said, "Just fine." We were all faking it. The older people complained about their aches and pains, but that was nothing new. The younger generations, though . . . we all seemed to be pretending to be fine. Like everyone was scared to criticize the current situation. And that freaked me out more than anything. It was like our freedom of speech had silently been revoked among our other lost rights.

The same DRI woman as last time took the podium and tapped the mic, making that awful feedback screech through the room again. I cringed until it was over.

"Good morning. Thank you for coming."

"Like we had a choice," Tater muttered from the side of his mouth.

"Shut up," I hissed. Without moving, I shuffled my eyes back and forth to make sure none of the Derps had looked our way.

The DRI woman began droning on and on about how they were working to ensure that each family would have equal and substantial amounts of food, and how they'd made outstanding progress sorting possible enemies from innocent citizens. Everything in me clenched in anger at that comment, since clearly they could not discern criminals from harmless, unarmed grandfathers. The entire room was fraught with taut tension.

My eyes wandered around the room and halted on a Derp staring straight at me. It took a moment for me to recognize the man across the room in a DRP uniform.

Julian!

A tiny smile graced his lips and he gestured to the side with his head. Seconds later, he slipped out through a side door of the gym. I looked up just as the DRI woman said, "I'm sure some of you have questions, and I can answer a few . . ." At least fifty hands shot up. This could take a while.

"You guys," I whispered to Tater and Rylen. "My friend Julian is here. He's a DRP! I'm going to talk to him real quick."

"Not without me," Tater whispered back.

Rylen motioned for Livia to go sit with our parents and he followed us. I glanced back as we walked toward the doors and saw Livia watching with pursed lips.

A huge, bald Derp stepped right in front of the door, gun across his back.

"Where are you going?"

"Uh . . . to the restroom," I said.

"All three of you?" The guys nodded and the Derp frowned. "You can't go without an escort."

I held my breath, waiting for Tater to say something like, "What are we, five-year-olds?" But thankfully he kept his mouth shut.

"I'll take them," said Julian, rounding the corner. He kept a straight face, bored even. It was so weird to see him in that uniform. What was he doing here?

The bald Derp moved aside. Another set of footsteps came rushing toward us and a sweet voice said, "Oh, can I please go too, sir? I'll be quick."

Remy! I held back a smile.

The Derp let out an annoyed huff and waved the four of us out the door of the gym. We followed Julian around the corner to the hall with the bathrooms, and we all looked around to be sure we were alone. Julian opened his mouth to talk, but Tater shook his head and pointed to a side door at the end of the hall. We followed him quickly through the door, which led to a back hallway where I'd never been.

Once we were in the back hall, Tater said, "This is the athletic storage wing. We used to sneak back here to skip class."

I looked at Julian. "You're a DRP?"

"Yup. They closed down the elementary school clinic when they ran out of resources. I talked them into giving me this job so I could get my parents some food, but they wouldn't let me work in my own city. I recognized the name of your town on the job list and requested it. I was hoping I'd see you today. Things are fucked up, Tate." His eyes were rounded like they'd get when we pulled up at a bad scene.

"What's going on?" Rylen asked.

"You guys need to get out of here. Slip out a back door or something."

My heart pumped. "Why?"

"They're not letting anyone go home. They're bussing everyone to some supposed safe shelter area."

"What?" Remy's round face turned a shade of porcelain white.

"The DRI say the whole town is under investigation and it's not safe for people."

"They're not shipping us anywhere," Tater said. He looked at me. "Come on, let's get Mom and Dad and Abuela and get the fuck out of here."

Julian grabbed his arm as he turned. "You can't get them out. Once you go back in there, you're stuck, man."

"I have to get Livia." Rylen's stricken face made my chest ache.

"We should go back in there," Remy said in a shaking voice. "If the town's not safe—"

"It's bullshit, Remy," Tater said. "The only thing wrong with this town is that it's overrun with those assholes."

Remy covered her mouth, trembling all over, her eyes darting to the door. I took her hand and she looked at me with unfocused eyes.

"We can't let ourselves be taken anywhere by them," I

said. "I don't trust them. Not after last night."

Her eyes squeezed shut and two tears streaked down. "But what if they're right? What if the bad guys are here? What if they're trying to keep us safe?"

"Rem, what if they *are* the bad guys? And what if they're trying to take us to some camp like the freaking Nazis?" I asked more harshly than I'd meant, causing her face to scrunch.

"What else can you tell us?" Rylen asked Julian. "How much time do we have?" I could see Rylen's eyes calculating, trying to figure out how he could get our loved ones safely out of that room.

"To be honest, they don't give us information until right before something happens, and even then we don't get the details of why. Just orders. We're told to assume everyone is the enemy. That every person we encounter is one step away from igniting a bomb. Anyone who questions us is not to be trusted." Through the wall were the sounds of bus engines and the hissing sputters of brakes next to the school building. "And as far as how much time? None."

My insides lurched and panic set in.

"Julian, please," I begged. "Can you go in there and try to get our family out?"

He pressed his lips together, but nodded. "I can try."

Remy grasped his arm and quickly gave her parents' names and where they were sitting, along with their descriptions. Julian's face was pinched with worry when he put his hand on the doorknob. He stared down at it as he jostled the unmoving knob.

"Shit!" Tater exclaimed. "I forgot this door locks from the inside!"

"Tater!" I hissed.

"What? It's been years! We used to put paper in the jamb

to keep it from locking." He grasped the top of his head with his hands and began to pace.

Rylen pointed down the narrow hall. "That door exits the side of the school." He looked at Julian. "Can you run around and go back in through the front?"

We all went still as voices sounded outside the door.

"We all need to get out," Julian whispered. "They'll check the entire school, and the bald one knows four people left for the bathroom. I'll go back in, but I have to try to avoid him."

I went up on my toes and gave Julian a quick hug. "Thank you. Please be safe."

"Yes, thank you," Remy said.

The five of us rushed down the hall. Julian carefully pushed the door open a crack and peered out into the sunshine, then opened it enough to stick his head out. "It's clear. You guys hide in that field." He pointed to the deadened cornstalks then took off. Julian ran toward the front of the building while the rest of us sprinted into the dry field. When we got deep enough in to be hidden, we all crouched.

"I'm gonna see what's going on," Tater whispered. He deftly moved, weaving seamlessly to avoid moving the stalks.

Remy gave a minute whimper, and I put a hand on her shoulder. "We're doing the right thing, Rem." She swallowed and nodded.

I looked at Rylen, whose jaw was set tightly. He looked primed and edgy, ready to run and fight at a moment's notice. I thought about Julian trying to sneak six people out of there, and my hope wavered. How could he possibly pull it off?

My guts felt like I was on a Tilt-A-Whirl, spinning and dropping as my heart raced. I generally tried to stay positive, especially when I was trying to keep someone else calm, but I felt an overwhelming need to make a Plan B. "What if he can't get them out?" I whispered. "What if they're taken away?"

"Then we'll follow them and get them back," Rylen said matter-of-factly. From the frozen, deadly look on his face, I knew he meant it. His confidence gave me a moment of peace. Even Remy was looking at him as if everything would be okay.

My peace was short-lived.

Voices carried to us from the front of the building where a long line of busses idled. Armed Derps were shouting orders. Feet shuffled along the sidewalks. From inside the building was a muffled, reverberating *crack*, followed by another. Remy gasped. My eyes shot up to Rylen, who had frozen.

"Was that a gunshot?" I whispered.

He gave a stiff nod, and I covered my mouth against a bout of nausea.

"God, please," Remy whispered. "Please." I reached for her and she wrapped a hand around my arm, pulling me close so she could press her face to my shoulder. I put my hand over hers.

"They'll be okay," I whispered.

As we crouched in the cornfield, full busses began to pull away. I stared at the side door, willing our loved ones to burst out, but it remained firmly shut.

"I want to go watch with Tater," I whispered.

"Me too," Remy said.

"All right," Ry whispered.

I led the way, moving slowly and carefully as I'd seen my brother do, until we got to the corner of the field where Tater was watching intently.

"I haven't seen them," he said before I could ask.

"Did you hear the gunfire?" Rylen asked him.

"Yeah." Their expressions were the grave masks of soldiers.

We watched as two more busses were filled, driving away.

At the same time, Tater, Rylen, and I jolted at the sight of Mom, Dad, Abuela, and Livia being shuffled among the herd of people down the walk toward the busses. Crap, Julian wasn't able to get them! I was relieved to see they were okay, but scared to death at the thought of them getting on a bus. So, where was Julian?

"Shit," Tater muttered. He started to stand, but Rylen grabbed him.

"If you walk out there now, they'll kill you," Ry said.

Tater clenched his fists.

"My parents!" Remy said, pointing. Sure enough, her dad had his arm around her mother, who appeared to be crying. Her dad kept looking around. Remy let out a sob. "He's trying to find me! I need to go!"

"Remy, you can't. Just like Tater can't. If we come strolling out of the field they'll know we tried to escape and they'll be suspicious of us. You saw how easily they kill, and you heard Julian say how they're taught to mistrust."

"I can say I just got here. That I was late."

Tater shook his head. "They've got your name on the list."

"We can't let them be taken," I said, watching as the line moved forward. All I could think about was gas chambers and body pits. I know it was morbid, but these people brought out the worst in my imagination.

"I'm going!" Remy shot up, and Tater grasped her around the waist with a strong arm, pulling her down until she was sitting on his lap. She struggled and he covered her mouth. He held down her arms when she clawed at his hand.

"Remy, calm down," I whispered. "Tater, don't hurt her!"

"I'm not! She freakin' cat-scratched me."

"Remy," I said. "Promise you won't yell or try to run, and he'll let you go." She breathed heavily through her nose, and her eyes shone with emotion.

Rylen took a knee beside her. "We can't go out there. How do you think your parents would feel watching you get shot?" Remy's eyes shut and all the fire went out of her. Tater carefully let her go and to my utter shock, Remy turned her face and buried it into Tater's chest. He froze in confusion until her body shuddered. Then he hesitantly put his arms around her.

"It's all right," he whispered into her hair. At the sound of his voice, Remy pulled back abruptly, as if a trance and been broken, and jumped off his lap, moving to crouch beside me and glare at him instead. He eyed her back just as hard.

"Focus," Ry told him.

I ignored them and watched our families. It looked like they'd end up on the same bus. My heart nearly stopped when the side door we'd come out of opened with a click. All four of our heads wrenched to the side, watching in horror as Julian came stumbling out with one hand holding his bloodied neck. He fell to his knees.

*Shit!*

Rylen cursed and I covered my mouth against a scream. The gunshots . . .

"Stay here," Tater said. "I'll get him." He moved fast through the field, disappearing from our view, then cut across the lawn toward the school at a sprint. He was out of sight of the people in the front of the school, but I prayed nobody would hear and come to investigate.

Within a minute, Tater had carried Julian into the corn field and I raced to meet them.

I skidded in the dirt to stop beside Julian's head. The side of his neck was gaping. It wasn't spurting, but I was guessing the worst of the bleeding had happened in the building. I immediately grabbed and held tight with both of my hands. This was not good. This was an artery.

"Julian, sweetie," I said. "Stay with me."

His glazed eyes peered up at me. He'd seen enough injuries to know.

"They . . . know . . . four are . . . gone." His words started as a rasp and ended in a gurgle that made the backs of my eyes burn.

"Julian." I swallowed the moisture that pooled in my throat. Blood seeped from beneath my hands.

"Safecamp . . . in . . . Mo . . ." His eyes fluttered.

"Where, Julian? Stay with us." I looked up at Tater and said, "Pat his cheeks."

Tater did, and Julian's eyes opened. "Mojave."

"They're taking them to Mojave Desert?" Rylen asked.

His eyes closed and he let out a barely audible sigh of, "Yeah." His chest heaved with great effort and he commanded, "Get . . . out . . ."

Julian went still, and his blood flow slowed beneath my fingers. I could barely see him through the tears that began to silently trail down my face. "No," I whispered. In two days I'd watched two people I cared about breathe their last breaths. I'd held their lives in my hands and been unable to save them. Remy sat at Julian's feet, staring at us from just above her knees, watching as the guy she used to flirt with died.

"No," I said louder. "Wrap his neck in something. One of your shirts." I grasped Julian's chin and tipped it up, pinching his nose to begin CPR.

"He's gone," Tater said. "He's lost too much blood."

"No." I bent to take his mouth, and Rylen pulled me back, holding me tightly.

"He's gone," Tater repeated. "You heard what he said. They're looking for us. We need to get the fuck away from the school."

Another bus pulled away, but we couldn't see it. I began panting, struggling to breathe.

"Oh, my God . . . that was their bus. They took them."

"We'll get them back," Rylen assured me. He looked at Tater and down at Julian. "We should take his uniform."

I watched, helpless, as my brother and Rylen stripped Julian's dead body down to his boxers and undershirt. I'd seen countless crime scenes and accidents, and watched people die. It was never easy, but never before had I felt such loss and desolation as I did at that moment. I'd sent Julian back into the school. He'd died trying to help us.

I put a hand on Julian's chest. "I'm so sorry, Julian."

The guys worked quickly to hide the blood, covering it in loose dirt and fallen stalks.

"Come on," Rylen whispered, touching my shoulder. "We have to get further into the field." Rylen bent as if he were going to hoist Julian's body up.

"What are you doing?" I asked.

"We can't leave his body. We'll take him and bury him when we can."

"Yeah," Tater whispered. "If they found his body without the uniform they'd know."

Tater helped Remy up, and the four of us moved just in time. We were halfway into the huge field when the side door banged open and stern voices rang out. We went completely still, sinking down. I looked, but all I could see were yellowed stalks, dirt, and sky. From the corner of my eye I saw Rylen on a knee, leaning to the side to balance the weight of Julian's body over his shoulder.

Shouts periodically filled the air, and it sounded as if

Derps were running around the perimeter of the field. What if they came out here? We might be able to outrun them, but they could blindly shoot into the field and we couldn't outrun bullets. Remy and I hunkered close, breathing fast, and I listened so intently it felt as if my eardrums throbbed.

We remained there for what seemed like hours, our bodies alert, until voices faded and eventually cars started, their tires crunching in the distance. Then silence rained down upon us and our reality became achingly clear.

They'd taken our families. And we were officially outlaws.

# THIRTY

E WAITED IN THE field awhile longer to be sure everyone was gone before we moved toward the farmhouse at the other end of the crops. The house was empty, of course, but we were there for one purpose: to bury Julian.

We stayed close to the edge of the cornfield in case we needed to run back in to hide. Remy cried quietly the entire time the guys and I took turns digging, and then lowered him into the ground, each holding one of his limbs. Then we covered him in dirt and stood there, exhausted in every way possible.

We moved closer as Remy said a quiet prayer for Julian's soul and for the safety of us and our families. When she finished, we stared at each other. My only comfort was knowing there were three people in front of me who understood exactly how I felt at that moment. We weren't alone. As long as we had each other, there was hope.

"Should we go back and see if our cars are still there?" I asked. If they weren't, we were screwed.

Tater and Rylen both nodded, and the four of us headed back through the dried stalks toward the school.

At the other end of the field, we stared out at the eerily silent school grounds. When we were sure not a soul was in sight, we darted to the parking lot.

Tater hissed, "Yessss," under his breath when we spotted the cars. Then he froze, scaring the shit out of me. "I don't have the keys."

"I've got one." I pulled Mom's set of keys out of my pocket and twisted Dad's car key from the chain, handing it to him. "We only have one key, so don't lose it."

He saluted me and jumped in Dad's SUV. To my surprise, Remy flung open the passenger door and jumped in beside him. *Traitor.* I looked at Rylen, who gave an amused shrug as we jogged to Mom's car and jumped in.

"Wait," I said. "Where the heck are we going?"

"Southwest to Mojave," he said simply, as if it were a tiny park and not a desert that spanned three states.

I rolled down my window and Remy did the same. Tater leaned forward to see me through the passenger window.

"We need to stay off the main roads."

Tater nodded. "I got this. Follow me."

We made it out of town and onto a back road quickly. The good thing was, a caravan of school busses could not possibly move very fast, so we had a decent chance of spotting them and keeping track. Especially with Tater's lead foot leading the way. We just had to keep out of their line of vision.

Rylen stared out the passenger window as I drove. Part of me wanted to fill the silence with words, but I let him be. After an hour of driving, my stomach gave an embarrassingly loud gurgle that filled the quiet car. The corner of Rylen's mouth came up as he turned to me.

"Sorry," I said, and he shrugged.

"We haven't eaten in almost a day," he pointed out.

He was right. I felt my body shaking a little, as it always did when my blood sugar got low. Next would come dizziness.

"Let me see if I can reach anything in the back," he said. Rylen climbed over the seat as nimbly as an obstacle course, and I forced myself not to check out his ass. He pulled up a lever on the back seat and pulled it down to reveal the contents of the stuffed trunk. "Bingo."

I heard him riffling around and then the seat clicking back into place. He unscrewed the cap on a bottle of water and handed it to me. I worked really hard not to snatch it away and moan as I drank it. I forced myself to stop halfway through the bottle and save the rest. I could have drunk five of those bottles at that moment.

Next he handed me a bag of turkey jerky and a chocolate chip granola bar.

"Oh, my God, I love you," I said. The moment the words left my mouth my face flamed and a wave of dizziness hit. I had to grip the wheel harder. Rylen laughed it off and tore open the granola bar, handing it to me before ripping the top off the jerky bag.

I felt him watching as I took an overly large bite and struggled to chew it. Since I couldn't talk, I pointed to the bag of jerky, then at his mouth.

"I don't want to eat all of your food," he said.

I forced myself to swallow so I could say, "Don't be crazy! You have to eat too. It's for all of us. You're part of this family, Ry. You always have been."

His eyes met mine, and pure emotion seemed to spill straight from his spirit into mine. The gratefulness and love he gave off took my breath away. I had to swallow and peer back at the road. I cleared my throat and swallowed again.

From the corner of my eye, I watched him put one piece in his mouth and start to close the bag, but I gave his hand a slap. "Eat more."

"Dang, boss lady." He shoved another piece in his mouth and I took one too.

Once I'd had enough to stop shaking, I asked the question I'd been thinking about all day.

"What do you think is really going on? I mean, safe houses? All I can think of are concentration camps. Am I being paranoid?"

Rylen rubbed a hand over his face. "I don't know, Pep. I can't wrap my mind around any of this mess." He shook his head. "I shouldn't have let Liv out of my sight. I should have kept her with me instead of sending her to sit with your parents."

"Ry . . ."

"She's just as strong as you, but I never give her enough credit. I try to protect her, instead of letting her grow, and now she probably thinks I abandoned her." He let out a gravely sigh. "I'm just glad she's with your folks and not alone."

"You don't need to feel guilty. I'm sure she knows you'd never purposely abandon her."

He made a dismissive sound. "Yeah, well."

"They'll take care of each other until we get them back." The words echoed in my mind: *get them back*. But how? What if we couldn't?

He must have had the same doubts because he went back to staring out his window in silence.

We'd been driving nearly an hour and a half through the middle of nowhere when I saw Tater and Remy leaning together and pointing. I looked over and saw a faint trail of high-blowing dust in the distance.

"Look!" I pointed.

He stared and a triumphant grin grew. "That's coming from the main road."

I couldn't keep the smile from my own face. "It has to be them." Our road seemed to run parallel, thought it was rutted with potholes and cracks that I constantly swerved to avoid. Remy turned around to smile at me through the back window and I gave her a thumbs-up.

After nearly two more hours of passing bordering small towns and hopping from dirt roads to side roads, we finally saw the bus caravan enter Amargosa Valley.

Rylen leaned forward and squinted. He had much sharper eyesight than me. "It looks like they've got the valley gated."

Tater pulled up at an abandoned gas station and we all jumped out. My legs and arms ached from digging the past two days and then sitting so long. Rylen stretched his arms. Tater opened the back of Dad's SUV and rooted around until he pulled out binoculars.

"I'm gonna get on the roof," he said. Rylen nodded. The two of them went around the small, square building until they found an HVAC unit that was strong enough to let them climb, and then Rylen boosted Tater up.

I walked back to the car to talk to Remy.

"I have to pee so freaking bad," she said, dancing in place.

"Go," I told her. "I'll watch for the guys."

She squatted next to the car while I peered up at my stealthy brother on the roof. When Remy finished, she covered for me.

"Guys have it so easy," I grumbled when I was finished. I reached into Dad's glove compartment for wet wipes to sanitize our hands.

"You're such a germaphobe," Remy said with a laugh when I handed her a wipe. After a second she got serious. "What do you think they're doing to them? I mean, I know you think it's something bad, but what if they really are just trying to keep people safe? What if they're good, and we're against them?"

I wondered how Remy's gut instincts could tell her something so much different than mine. She'd always been trusting where I was cautious, and many times my caution had turned out to be unnecessary. What if she was right and we'd made enemies of the good team?

And then I remembered Grandpa Tate and Julian. I swallowed hard and shook my head. Plenty of times Remy's trusting instincts were wrong, and she was burned.

"They're manipulating people and using scare tactics to control them. There's nothing good about that, Rem."

"But maybe they *have* to be like that because people are so stubborn and it's the only way to force us to let them do what's best for us."

I stared out at the distance, at the valley pass between two rocky mountains where the busses had disappeared. Before I could answer, I heard the thud of feet hitting the ground and knew the guys were coming back.

Tater nodded at us. "It's gated. This is where they're holding them."

I let out a breath. We knew where they were. This was a great first step, but now would come the hard part. I looked up at the sky which had already started to dim.

"We need to figure out where to stay tonight, somewhere away from here."

Tater nodded. "I saw signs for Ash Meadows National Wildlife Refuge not far from here."

"We can stay there tonight," said Rylen, "and come out early in the morning to scope out the camp."

I shivered when he called it a camp.

"Let's go," Tater said. "I'm starved."

We came to the state park down the road. The gates were unmanned, of course, so we moved the barrier aside and drove in, careful to move the barriers back into place so nobody would know someone was there.

When we came to the open landscape, Rylen whistled. "Damn, that's pretty."

Ash Meadows was stunning with its hills and mountains with both desert beauty and greenery in its shrubs and ash trees. We followed the road as far as it could take us toward the mountain and then parked beneath a copse of trees near a hiking trail into the mountains. The entrance of the trail said "Point of Rocks" and had a board with information, a map, and brochures. I took a brochure and shoved it in my back pocket.

"Do we need two tents?" Tater asked. "This one fits six."

"Just one," Remy said. "Less work."

I looked at the darkening sky. "We need to hurry. It'll be night soon."

We grabbed as much as we could carry and ascended the trail until we came to a semi-flat area surrounded by ash and pine trees. We got the tent up quickly and broke out the gas stove to heat baked beans and Vienna sausages in their cans. We could have eaten them cold, but Tater was feeling fancy.

On our way up we'd passed signs that mentioned a desert oasis, and looking down at the view, I could see why. Amid the mountains and desert plains, scattered with dry shrubs and ash trees, was a spring. In the setting sun it glittered an icy blue. Movement by the spring made my heart nearly stop until I realized it was a four-legged animal with huge horns.

"Look!" I whispered.

We all peered down.

"Bighorn sheep," Rylen breathed.

"They're drinking the water," I said, worried.

"Doesn't look like it's hurting them," Remy remarked. "Yet."

Tater nodded. "Not sure they'd bother poisoning these springs when people don't live out here."

I pulled the brochure from my back pocket and read through it.

"That's King Spring. It says the water from these streams come from an underground aquifer. Fossil water that takes thousands of years to move through the ground." I looked out at the springs. "Do you think it's safe? Could we actually bathe in it?"

"Oh my gosh," Remy said longingly. "That would be so awesome. We got those vaccinations, so we should be safe, right?"

"There are different strands," I said. "Bacterial, viral, we're not protected against everything."

We watched the sheep roam freely, and I envied their lack of care.

"I'll jump in that shit," Tater said.

I rolled my eyes at him. "Not it on taking care of you when you break out in hives."

Rylen chuckled.

If I weren't so exhausted, and feeling so worried about my family, I might have gone to explore.

Right now, all I wanted to do was sleep. I was the first to climb into the tent and bury myself inside a sleeping bag. I don't even remember closing my eyes, but my brain shut off hard, and I was thankful for it.

During the night I felt Remy press her body flush behind me, but she felt bigger than normal. And then her unusually heavy arm slung over my waist. If it wasn't pitch-black in the tent, I would have figured it out sooner. It was the scent of him that made me realize. 'Wide awake me' might have discretely removed his hand and put some space between us. 'Exhausted me' scooted closer, garnering his heat through the thin sleeping bag separating us. I fell back asleep with the feel of his breath on my neck.

It was still dark when a barely audible low groan from the back of Rylen's throat made my eyes flutter. My sleeping bag had slipped down, and we were both covered by Ry's blanket. In a moment of shock, his strong hand grasped my hip, and he pressed the hardened length of himself against my ass. His mouth came down on my neck and I felt his lips, soft in contrast to the light scratchiness of his facial hair. The heat of his tongue flicked against the skin of my neck just as his hips grinded against me and he held me hard. I gasped as the heat of arousal shot through me so powerful it was almost painful. The sound of my shocked breath froze him. For one split second we were still touching, and I felt him everywhere: his lips, his hand, his really hard—

Rylen sat up in a rush and whispered hoarsely, *"Fuck."*

A solid beat passed before he unzipped the tent and pushed out, zipping it back. His footsteps sounded like he was going toward the path, walking fast. My heartbeat was pounding in my ears and throat, and every sensitive place on my body. Oh, my God.

Tater sat up, but Remy kept sleeping.

"What's wrong?" he asked.

It took me a second to find my voice. "He's probably going to the bathroom."

Tater sighed and fell back. In seconds he was lightly snoring again.

I tried to relax, but it was impossible. I lay there with my eyes wide open, more turned on than I'd ever been and wishing the sensation would go away. Rylen had been asleep. He probably thought I was Livia. That heated moment had not been meant for me.

But OH MY GOD. Now I knew exactly what I was missing out on, and I would never forget. But it sucked to know he was out there right now, probably feeling embarrassed and ashamed. Should I go to him? Tell him it was no big deal? No. Because it kind of was a big deal. And I hadn't tried to stop the moment from happening. At all. So I lay there feeling all the things for what seemed like forever.

When I finally heard Rylen coming back, I yanked my sleeping bag all the way back up. I flipped to my side and lay still, pretending to sleep. He unzipped the tent and whispered in a deep voice, "*Tater.*" I heard him shaking Tater's foot, and my brother groaned.

"Come on, bro," Ry whispered. "It's four. Let's scout."

Remy stirred and said, "What's going on?"

"You can keep sleeping," Tater told her. "We're going to do some recon and be back to plan together."

"I wanna recon," she slurred.

"We're just getting a lay of the land," Tater whispered.

He closed the tent flap, and I listened as they gathered their things and crunched their way down the path. A minute later the car started and drove away. Once Rylen was far away, I managed to fall back asleep.

Dawn was lightening the horizon when my eyes flitted open again. Remy was breathing soundly next to me. I shuffled out of the warm bag and felt immediately cold as I opened the zipper and stepped out. I would need to get my fleece jacket from the car, but for now I was focused on the small tin kettle on the gas stove and the two mugs with packets of premade vanilla latte powder inside.

I'd bet my life Rylen set that up for us. I rubbed my arms as I waited for the water to heat and then turned off the stove and poured two steaming mugs. When I opened the tent, Remy was sitting up, her blond waves a tangle around her face. She let out an animalistic sound when she saw the steaming mug, and it made me giggle. I handed her a cup, and we cuddled into our bags as we sipped.

I tried, and failed, not to think about what had happened in the night. I would deal with it and try to deflate the situation when Rylen returned. I normally didn't like to share personal stuff, but I needed Remy's help to make sure this didn't happen again.

"Hey, Rem?"

"Hm?" She took a sip.

"Can you sleep next to me from now on?"

Her eyebrows scrunched. "Why? What happened?"

"I mean, nothing. I think maybe Rylen was dreaming last night or something, and he got a little snuggly—"

"Oh, my freaking Gosh, Amb . . . did he have morning wood?"

I took a calm sip and said, "Maybe."

Remy rocked back, her laughter splitting the air. "That is classic! The poor guy. He's so freaking noble, he's probably beating himself up about it."

"Yeah, well. Sleep next to me from now on, 'kay?"

She grinned. "You liked it."

I took a sip. Shrugged. Took another sip.

"You liked it *a lot*," she corrected.

I sighed. "Let's drop it. It didn't mean anything. He was asleep."

She smiled softly to herself as we drank our coffee in the quiet morning.

"How long have they been gone?" Remy asked.

"I'm not sure. An hour, maybe? No more than two."

When we finished our coffee, savoring every drop, we hiked down to Mom's car and got my jacket, plus a sweatshirt of Tater's for Remy. My eyes landed on the shower stuff in the trunk and I asked, "Want to take the big pot and gas stove down to the spring so we can wash up?" I felt really grimy.

Her face scrunched. "I guess. I wish it wasn't so cold out."

"Me too. Let's make it quick."

We ran back to camp for the stove, and grabbed the pot, towels, clothes, and soap from the trunk. The hike down to the spring was awesome. Part of the Preserve were wetlands from the springs, so they'd built boardwalks to cross over marshy spots.

We got to the clear pool of water and I scooped a heavy potful, then placed it on the fire. Remy was reading a placard stand.

"It says people aren't allowed to swim here because it disturbs the algae for pupfish. Ooh, I want to see a pupfish!"

We dropped to our hands and knees and stared down into the pool until we both pointed at the same time to a tiny, inch-long fish. Then another. There were a bunch. When our water warmed, I carried the heavy pot away from the pool so the soap wouldn't get in. Remy laughed at how I walked bowlegged to keep the hot pot from hitting my knees.

"You first," I told her.

She looked around. "Should I get all naked out here? What if they come back?"

"It's up to you. If you want wet undies, go for it. Otherwise, strip."

"But I haven't shaved in, like, ages."

I rolled my eyes. "I swear I won't stare at your sasquatch crotch."

She gasped dramatically. "It's not sasquatch!"

I started giggling at her defensive, and she laughed too, giving me a shove.

"Oh, fine. Whatever." She took everything off and turned

her back to me, rubbing her arms. "Hurry. I'm freezing."

I focused on her hair, pouring just enough water over her head for her to start a lather, which she used to quickly wash her body. Then I scooped cupfuls and began to pour them slowly over her head until it looked like the soap was gone. It took more than half the pot. But she had a lot more hair than me, so it should be okay.

"Done." I bent and grabbed a towel, tossing it at her. She wrapped it around her body, cinched it under her arm, and squeezed out her hair.

"Your turn," she said. "I'm not dressing until we're done 'cause I don't want it splashing on my clothes."

Now that it was my turn to get naked I suddenly felt modest. Remy was curvier and more confident in her body than I'd ever been. She put a hand on her hip and regarded me smugly.

"Not so easy, is it? Just turn your skinny butt around and do it."

I sighed and turned, ready to get this over with. But first I peered around to be sure the guys weren't coming. It was just us and Mother Nature. I quickly undressed.

"Oh my gosh," Remy said in a happy voice. "You have the cutest mole right here!" I felt her finger poke the center of my right butt cheek and I jumped.

"Ah! No touchy! Just hurry up—it's cold!"

"See, I told you!"

We were laughing hysterically at ourselves as she began pouring water over me. It was the most ridiculous thing ever. Who would have thought Remy and I would ever have to shower each other?

"Make sure you wash your sasquatch," she sang.

"Shut up!" I was dying. My ab muscles hurt from laughing and Remy totally missed me with her next pour, dumping it at my feet as she slumped over in a fit of humor. "Give me that, crazy." I took the cup and did the rest of the pouring myself since we were almost out of water. Finally I was clean. Except my feet, but not much could be done about that. I'd brush them off when they dried.

We stepped away from the mud we'd created and moved to the boulder that held our clothes. I scrubbed the towel over my head first, then my body. Remy and I were both shivering as we reached for our clothes and hurriedly tugged them on. Then we took turns brushing our wet hair.

We were gathering our things when I heard a throat being cleared. I stood and spun toward the noise, expecting to see Tater's amused face, but what I saw instead made my blood freeze. The far side of the pool was lined with huge rocks, and behind them stood five guys in camo. A sixth, beefy guy was crouched on top of the middle boulder with a handgun propped on his knee and a grin on his face. Remy sucked in a harsh breath and moved closer to me.

How long had they been there? I'd glanced this direction before my shower began, so they had to have snuck up stealthily and hidden behind the rocks.

"What do you want?" I asked, moving instinctively to block Remy. I really, really should have brought Grandma's gun down here with me.

The big guy with the gun kept a smile glued on his face, but his eyes were hidden beneath a camo hat pulled low over his forehead. "You girls with the Disaster Relief Initiative?" he asked casually. He had a seriously southern drawl.

I swallowed hard. They didn't look like Drips, and they weren't in Derp uniforms. Their camo actually looked like authentic military gear. And they were sporting overgrown buzz cuts. My heart started to calm when I realized they might be safe, but I could feel Remy's terrified breaths on my neck.

"No," I said. "Are you?"

"Let's just say, not the current government."

I looked at the other faces: hard, expressionless, careful. "You guys are Army."

The guy gave me a real grin now. "Four of us."

A solid African American with wide shoulders and a narrow waist lifted his chin. "Marines." A shorter, leaner guy on the end with auburn hair and freckles said, "Air Force."

"What's your name?" I asked the main guy.

"Sergeant Ray Harris. But most people just call me—"

"*Texas Harry*," called a voice from the other side of us.

"Tater!" Remy gripped my arm.

Everyone turned and watched Tater and Rylen materialize from behind two trees with rifles in their hands. A wave of relief crashed over me. Tater kept his eyes on the newcomers while Rylen glanced at me. I gave him a nod to show we were okay.

"No fucking way," Texas Harry said. "Tate Bait?" He hopped down from his rock and loped around the pool toward Tater. The other guys, as well and me and Remy, started walking over too, but carefully. The two of them met in a back-slapping hug. "I thought you were at Benning." The guy dwarfed Tater, and my brother was no shorty.

"I was," Tater said. "But my family's here, so I hitchhiked back when Benning closed. What are you doing up here from Huachuca? I figured you'd go back to Texas." I recognized that base name. It was in Arizona.

Sergeant Harris snorted. "I did. Whole fuckin' place where I grew up was a ghost town. Then I heard on the radio people were being taken to Nevada."

"They actually said that on the radio?" I asked.

He gave a nod. "Underground station. Been shut down since then, though."

A lull passed as everyone looked around and sized each other up. The guys all nodded, as if passing one another's assessments. Then they made introductions.

The marine was Sergeant Devon Price. The airman was Second Lieutenant Sean Wilcott, and the other three army soldiers were Sergeants Matt Nelson, Mark Mahalchick, and Josh Depaul.

Everyone seemed safe enough for us to speak openly.

Remy and I turned to Tater and Rylen. "So?" I asked. "How did it go?"

They addressed both us and the new guys. "They've got a whole town set up in that pass between the mountains. All gated. All guarded."

"Up where they're taking all them busses?" Texas Harry asked with a nod. "Supposedly they got those kind of places set up all through the countryside, away from cities. You know someone there?"

Tater's face went hard. "My parents. My grandma. His wife." He inclined his head to Rylen, who stood with his arms crossed. "Remy's folks." He looked at Remy, and all the guys turned to stare at her. Remy eyed them skeptically.

"You guys saw us washing, didn't you?" It burst out of her like she'd been holding it in.

The guys all looked down or to the side, anywhere but at us. Some scratched their necks. I felt my face go hot.

"Say what?" Tater asked. Rylen stared hard from guy to guy.

Texas Harry gave an unapologetic slow grin. "We didn't see . . . much. And we stayed behind the rocks."

Remy crossed her arms. "Pervs." My face was on fire. I hoped they hadn't heard the stupid sasquatch commentary.

"Wait, hold up," Tater said. "Y'all got to see Remy naked?"

I whacked Tater on one arm while Remy slapped his other shoulder. He jumped away, shielding himself. "I'm just saying! That is *wrong*. You should be ashamed of yourselves."

He tried to look serious, but the guys all laughed now, and while I still felt a bit violated and embarrassed, even Remy rolled her eyes and seemed to relax some. Rylen gave me that serious look of his again, like he was making sure I was okay. I let out a huff of air and gave him another nod. We had bigger issues.

"What else did you find out?" I asked.

"There's only one entrance and exit," Rylen said. "It looks like they've got new, basic buildings set up, like barracks or apartments. They had all the people lined up—"

"Looked like thousands," Tater added.

"And they were leading them into a couple of big warehouse buildings."

My heart raced. "What are they doing in there?"

Ry shook his head. "We didn't hear any gunshots or see any bodies being carried out. My guess is they're putting the people to work."

"Like concentration camps," I whispered.

"No," Remy said fiercely. "These are not Nazis, Amber. How do you know they're not just keeping them safe? Giving them food and beds or something."

The marine, Devon, spoke up in a smooth voice. "They may not be Nazis, but they're evil as hell. I've seen 'em line people up and execute 'em."

Remy gave him a horrified look. "Were the people bad?"

"Bad? Not unless you call five jarheads refusing to leave their post *bad*."

Everyone stared at him in horror.

My voice came out raspy. "What happened?"

"DRI came in and closed down the Yuma base, and it didn't feel right. How you gonna dismantle military in a time like this, and just tell everyone to go home? Naw, man. We wanted to stay. We couldn't find none of our officers—it was like they were wiped off the face of the earth—"

"Yeah, same thing in Benning." Tater looked at the auburn haired guy, Sean. "You're an officer, right?"

"Yes, but I was on leave, so I have no idea what went down on base."

Everyone turned back to Devon, who continued. "We wanted to do something, but they weren't having it. Kept telling us to leave. Five men refused to stand down, and they took them out. Bam, bam, bam, down the line. Then they turned to us like, *anyone else want to stay?*" Devon finished and crossed his arms, matching Rylen's stance.

My stomach turned. "Maybe they killed all the officers so they couldn't lead their troops."

"No." Remy looked like she was about to lose it. "That's a really big assumption to make."

"These are conclusions based on facts, Rem."

"Stop!" Her voice shook, and I knew she was near tears, freaked out.

Remy grasped her wet clothing and towel to her chest and rushed away in the direction of our camp. I sighed and let my head fall back.

"Your friend still believe in unicorns, too?" one of the Army guys asked with a laugh, Josh, I think. He sounded like a New Yorker, that tough edge to his voice, and gray eyes that looked like they'd seen some rough stuff. He had dark hair and a Roman-curved nose.

"She's not stupid. She just doesn't want to believe the worst of people."

"We call that naïve where I'm from."

I speared him with a glare. "Leave her alone."

He shrugged and turned away. I looked at Tater and Ry.

"So what's our next step? We need to make a plan, right?"

They both nodded, and Texas Harry cut in. "You trying to break them out?" He whistled. "Gonna need one hell of a plan for that."

"Damn straight," Tater said with a sigh. "But first, food."

Every single set of male ears seemed to perk at that word, and I kind of wanted to punch Tater. Six extra manly mouths to feed? Our food would be gone in two days.

The Texan eyed the rifle in Rylen's hand. "Shoot some rabbits and I'll skin 'em."

Rylen tipped his chin down. "Deal."

"We can't shoot the gun," I said. "Someone will hear."

"We're miles from them," Texas Harry assured me. "And we've been scouting this area for nearly thirty-six hours. Not a soul out here but us."

Still, I was nervous. Being anxious had become a way of life now, and it sucked.

# THIRTY-ONE

EMY AND I SAT in the tent while the guys roasted two bunnies over the smoking fire. I didn't expect rabbits to smell so good, but they did.

"I'm sorry I keep freaking out," Remy whispered.

"I love it that you're an optimist," I told her. "And I hope you're right. But you know I'm a cynic by nature, and after everything I've seen . . . it just doesn't add up for me."

She picked at her old nail polish, flecks of teal falling off.

"What about these guys?" she whispered. "Do you trust them?"

"Yeah, I think they're legit. Do you?"

She nodded. "I feel like an idiot for spazzing in front of them. Not exactly a great first impression."

"Their first impression was you naked. I'd say it was probably pretty great."

She covered her mouth against an embarrassed smile. "I can't believe they were watching."

"I know." I shook my head. "Let's just go out there. It'll blow over. We need to stick together and play nice."

She huffed a sigh, and we stood up. The tops of our heads skimmed the low tent ceiling. I unzipped the opening, and we climbed out. The guys regarded us and went back to their low conversations. But Rylen wouldn't look my way.

"Food's almost ready," Tater said.

I gave him a smile. "Thanks." Remy and I went over and sat beside him on some rocks.

The six military guys had quite a few belongings, which they'd hidden before they approached us at the water earlier. They had some food and sleeping bags from what I could see of their giant green rucksacks.

When lunch was ready, we all ate rabbit with our fingers, then passed around a pot and raised it to our lips for mouthfuls of warm kidney beans. Ugh. Gross. But it did the trick. We could hardly complain when our stomachs were full.

The shortest, stocky Army guy, Matt, stood up and stretched his barrel chest. "I'm gonna go jump in that water down there."

"That sounds hella nice," the tall, skinny Army guy said. I think his name was Mark.

Texas Harry slapped Mark on the back of the head. "What I'd tell you 'bout that Cali-hella shit?"

Mark laughed. "Don't hate, cowboy."

The new guys made me wonder if there weren't groups like this of displaced military personnel all over the country. I wished there was a way to get us all together and figure this mess out. It was all so strange, so mysterious. No matter which way I looked at the events of the past month, I couldn't figure it all out. All I knew was that something wasn't right.

All six of the men grabbed their towels and ran down the mountainous path. From afar we saw them strip down and jump in the clear water. Tater went in the tent to grab a cat-nap, leaving Rylen sitting alone on a rock near the fire.

"They're going to disturb the algae that feeds the pup-fish," Remy whispered to me.

I almost laughed. I was really relieved she hadn't said that in front of the guys. "New algae will grow."

"I guess." She sighed. "I'm going to do some yoga. Want to come?"

"Um, no," I told her. "But thanks. You enjoy."

I thought about disappearing to the tent so Rylen wouldn't feel awkward, but we needed to get this convo over with. So I made my way over and sat quietly beside him on the rocks. He fiddled with a twig between his fingers.

After a long while he asked, "You don't do yoga?"

I gave a laugh. "No. You?"

"Hell no."

We watched the guys climb onto the rocks and jump in. From afar I saw five various shades of white asses and one brown one.

"Look, Pepper—"

"What do you think of those guys?" I asked.

He paused. "Typical military dudes. They're solid."

"I think so too." His eyes burned into me. I cleared my throat and reluctantly turned to melt into the regretful look in his eyes.

"I'm sorry about last night."

I shook my head. "We were asleep. I don't even . . ." I waved a hand like I barely remembered. His face remained fiercely remorse as he studied me. He must have been satisfied that I wasn't mad because he finally looked away.

"It won't happen again," he whispered. My stomach sank with disappointment that I should not have felt.

A cloud passed over. I grabbed my arms, shivering. "Are you worried about her? About Liv?"

He picked up another stick and tossed it on the fire. "I

know she'll be fine as long as she has your parents and grandma, but I worry what the Drips and Derps are up to. I wonder what they'll do to everyone. That's the part I can't stop thinking about."

"Me too." I held my hands out to the fire. "What do you think today's date is?"

He shook his head. We tried to calculate, starting from Thanksgiving when we lost power. So many of the days melded together.

"Damn," Rylen said. "It's almost Christmas."

Sadness engulfed me at the realization that our holiday traditions wouldn't be happening this year. Our family might not even be together. Grandpa and Len were gone. This was all so unbelievably wrong. Rylen's eyes were unfocused as he stared at the fire. I stared at his profile. Every line of his unshaven face. Every muscle that flexed from his forearms up to his biceps as his fingers fisted and unfisted. If he were mine, I would touch him. I would reach out to comfort him. I would turn his face to mine and kiss him while we had this moment alone. For a few moments we could forget about our worries and lose ourselves in each other's touch. I would give him anything he wanted.

I looked away.

The chasm growing inside of me was too deep. I feared nothing could ever fill it. I feared I would always feel this emptiness, my losses echoing inside an endless canyon.

Rylen's mind seemed to clear, and he turned to me, his eyes the same color as our winter sky, a cloudy blue, swirling with unspoken thoughts and emotion.

"Do you have any regrets, Pepper?"

Feelings burned up my neck and into the back of my eyes. "Just one," I whispered. *I should have told you.*

"Yeah, me too." His eyes speared me. "Just one." Then he

looked at the fire again.

I turned my burning gaze to the fire too. My chest and neck were so tight I would snap if I breathed too deeply.

I expected him to drop it, but he didn't. He poked the fire with a stick and said, "Remember that time me and Tater came home drunk from that party and you were on the tire swing?"

It'd been a long time since my stomach did the truffle-shuffle. I could hardly force a response as I recalled that night. "Yeah?"

"I almost…" He let out an embarrassed laugh. "I almost kissed you." He shook his head. "I thought you were going to punch me—"

"What? That's not what happened. *I* was the one who almost kissed *you*."

He turned to me, his eyes narrowed. "No—"

"Um, yes."

"I remember the look on your face, Pepper. You were pissed."

I let out a frustrated sound of exasperation. "I was mad at Tater! Remember I grabbed your shirt," I grasped the fabric at his chest to reenact, "and pulled you?" I tugged him close.

Our eyes suddenly stuck like glue, our breathing hitching and accelerating in tune as we remembered how close we'd come then and how close our faces were now.

"That's not how I remember it," he whispered.

"I was the sober one," I whispered back. "I remember every detail."

His Adam's apple bobbed as he swallowed. I let go and turned my head back to the fire, feeling wrecked with regret. How could we both remember that moment so differently? "It doesn't matter now, Ry. It's in the past."

From the corner of my eye I saw him run a hand across

his scruffy face, up over his hair and down to his ear where he pinched his lobe in his fingers. It took forever for my pulse to settle.

Time passed in a bubble of tense silence until Remy and the guys came back, and Tater trudged out of the tent. I plastered on a fake smile, glad for the distractions from my thoughts. I avoided Ry's eyes for a while and tried really hard not to think about it.

The new guys looked fresh and clean with wet hair and towels flung over their shoulders. They hadn't bothered to put shirts back on, despite temps I thought were way too cold for that. They were a fit bunch of guys. New York Josh winked at Remy and she gave him the scowl she used to reserve for Tater. He chuckled to himself.

Rylen stoked the fire, and we all gathered around.

"Let's plan," Texas Harry said.

"Do any of you have binoculars?" Tater asked.

"Roger that," said Matt.

"*Yessss,*" Tater hissed. "That's what we need. We couldn't make out any details inside the camp this morning. Let's go back tonight after dusk and check it out again. We have to park and hike. Who's in?"

Everyone raised their hand but Remy. She looked around and blushed. "I'll hold down the fort here. I'll just be in the way if I come."

"I'll stay here with you," I said to make her feel better, but I immediately kicked myself. Damn it. I'd really wanted to go. The grateful look on her face made me glad I'd offered to stay, though. She'd be too freaked out here alone.

"We'll need to take both vehicles," Rylen said. "Do you guys have a car? I'd rather not leave the girls without emergency transportation."

New York Josh slapped the marine, Devon, on the

shoulder. "We've got big D's grocery getter."

Everyone laughed as Devon glared at Josh. "Don't be talking shit about my mama's van."

I had to laugh now. "Are you guys driving around in a minivan?"

Devon raised his chin. "That thing will outlast all y'alls cars. I guaren-damn-tee it." The thought of six big military men cramming in a minivan was just too funny.

Once everything was settled, we went down and got the other tent. One of the guys had a smaller tent in his pack, too, and a tarp for the others to sleep under the stars in their sleeping bags.

"Hope you don't wake up with a snake in your sleeping bag," Remy told them.

Texas Harry raised an eyebrow. "D sleeps with a big ole snake in his bag every night."

The guys practically fell over each other laughing. Devon's chuckle was deep. Remy put a hand on her hip and said to the Texan, "Well, I hope it slithers over and bites your ass."

He pulled a face. "His snake don't like me. But you probably better watch your pretty little one."

Tater waved a hand. "Big D better keep his damn snake outta my tent."

Devon threw his head back, showing rows of gorgeous white teeth. "Ya'll can quit worrying 'bout my snake. I got him trained like a trick pony."

Rylen sputtered on the drink he was taking from his bottle of water and another round of raucous laughter rose up.

The guys went back and forth, sparing words, one-upping each other until all of our stomachs hurt. The humor was cathartic. Our group seemed to emit a newly charged sense of energy and urgency. Because *this* was life. Laughter, love, friendships. We had a way of life to protect. We weren't perfect by any means, but we were *good*. And we sure as hell weren't giving it up without a fight.

# THIRTY-TWO

I T FELT LIKE THEY were gone forever. We stamped out the fire when it got dark, not wanting to attract attention from afar. Though we were well protected by mountains, I wasn't taking any chances. Remy and I bundled in our sweatshirts and went in our tent. We lay back in the darkness and stared up.

"You know," Remy said. "As much of a jerk as that guy Josh is, he's kind of cute, isn't he?"

"I guess they all kind of are, in different ways."

"Well, they're all giving off major vibes toward you. Except Sean," Remy said matter-of-factly, "he's gay."

"You think so?"

"My gaydar is blaring."

I thought of the quiet, freckled officer with perfect posture. He was a couple inches taller than me, but short by male standards. Probably the most cut of all the guys, like, super low body fat. And, yeah, he took good care of his auburn locks. Remy could be right. He was the only one who didn't ogle her boobs or make crass jokes though he'd shared in the laughter.

"Well, don't say anything," I told her. "Some military guys are weird about that. I know Rylen and Tater wouldn't care, but you never know about the others."

"I won't." She paused. "So . . . which one do you like best?"

I sighed. "I don't know. None of them."

"You just said they were all cute."

"They are, but that's the last thing I need to worry about right now."

She gave a feminine grunt. "There is nothing better to distract you from the Apocalypse and Mr. Nonavailable than a hot guy."

I rolled onto my side to face her, making out her silhouette. "Is that what you think this is? The Apocalypse?"

"I mean . . . I was just joking, but . . ." Her voice got serious. "It could be. My dad thinks it is."

A zinging chill went up my spine. I grasped my neck to massage it away. Outside of the tent I thought I could hear shuffling.

I sat up and whispered, "Do you hear that?"

She sat up too. "It's just the guys, right?"

I pulled Grandma's pistol from beneath my pillow.

"What's that?" Remy asked.

"Protection." I reached for the tent zipper and slowly pulled it down.

She gasped. "You have a gun? Be careful!"

"I will. Stay in here."

I went out and slipped behind a tree, racking the slide with a *click*. Down the trail I could see a group of shadowy bodies making their way up to our camp. One huge guy and one super tall guy stood out from the others: Texas Harry and Mark Mahalchick. I let out a breath and called to Remy,

"It's them." She slipped out of the tent and zipped it back up.

When they got up to us, the guys all eyed the gun in my hand.

"You packin' heat?" Josh asked, sounding impressed. I clicked the safety back on. Devon whistled. "She was 'bout ready to take our asses out."

"My sister knows how to shoot, too," Tater said. I almost "aww'd" out loud from the compliment.

We all ended up back around the dead fire in a circle to talk since we'd pulled up rocks and logs for makeshift seats.

"So?" I asked.

"We literally saw nothing," Tater said. "Nothing interesting, anyway. There were Derp guards patrolling, but since we got there right after dark, all the people were indoors. It was quiet."

"The busses are gone," Rylen noted. "Only three white vans are there now."

"From what we could see, they have about twenty Derps," Texas Harry said. "And you said a couple hundred townspeople?"

Tater nodded. "They could overpower them if they wanted, but I know they won't."

No, I didn't think they would either. They wouldn't want to take the chance of getting a bunch of their people killed if they weren't in direct, known danger. Plus, they were half-starved, unless they were giving them full rations now, which I doubted.

"I think our best bet would be to cause a distraction away from their encampment," Rylen said. "Draw as many Derps away from the camp as we can, toward a diversion of some sort."

"What kind of diversion?" I asked. "Like a big ass fire or something?"

"Exactly," Rylen said. "Something close enough to make them feel threatened and want to check it out, but far enough to give us time to come around from the other side and storm the front gate."

"What if everyone starts shooting?" She sounded horrified. I tensed, waiting for the guys to verbally attack her naiveté again, but they were respectfully quiet.

"None of us wants to kill," Texas Harry said. "But if it comes down to them or us, we won't hesitate."

Shooting was a given. The guards would feel threatened. So would our guys. Sudden fear seized me. Twenty guards against our eight guys and me. And that's if Remy would let me out of her claws so I could help the cause.

I rubbed my forehead.

"I think this night calls for a drink," Texas Harry said. He pushed to his feet and went over to his pack, rifling through and joining us again with a huge bottle.

"Jack?" Tater asked. "Hell yeah, bro."

Before anyone could do or say anything, Remy reached over and grabbed the bottle from Texas Harry. She unscrewed the cap and held the bottle with two hands as she tipped it up and chugged.

"Remy!" I said. She brought it down and her whole body gave a violent shiver. She let out a loud breath and smiled. All at once the guys broke into cheer, clapping and slapping their legs.

It was on.

I was the only one not drinking. And honestly, I wanted to. I wanted to get so wasted that my worries would crawl away from me and pass out in a sea of nothingness. But the problem was, we did not have enough water resources to keep us hydrated against the alcohol. I couldn't say that to them, of course. This beast would not be stopped. Even

Rylen was drinking. They would probably end up draining every single bottle of water tomorrow, which made me itchy all over. I wanted to smack some sense into them.

But they were having fun. And fun was a rarity we needed.

# THIRTY-THREE

THE FUN WAS GETTING out of hand. All of the guys were hitting on Remy. Except Rylen, of course, and Sean, who sat with the group and grinned without saying much. But the rest of them were like freaking peacocks with their feathers fanned, strutting around her. Remy ate up the attention like a starving woman. Her face was going to hurt tomorrow from smiling and laughing.

Rylen and I sat together on our rocks, watching as the other guys told animated stories of all the manly things they'd ever done—how much they could lift, how far they could shoot, how many IUD explosions they'd escaped—everything but the size of their junk, but that would probably come up now that we were nearing the bottom of the bottle. Everyone took one last swig, and then the liter was empty.

Tall Mark grinned at Remy with his wrists hanging lazily over his knees. "So, what were you studying in school?"

"Biology," she said. "I wanted to be a middle school science teacher."

Mark made a face and some of the other guys hissed. "Why would you want to do that?"

"Middle schoolers are awesome!" Remy said with passion. "They're right at that age where they're trying to figure out who they are and what their place is in the world. And science is all around them. It's like a constant that keeps them grounded and helps them make sense of their changing bodies and emotions, and—"

"You do realize all them little boys are gonna be having wet dreams about you, right?" Texas Harry asked.

Remy's mouth popped open, appalled, as the other guys fell over laughing.

"That is disgusting!" she yelled. But she couldn't stay mad long. In seconds, she was laughing with them. "I'll put my hair up in a bun and wear a mumu."

"Won't matter," Mark said. "Boys have legendary imaginations."

Another round of laughter.

Short Matt was the drunkest of the bunch, his head lolling and his words slurring. "I once jerked off thinking about my English teacher on a stripper pole. I think she was, like, sixty."

More falling over raucous laughter.

"You've got issues, sweetie," Remy said.

"I was twelve!" His goofy, lopsided grin made her reach out and pat his cheek. Everyone *"Awwed"* and then a comfortable lull passed.

Texas Harry rubbed the thick facial hair growing across his cheek. "Man . . . I really need to shave this sasquatch."

A beat of absolute, horrible silence passed, in which my stomach plummeted deep inside me, and then Remy's voice and spluttering gasps filled the air, "You! You dirty perv! You were listening and watching us! I knew it." Absolute hysterical laughter ensued.

*Shit!* My face flamed and I was glad it was dark enough to hide the worst of my embarrassment.

"What are you guys talking about?" Tater asked with a bemused smile.

"Nothing," I said loudly.

"It's obviously *something*," Rylen said.

I was desperate not to have the sasquatch comment explained. "No, it's really nothing. They overheard mine and Remy's stupid conversation when we were showering."

Sean stood up and stretched. "On that note, I'm going to hit the sack."

"Always first to bed," Texas Harry said. "G'night, Sleeping Beauty."

"Yeah, yeah," he laughed softly, giving a mock-salute. He disappeared into the one-man tent.

"What's with the sasquatch comment?" Tater would not let it go.

"Oh my freaking gosh," I said. "Just drop it. They're joking around with us." I stood up. If the sasquatch explanation came to light, I really didn't want to be sitting next to Rylen. "I'm going to bed."

"Wait, I have an idea," New York Josh said. He turned the big bottle onto its side on a patch of dirt and gave it a spin.

"Oh, no," Remy said. "Not if I'm the only girl. I'll play if Amber plays." She looked at me, her eyes pleading in the moonlight. I walked over, but stopped and kissed the top of her head.

"Not on your life," I told her.

Everyone but Tater and Rylen *booed* me. I smiled and shrugged. "Good night, everyone."

I made my way to the tent, feeling a strange sense of sadness and regret. I wanted to be able to have fun like Remy. Would I ever be able to? I hated feeling so boring.

I'd almost zipped the flap closed when I saw a hand grasp the opening. "Mind if I join you?" Rylen's voice reverberated through the nylon door, making me shake on the inside.

"Yeah, sure." I unzipped it and he climbed in, leaving his shoes outside of the tent just as I had.

I was very aware of his nearness in the small space as we both took spots against the far sides, leaving room between us for Remy and Tater. Voices and laughter came to us from where the others sat up the hill, but I couldn't make out full details of their conversation. I lay down on my side, facing him, and he lay on his back. It was dark, but my eyes had adjusted to the small light given by the moon, stars, and campfire. I squinted and saw that he'd closed his eyes.

Rylen had had at least eight shots from the liter of whiskey. The tent's air quickly filled with the faint smell of Jack Daniels and Rylen Fite. I can't say I hated the combination. In fact, it kind of gave me my own personal buzz.

We were quiet so long that my body started to relax and feel heavy with sleep. And then Rylen whispered.

"I don't think she's happy."

My ears perked and my heart sped up. "What?"

It took a moment, but he finally replied in that same low, quiet tone. "I don't think she wants to be married to me."

For a few seconds all I heard was my heart pounding in my ears. He had to be drunk to bring up something so major. Something so private.

"I doubt that, Rylen," I whispered.

"I mean it," he whispered a little more strongly. "I keep thinking back to Guatemala . . . she told me that she told you."

"Yeah," I breathed, still shocked he was talking about this.

"We were caught up in the moment, you know? She was scared for her life, and I was pissed off by the injustice of it—and we just sort of clicked. We clung to each other. It was like no one else in the world could understand."

"You don't have to tell me any of this," I said. I was so afraid he would wake up and regret this conversation. I didn't want him to be ashamed or awkward about it tomorrow.

"I want to," he insisted. "I can't talk to anyone else." He sat up and rubbed his face, roughly running his hands through his hair. We ended up facing each other, and I clasped my hands in my lap to keep them from trembling.

"Okay," I said. "Tell me why you think she could possibly regret it."

"In Guatemala, I put her up in a hotel to keep her safe, and I'd visit her at night after work. When it was getting close to time for me to leave, she asked me to bring her to a neighboring town where she had a cousin she could stay with. I didn't like that idea. It was another small, old school town, just like hers, where people basically made their own laws. Her dad could have found her there. Or word would travel and she'd end up shunned. I told her I could bring her to the U.S. It wasn't until we went to the local town council to get her paperwork that I realized those fuckers would do anything to make a buck. They said she couldn't leave unless she was going with a legal spouse."

"Is that really the law?" I asked.

"No clue. Some towns in the world are so corrupt that they make their own laws to suit their needs. And of course a marriage license was pricey. It made the local government some money. At that point I would've done anything to keep her safe. God, Pepper, if you could have seen . . ." He looked up, and I could make out his eyes on me. "I know she's been kind of shy since she's been here, but when I saw her being beaten, she was fierce. Her chin was up, and she did not want to show pain. She wouldn't give those bastards the satisfaction of seeing her cry. She was so strong, and all I could think was, *Damn, that could be Pepper."*

He looked down and I swallowed several times, fighting the emotion pooling inside of me. I had no idea what to say. No idea how to feel—only that I was overwhelmed.

"When we were at the hotel, I didn't try to touch her because she was so hurt. She was black and blue all over, covered in cuts. On the second day, she kissed me, but it felt like she was trying to thank me or pay me, so I stopped it. I think it hurt her feelings. I tried to explain it in Spanish as best as I could, that she didn't owe me, but I'm not sure she understood. And next thing I knew, we were married and flying to the U.S."

My heart was lodged so far up my throat, I couldn't even swallow.

He scrubbed the top of his head with his fingers again. "We've been married six weeks and we've never . . . we haven't been together. We've only kissed."

A giant, dry blast of air got stuck in my constricting lungs. Rylen and Livia hadn't had sex. I was relieved and shocked and saddened for them both. I pushed words out of my mouth. I had to be supportive.

"It makes sense, Ry. You kind of had to rush the wedding, and then there was the pregnancy stuff. But now it'll sort of be like you're dating. We'll get her back, and you guys can get to know each other." I paused. This was killing me. "You'll work your way up to the other stuff."

"I don't think she wants to." He sounded pained. "I know she cares. She genuinely does. But whenever we've tried to get physical, it feels . . . forced." He shook his head. "She's a good girl. I want to make her happy."

I swiped my leaking eyes with the backs of my hands. Oh, God, I couldn't talk. I couldn't handle this. I tried to inhale as quietly as possible, to fill my chest with a cleansing breath of Rylen-scented air.

"Everything will work out," I whispered. "I'm sure there's nothing wrong. The world is a mess right now. It's probably having an effect on lots of marriages, much less brand new ones with language barriers."

"Maybe." I thought I could see his head shake. "I don't know."

I reached into my bag by my feet and pulled out a bottle of water. I unscrewed it and took a big gulp, and then I handed it to Ry. "Drink all of this and get some rest."

He gave a chuckle. "Yes, ma'am."

A loud burst of laughter and yelling came from outside as Rylen finished the water and lay on his back. I watched his shadowy form, and within a minute his breathing became louder and steady. He was asleep.

I pushed my legs into the sleeping bag and sighed in contentment at the warmth. I wished I could fall asleep as fast as Ry, but his words were galloping through my mind, and the voices of everyone outside rang in my ears. Why was life so unfair? Why did everything have to be so wrong? The only thing worse than Rylen being married was Rylen and Livia being stuck in an unhappy marriage. As much as it killed me to think it, I would rather they fell fast in love and humped like bunnies than to be in this in-between asexual phase, being unhappy and refusing to part ways. Maybe if they were truly in love, it would force me to move along.

After a long while of wallowing in my thoughts, things seemed to quiet down outside. Sounds of shuffling feet and grumbling, and zippering sleeping bags filled the night air. If everyone was getting ready for bed, that meant Remy and Tater would be in soon. I wished I could fall asleep, because everyone in the camp was probably going to snore like crazy tonight. If they fell asleep before me and I had to listen to that, I was screwed.

A few minutes later I thought I heard Remy crying. I sat up and listened harder. She was whimpering somewhere nearby. Just as I was about to jump up and find her, the whimpering turned to rhythmic moans of *"uhn, uhn, uhn."*

Oh, my God! Was Remy having sex with one of them in the other tent??

No way. I listened harder and heard Texas Harry say, "Lucky bastard," from a little further away, followed by murmurs and low laughter. So, it wasn't him. Josh, maybe?

Remy gave a particularly loud shout of ecstasy and Rylen sat straight up, head swiveling side to side. "What was that?"

"Uh . . ."

*"Yes, oh God, yes. Tater, uuuhng!"*

"Oh, my God." I slapped a hand over my mouth.

Rylen fell heavily onto his back and flung a forearm over his eyes. "Ah, Tater, you motherfucker."

My thoughts exactly. What were they thinking? They annoyed the hell out of each other! Stupid whiskey and its stupid inhibition lowering ability. Now we'd have awkward drama on our hands on top of everything else going on. I knew Remy. It was never just a hook-up for her. All hook-ups came with drama.

They got quiet, and my heart started to slow, and then *bam*. They were at it again, faster and louder. When I heard skin smacking and Tater's grunting, I slammed my pillow over my head and squished it against my ears to block out all sound. I stayed like that until long after the sounds had stopped, with my arm muscles shaking from the exertion of holding down the pillow, until I was finally exhausted enough to fall asleep. Small mercies.

# THIRTY-FOUR

I WOKE AT DAWN to the distant sounds of retching.

Rylen never stirred as I sat up and slipped out of the crinkly sleeping bag. The tent zipper seemed so loud in the quiet morning. I reached back and grabbed my sweatshirt, pulling it over my head. One of the guys in the outside huddle of sleeping bags stirred, but nobody got up.

I made my way down the trail toward the sounds until I found Remy behind a tree, bent over on her knees, one hand on the ground, one hand holding back her mane of wild blond waves. Her whole body shook. She didn't look up as I squatted next to her and gathered her hair.

"I think I'm dying," she croaked.

Aside from fast-food French fries, there was nothing I could give Remy to make her feel better. She wouldn't drink water or eat anything when she felt like this. Only time would help her. The next couple hours would be miserable.

"You'll be okay," I whispered.

I looked at the ground, but it was only liquid and yellowish acid. She hadn't eaten much yesterday, which made it all the worse.

"Is everyone still asleep?" She sounded hopeful.

"Yeah."

She sat back on her heels, wiping her face with her eyes closed. I so wanted to give her a hard time about Tater, and to kick her ass for making me listen to them having sex, especially while I was stuck next to Rylen. But I didn't have the heart. Once she was feeling better, it would be *on*.

When her stomach finally settled, she crawled over and leaned back against the trees. Her eyes stayed shut, and I began to wonder if she was avoiding looking at me.

"Can I get you anything?" I asked.

"No," she whispered. "Not yet." Her hand reached out toward me and I took it. She was warm despite the chill of the morning.

I cleared my throat. "So . . . how much do you remember from last night?"

She gave a dry, lackluster chuckle. "Enough." One eye cracked open and focused on me. "How mad are you?"

I let out a heavy sigh. "I can't say I'm excited. I figured you'd pick any of those guys over my idiot brother. I thought he annoyed you."

Now it was her turn to sigh, but her exhale sounded dreamy. "He did back in the day. But not anymore. Not since he came back."

"Great. Well, just for the record, I never want to hear him having sex again."

Her eyes shot open and bugged out. "You could hear us?"

I stared at her. "Um . . . like, every detail. I slept with a pillow over my head."

She gave her embarrassed giggle, but the sound quickly changed to a gag and she was bending over again. Nothing came out, just dry heaving, and then she was giggling again and grabbing her aching head.

"You're a hot mess," I said.

When she finally settled, she leaned her head back again. "Amber." Another sappy sigh. "I could fall *so hard* for him."

Oh, no. No, no, no. My brain went on high alert. This never, ever ended well. Remy, in her own way, was a player, just like Tater. If a guy fell hard for her, she'd find some flimsy reason to break things off. If a guy decided he wasn't into her anymore, it affected her on a deep level. It was like a desperate, sickening mental game she played, a punishing cycle. Pretty sure this was her way of dealing with Daddy Issues.

I was so freaking glad not to have Daddy Issues.

"Just take things slow," I told her. "There's so much going on right now. It's fine to have some fun when we can, but it's probably not the best time to be worrying about a guy." Especially my brother.

"I know," she said, probably just to appease me. She wrapped her arms around her waist and pulled her knees in tighter, still shaking.

"You should try to lay back down," I told her.

"I don't want Jacob to see me like this."

I forced myself not to roll my eyes. "Just get back in the tent with Rylen, then."

"But what if Tater thinks I'm avoiding him?"

Now I did roll my eyes. "You're overthinking this. Tater is not going to care what you look like. He's going to be just as hungover as you and everyone else up there. Just do what you need to do to feel better."

"Always so logical," she whispered. Followed by, "Oh, my head."

I helped her to her feet and she held my arm as we walked up together. She stopped twice and bent over, looking like she was going to heave again. We finally made our way up to camp, and blessedly everyone was still asleep. Remy stared at both tents a few minutes before she made her way, hunched like an old lady, and climbed into Tater's tent.

I rubbed my temples. Coffee. I needed caffeine stat. And though my gut was calling out for food too, I knew if I filled it with liquid I could trick it into shushing for a little while. I walked with care between sleeping bags and filled the tea kettle with water from a gallon jug. Then I turned on the gas burner and sat on a log to wait.

I felt eyes on me and was startled to see every single guy awake in their beds, watching me. Their faces appeared miserable: ashen skin, messy hair, arms splayed like they were too lethargic to do anything more than watch me.

"Um, hey," I said. "You guys want coffee?"

Five sets of eyes widened.

"You got coffee, for real?" Devon asked.

"It's going to be weak, but yeah," I told him. I had to ration it.

Slowly, the guys stretched and sat up, looking achy, and went off in different directions to use the trees. Sean came out of his tent, looking fresh and well rested. We gave each other a polite nod before he left to find a tree, too.

When the water was hot, I pulled out our paper cups and poured for everyone, putting half a scoop of instant coffee. I also tore open a packet of sugar and poured it in mine. It was weaker and less sweet than I liked it, but it was still so good. I didn't know how I would survive when this stuff ran out. These guys had no idea how lucky they were I was willing to share.

When I saw Tater practically stumble out of his tent, I jumped up with my coffee and ran to meet him. He put up a palm to stop my progress, while holding his head with his other hand.

"Let me pee first."

I waited impatiently. When he came back, still disheveled, I took him by the wrist and pulled him down the trail out of ear shot of the others.

As I was about to speak, he snatched my coffee and drank half. I snatched it back and was pissed when a little sloshed over the edge.

"Tater! You cannot mess with Remy's mind!"

He stared at me blankly. "We're just having fun."

"No. It's never just fun with her. You're going to hurt her and make everything awkward."

"Ah, come on. How do you know she won't be the one to hurt me?" He gave me his droopy puppy eyes.

I smacked his arm then pointed at him. "I am immune to your cuteness. No more hookups unless you really do like her."

"Amb—"

"I'm serious! I will kick your ass, Tater!"

He reached for my coffee again, and I curled my arm and body around it like freaking Gollum protecting his *precious*, and snarled, "Go make your own."

I heard footsteps and looked up, still curled around my paper cup. The image of Rylen in fitted nylon running pants and no shirt made me straighten so fast my coffee sloshed over again. Damn it!

I licked my hand.

Tater walked away, narrowly dodging a punch from Rylen, who made his way down to me. He kept coming when I thought he would stop, ending up way too close. Rylen had a way of sliding into my personal bubble and making my skin prickle with heat. His head tilted down toward mine and he spoke in a low voice.

"I'm sorry about last night, Pepper. Again." He tugged on

his earlobe and gave his head a shake. "I don't know what the fuck is wrong with me."

I brought the coffee up to my lips and gave a shrug. "Nothing to be sorry about."

"I said too much." He straightened and ran a hand through his hair, which was longer than I'd seen it in years.

I didn't want to relive the conversation, but I needed to take away his worries so we could move past this apology. "You obviously needed someone to talk to, and I'm glad you felt comfortable enough to confide in me, drunk or not."

He let out a dry laugh. "Definitely drunk."

"Yeah, well." I shrugged again. "You weren't alone." I downed the rest of my coffee, then felt sad that it was gone.

"Thanks," he whispered.

I opened my mouth to respond, but a high-pitched shriek split the air. Remy.

Rylen and I sprinted up the path to the camp and found all of the guys in a semi-circle and Remy in the tent entrance, staring down. I pushed through. Her terrified eyes went up to me and back to the ground. "It's a scorpion!"

I looked down at the nearly-translucent beige creature, about three inches long. Then I ran forward and stomped it. Remy screamed and the guys hollered. I felt it crunch through my sneaker bottom and I shivered all over. I lifted my foot, but the damn thing was still moving, so I proceeded to do the Mexican hat dance on that sucker until it no longer moved. I looked up in to the guys' faces. They stared at me.

"Pussies," I muttered, kicking the scorpion to the side so Remy could get out.

She grasped me in a hug. "My hero!"

"That thing could've killed somebody," Devon said. "I ain't sleeping on that ground no more. I call the backseat of the van."

"Scorpion stings are like bee stings," I said. "They're not going to kill you."

Still, they all looked skeptical. I turned to Texas Harry. "Don't you have scorpions in Texas?"

"Yes, ma'am," he said. "But I use 'em for target practice. Didn't think the little lady would take kindly to me shooting by her feet."

"Thanks for that," Remy said.

"It's rattlesnakes you need to watch out for," I told the group at large. "I don't have any antivenom, so if you get bitten you're screwed. That really could kill you, or do major damage."

"I call passenger seat in the van," New York Josh said.

"Or," I said over everyone's sudden chatter. "The other tent will be free tonight. Four of you can fit in there. Remy and Tater will be back in the other tent with me and Ry."

Remy pushed her hair behind her ear and looked down as several guys chuckled. A pink blush spread across her face.

"You're such a mean camp Mama," Short Matt said. "Taking the fun out of everything." He gave me a green-eyed wink.

I winked back. "Don't forget it." I looked around at their miserable faces and slumping bodies. "And in the meantime, Mean Mama will make you something to eat. After this, you're on your own."

The plan that evening was to return to the DRI "Safe House" area to do more recon. We needed to figure out exactly where we would set off a fire, and where our people needed to be stationed during it, and how to best get to those areas without detection.

"I'm going this time," I said during our early dinner. We were down to two meals a day: a late breakfast and an early dinner, with no snacks in between.

"I'm not staying here alone," Remy told me.

"Then come with us," I said.

She peered down at her salty square cracker, and I could tell she didn't want to come, but her fear of being here alone was greater. A strand of her hair fell and brushed her arm. Remy jumped and slapped her arm, then relaxed when she saw it was just her hair. I had to giggle. She glared at me, but eventually broke into a smile. She'd been freaked out about the scorpion all day.

"Man, I haven't shit in two days," Tater blurted out of nowhere.

"Right?" New York Josh said to Tater. The others nodded.

Remy crinkled her nose. "TMI."

"Your body needs everything you're intaking," I said.

"What are you, a doctor?" New York Josh asked. I was starting to be able to read him. He always sounded like an asshole, but he wasn't trying to be. He was just naturally a hardass with dry wit.

"She's an RN," Rylen said. "A paramedic."

New York Josh gave me an appreciative once-over. "All right. That explains the fearlessness."

My chest heated at the compliment and his lingering look. Remy was right—he was good looking with those Italian features.

"Hella good to have a nurse on hand," Tall Mark said.

Texas Harry slapped the back of his head.

I savored my last cracker and brushed my hands off. It was time to get ready to go. I was excited to finally have a hand in the scouting and planning.

We cleaned up and got ourselves ready, gathering all the gear we'd need. Remy and I both put our hair up in pony-tails. I saw her hands trembling, and took her fingers in mine.

"Everything will be fine," I told her. "We're just looking to-night, 'kay?"

"Okay," she whispered. Her eyes drifted from my face over my shoulder and stopped. I turned to see Tater approaching and felt Remy's hand tighten around mine.

Tater kept his gaze firmly on me. "You ready?"

"Yeah." I waited for him to acknowledge Remy too. When he didn't, I said, *"We're* ready."

He gave me a nod and left to join the guys. Remy's face fell.

"He hasn't looked at me or talked to me all day."

Shit, shit, shit. He'd taken my advice not to lead her on, but blatantly ignoring her was going to cause problems too.

"I don't know what to say about him, Rem. Last night you guys were having fun. Today, he's focused on trying to break our families out. Don't take offense, 'kay?"

She continued to frown. "'kay."

We took two vehicles: the guys' minivan, and Mom's se-dan. Tater and Rylen sat in front with Tater driving. Remy held my hand in the backseat the whole way. I had to admit, I shared in her fears now. The moment we'd left state park land, a sudden vulnerability overtook us. I found myself star-ing out of the window, watching for any sign of other cars or people or life, in general. The others seemed to be doing the same.

The sun drooped behind distant mountains, blanketing us in cool dimness. We drove slowly, trying not to kick up too much dust. Tater and Texas Harry parked behind a hill with a few scraggly evergreens, hidden from the main road, but within walking distance of the gas station. We all got out, closing doors behind us with care.

My heart picked up and leveled off at a quick thump that forced my breaths to become shallow. We weren't safe out here. My flight or fight instinct was begging me to flee, but not alone. I needed all of my loved ones to flee with me, away from this evil sense of dread. A strong hand enveloped my shoulder and I looked up at Rylen.

"It's all right," he said.

I took a deep breath and shook my arms out. The darkness would not leave me.

A longing deep and powerful hit me right in the gut, stopping my breath—it was a longing for my parents, for Abuela. I closed my eyes and years of unconditional love filled me. The longing stretched into a bone-deep need for my family to be one again. My jaw was clenched tight. Icy fear for them hit me in a rush, making my eyes burst open. A violent shudder overtook me and I hated, absolutely *hated*, the DRI for making me feel this way.

Rylen, Tater, and Remy were watching me.

"Amber, calm down," Tater said. "Everything's okay."

"No," I whispered. "We need to get them out of there."

"I know," he said. "And we will. If we can get all the info we need tonight, we'll be able to break them out tomorrow or the next day."

I forced another deep breath. I had to shake away the bad feelings or I would only be a hindrance. "Okay. I'm sorry. I don't know what's wrong with me."

Tater bent his knees to come eye-to-eye with me and said, "You're solid. Gimme some." He stuck out his fist and I bumped it with mine. Remy shifted next to us, her arms wrapping around her waist. Tater looked at her and hesitated, like he wanted to bump knuckles with her, too, but instead he just gave an awkward half-smile and turned away to jog to the other guys.

Remy frowned. "What the hell? I have cooties now?"

"He doesn't know how to act," Rylen said. He gave Remy

an apologetic look. "Let's go."

The night was filled with a lot of walking and hiking, most of it spent hunched over and trying to be as small and stealthy as possible while we sweated out every drop we'd had to drink that day. If we'd tried to do this in the daytime with the sun shining, I'm afraid some of our group would have passed out.

We finally worked our way pretty close. I felt worthless, not knowing a lot of the military lingo they used as they chose coordinates of the best places to station themselves and who would go where. All I could do was stare down at the camp in the valley, which looked so small from where we were.

A full moon shone above us, along with a clear sky of twinkling stars. It gave us just enough light to make out the maps.

"That hill, right there," Matt said, "would be perfect for the fire."

"It's too far," Mark countered. "This one's better."

"That's too close—"

All at once we lifted our heads and listened. A sound was coming from far off, like wind or a whirring whistle.

Rylen whispered, "Jet. Get down."

Everyone scuttled, trying to find trees or rocks or bushes to anchor ourselves near. And sure enough, within a minute a plane flew over and it was so low, so loud, that it shook the ground beneath us.

"Fucking hell, it's Air Force!" Rylen said. "Two fighters!"

Mark started to jump up and holler, but Matt grabbed him and yanked him back down. "Stay put, brah. Wait and see what they do."

The Air Force! Absolute unadulterated joy poured

through me and I nearly laughed. The Air Force was here to stop the DRI!

From my vantage point I could see the camp. To my glee, Drips and Derps were running for the camp gates. They exited and locked the gate behind them. They rushed toward the white vans outside.

"They're leaving!" I whispered loudly.

Mere seconds after they'd piled into the vans and sped away, loud sounds came from the camp. Abruptly, a sea of people poured forth from the building, like they'd broken out of it, and they were all screaming, running for the gates.

"Oh, my God, everyone is freaking out," I said. Our group rushed over to see. "They're going to trample each other!" Remy said. "We have to go down there!"

To my surprise, nobody objected. As a group, we came out over our hill and began rushing down the steep decline. I heard the whir of the jets coming back. This time we all cheered when we saw them getting closer. They'd chased away the Drips and Derps. Now we could get these people out and find out exactly what the hell was going on with this country.

We were still a good distance away, sprinting, but even from afar it was clear there was panic at the camp gates. Some were trying to climb over, but the tops were circled in barbed wire. I wanted to yell for them to wait a damn second and we'd be there to help, but they wouldn't have been able to hear us.

As the jets neared, hovering lower enough to get a good look, I fought the urge to cover my ears against the noise of them. But then I wished I had. And I wished I'd covered my eyes too.

The flash of light hit first, and it seemed like forever before the sound blasted us backward onto our asses. Heat came next, rolling over us, mixed with dust and dirt and rocks. I covered my head and rolled to my stomach. A sudden flash-back of the hospital bombing caught me in a giant, tight fist.

But this could not be a bombing. The U.S. Air Force was here. Had the DRI set off bombs within the camp?

The camp . . . holy fucking shit.

I pushed to my knees and tried to open my eyes, but it was like a windstorm. I couldn't see a thing. I forced myself upward, keeping an arm across my face, and moved in the direction we'd been going. At least, I was pretty sure it was the right direction.

I heard coughing behind me, and moans.

"Amber?" I heard Remy say, but I couldn't stop. I couldn't go back. She was alive and okay, but the camp . . .

"Amber!" she screamed.

"I'm fine!" I yelled over my shoulder. "Stay here."

"I got you," I heard Tater say to her.

Once I knew I was moving in the right direction, I picked up my pace. I pulled my T-shirt up over my nose so I could breathe, and I jogged. Seconds later I heard feet hitting the dirt to my right, then my left, then behind me.

"They dropped a bomb," I heard Rylen say to my left. "They dropped a fucking bomb on camp."

"Are you sure?" I yelled.

"I saw it fall, too," Texas Harry shouted.

Oh, my God. No. I dropped my shirt and flat out ran. Sand whipped my face, but I couldn't feel it.

Please God.

Not this.

Not my family.

No. NO.

I refused to let it be true.

My eyes burned from the sand. Tears streamed down and

I coughed as I ran. My foot hit something hard and I stumbled, going to one knee. Rylen hiked me back up by the arm and I kept running.

"Whoa, whoa!" Texas Harry yelled from in front of us. "Hot metal! Watch your step. I think it's the gates, but it's all twisted. Just burnt my fuckin' shin."

I slowed and could make out bits of what he meant. It looked nothing like a gate, just twisted chunks of silver debris. My stomach plummeted and my soul cried out in agony. If this was what was left of the gate, and all those people had been gathered at it . . .

I grabbed my knees, coughing. My parents might not have been at the gate. They weren't easily panicked. What if they'd stayed in the building? I pushed forward, making my way around the debris.

Rylen was at my side. "Pepper . . ."

"Have to find that building," I said.

"Pepper, look." His voice was so sad. I shook my head. I didn't want to hear that.

"No, they're hiding somewhere."

"Pepper, *look.*" He came up behind me and took me by the shoulders, pointing me in the direction of the building. Through a swirl of dust and smoke, I could make out the remnants of one partial wall. "It's gone."

"No!" I yelled, and broke away at a sprint. I fell twice over rocks or ruins, but never saw a single body. When I got to where the metal wall stood, it gave a creaking shudder and fell to the earth with a *whoosh.* There was nothing. Chunks of stuff that was probably cots or something. And my skin was so hot. The ground was hot, like it was on fire. All I could smell was char and cinder.

"We have to get out of here—"

"They're here!" My head pivoted from side to side. Each

wisp of smoke was like Mom walking toward me, Abuela reaching out her arms for me, Dad waving to let me know he was fine. I was numb to the burning of my skin.

Rylen bent and scooped me into his arms.

I struggled and push against his chest. "I need to find them!" He ran, ignoring me, and I pounded my fists against his shoulders. "Damn you, stop!" Sobs rose and I nearly choked as I cried and screamed. "Put me down!" Still, he held tight, and ran.

"Rylen, please, please," I begged through tears. "I need to get them. They're somewhere. Oh, my God . . ." My face fell against his shoulder and I bawled against his neck. *"Oh, my God . . ."* My hands tightened, fisting his shirt in my palms, holding him like a lifeline as my mind threatened to shatter into unfixable pieces.

He never said a word. Just ran.

# THIRTY-FIVE

PPARENTLY, GRIEVING WAS LIKE being drunk. Whole pieces of time went missing.

I don't remember making it back to the car. It wasn't until we were nearly back to the state park that I became aware of Remy's arms around me, my shirt damp with her tears. And all I could do was look at the brown cloth seat below me and think, *This car is really clean*. It was the cleanest thing I'd ever seen. Mom did a good job of . . .

All at once my chest ripped open and my insides shattered, like a bomb going off inside of me all over again. An animalistic sound tore from my throat and Remy tightened her grip around me. My own arms, which had already been around her, clenched as if my life depended on holding her.

In the passenger seat, Tater was bent over, clutching his head. Rylen, driving, met my eyes in the rearview mirror. The dashboard lighting made his skin glow in the darkness. But his face was dirty. His eyes red.

Livia.

"Did they find anyone?" I whispered.

"No," Rylen said.

Remy let out a low wail that I felt on a soul level. Had our parents been at the gates? Based on how they were trying fervently to get out, they had to have known something bad was coming. They must have been terrified. If only we could have gotten there sooner. If only we hadn't assumed we had more time—we should have tried to break them out right away instead of planning and waiting.

When we got back to our trail area, it no longer seemed like the benevolent, safe, fun place we'd left hours before. Everything looked sinister in the darkness. Trees were Derps with guns. Chirping bugs sounded like they were laughing at us. I tried to help Remy out of the car, but she shook her head and refused to budge. Tater also remained in the front seat. Rylen got out first and I faced him. Something dark was on his T-shirt collar and across his shoulder. Blood? Was he injured?

I went up on my toes and gently pulled the fabric aside. In the darkness I could scarcely make out bloodied marks, like he'd been clawed. I sucked in a painful breath.

"Ry . . . Oh, God, I'm sorry." I had shredded his skin while he carried me. He gently pulled my hand away and held my wrist.

"It doesn't hurt."

My jaw clenched to keep it from trembling.

"I need a minute," he whispered. Rylen squeezed my hand and let me go to walk into the trees, disappearing. My heart constricted.

I went around the car and opened the passenger door. Tater turned his head up to me, and when our eyes met, I shattered all over again. He stood and enveloped me. This boy, *man*, who'd driven me crazy my whole life—only he felt exactly what I felt—only he knew exactly what I'd lost.

Because he'd lost them too. And they meant just as much to him.

We clung to each other, crying, and I was so thankful he was alive. I didn't know what I'd do without Tater. When we finally calmed, I looked into the darkened back window at Remy, who was curled up in the fetal position. Without a word, Tater opened her door and climbed in, gathering her into his arms. He kissed her head, and down her cheek, and then gently on her lips, then took her in a hug again. It felt so intimate and private that I left them to be alone.

I felt strangely disembodied as I walked the dark path up to our camp, like a branch without its tree. No roots to anchor me. No trunk to hold me up. Who was I without my mom and dad? That's not a person I ever wanted to be.

I sat absently on a log while everyone slowly made their way up into the camp. After a long while, we all gathered in a circle. Rylen was the last to join us, coming from the darkness of the trees. He sat a little further back than the rest of us. We were all silent until New York Josh finally relented.

"What the fuck was that?"

Texas Harry huffed air through his nose. "Either the U.S. Air Force is with them, and against us, or they got their paws on one of our fighters."

"Not just one," I said. "There were witnesses in Vegas who said two planes dropped bombs there in the very beginning. So, either they've had infiltrators a long time, or . . . I don't even know." My chest hurt too much to finish a thought.

"So what do we do?" Tater asked.

"We infiltrate back," Rylen said. His hands hung heavy over his knees, weary eyes lifted up to his longtime best friend. "And we search out others like us."

Sean stood up and went to his tent. Seconds later he came back out with a small portable radio. "I listen to this thing every night. Mostly it's DRI propaganda, but sometimes there are actual broadcasts that pop up. They're usually down within a day, though." We waited as he turned it on and began the slow search through the airwaves. A voice hit the air loud and clear, and my chest constricted. Senator Navin.

"—safe bases for survivors. I want to personally thank all who have made this a smooth transition. It is imperative that we condense our population to maximize safety while we root out the remaining Outliers. Go to your local police station immediately to find a DRI personnel who can get you to the nearest safe base."

"Do you think he's in on it?" Matt asked. "Or do you think he's being used by them?"

"Nobody's that stupid," Josh said. "He's their *leader*. Their fucking spokesman."

"Senator Navin has always been a good man," Remy said thickly. "I don't think he knows. I think he believes what he's saying. Somebody has to be lying to him. He must not know. I mean, it could have been some shady, random, individual who decided to steal a plane and bomb people today—"

"Dude!" Josh said with a laugh.

"Don't," I warned him with a sharp glare. "We don't know. Anything could be possible. Everything is speculation at this point, and there's no use arguing when we don't have all the facts." I looked at Sean. "Can you keep searching?"

He flicked away from the senator's voice and was met with differing variations of white noise. He seemed to turn and turn the dial forever until it was quiet, and he paused. Static came again, then silence. Static. Long pause. Static, short pause, static, short pause. After a few seconds of it, there seemed to be a purposeful tempo to the stops and starts. Everyone sat up straighter.

Rylen jumped to his feet and put up a palm to let Sean

know not to move it.

"S.O.S." Rylen said. "Morse code."

"Holy shit," Texas Harry said. "You can understand that?"

Rylen nodded, his eyes distant as he listened.

"Yeah," Matt said. "I know code too. It keeps repeating S.O.S."

My heart banged in my chest. I didn't think anyone used Morse Code anymore. Dad said it was sort of a lost art with all the advancements in technology. My stomach dipped at the thought of Dad sitting in his recliner, watching those history shows and spouting random knowledge to anyone listening.

"Wait," Ry whispered. "Whiskey . . . Oscar . . . Romeo . . . Lima . . . Delta."

"World," Matt said.

Rylen continued to concentrate on the static breaks. "Uniform . . . November . . . Delta . . . Echo . . . Romeo."

"Under," Matt whispered.

"Alpha . . . Tango . . . Tango . . .

Alpha . . . Charlie . . . Kilo."

"Attack." Matt swallowed.

"Oh my gosh." Remy reached for my hand.

Rylen leaned closer to the radio. "Delta . . . Papa . . . Golf. Hotel . . . Oscar . . . Oscar . . . Alpha . . . Hotel. DPG Hooah?"

"Hooah!" The Army guys shouted and jumped up to smack hands and chest bump and every other celebratory thing. The sound of the word *hooah* even made me smile for a second.

"Sh!" Sean ordered. Everyone settled down and looked back at the radio, but all that came out now was uninterrupted static.

"Whoever it was shut down signal," Sean said. "Trying not to be detected."

"DPG is a base," Josh said. "Dugway Proving Ground."

"Utah," said Tater and Matt together, then they fist bumped.

Texas Harry pulled out a map and spread it open. "We'd have to go northwest to get there. Probably seven or eight hours by car. No way we have enough gas, though."

"Let's break into that gas station and see if we can get the pumps working," Tater suggested.

Everyone nodded, and I bit my lip.

"How are we going to drive to Utah without being caught?"

"Back roads," Rylen said. "Desert routes. DPG is in a desert region. We keep someone in the lead car on lookout with the binoculars."

My insides twisted with fear at the thought of leaving our safe haven, but the thought of being with others like us—uniting with allies and trying to stop whatever the hell was going on here—that desire was so much stronger than my fear. I didn't just want answers anymore. I wanted action. I wanted to stop these bastards and end their lives for what they'd taken from us.

*World under attack.*

We'd been under attack for the past month, but those words felt so loaded. Like they knew something. Like they knew exactly *who* was attacking.

"Let's leave now," I said. "We can drive through the night."

"Hooah." Texas Harry spun a finger through the air like a lasso. "Round up, boys."

I looked at Rylen, Tater, and Remy, at their smudged faces and dusted clothes. But mostly I looked at the sorrow in their eyes reflecting in the moonlight.

"We have to stick together," I whispered, my voice breaking. "I can't lose any of you."

The four of us came together in a sort of huddle, a four-way embrace.

"We got this," Tater said.

Tears were already streaming down Remy's face, and I fought back another wave of my own. I swear, I wasn't usually this weepy, but I felt like we were living in Hell and could not find the exit.

Rylen gritted his jaw and closed his eyes like he was holding back a flood of emotions.

I took a deep breath. "Let's break down the tents and get out of here."

It was time to leave the Mojave and all its nightmares in the dust.

# TO BE CONTINUED . . .

Look for UNREST, book two of the
UNKNOWN series, in winter 2017

# ABOUT THE AUTHOR

Photo Credit: Anastasia's Photography Eastern Shore

WENDY HIGGINS RECEIVED HER degree in Creative Writing from George Mason University, and a Masters in Curriculum and Instruction from Radford University. She taught high school English until becoming a mom and full-time writer. Wendy is the *New York Times* bestselling author of the *Sweet Evil* series and *The Great Hunt* duology from HarperTeen, along with her independently published Irish fantasy, *See Me*. Wendy lives on the Eastern Shore of Virginia with her veterinarian husband, daughter, son, and their lil dog Rue.

Feel free to contact Wendy at:
wendyhigginswrites@gmail.com
Website: www.wendyhigginswrites.com
Facebook: www.facebook.com/WendyHigginsWrites
Twitter: @Wendy_Higgins
Instagram: @WendyHigginsWrites

# ACKNOWLEDGMENTS

FIRST OFF, THANK YOU for reading. You keep me going, book friends. Hugs all around!

To Gwen Cole: fist bumps chest bumps squeezy hugs Your early excitement was exactly what I needed! And huge gratitude to my next beta readers, lovely author Cindi Madsen, and fellow readers Meredith Crowley and Jill Wilson. I would never have the nerve to publish without your valuable feedback first.

Major props to the girls at Perfectly Publishable for their editing and formatting skills and timely professionalism.

Jennifer Munswami, I love, love, love your cover art and graphic teaser work. I don't know what I'd do without you!

As always, I could not chase my dreams without the full support of my family. Nathan, Autumn, Cayden, my parents, in-laws, and siblings, and my wonderful friends Courtney, Brooke, Ann, Jo, Nelly, Holly, Hilary, Christine, Dani, Carol, Meggie, Kristy, and Val. I am so freaking lucky and blessed. God is good.

And to the boy who I spent four years head-over-heels in love with from the 8th-11th grades, but who treated me as a sister and was completely clueless of my affections until I finally kissed him, thanks for the inspiration.

CPSIA information can be obtained at www.ICGtesting.com
Printed in the USA
LVOW10s1952150916

504774LV00020BA/1289/P